SPARKS!

WRITTEN BY **IAN BOOTHBY**

ART BY **NINA MATSUMOTO**
WITH COLOR BY DAVID DEDRICK

An Imprint of
SCHOLASTIC

Dedicated to the real-life Charlie and August!
—Ian Boothby and Nina Matsumoto

Text copyright © 2018 by Ian Boothby
Art copyright © 2018 by Nina Matsumoto

Library of Congress Control Number: 2017943774

ISBN 978-1-338-02947-5 (hardcover)
ISBN 978-1-338-02946-8 (paperback)

10 9 8 7 6 5 4 3 2 1   18 19 20 21 22

Printed in China   38
First edition, March 2018
Edited by Adam Rau
Color by David Dedrick
Book design by Phil Falco
Creative Director: David Saylor

CHAPTER ONE

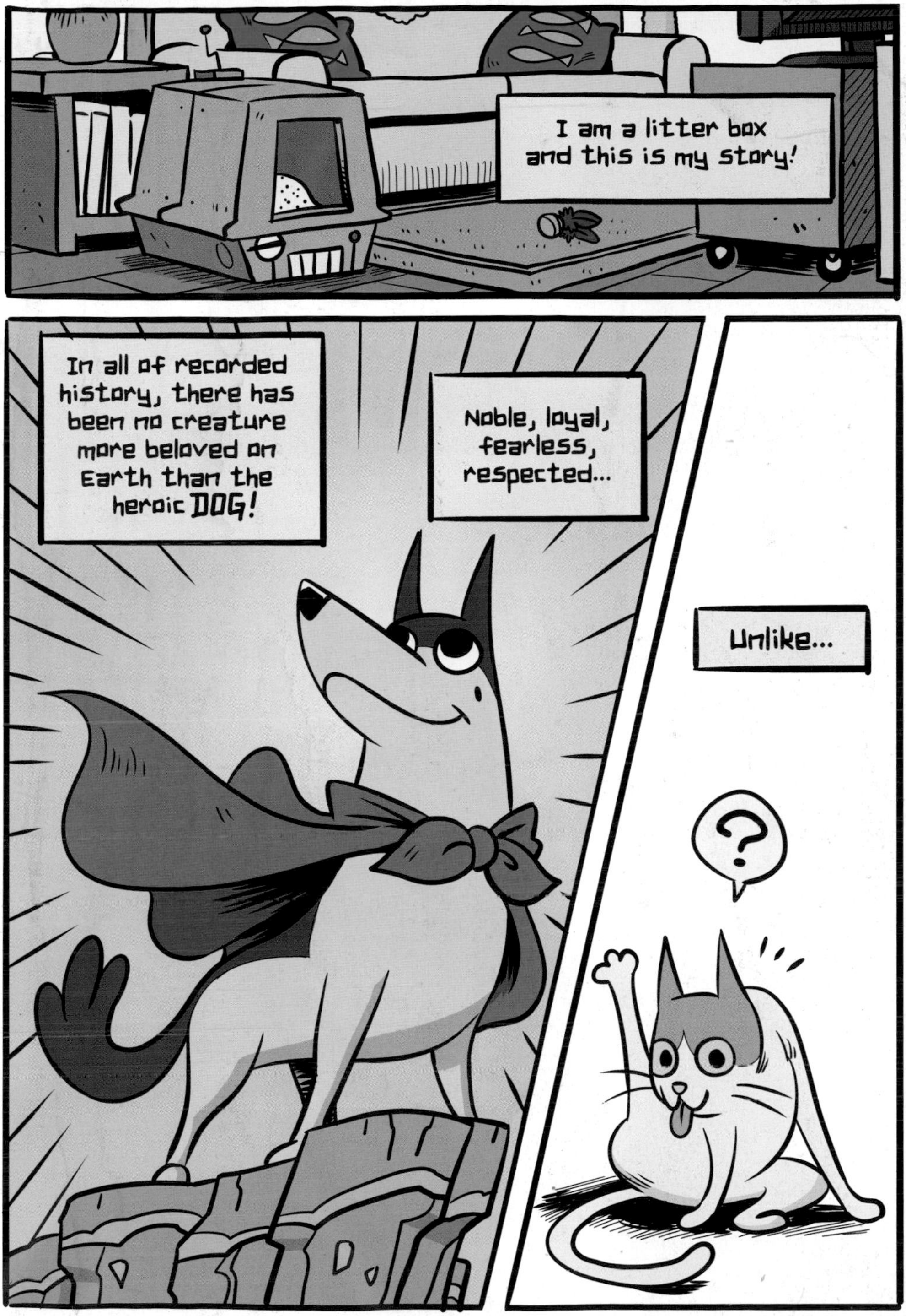
I am a litter box and this is my story!
In all of recorded history, there has been no creature more beloved on Earth than the heroic DOG!
Noble, loyal, fearless, respected...
Unlike...
?

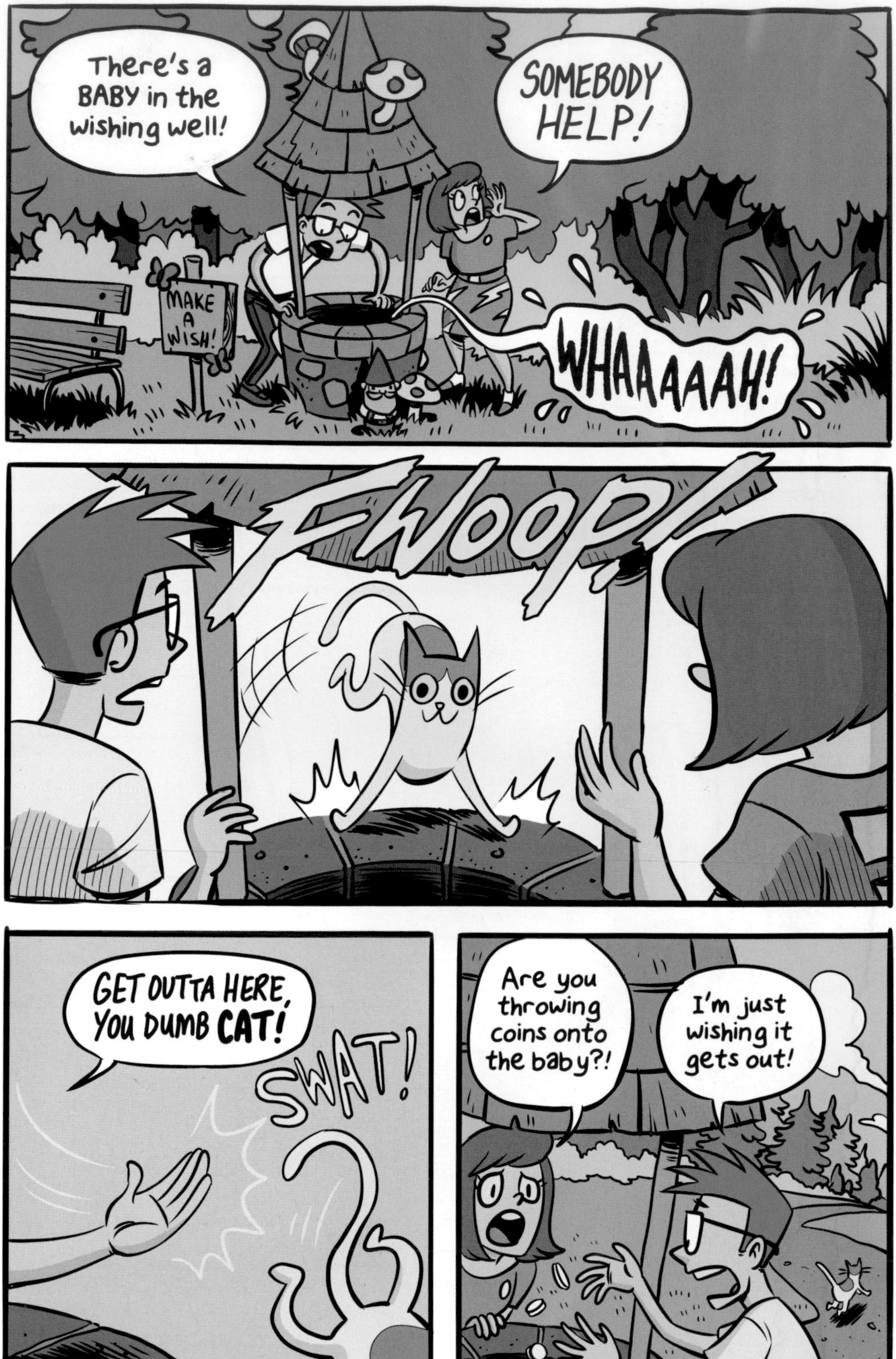
There's a BABY in the wishing well!
SOMEBODY HELP!
MAKE A WISH!
WHAAAAAH!
FWOOP!
GET OUTTA HERE, YOU DUMB CAT!
SWAT!
Are you throwing coins onto the baby?!
I'm just wishing it gets out!

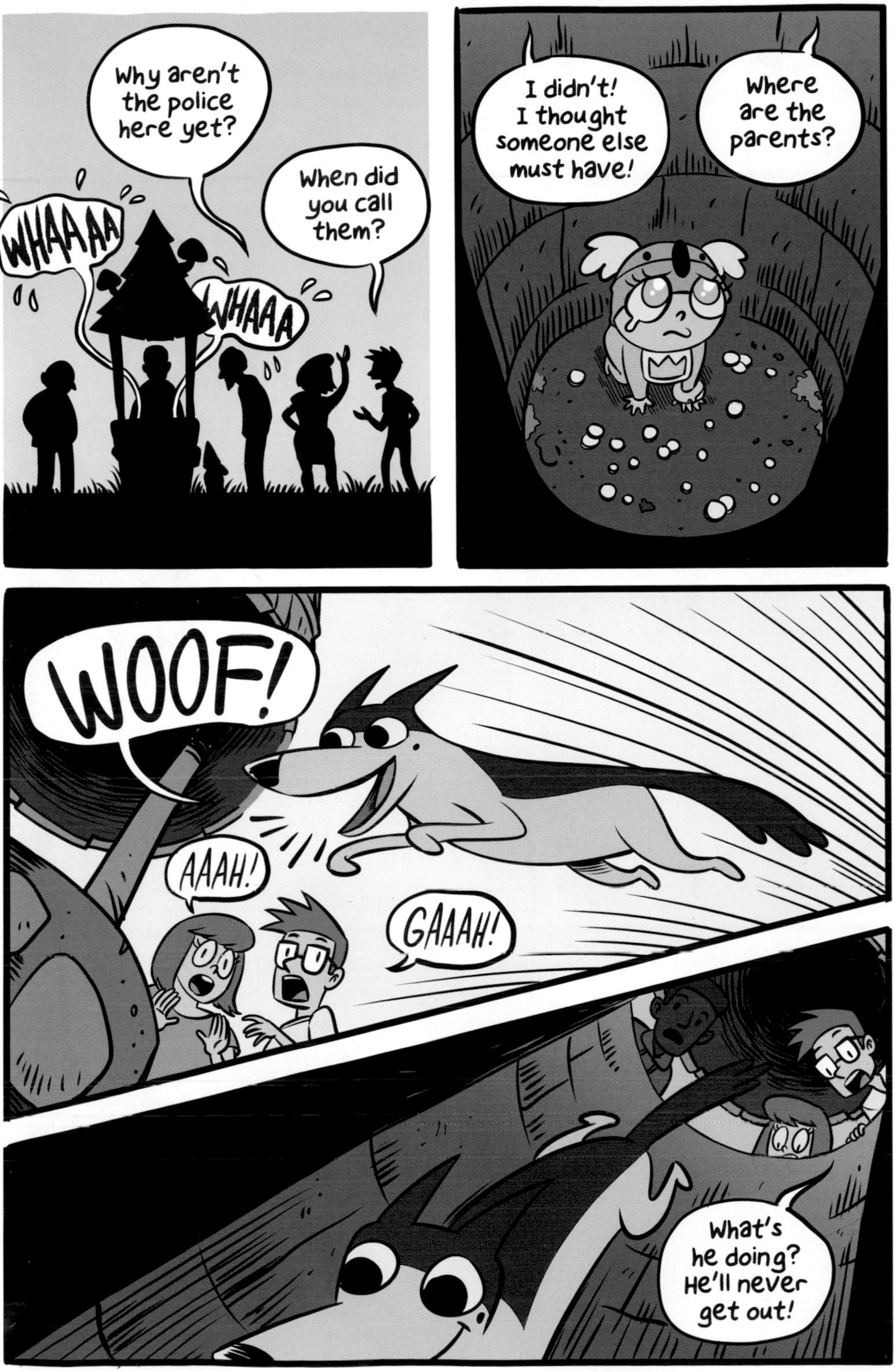
Why aren't the police here yet?
When did you call them?
WHAAAA
WHAAA
I didn't! I thought someone else must have!
Where are the parents?
WOOF!
AAAH!
GAAAH!
What's he doing? He'll never get out!

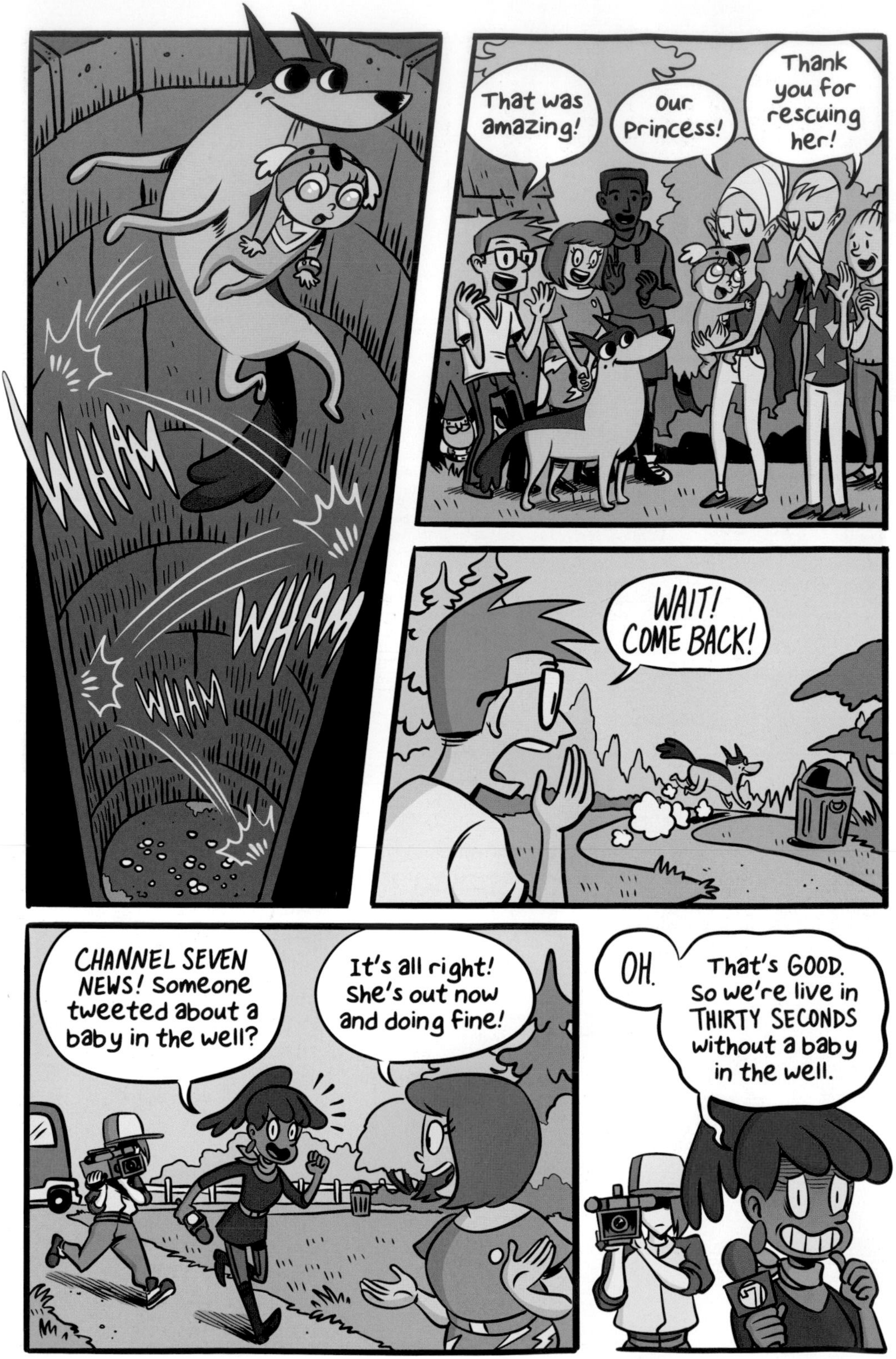
WHAM
WHAM
WHAM
That was amazing!
Our Princess!
Thank you for rescuing her!
WAIT! COME BACK!
CHANNEL SEVEN NEWS! Someone tweeted about a baby in the well?
It's all right! She's out now and doing fine!
OH.
That's GOOD. So we're live in THIRTY SECONDS without a baby in the well.

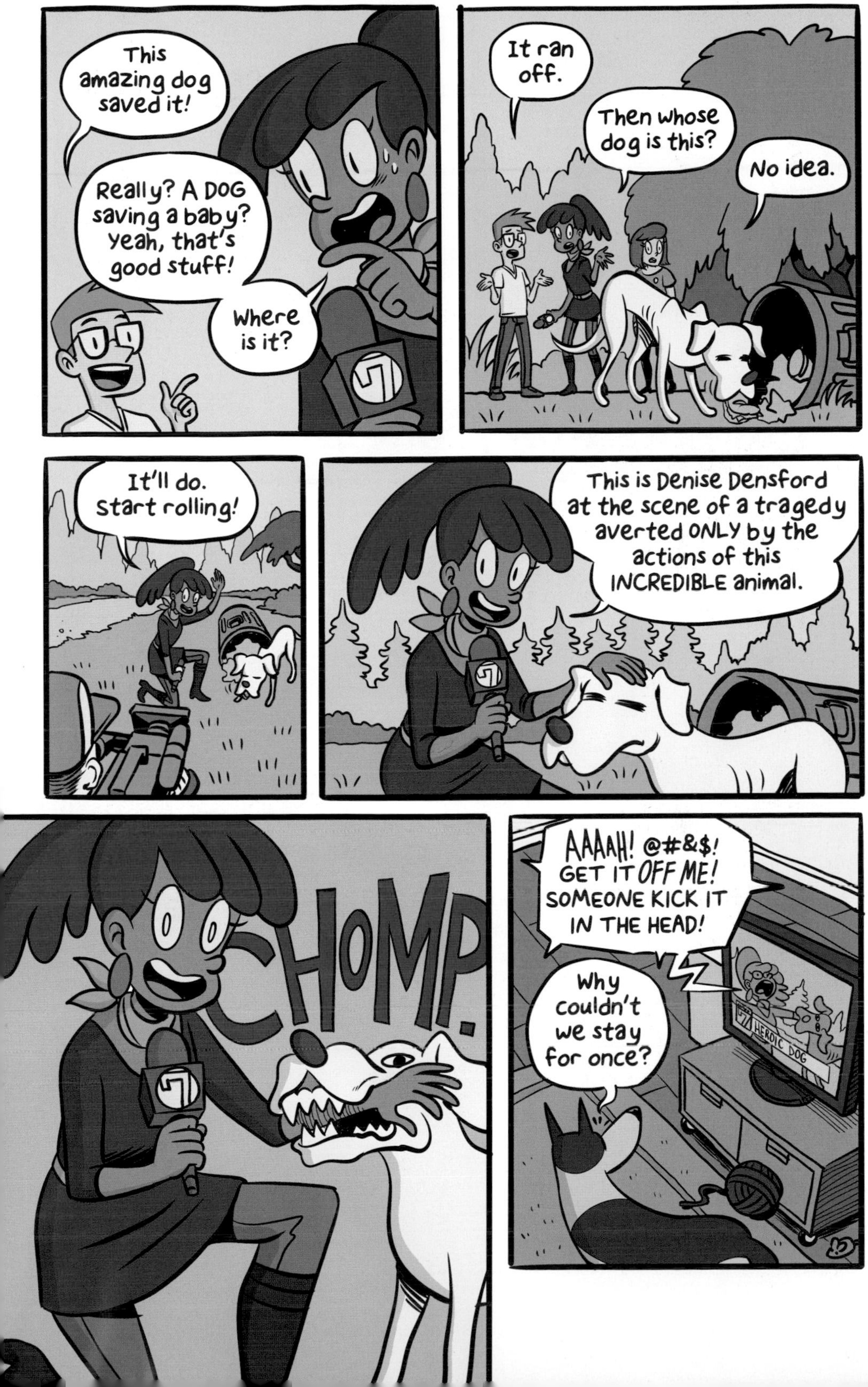
This amazing dog saved it!
Really? A DOG saving a baby? yeah, that's good stuff!
Where is it?
It ran off.
Then whose dog is this?
No idea.
It'll do. Start rolling!
This is Denise Densford at the scene of a tragedy averted ONLY by the actions of this INCREDIBLE animal.
CHOMP.
AAAAH! @#&$! GET IT OFF ME! SOMEONE KICK IT IN THE HEAD!
HEROIC DOG
Why couldn't we stay for once?

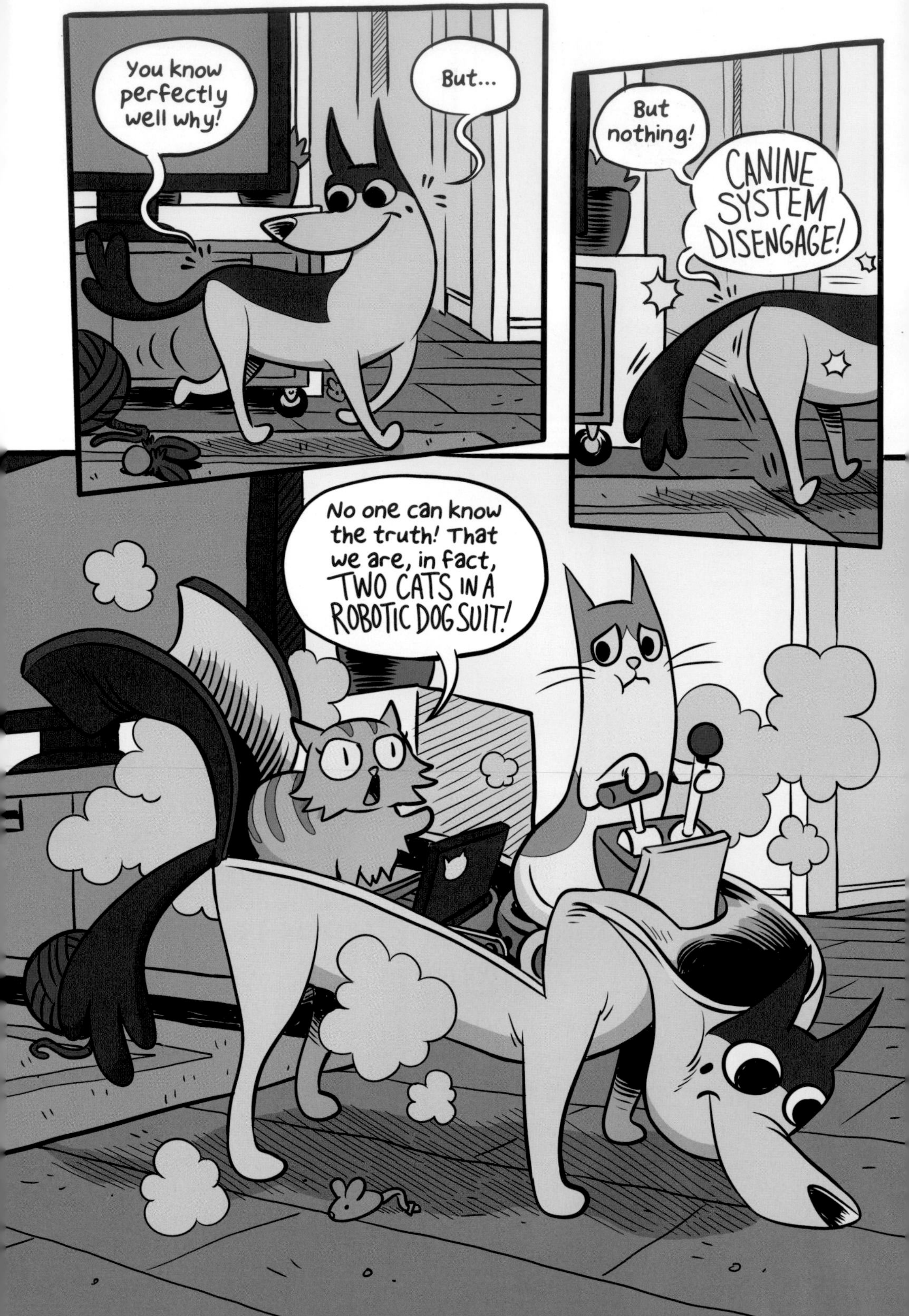
You know perfectly well why!
But...
But nothing!
CANINE SYSTEM DISENGAGE!
No one can know the truth! That we are, in fact, TWO CATS IN A ROBOTIC DOG SUIT!

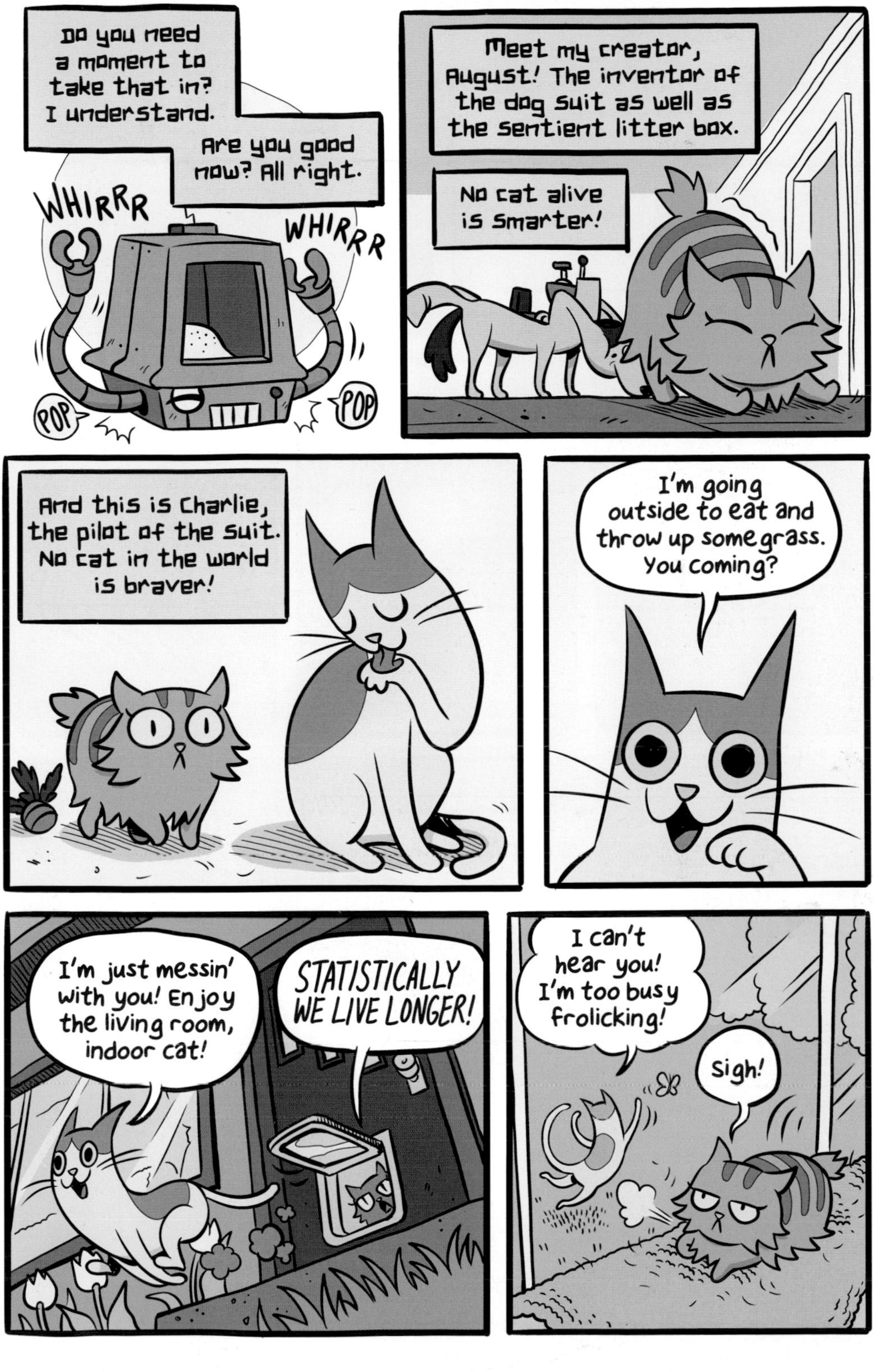
Do you need a moment to take that in? I understand.
Are you good now? All right.
WHIRRR
WHIRRR
POP
POP
Meet my creator, August! The inventor of the dog suit as well as the sentient litter box.
No cat alive is smarter!
And this is Charlie, the pilot of the suit. No cat in the world is braver!
I'm going outside to eat and throw up some grass. You coming?
I'm just messin' with you! Enjoy the living room, indoor cat!
STATISTICALLY WE LIVE LONGER!
I can't hear you! I'm too busy frolicking!
Sigh!

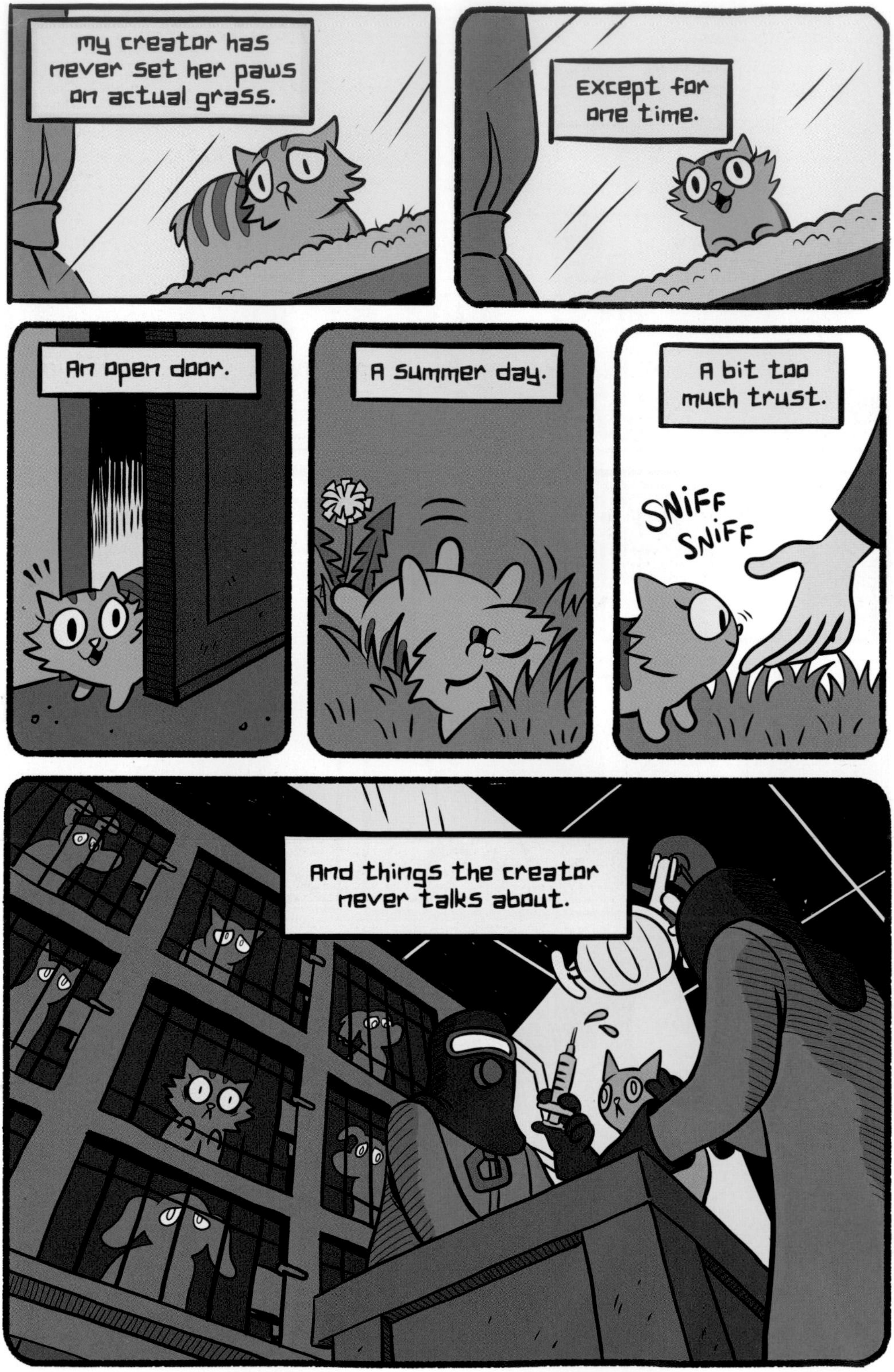
my creator has never set her paws on actual grass.
Except for one time.
An open door.
A summer day.
A bit too much trust.
SNIFF SNIFF
And things the creator never talks about.

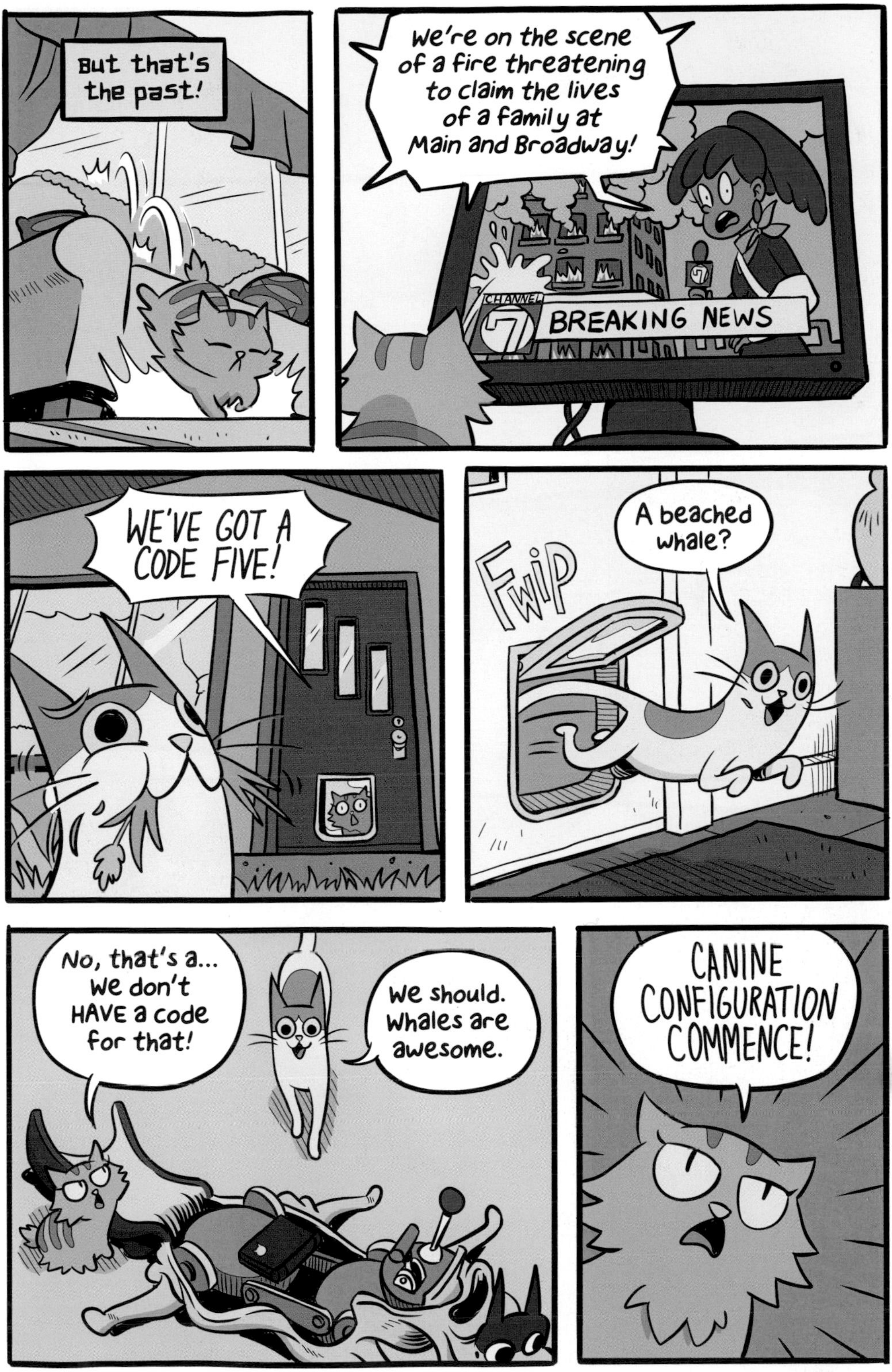
But that's the past!
We're on the scene of a fire threatening to claim the lives of a family at Main and Broadway!
CHANNEL 7
BREAKING NEWS
WE'VE GOT A CODE FIVE!
Fwip
A beached whale?
No, that's a... we don't HAVE a code for that!
We should. Whales are awesome.
CANINE CONFIGURATION COMMENCE!

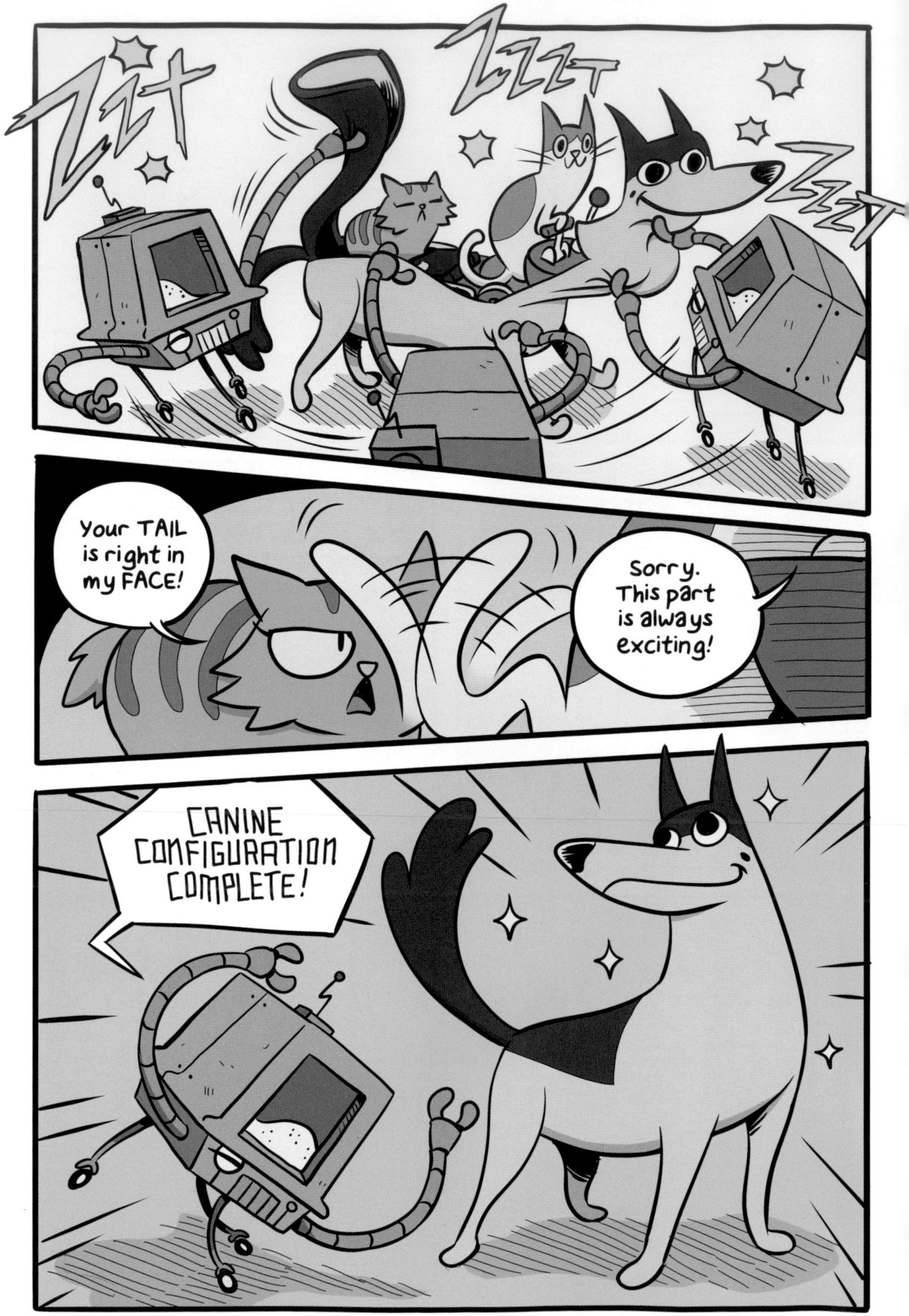
ZZT
ZZZT
ZZZT
Your TAIL is right in my FACE!
Sorry. This part is always exciting!
CANINE CONFIGURATION COMPLETE!

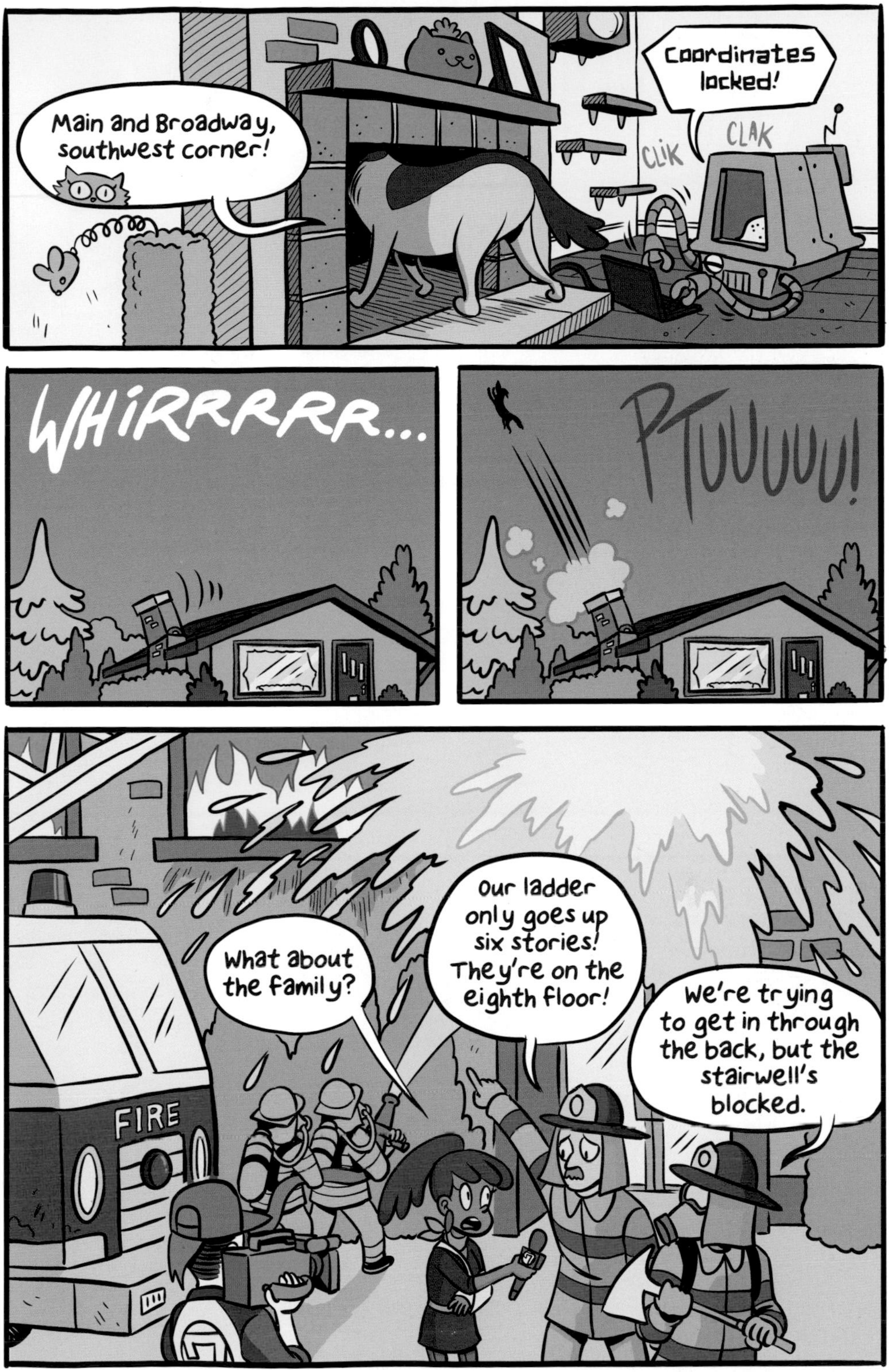
Main and Broadway, southwest corner!
Coordinates locked!
CLIK
CLAK
WHIRRRRR...
PTUUUUU!
What about the family?
Our ladder only goes up six stories! They're on the eighth floor!
We're trying to get in through the back, but the stairwell's blocked.
FIRE

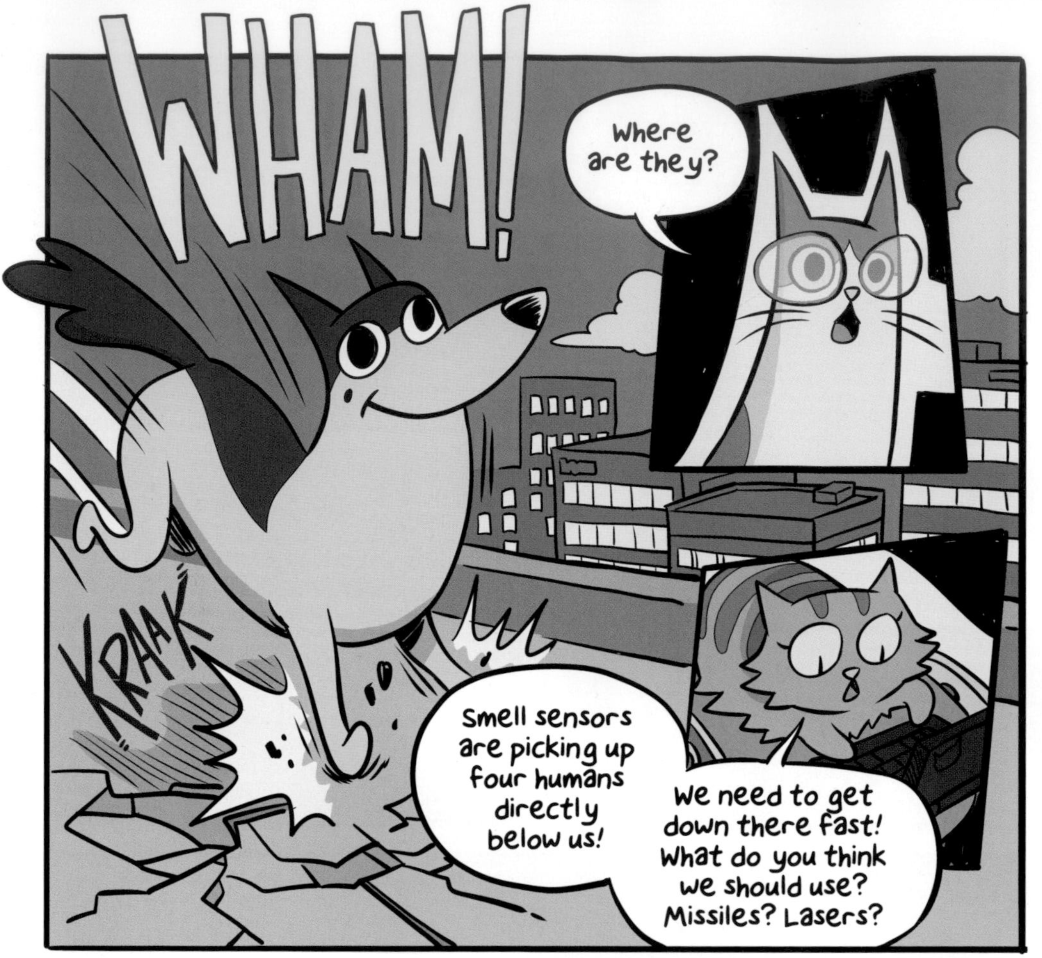
WHAM!
Where are they?
KRAAK
Smell sensors are picking up four humans directly below us!
We need to get down there fast! What do you think we should use? Missiles? Lasers?

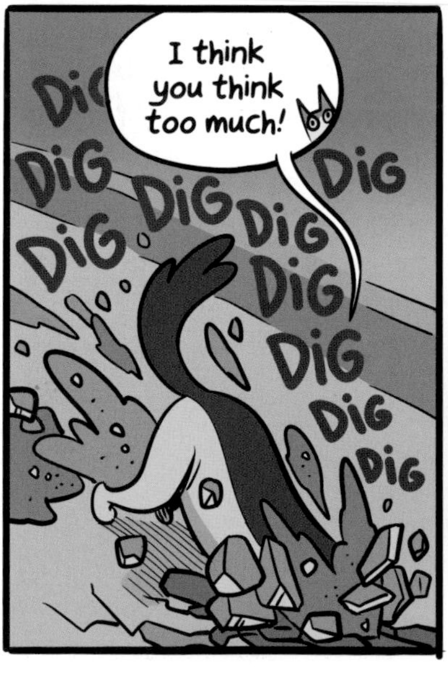
I think you think too much!
DIG DIG DIG DIG DIG DIG DIG DIG DIG DIG

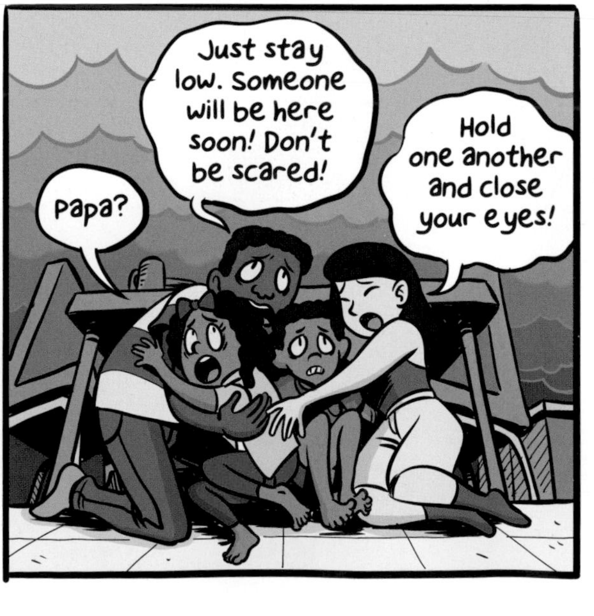
Papa?
Just stay low. Someone will be here soon! Don't be scared!
Hold one another and close your eyes!

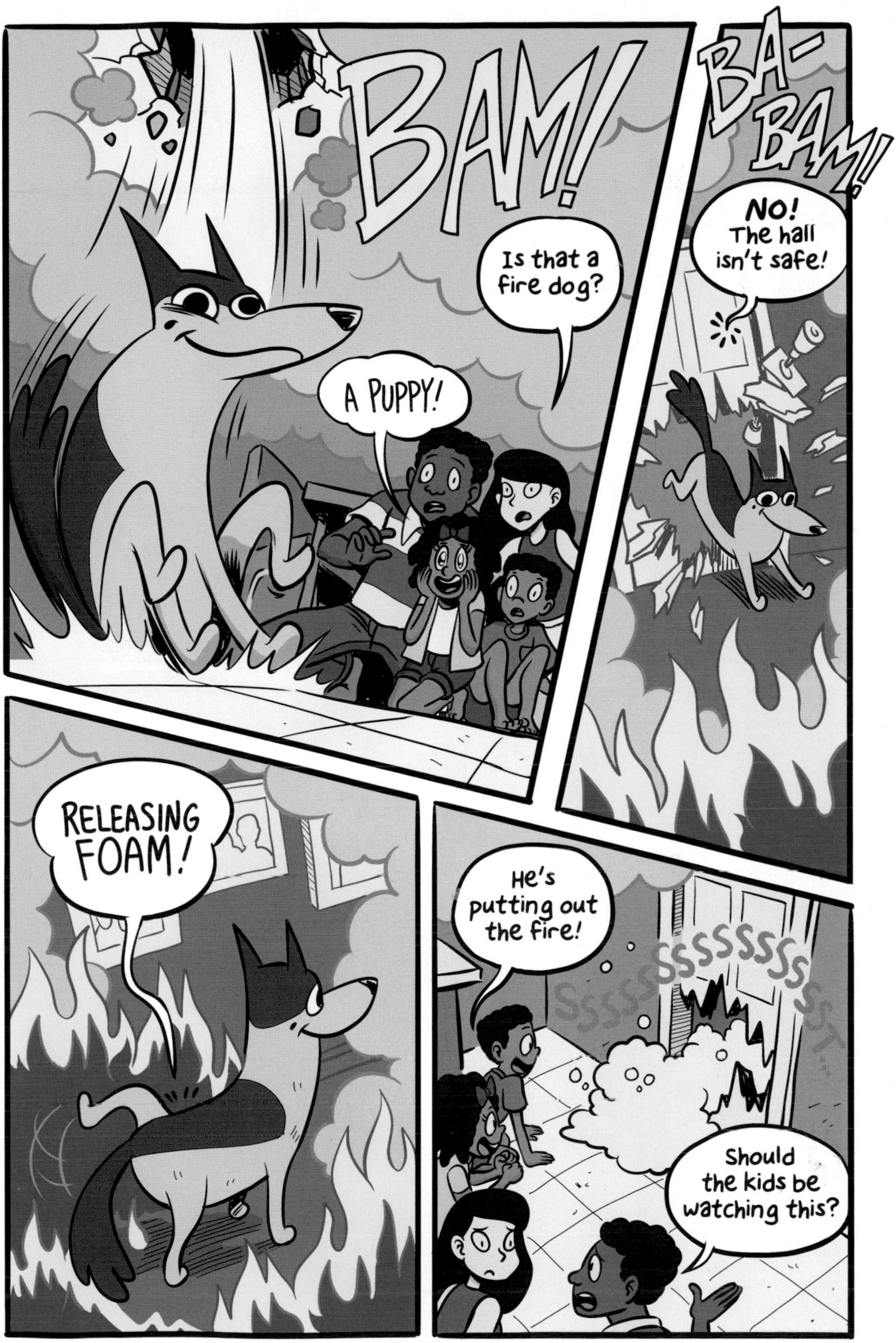
BAM!
Is that a fire dog?
A PUPPY!
BA-BAM!
NO! The hall isn't safe!
RELEASING FOAM!
He's putting out the fire!
SSSSSSSSSSSSSSSST...
Should the kids be watching this?

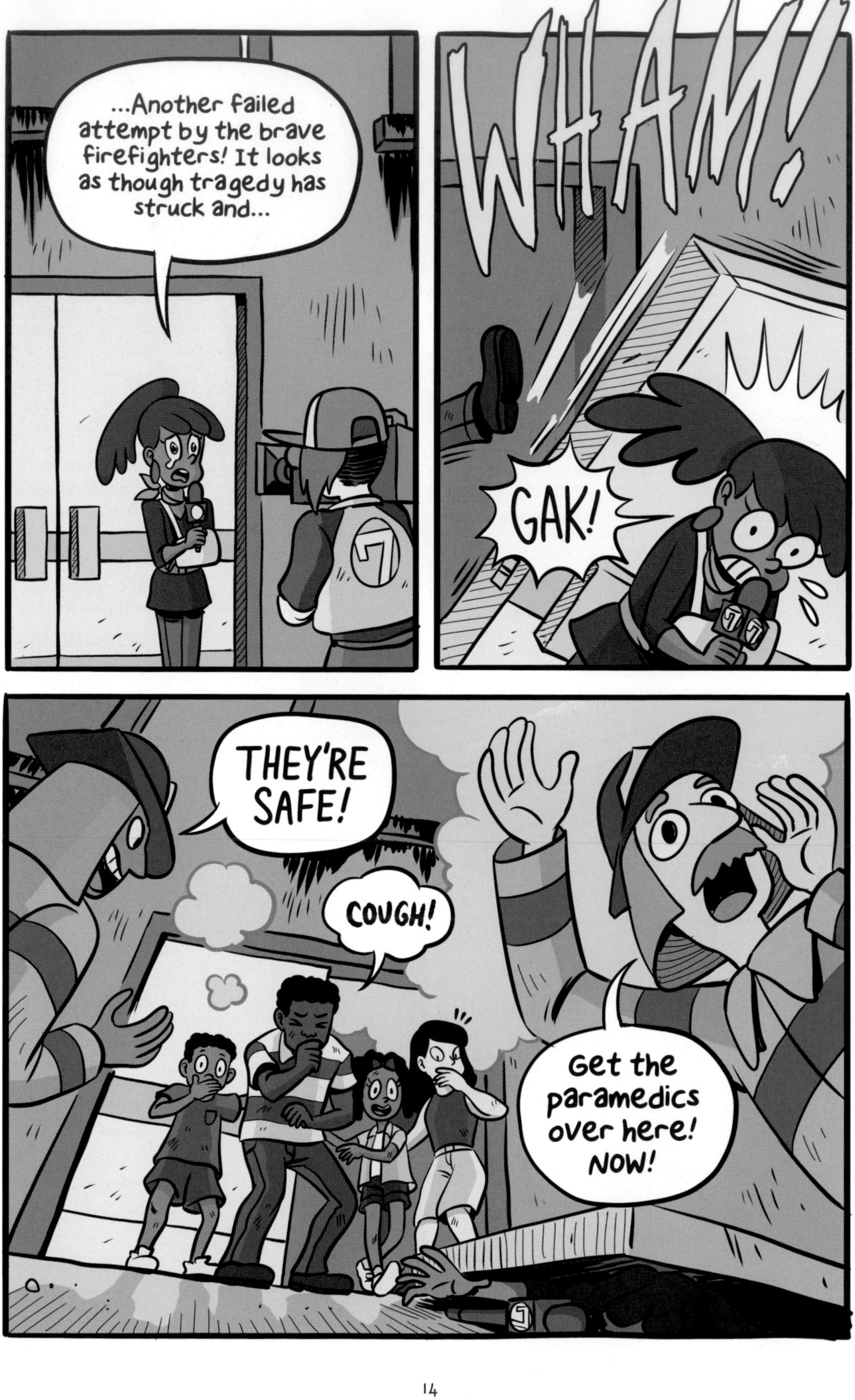
...Another failed attempt by the brave firefighters! It looks as though tragedy has struck and...
WHAM!
GAK!
THEY'RE SAFE!
COUGH!
Get the paramedics over here! NOW!

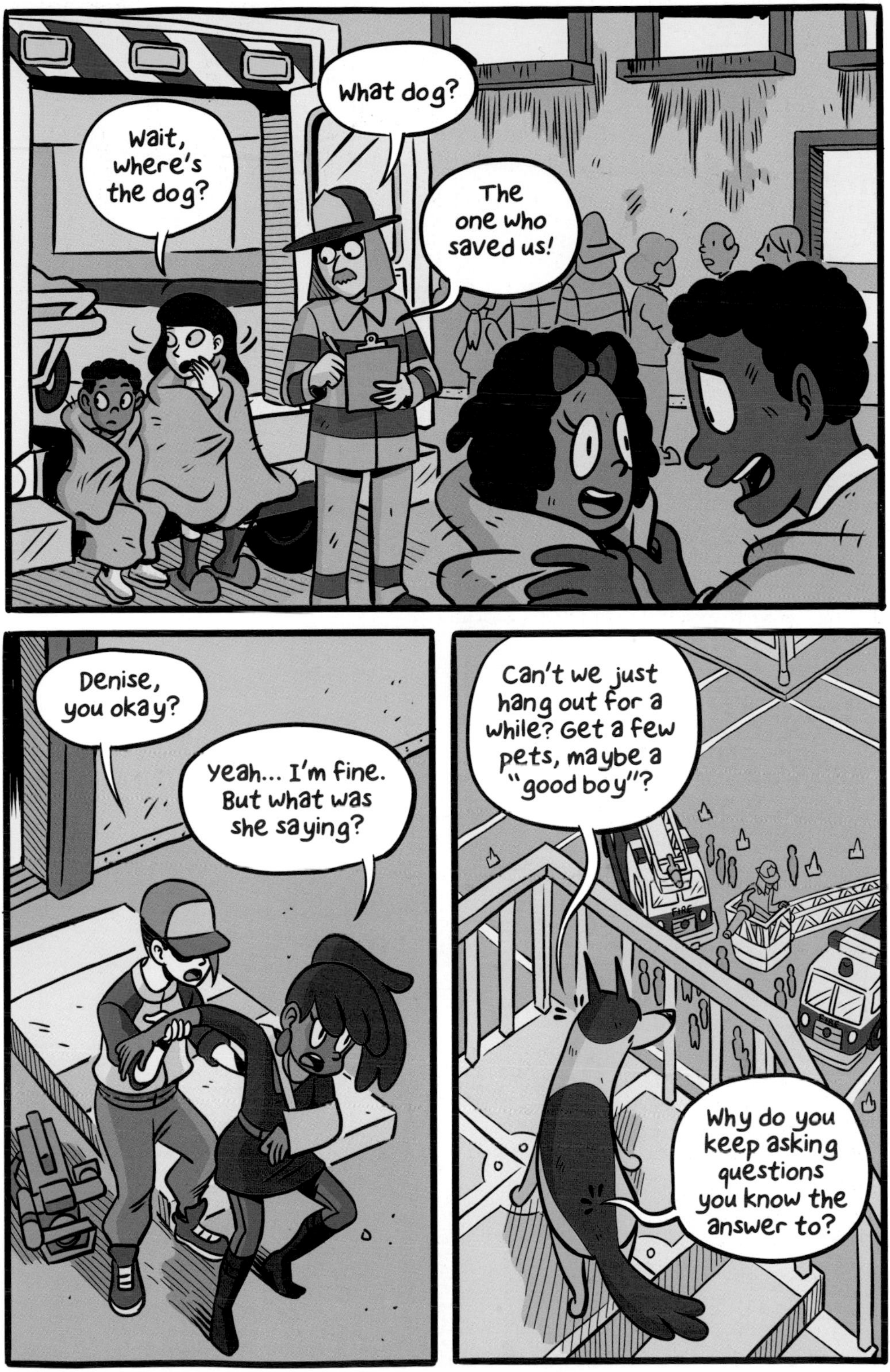
Wait, where's the dog?
What dog?
The one who saved us!
Denise, you okay?
Yeah... I'm fine. But what was she saying?
Can't we just hang out for a while? Get a few pets, maybe a "good boy"?
FIRE
FIRE
Why do you keep asking questions you know the answer to?

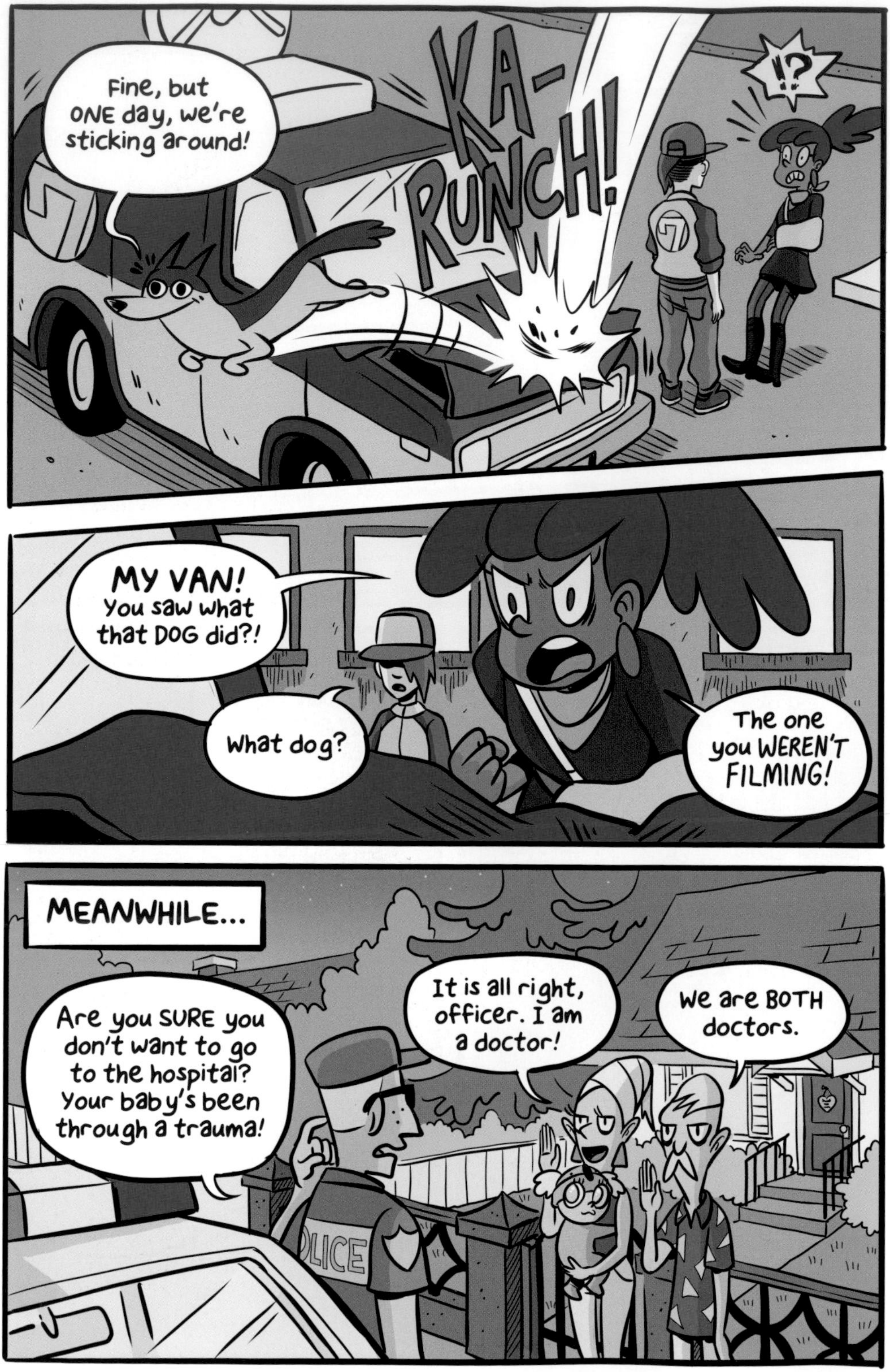
Fine, but ONE day, we're sticking around!
KA-RUNCH!
!?
MY VAN! You saw what that DOG did?!
What dog?
The one you WEREN'T FILMING!
MEANWHILE...
Are you SURE you don't want to go to the hospital? Your baby's been through a trauma!
It is all right, officer. I am a doctor!
We are BOTH doctors.
POLICE

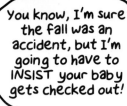

You know, I'm sure the fall was an accident, but I'm going to have to INSIST your baby gets checked out!

Just to be safe!

of course.

safety first.

I'm going to radio the hospital. Let them know we're on the way.

If you want to gather any of the baby's things...

Would you mind holding this for us while we do that?

Sure. What is it?

POP

A TEMPORARY BLACK HOLE with a radius of three meters.

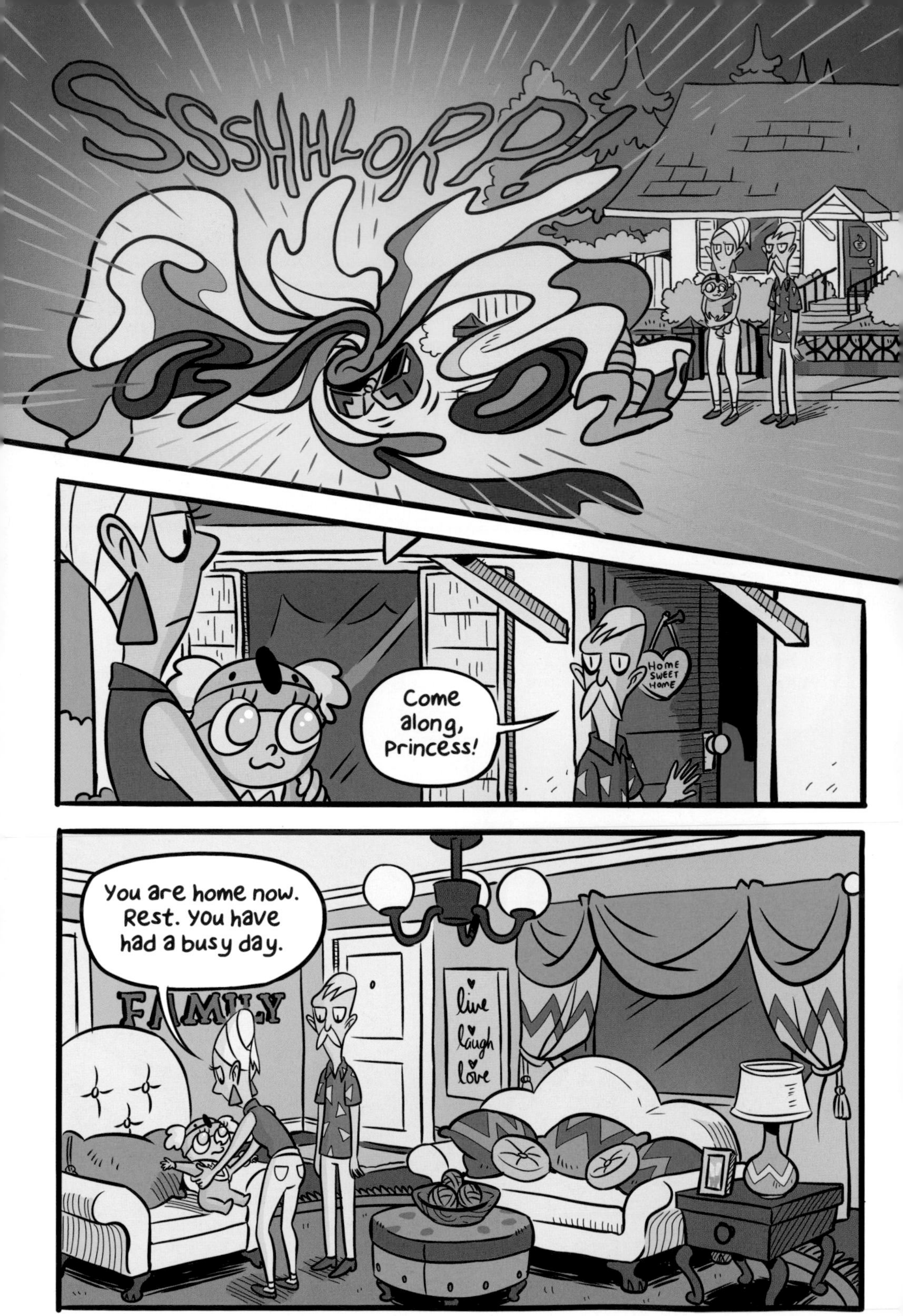
SSSHHLORPP!
HOME SWEET HOME
Come along, Princess!
You are home now. Rest. You have had a busy day.
FAMILY
live laugh love

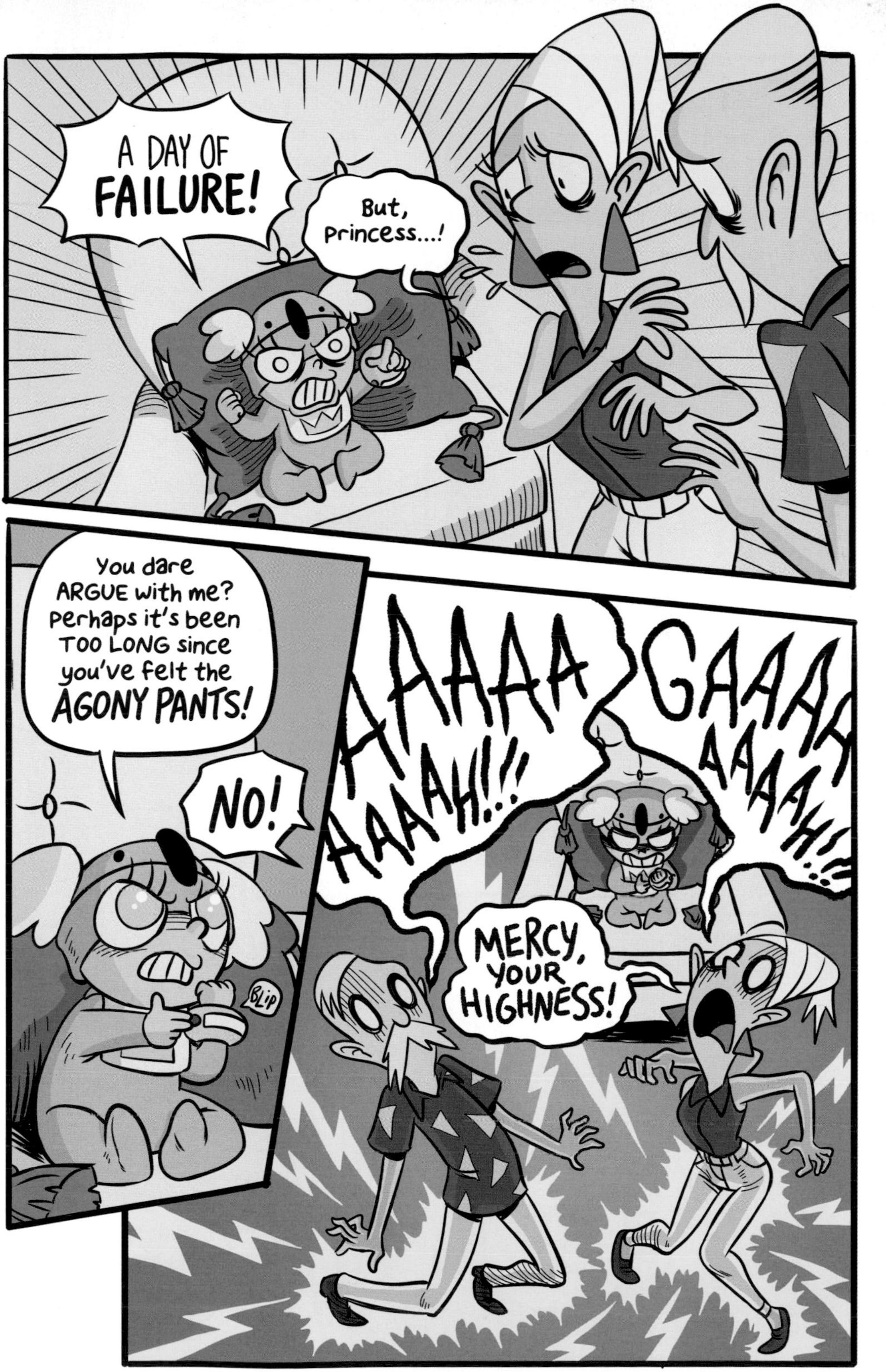
A DAY OF FAILURE!
But, Princess....!
You dare ARGUE with me? Perhaps it's been TOO LONG since you've felt the AGONY PANTS!
NO!
BLIP
AAAAA HAAAH!!!
GAAAA AAAAH!!!
MERCY, YOUR HIGHNESS!

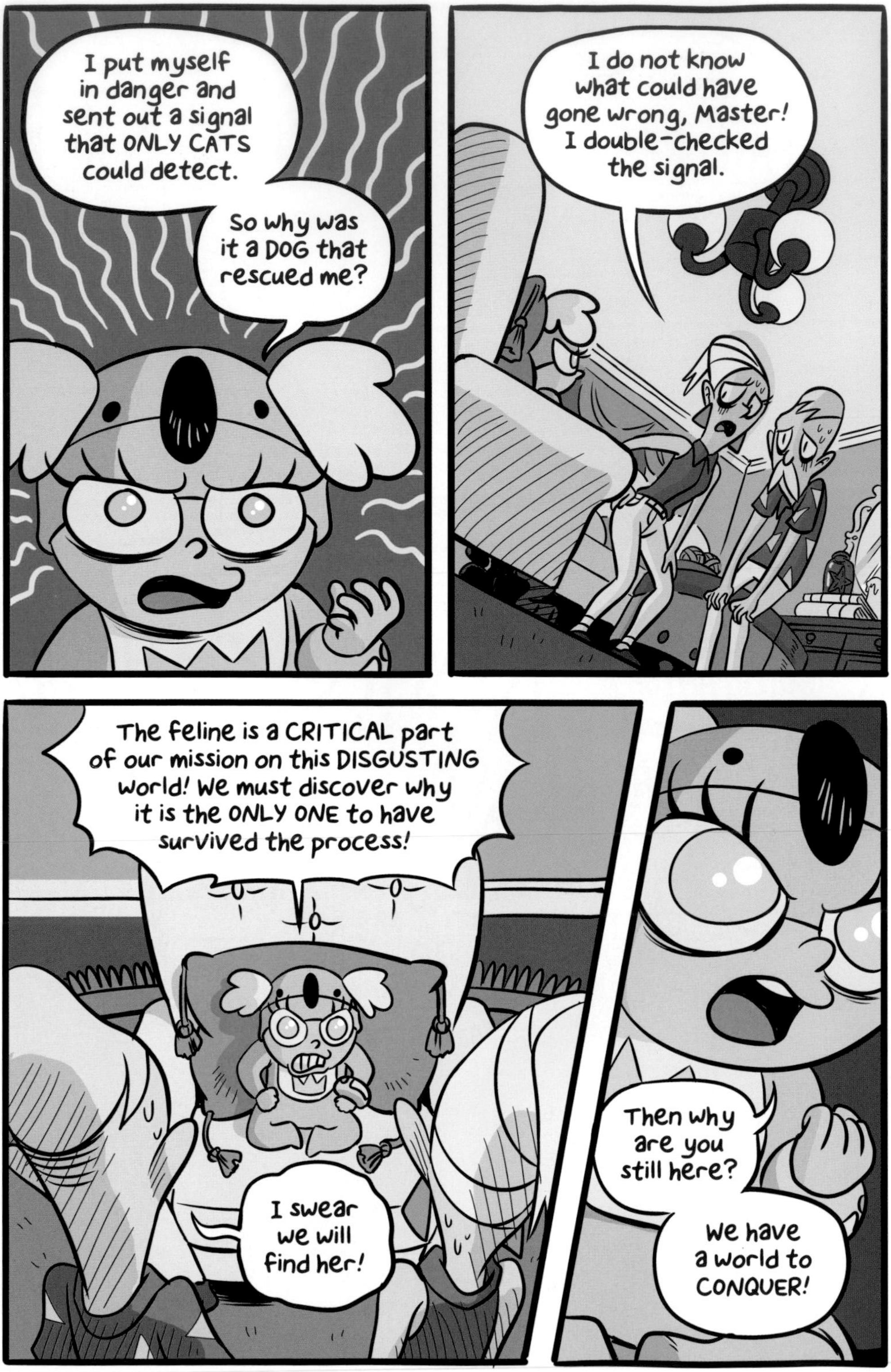
I put myself in danger and sent out a signal that ONLY CATS could detect.
So why was it a DOG that rescued me?
I do not know what could have gone wrong, Master! I double-checked the signal.
The feline is a CRITICAL part of our mission on this DISGUSTING world! We must discover why it is the ONLY ONE to have survived the process!
I swear we will find her!
Then why are you still here?
We have a world to CONQUER!

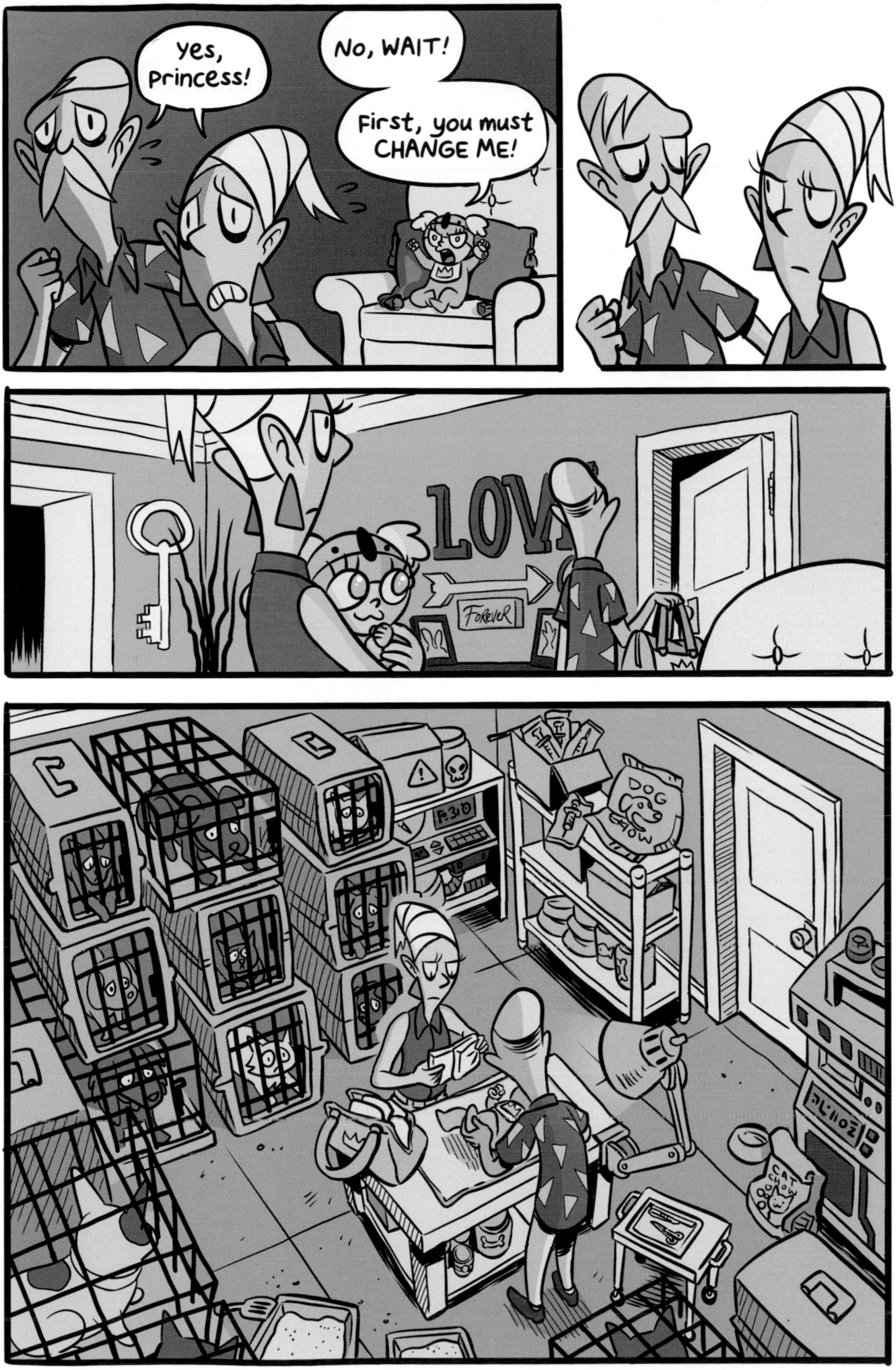
yes, princess!
No, WAIT!
First, you must CHANGE ME!
LOVE
FOREVER
DOG CHOW
CAT CHOW

CHAPTER TW

FAMILY
live
laugh
love
FAMILY
live
laugh
love
I HAVE AWAKENED!
live
laugh

Greetings, oh mighty and perfect Princess. Did you sleep well?

How would YOU sleep if you had to live like a MEWLING INFANT?

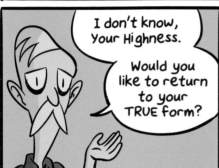

I don't know, Your Highness.

Would you like to return to your TRUE form?

No. We can't risk being discovered so close to the fruition of our plan!

All our YEARS of experiments have led to one thing!

A DEVICE THAT CAN CONTROL EVERY ANIMAL ON EARTH!

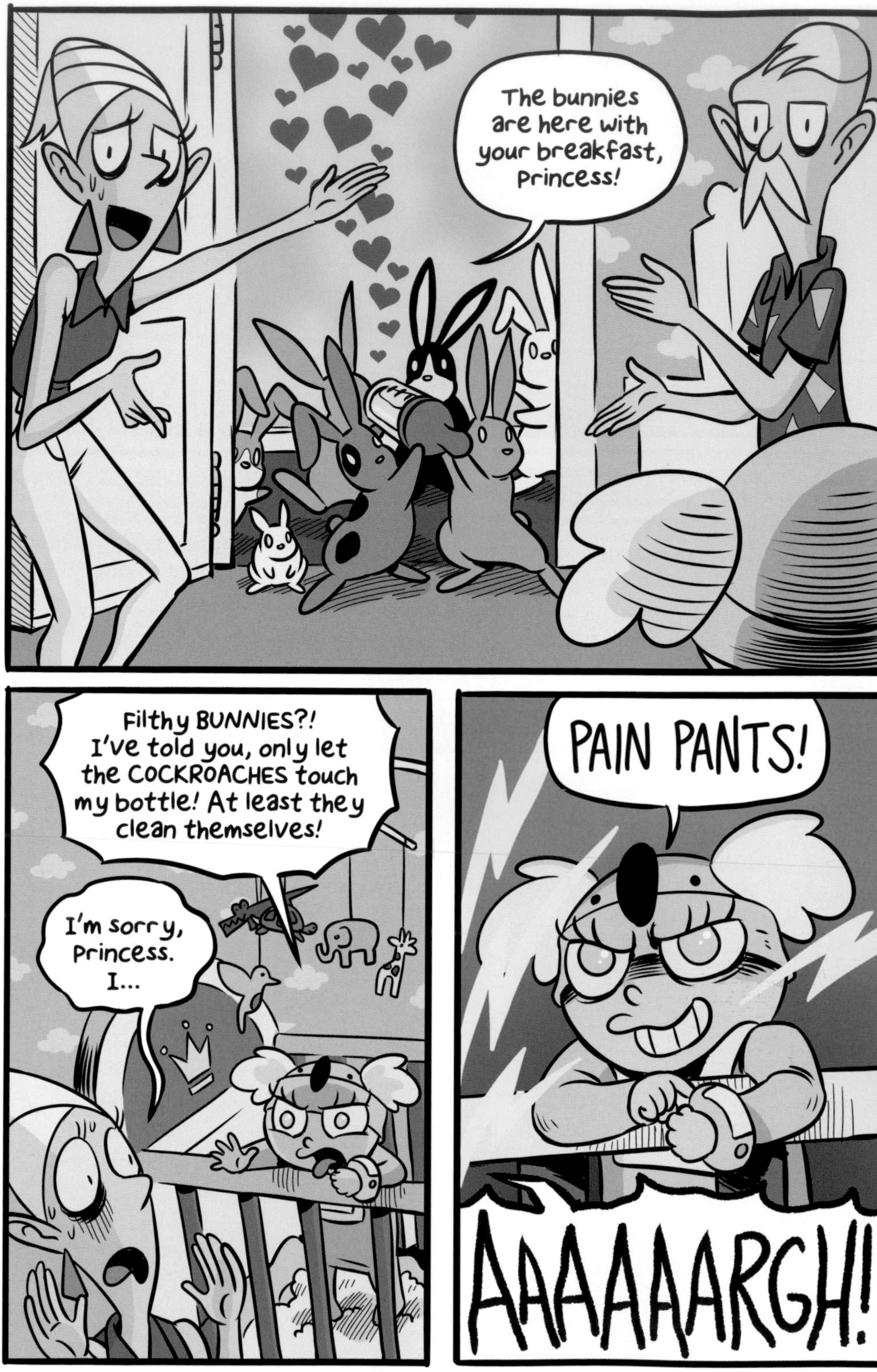
The bunnies are here with your breakfast, Princess!
Filthy BUNNIES?! I've told you, only let the COCKROACHES touch my bottle! At least they clean themselves!
I'm sorry, Princess. I...
PAIN PANTS!
AAAAAARGH!

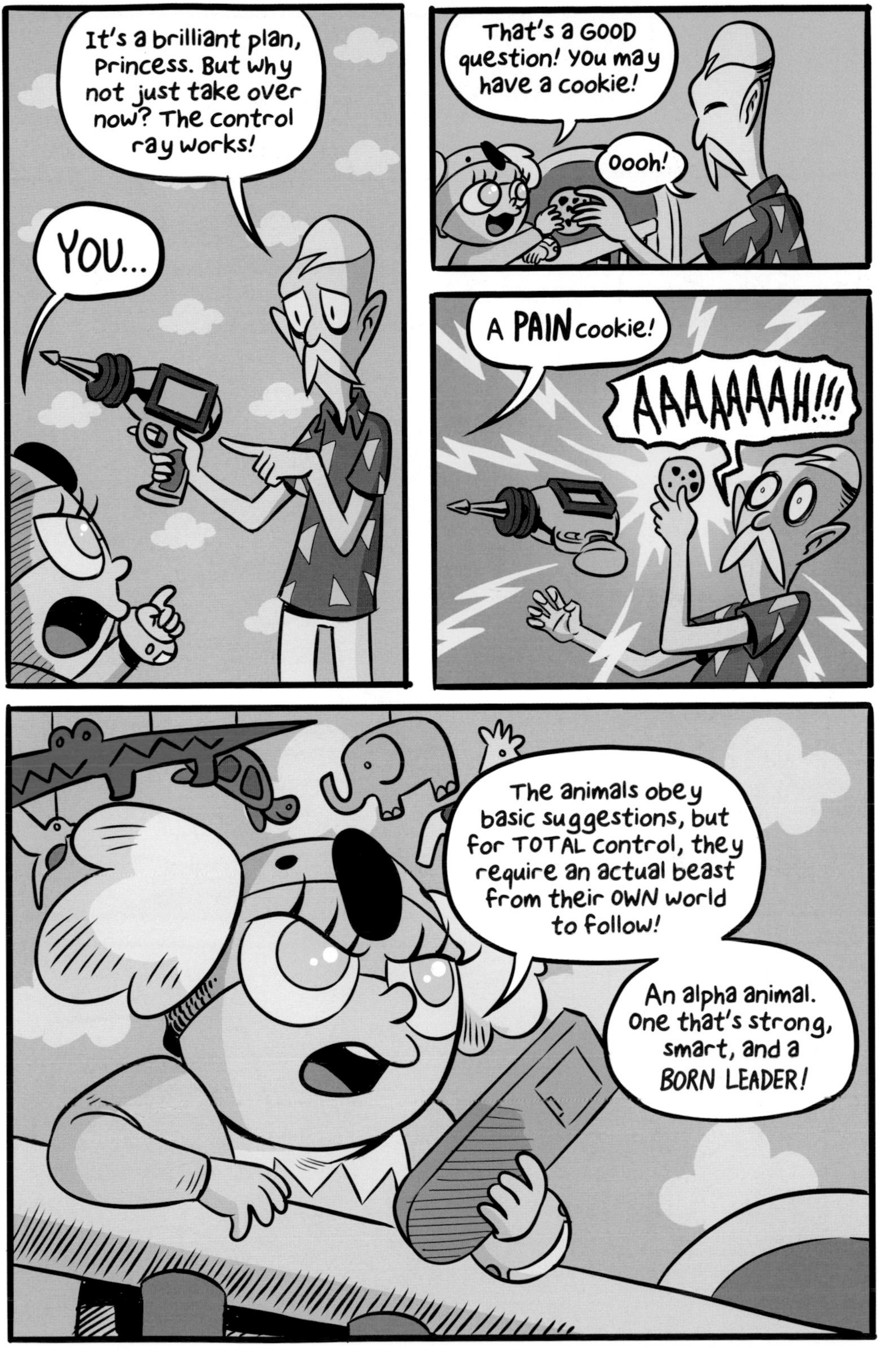
It's a brilliant plan, Princess. But why not just take over now? The control ray works!
YOU...
That's a GOOD question! You may have a cookie!
Oooh!
A PAIN cookie!
AAAAAAAH!!!
The animals obey basic suggestions, but for TOTAL control, they require an actual beast from their OWN world to follow!
An alpha animal. One that's strong, smart, and a BORN LEADER!

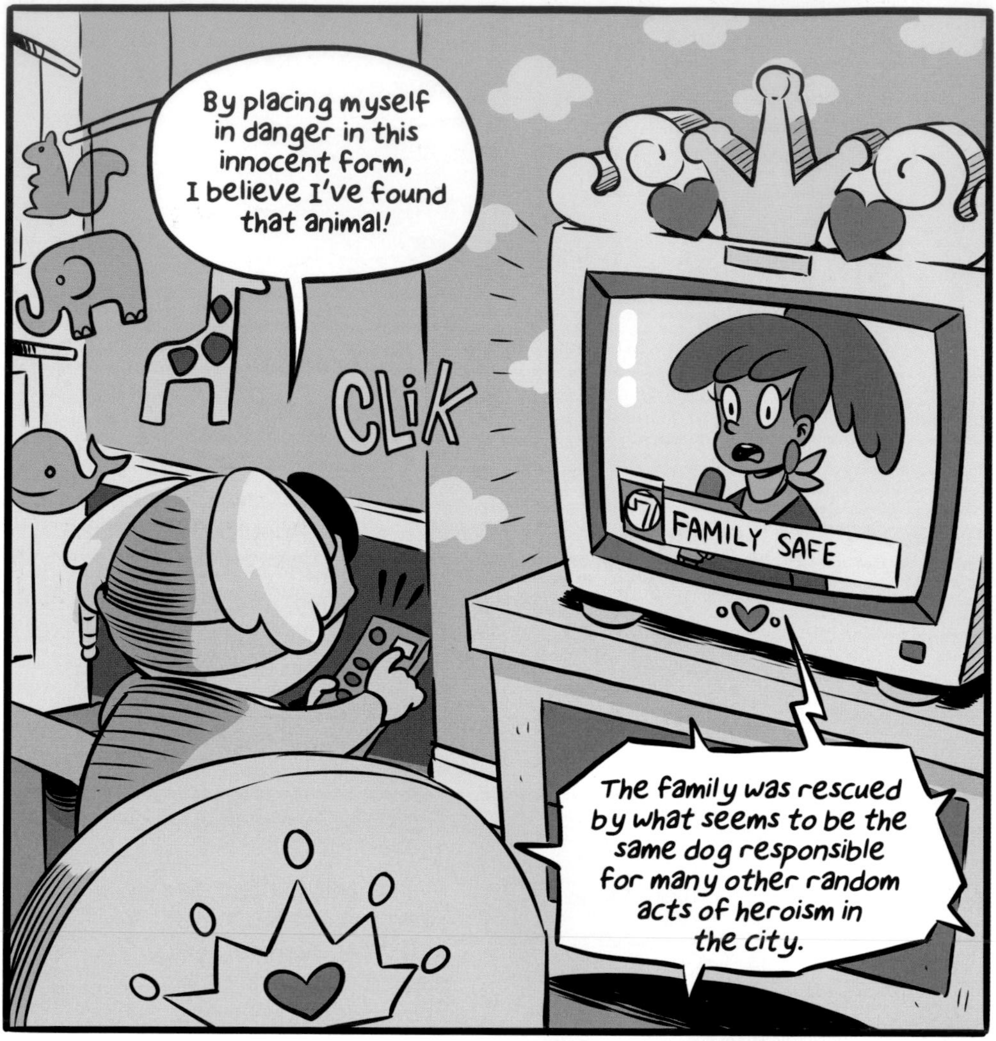
By placing myself in danger in this innocent form, I believe I've found that animal!
CLIK
FAMILY SAFE
The family was rescued by what seems to be the same dog responsible for many other random acts of heroism in the city.

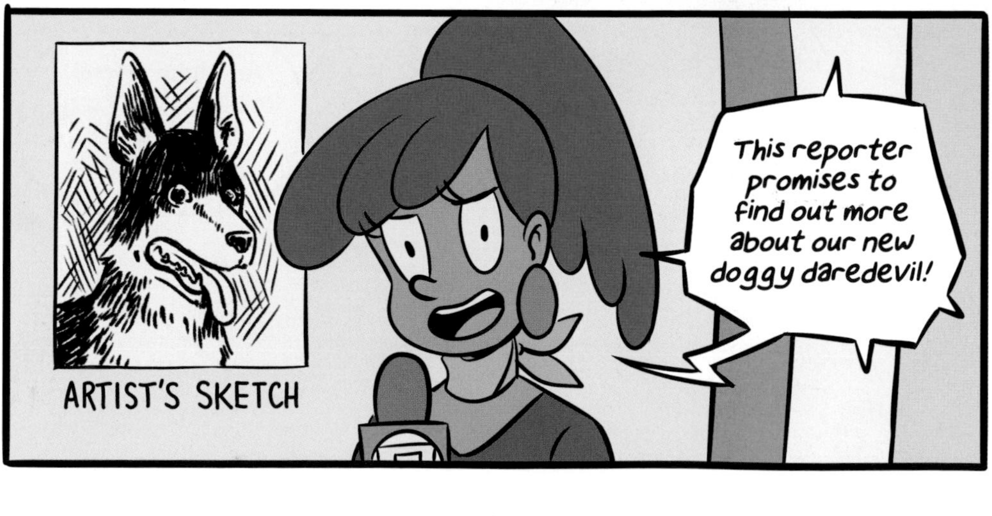
ARTIST'S SKETCH
This reporter promises to find out more about our new doggy daredevil!

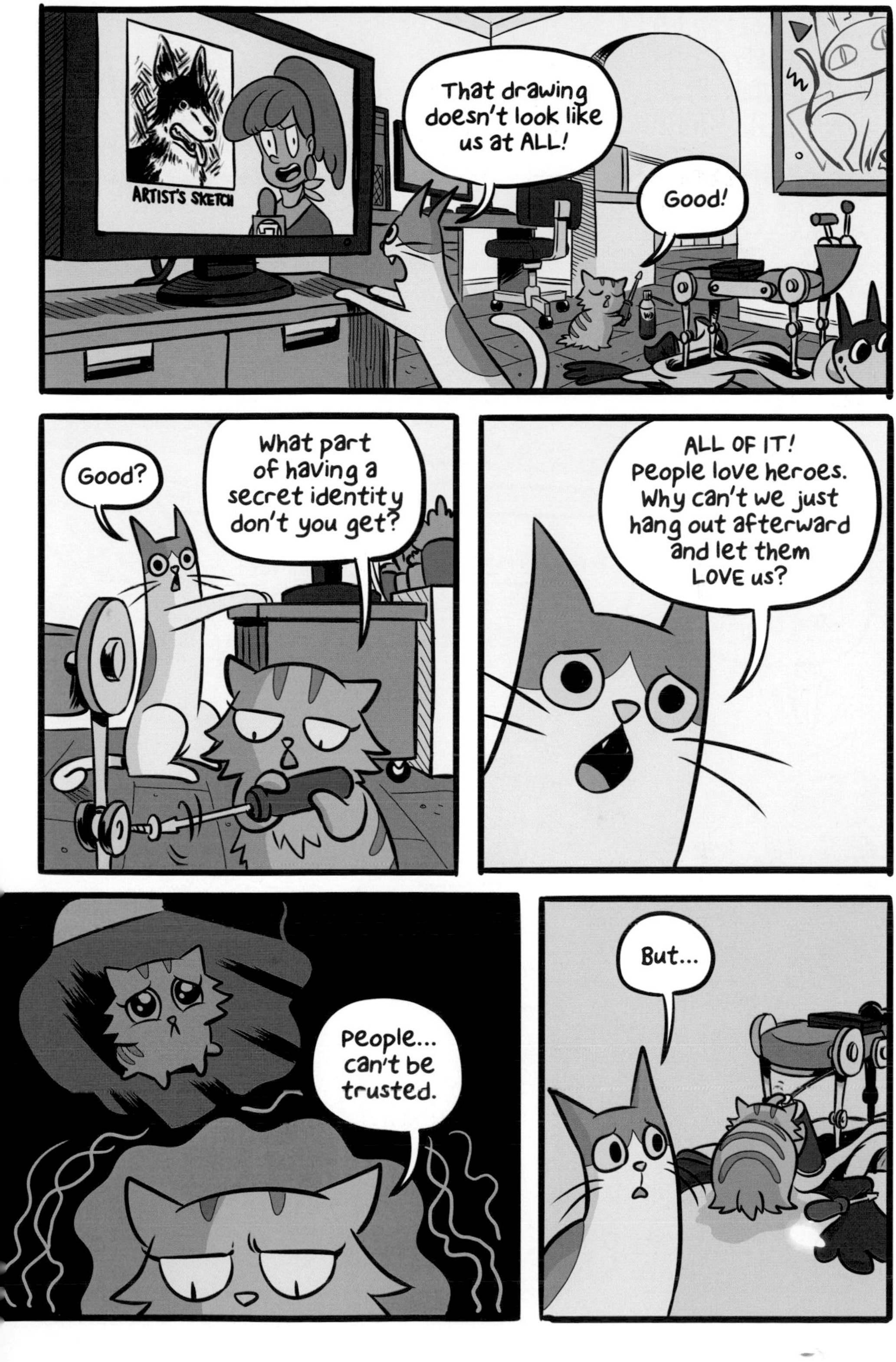
ARTIST'S SKETCH
That drawing doesn't look like us at ALL!
Good!
Good?
What part of having a secret identity don't you get?
ALL OF IT! People love heroes. Why can't we just hang out afterward and let them LOVE us?
People... can't be trusted.
But...

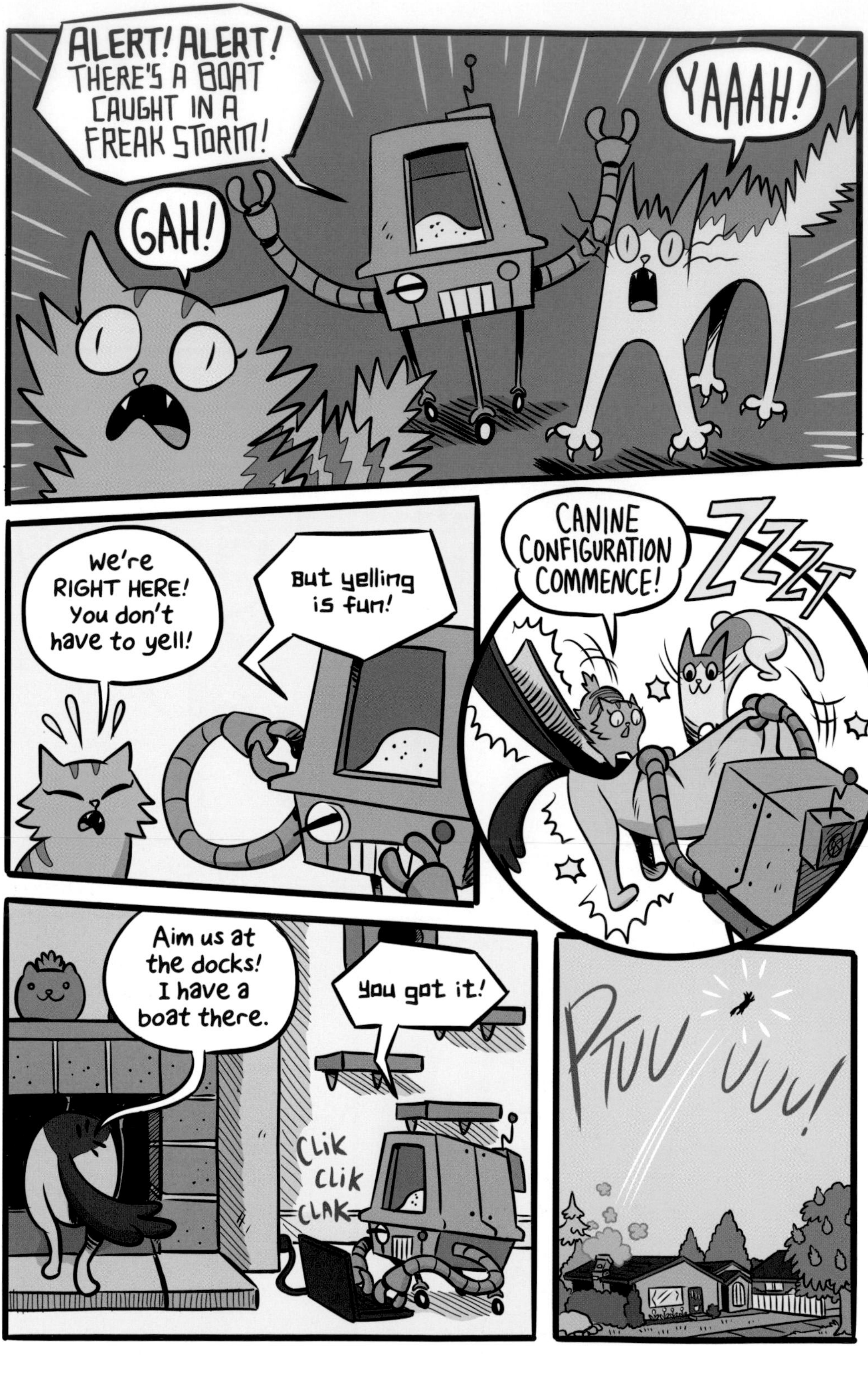
ALERT! ALERT! THERE'S A BOAT CAUGHT IN A FREAK STORM!
YAAAH!
GAH!
We're RIGHT HERE! You don't have to yell!
But yelling is fun!
CANINE CONFIGURATION COMMENCE!
ZZZZT
Aim us at the docks! I have a boat there.
You got it!
CLIK
CLIK
CLAK
PTUUUUU!

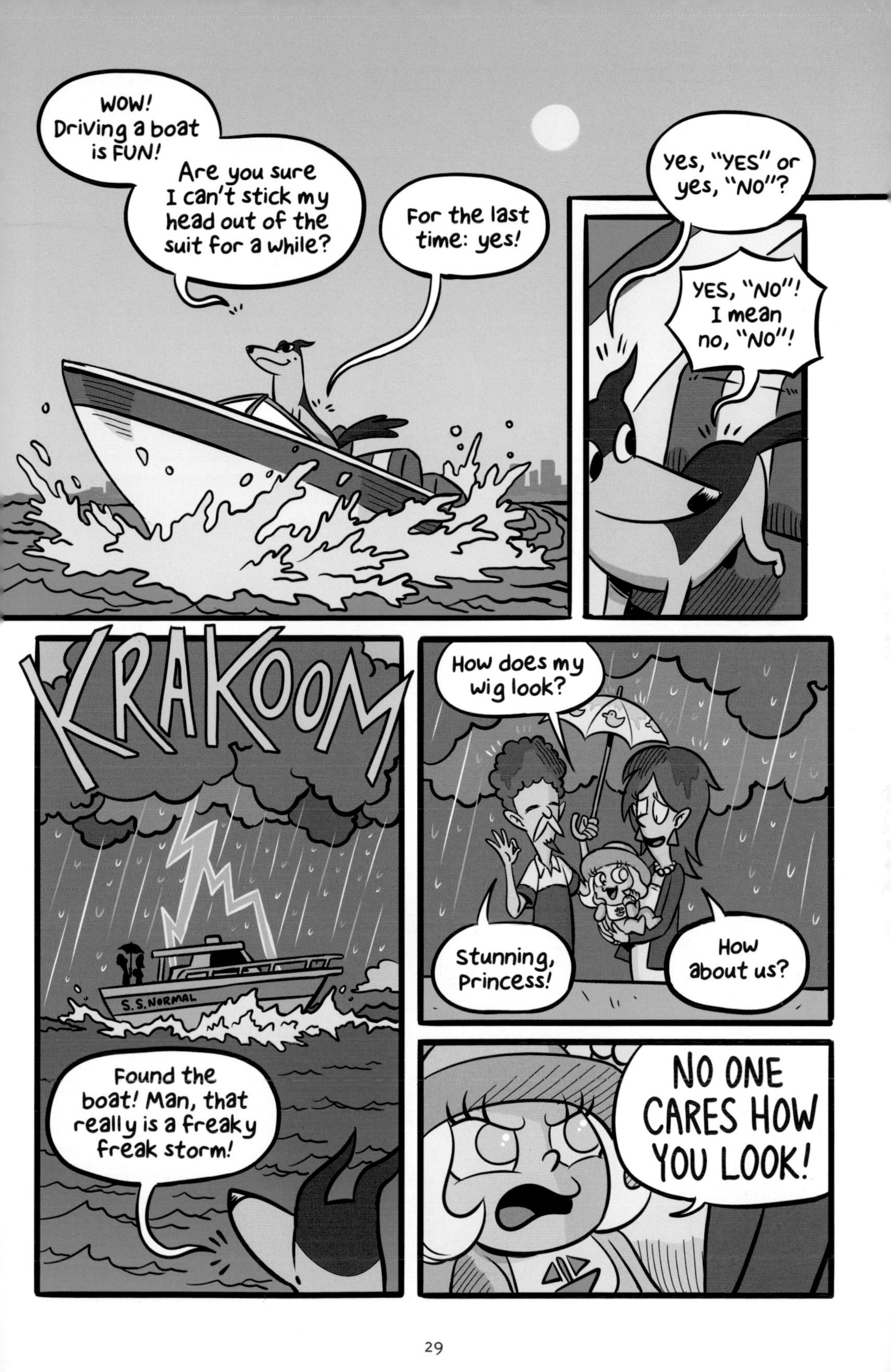
WOW! Driving a boat is FUN!
Are you sure I can't stick my head out of the suit for a while?
For the last time: yes!
Yes, "YES" or yes, "NO"?
YES, "NO"! I mean no, "NO"!
KRAKOOM
S.S. NORMAL
Found the boat! Man, that really is a freaky freak storm!
How does my wig look?
Stunning, Princess!
How about us?
NO ONE CARES HOW YOU LOOK!

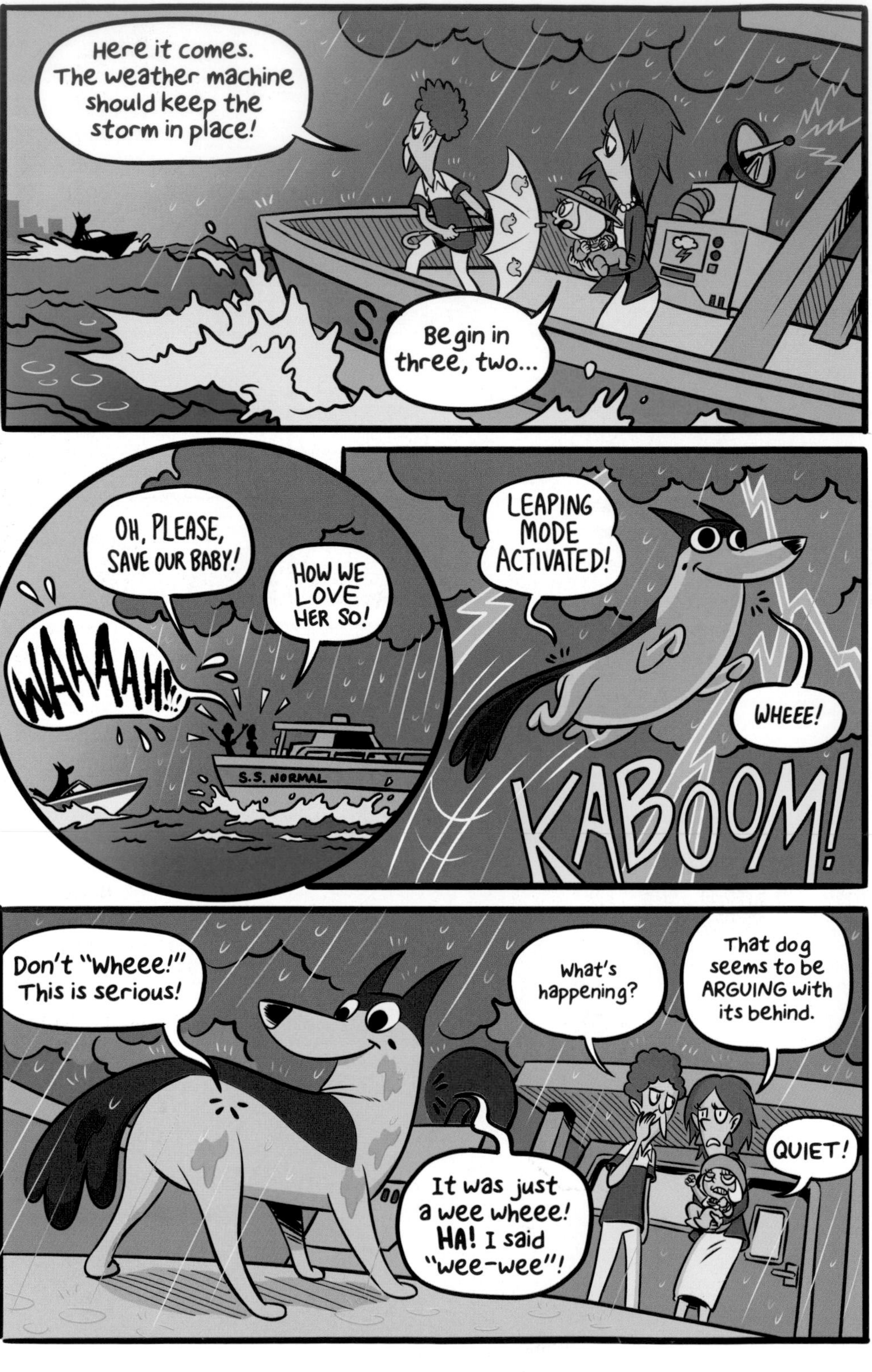
Here it comes. The weather machine should keep the storm in place!
Begin in three, two...
S.S.
OH, PLEASE, SAVE OUR BABY!
HOW WE LOVE HER SO!
WAAAAH!!!
S.S. NORMAL
LEAPING MODE ACTIVATED!
WHEEE!
KABOOM!
Don't "Wheee!" This is serious!
What's happening?
That dog seems to be ARGUING with its behind.
QUIET!
It was just a wee wheee! HA! I said "wee-wee"!

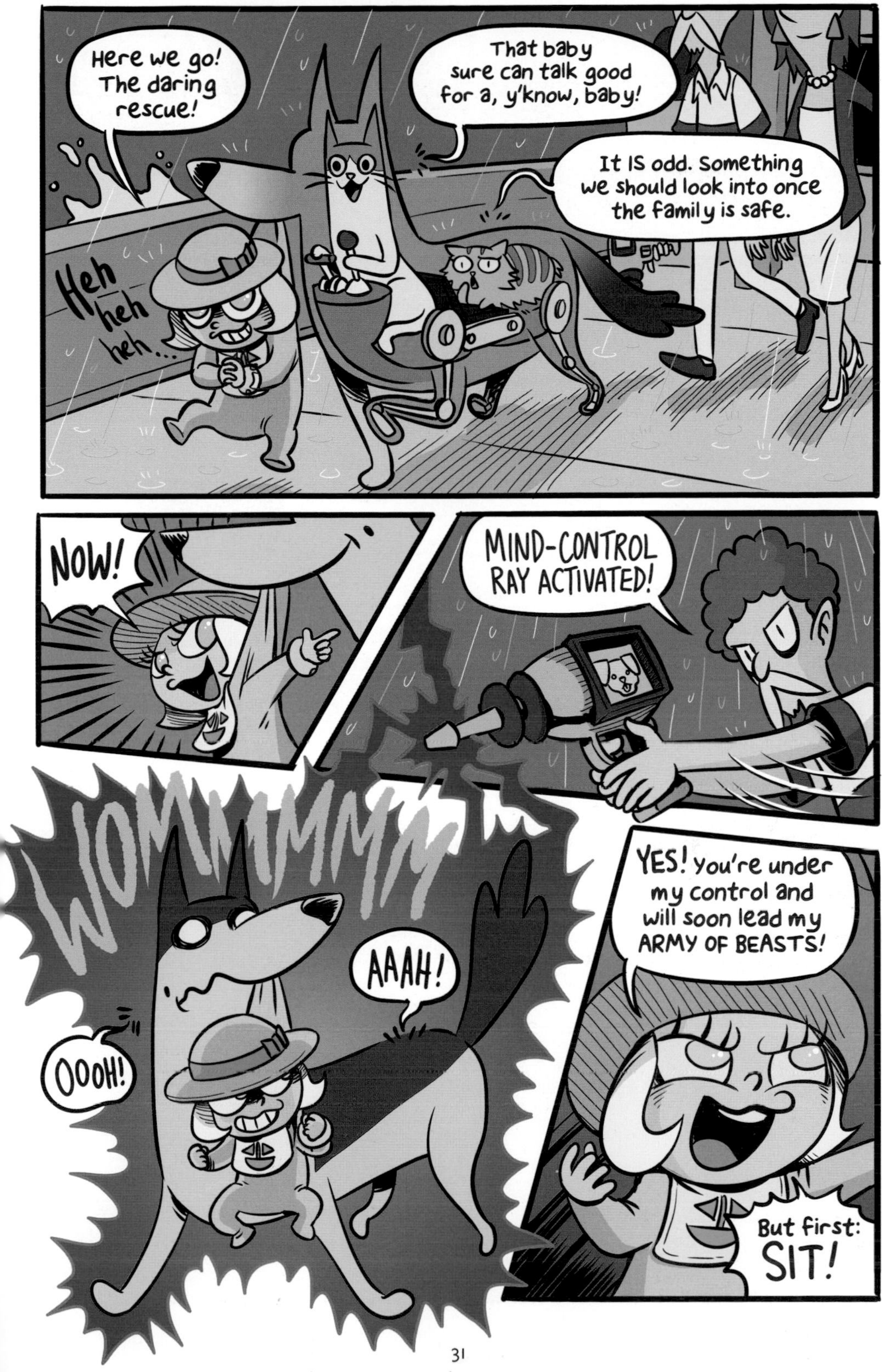

Here we go! The daring rescue!
That baby sure can talk good for a, y'know, baby!
It IS odd. Something we should look into once the family is safe.
Heh heh heh...
NOW!
MIND-CONTROL RAY ACTIVATED!
WOMMMMM
AAAH!
OOOH!
YES! You're under my control and will soon lead my ARMY OF BEASTS!
But first: SIT!

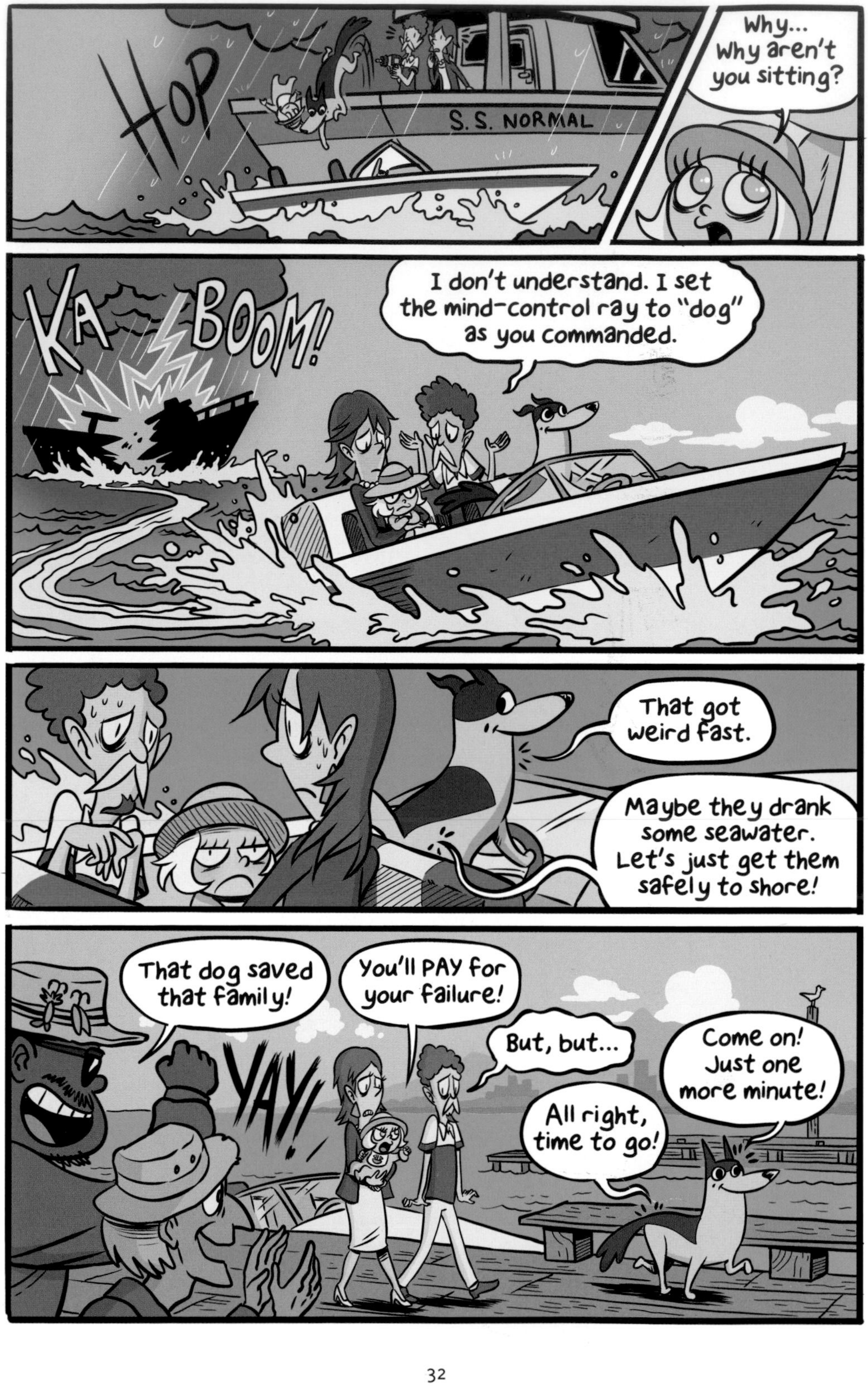
HOP
S.S. NORMAL
Why... Why aren't you sitting?
KA BOOM!
I don't understand. I set the mind-control ray to "dog" as you commanded.
That got weird fast.
Maybe they drank some seawater. Let's just get them safely to shore!
That dog saved that family!
YAY!
You'll PAY for your failure!
But, but...
All right, time to go!
Come on! Just one more minute!

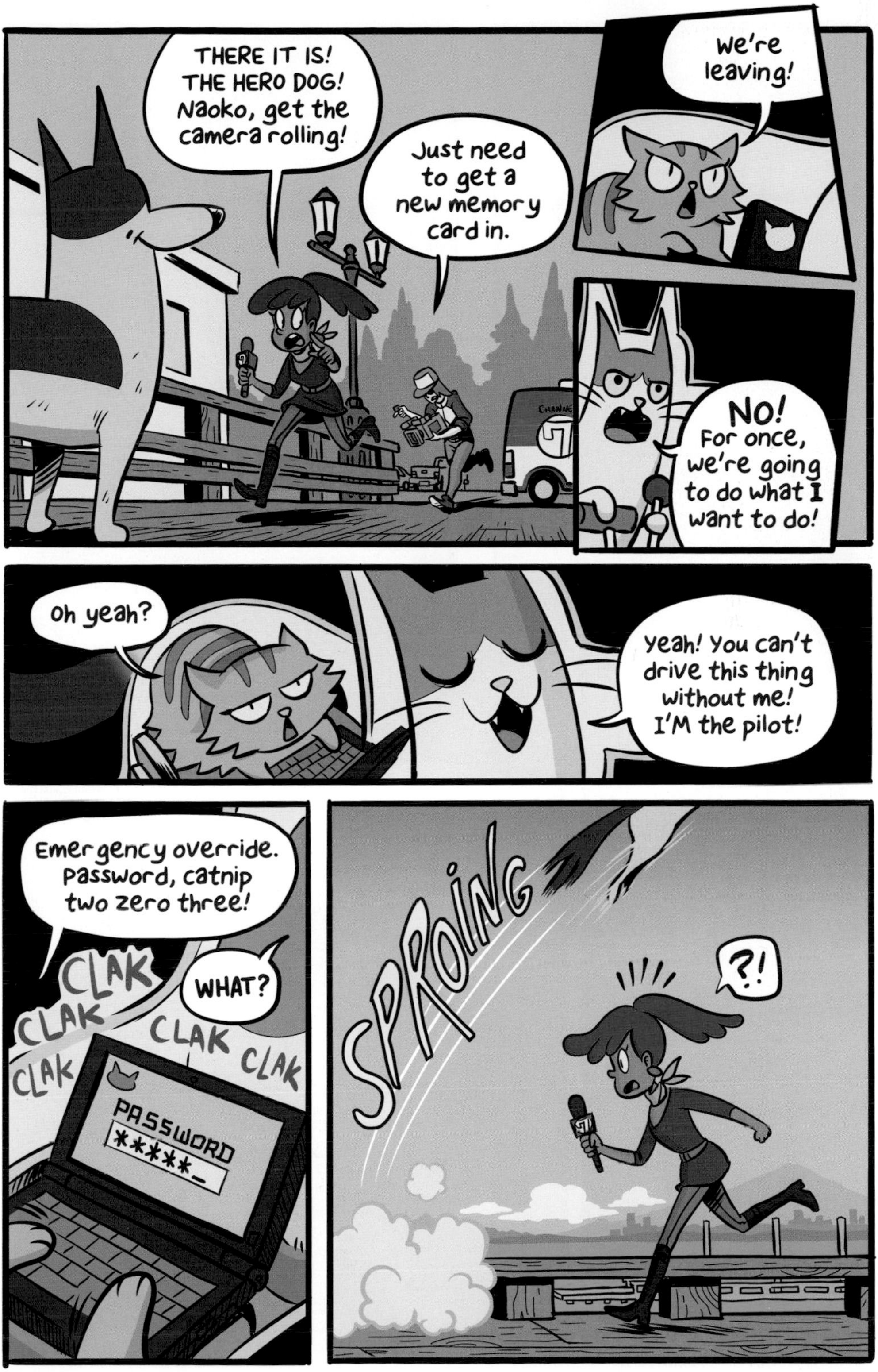
THERE IT IS! THE HERO DOG! Naoko, get the camera rolling!
Just need to get a new memory card in.
We're leaving!
NO! For once, we're going to do what I want to do!
Oh yeah?
Yeah! You can't drive this thing without me! I'M the pilot!
Emergency override. Password, catnip two zero three!
CLAK CLAK CLAK CLAK CLAK
WHAT?
PASSWORD
*****_
SPROING
?!

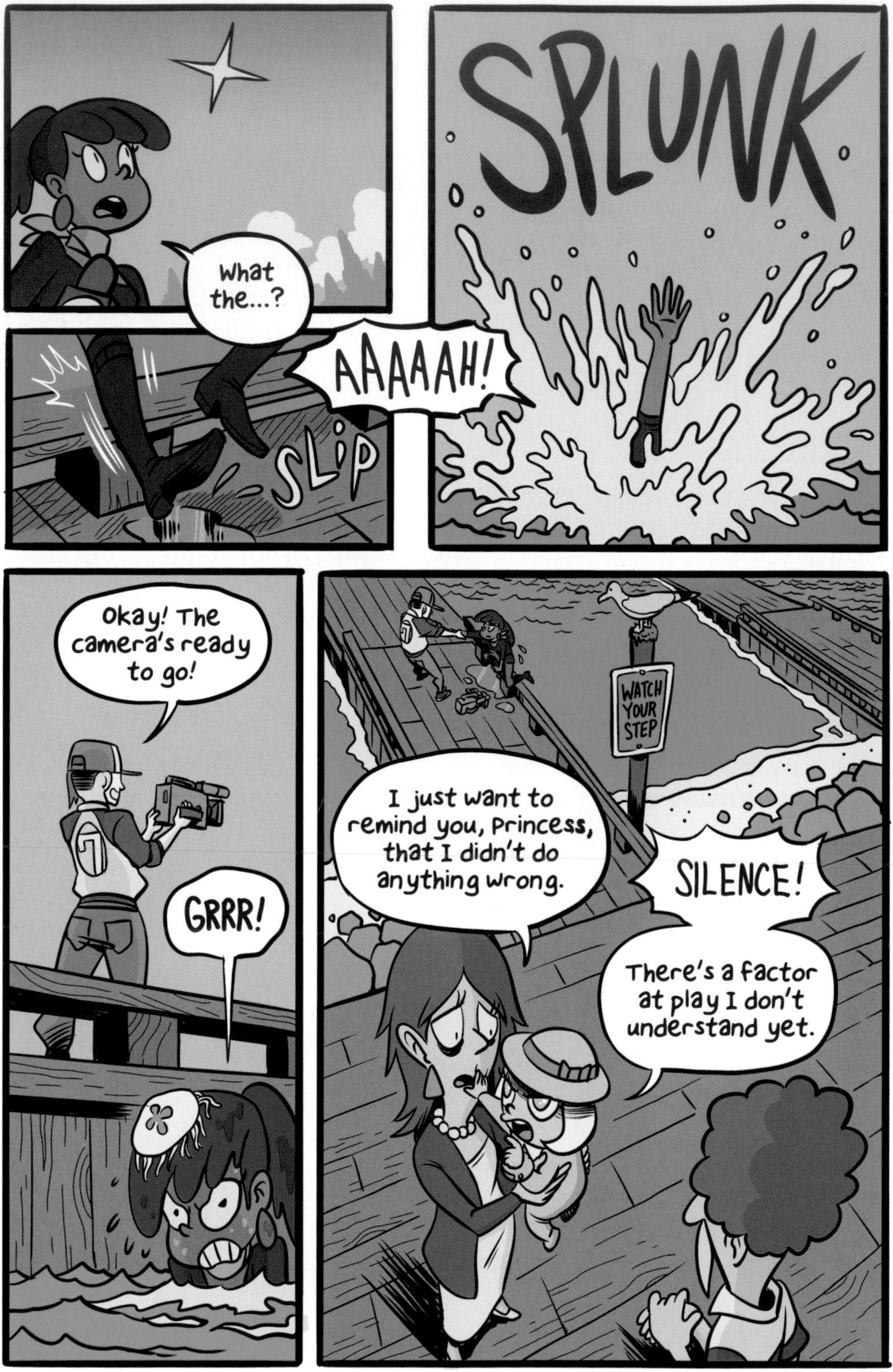
What the...?
AAAAAH!
SLIP
SPLUNK
Okay! The camera's ready to go!
GRRR!
WATCH YOUR STEP
I just want to remind you, Princess, that I didn't do anything wrong.
SILENCE!
There's a factor at play I don't understand yet.

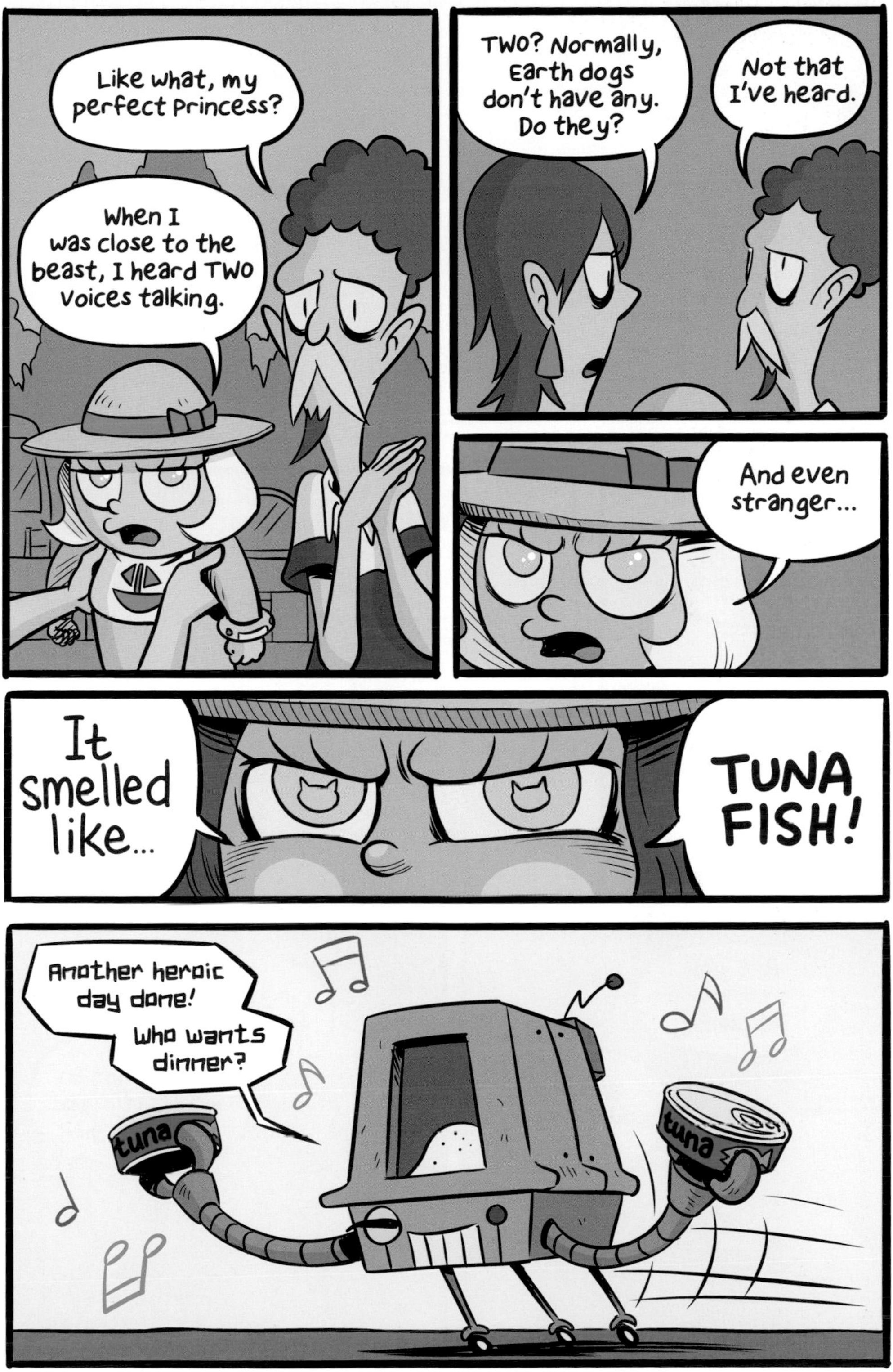
Like what, my perfect Princess?
When I was close to the beast, I heard TWO voices talking.
TWO? Normally, Earth dogs don't have any. Do they?
Not that I've heard.
And even stranger...
It smelled like...
TUNA FISH!
Another heroic day done!
Who wants dinner?
tuna
tuna

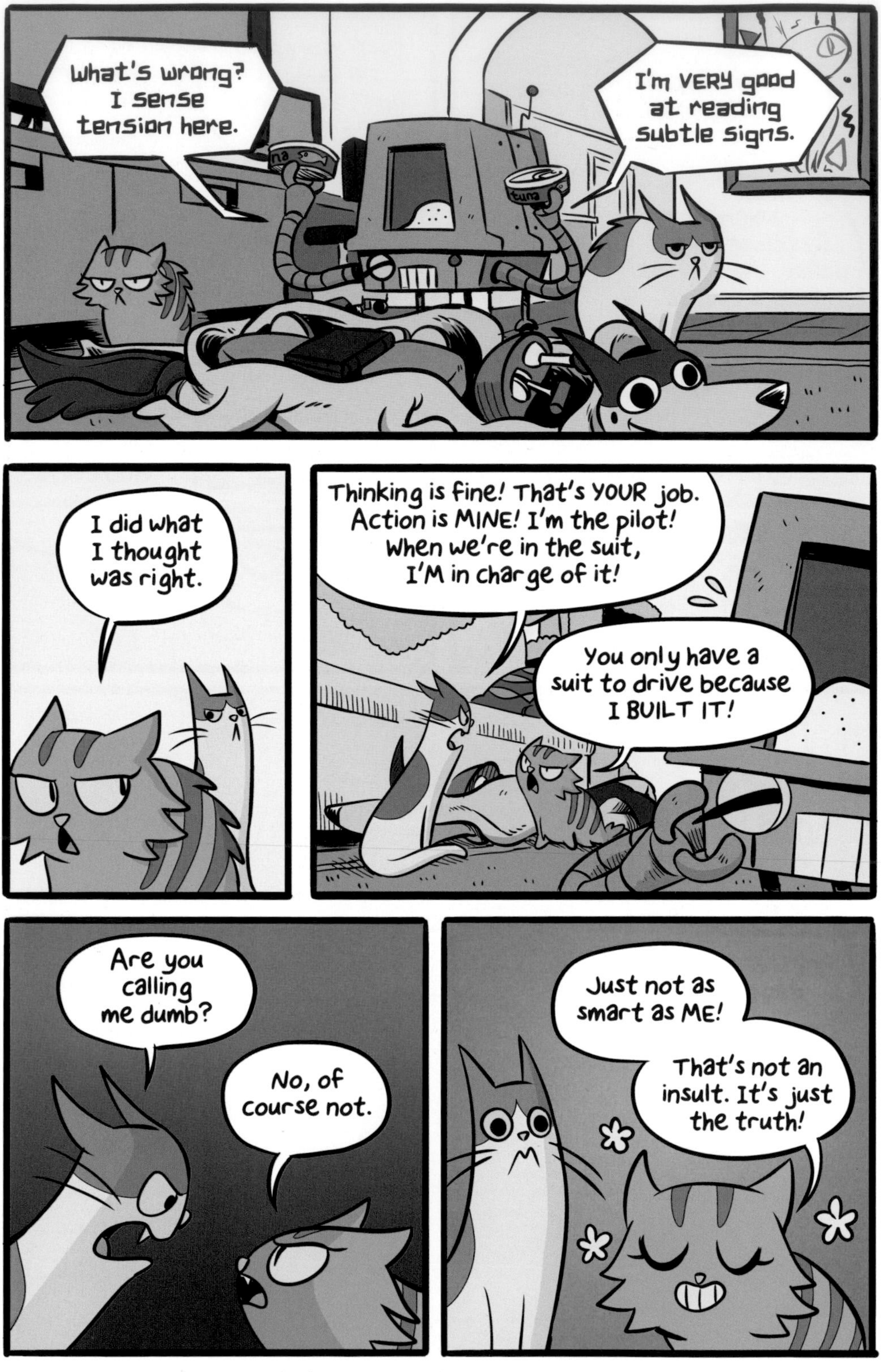
What's wrong? I sense tension here.
I'm VERY good at reading subtle signs.
tuna
tuna
I did what I thought was right.
Thinking is fine! That's YOUR job. Action is MINE! I'm the pilot! When we're in the suit, I'M in charge of it!
You only have a suit to drive because I BUILT IT!
Are you calling me dumb?
No, of course not.
Just not as smart as ME!
That's not an insult. It's just the truth!

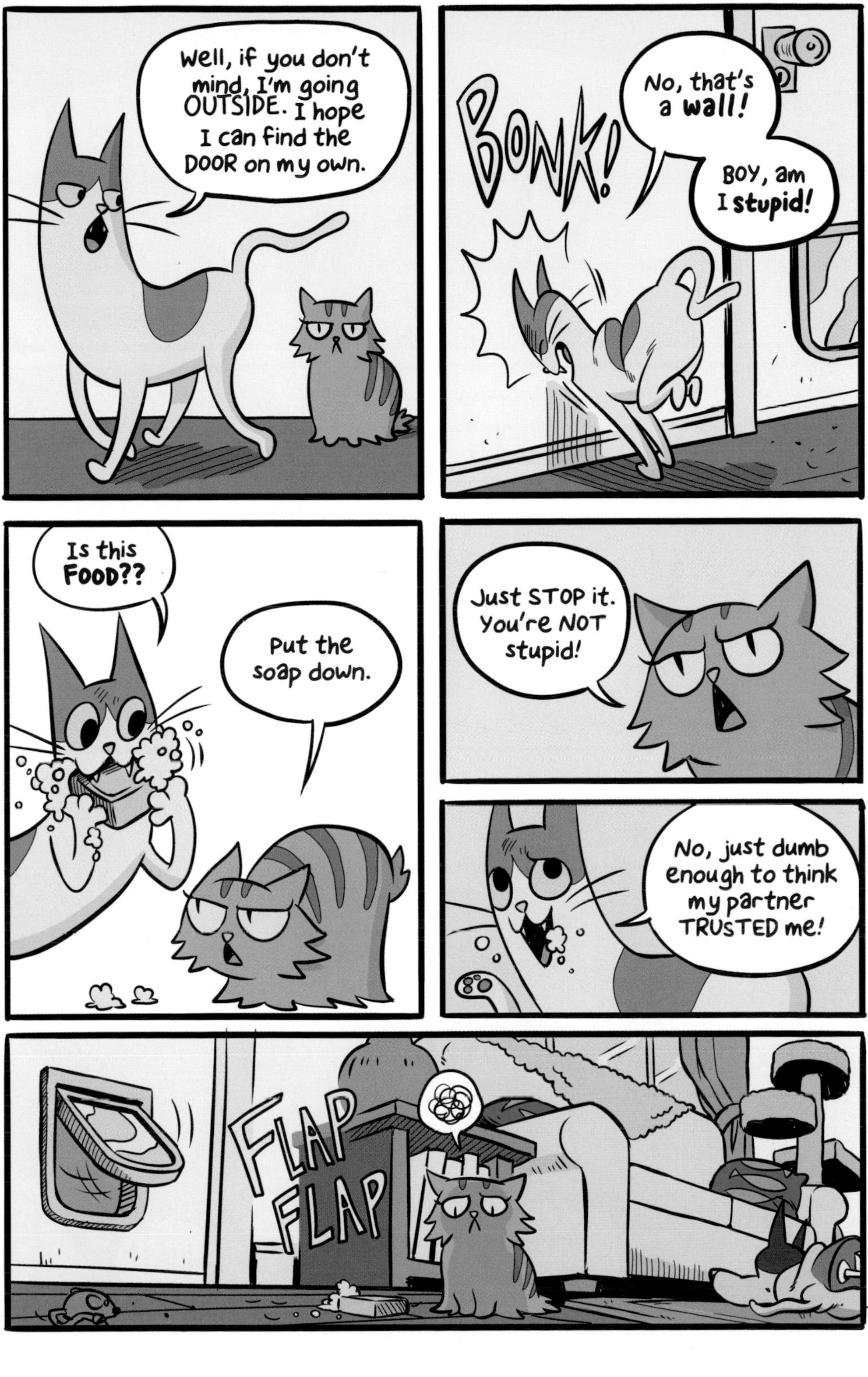

Well, if you don't mind, I'm going OUTSIDE. I hope I can find the DOOR on my own.
BONK!
No, that's a wall!
BOY, am I stupid!
Is this FOOD??
Put the soap down.
Just STOP it. You're NOT stupid!
No, just dumb enough to think my partner TRUSTED me!
FLAP FLAP

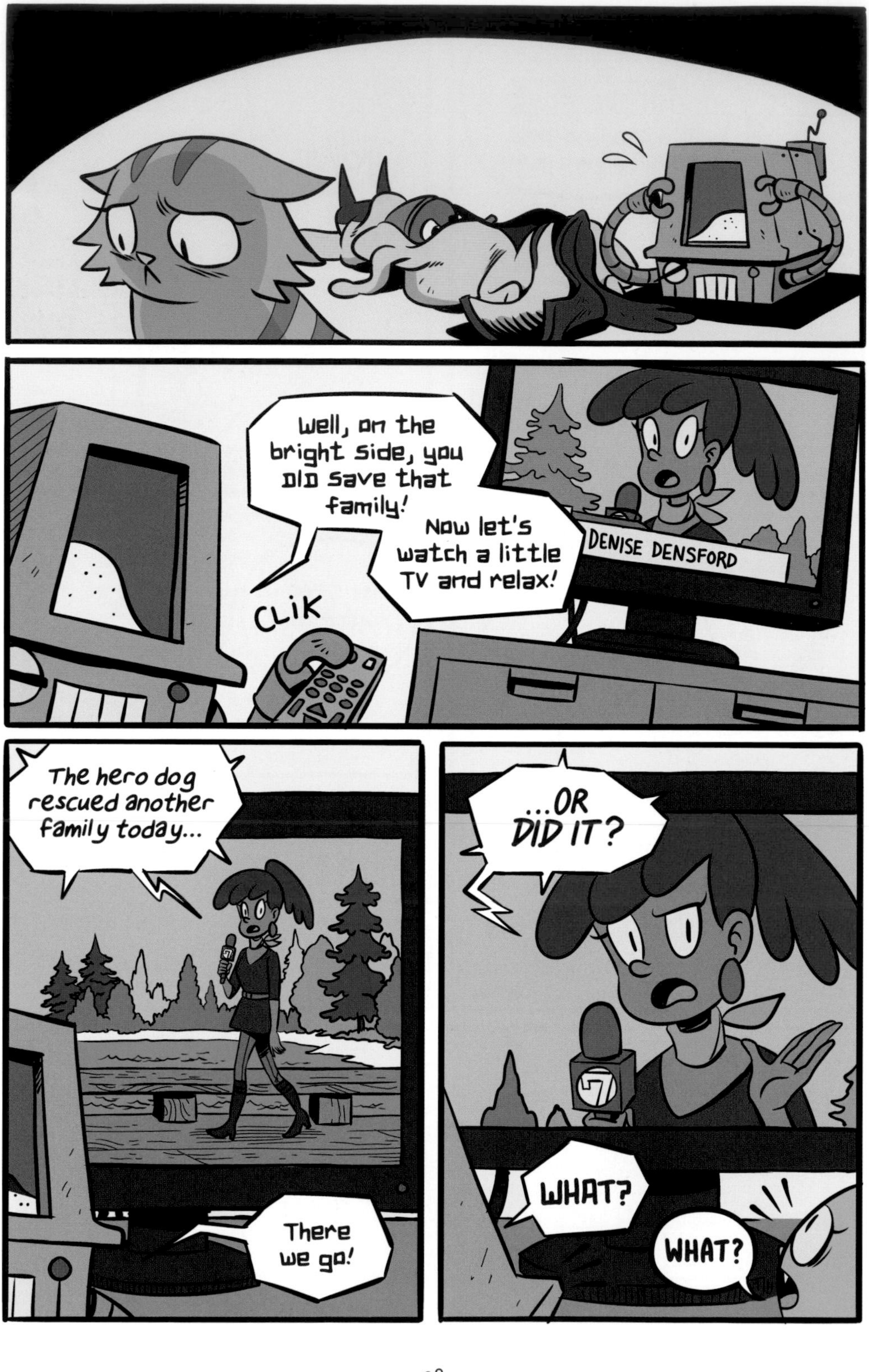
Well, on the bright side, you DID save that family!
Now let's watch a little TV and relax!
DENISE DENSFORD
CLIK
The hero dog rescued another family today...
There we go!
...OR DID IT?
WHAT?
WHAT?

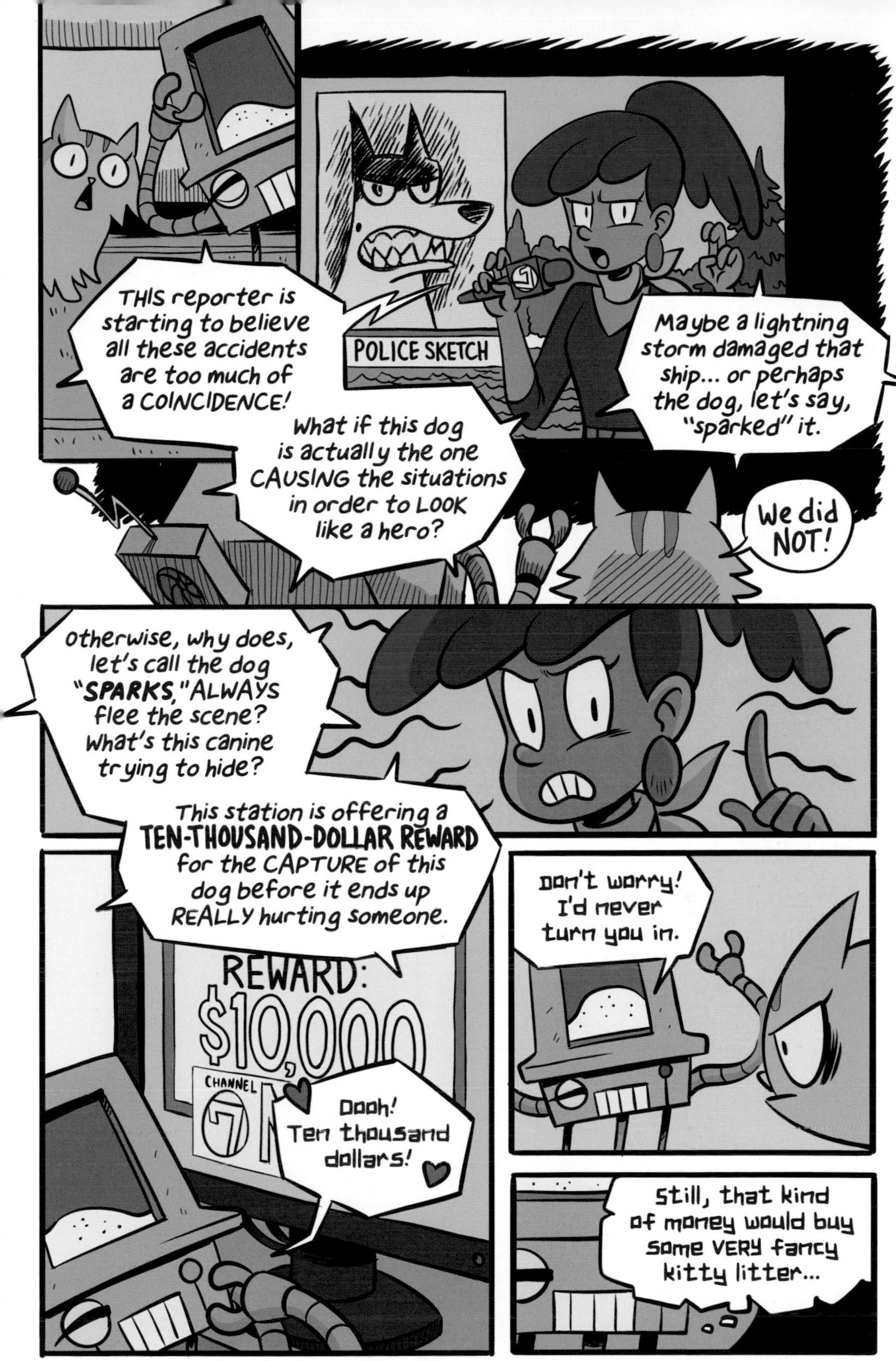
THIS reporter is starting to believe all these accidents are too much of a COINCIDENCE!
POLICE SKETCH
Maybe a lightning storm damaged that ship... or perhaps the dog, let's say, "sparked" it.
What if this dog is actually the one CAUSING the situations in order to LOOK like a hero?
We did NOT!
otherwise, why does, let's call the dog "SPARKS," ALWAYS flee the scene? What's this canine trying to hide?
This station is offering a TEN-THOUSAND-DOLLAR REWARD for the CAPTURE of this dog before it ends up REALLY hurting someone.
REWARD: $10,000
CHANNEL 7
Oooh! Ten thousand dollars!
Don't worry! I'd never turn you in.
Still, that kind of money would buy some VERY fancy kitty litter...

CHAPTER THREE

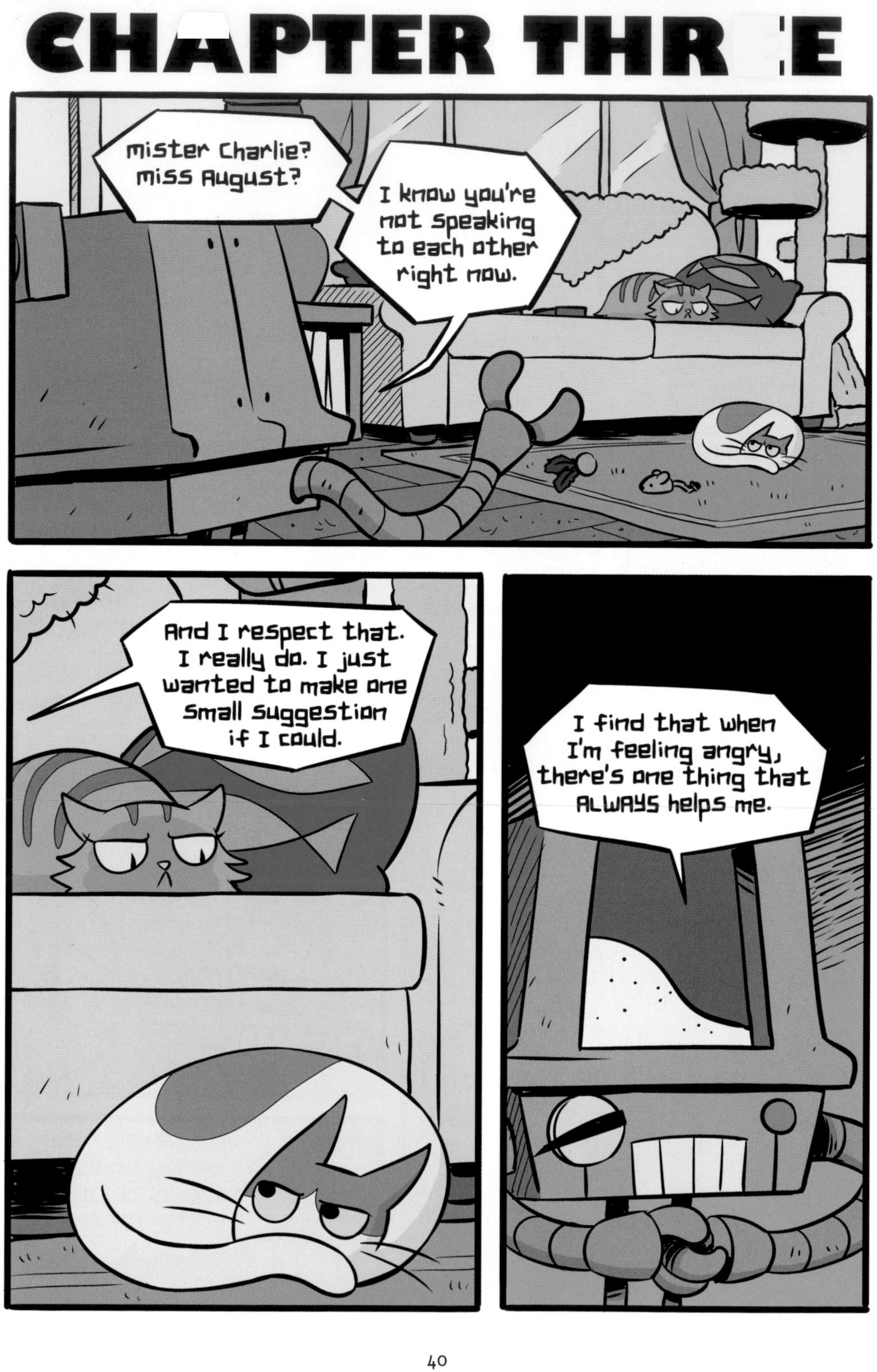

mister Charlie? miss August?
I know you're not speaking to each other right now.
And I respect that. I really do. I just wanted to make one small suggestion if I could.
I find that when I'm feeling angry, there's one thing that ALWAYS helps me.

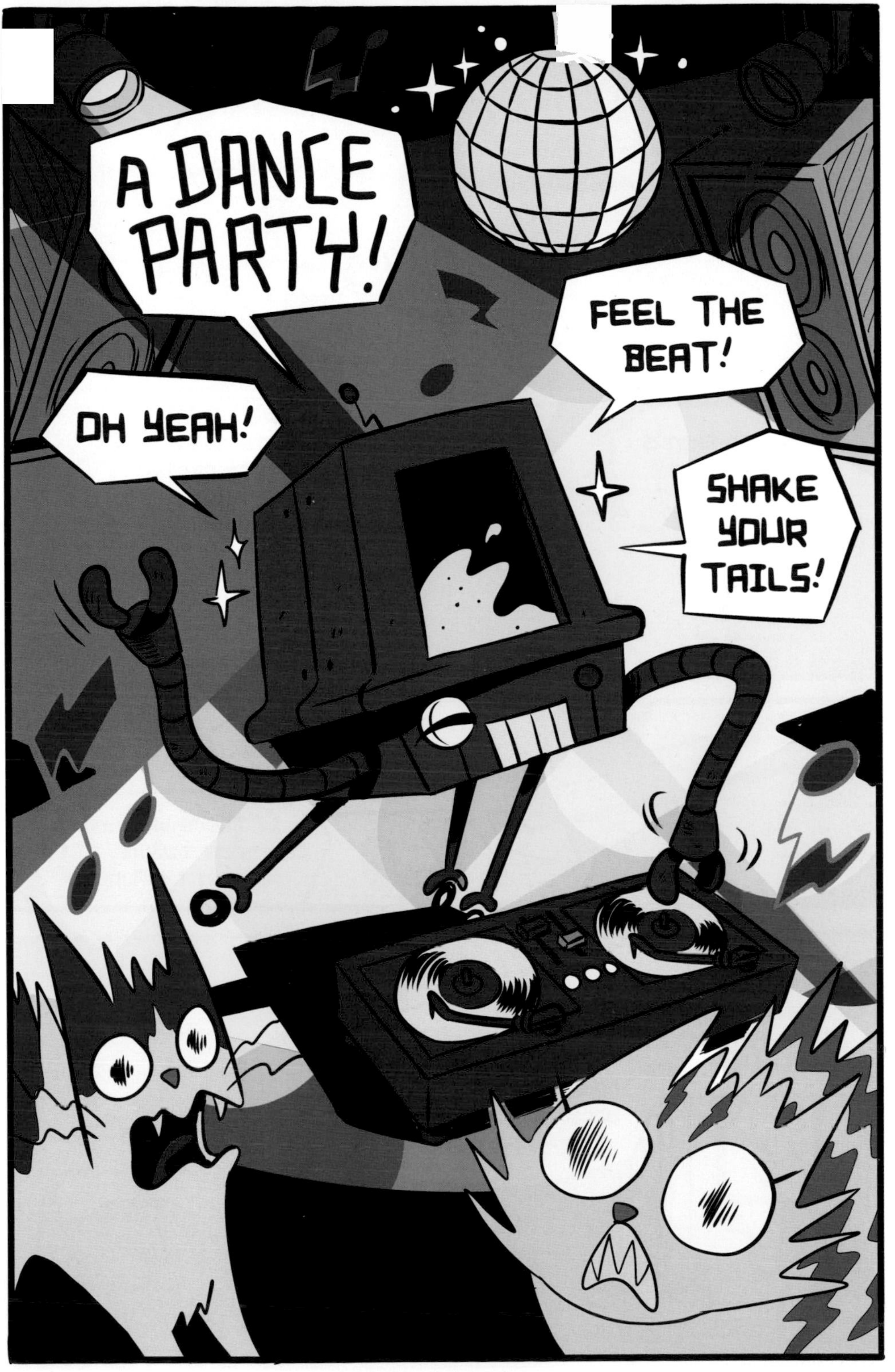
A DANCE PARTY!
FEEL THE BEAT!
OH YEAH!
SHAKE YOUR TAILS!

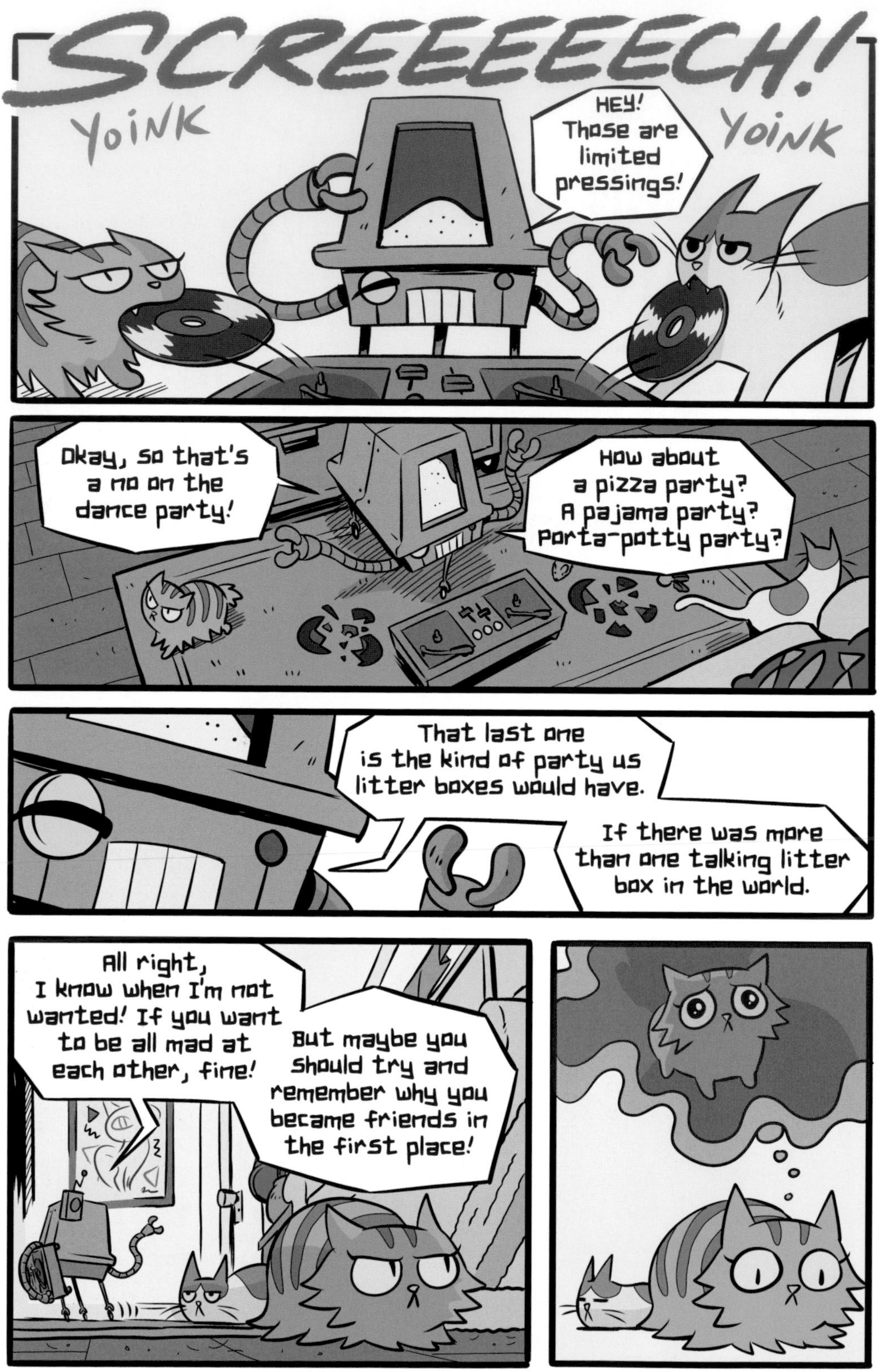

SCREEEEECH!
YOINK
HEY! Those are limited pressings!
YOINK
Okay, so that's a no on the dance party!
How about a pizza party? A pajama party? Porta-potty party?
That last one is the kind of party us litter boxes would have.
If there was more than one talking litter box in the world.
All right, I know when I'm not wanted! If you want to be all mad at each other, fine!
But maybe you should try and remember why you became friends in the first place!

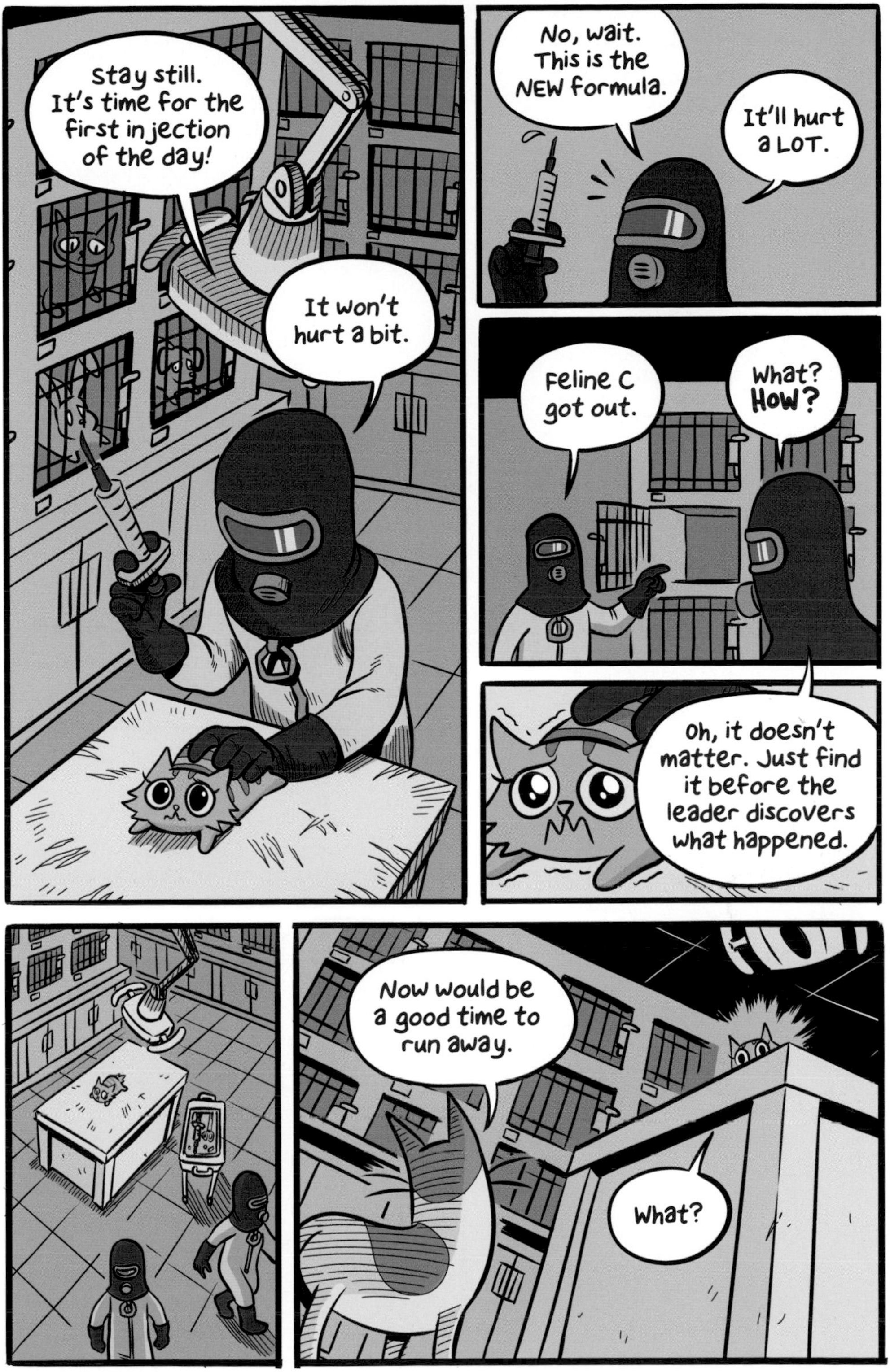
Stay still. It's time for the first injection of the day!
It won't hurt a bit.
No, wait. This is the NEW formula.
It'll hurt a LOT.
Feline C got out.
What? HOW?
Oh, it doesn't matter. Just find it before the leader discovers what happened.
Now would be a good time to run away.
What?

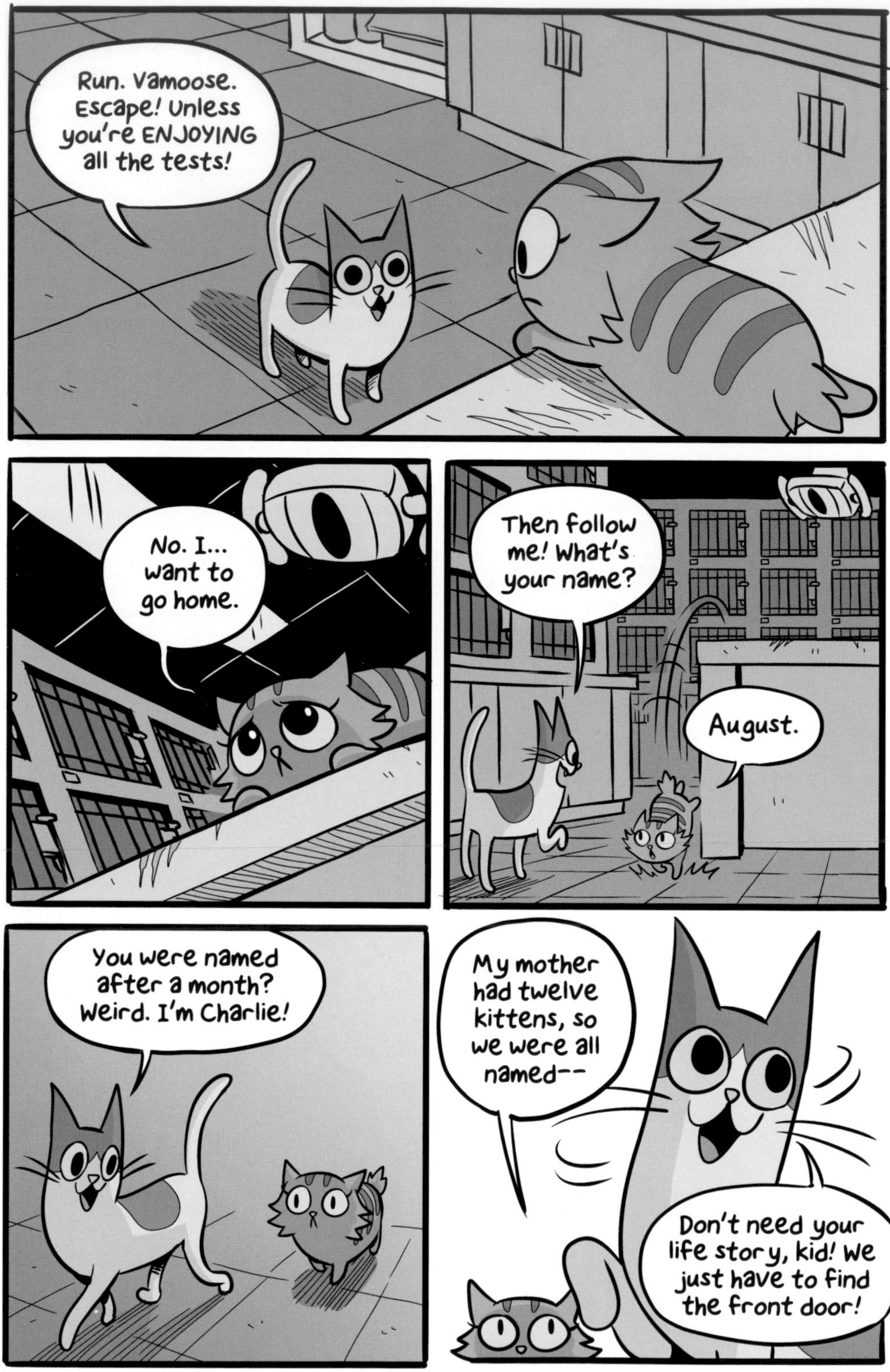
Run. Vamoose. Escape! Unless you're ENJOYING all the tests!
No. I... want to go home.
Then follow me! What's your name?
August.
You were named after a month? Weird. I'm Charlie!
My mother had twelve kittens, so we were all named--
Don't need your life story, kid! We just have to find the front door!

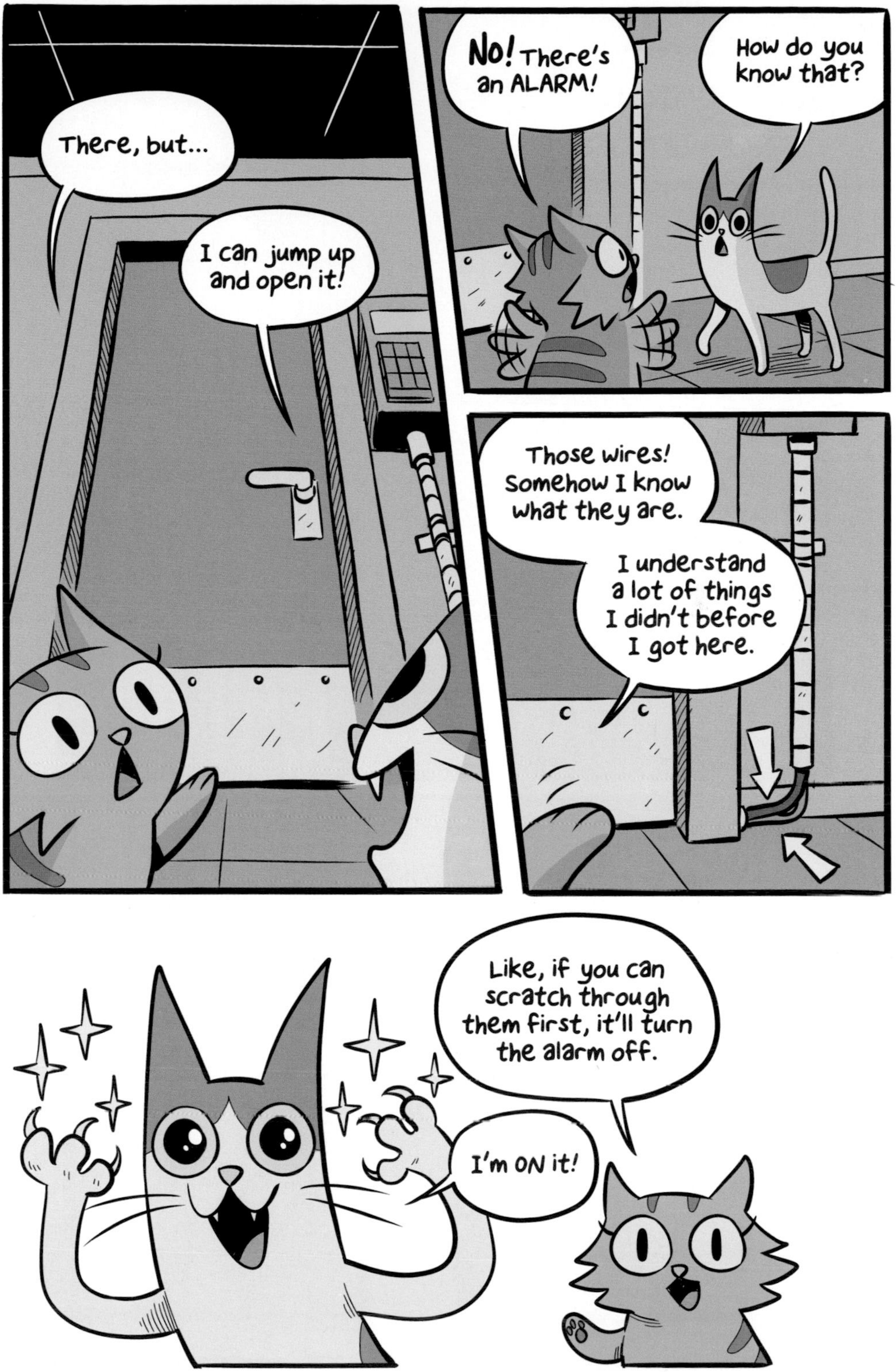
There, but...
I can jump up and open it!
No! There's an ALARM!
How do you know that?
Those wires! Somehow I know what they are.
I understand a lot of things I didn't before I got here.
Like, if you can scratch through them first, it'll turn the alarm off.
I'm ON it!

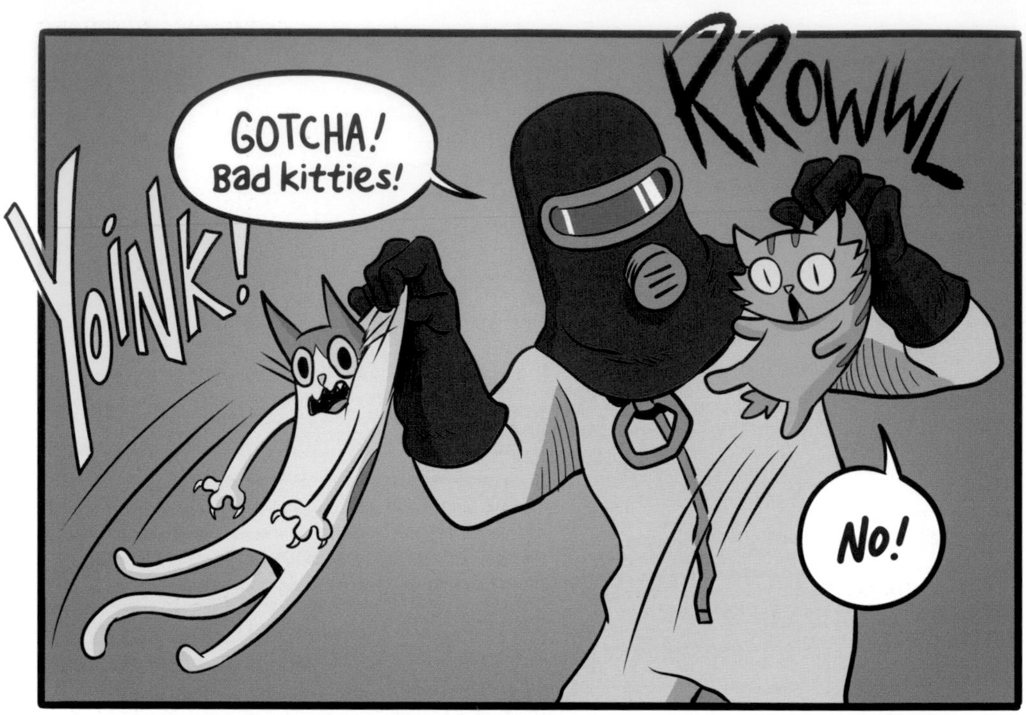
YOINK!
GOTCHA! Bad kitties!
RROWWL
No!

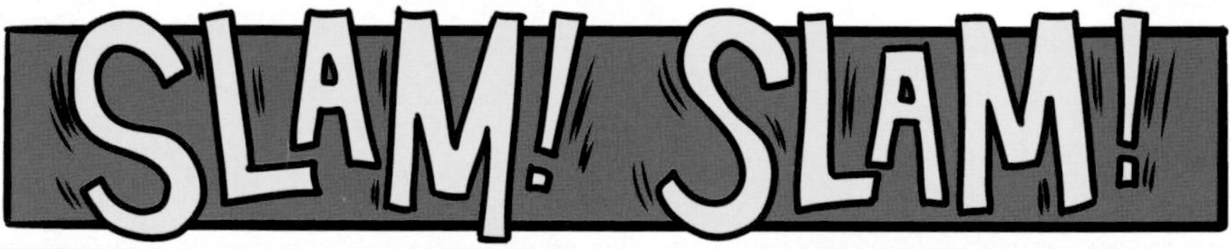
SLAM! SLAM!

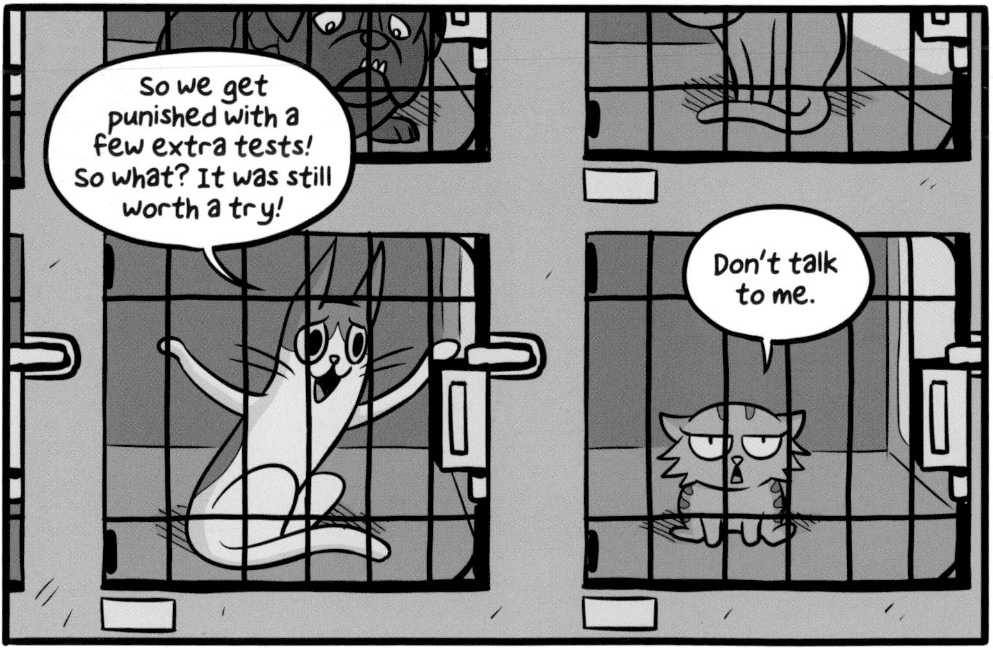
So we get punished with a few extra tests! So what? It was still worth a try!
Don't talk to me.

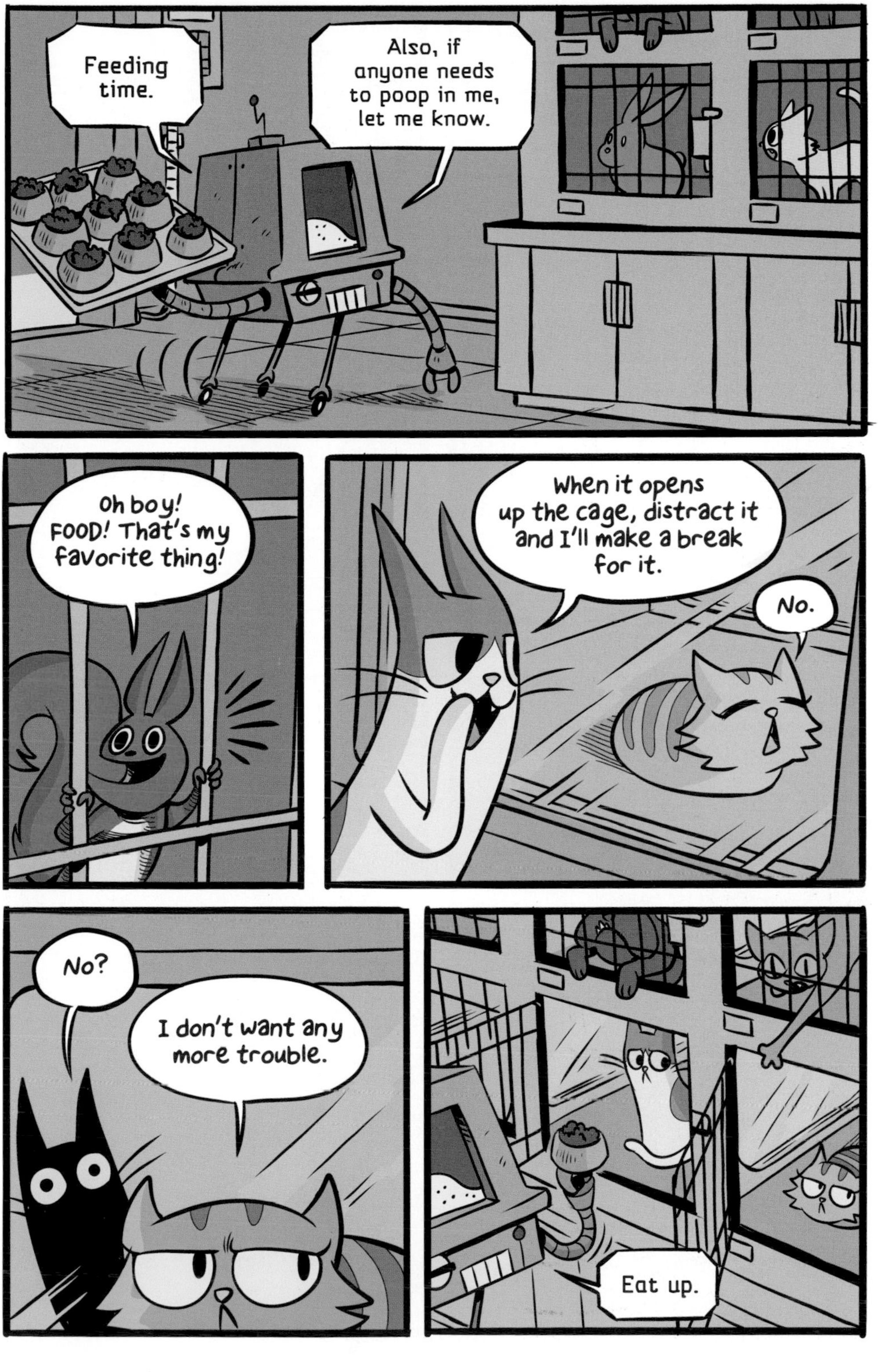
Feeding time.
Also, if anyone needs to poop in me, let me know.
Oh boy! FOOD! That's my favorite thing!
When it opens up the cage, distract it and I'll make a break for it.
No.
No?
I don't want any more trouble.
Eat up.

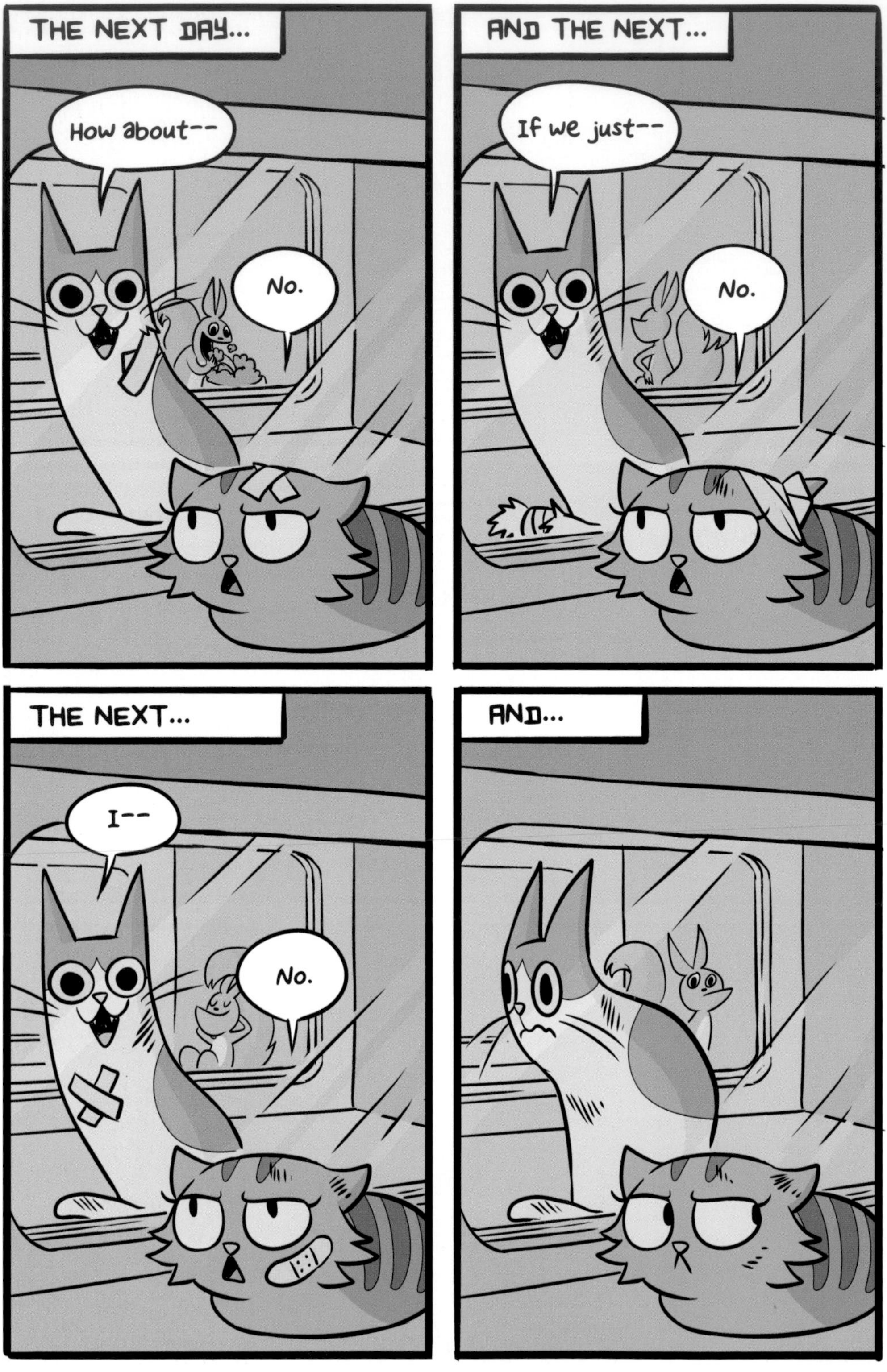
THE NEXT DAY...
How about--
No.
AND THE NEXT...
If we just--
No.
THE NEXT...
I--
No.
AND...

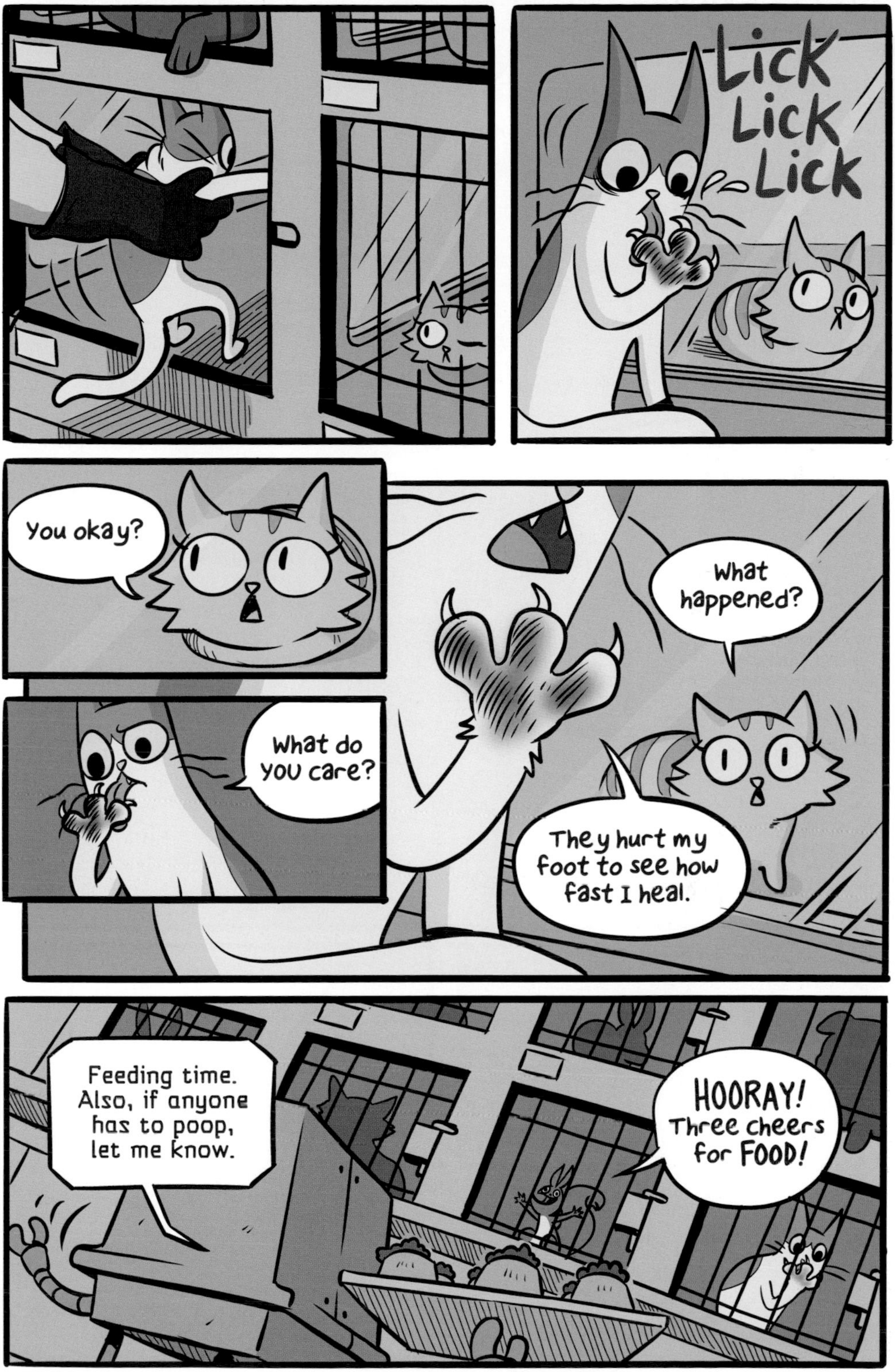
Lick
Lick
Lick
You okay?
What happened?
What do you care?
They hurt my foot to see how fast I heal.
Feeding time. Also, if anyone has to poop, let me know.
HOORAY! Three cheers for FOOD!

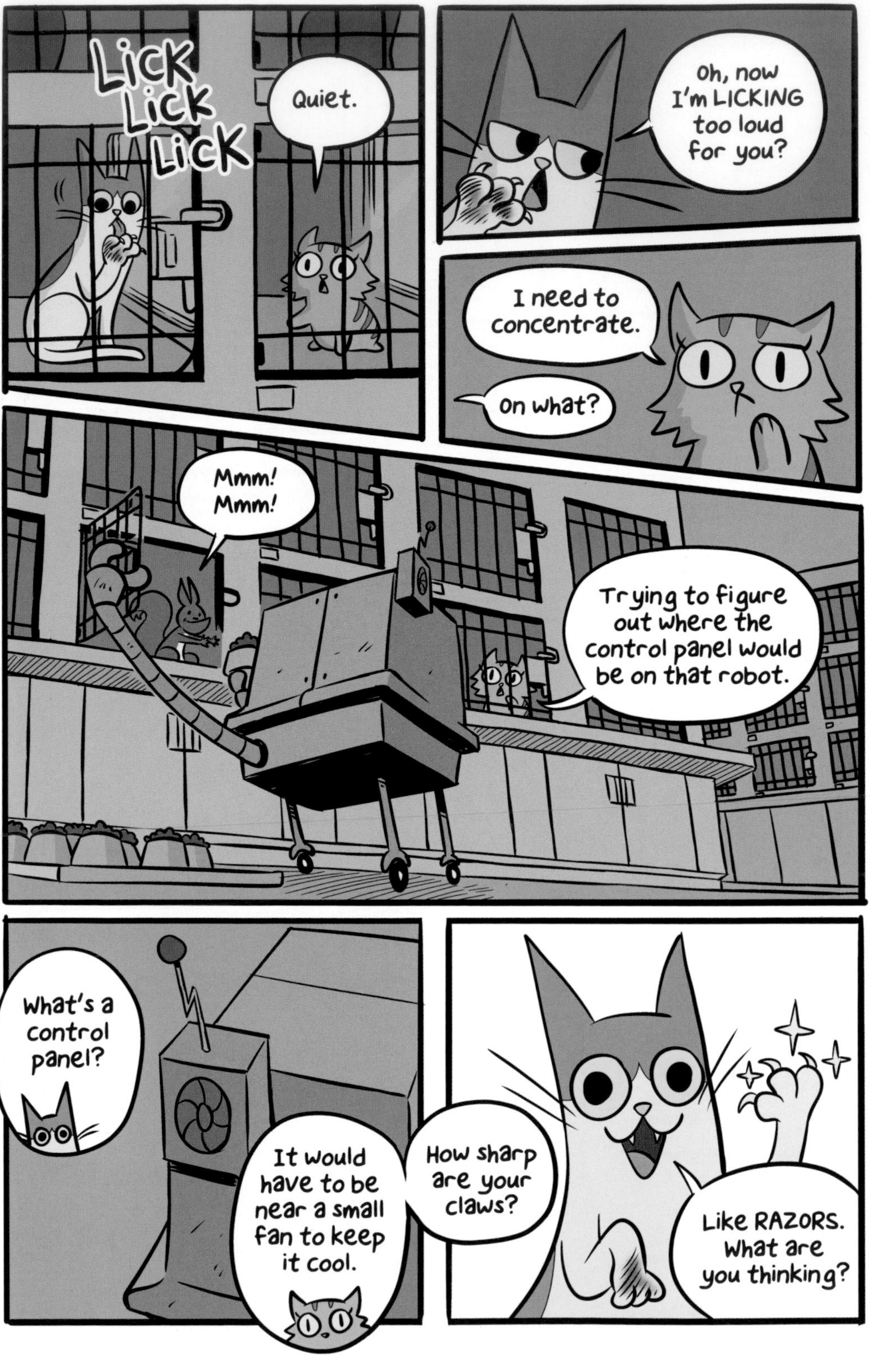
Lick
Lick
Lick
Quiet.
Oh, now I'm LICKING too loud for you?
I need to concentrate.
On what?
Mmm! Mmm!
Trying to figure out where the control panel would be on that robot.
What's a control panel?
It would have to be near a small fan to keep it cool.
How sharp are your claws?
Like RAZORS. What are you thinking?

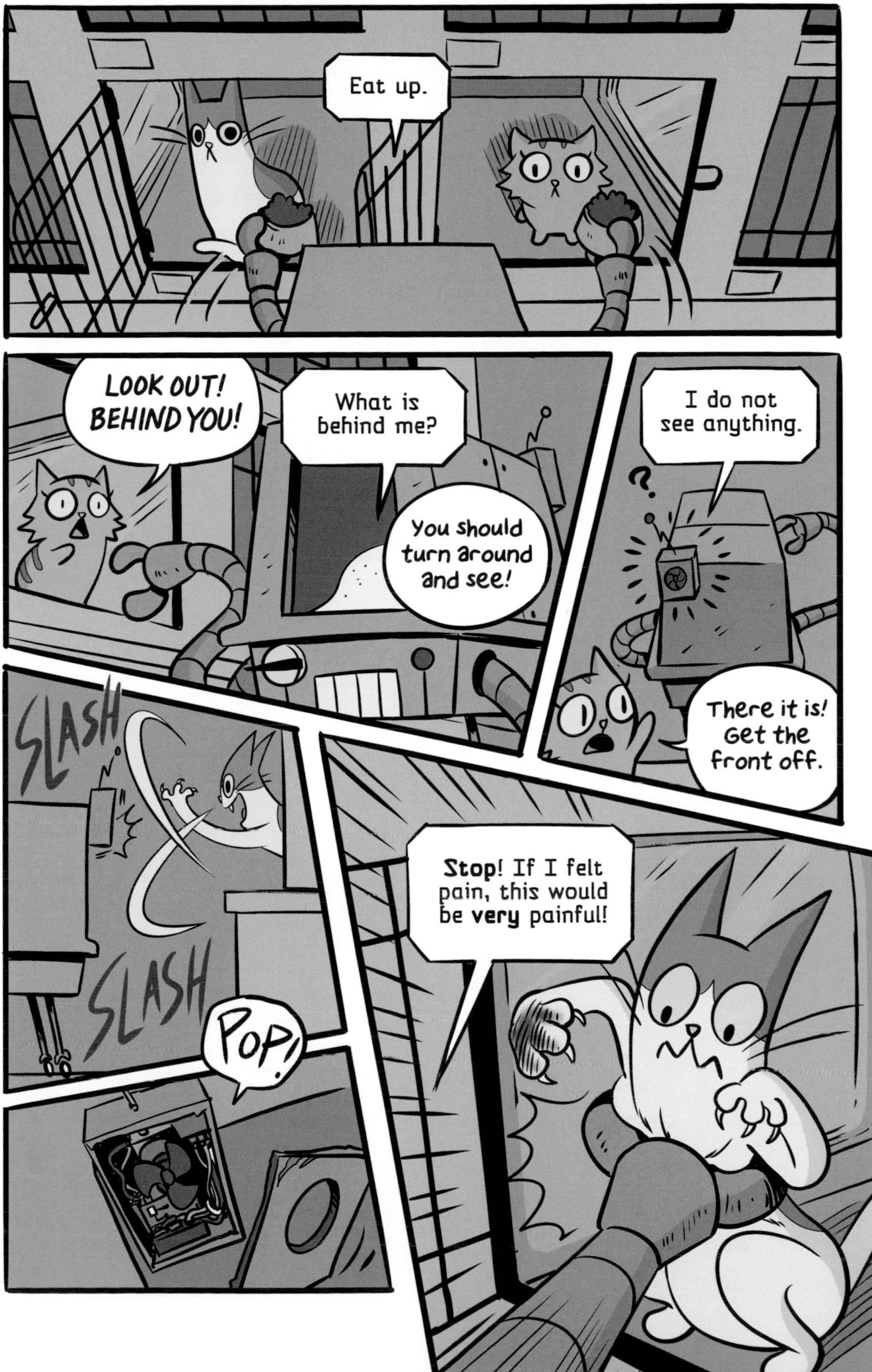
Eat up.
LOOK OUT! BEHIND YOU!
What is behind me?
You should turn around and see!
I do not see anything.
?
There it is! Get the front off.
SLASH
SLASH
POP!
Stop! If I felt pain, this would be very painful!

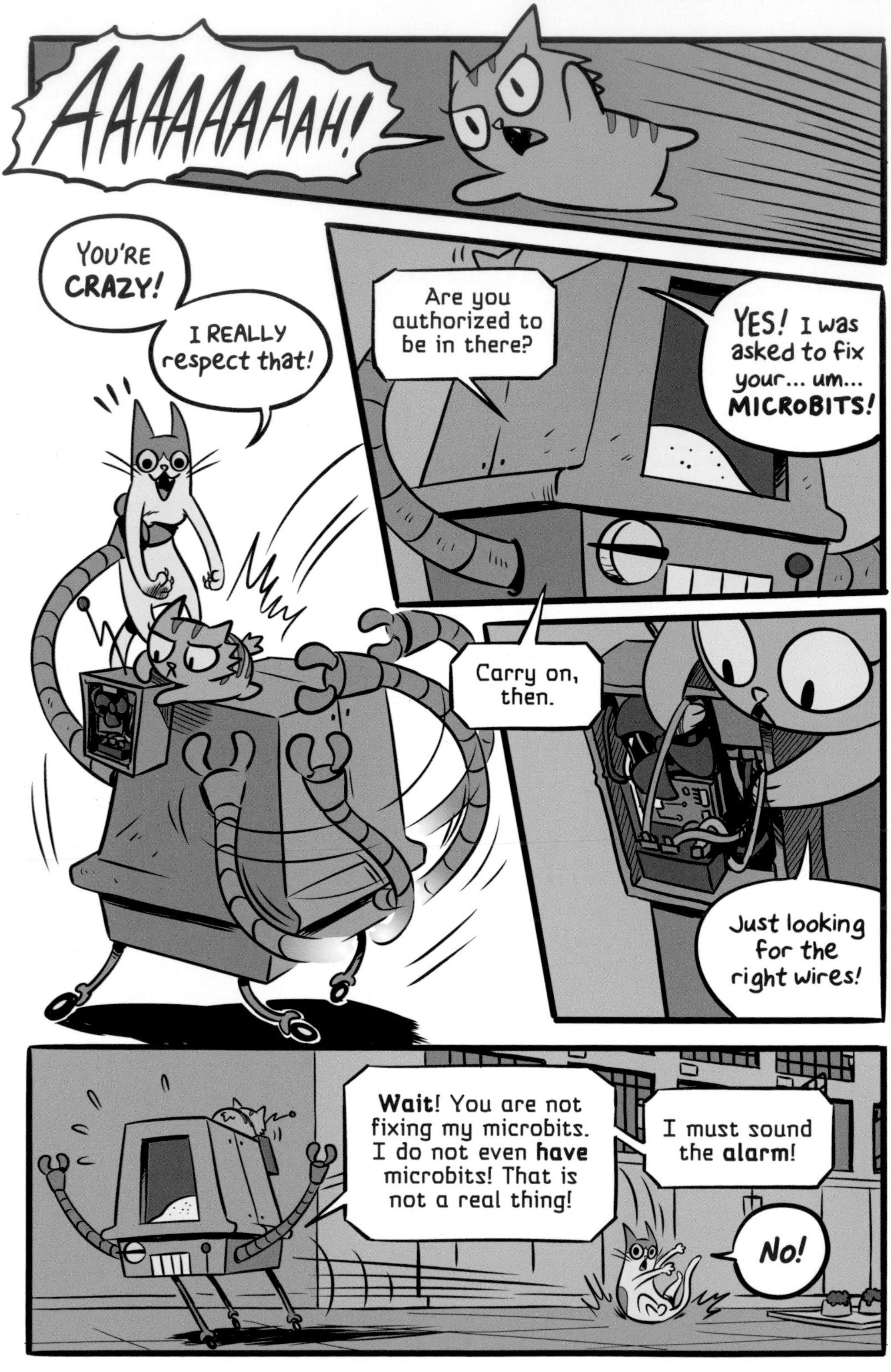
AAAAAAAAAH!
YOU'RE CRAZY!
I REALLY respect that!
Are you authorized to be in there?
YES! I was asked to fix your... um... MICROBITS!
Carry on, then.
Just looking for the right wires!
Wait! You are not fixing my microbits. I do not even have microbits! That is not a real thing!
I must sound the alarm!
No!

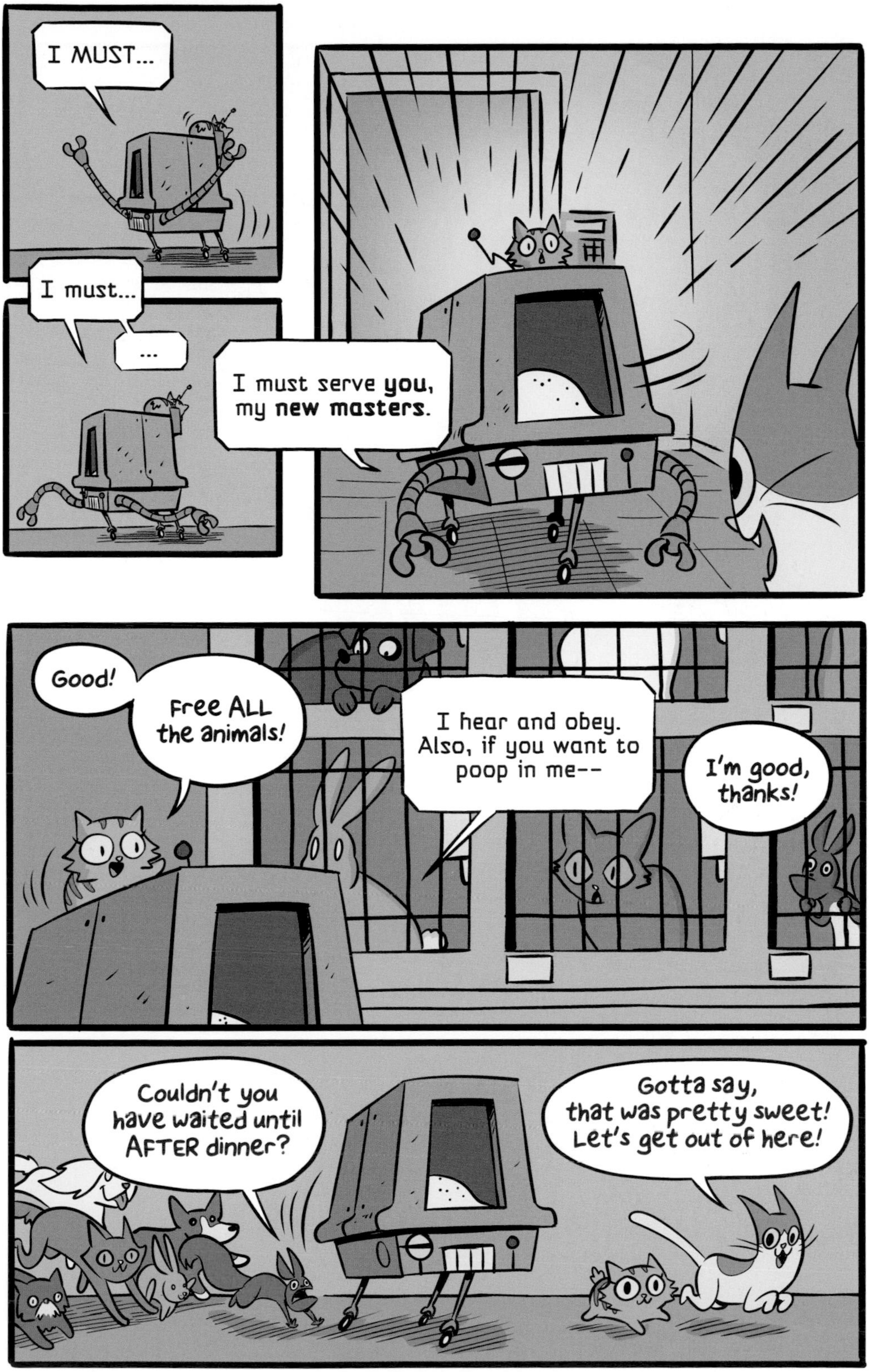
I MUST...
I must...
...
I must serve you, my new masters.
Good!
Free ALL the animals!
I hear and obey. Also, if you want to poop in me--
I'm good, thanks!
Couldn't you have waited until AFTER dinner?
Gotta say, that was pretty sweet! Let's get out of here!

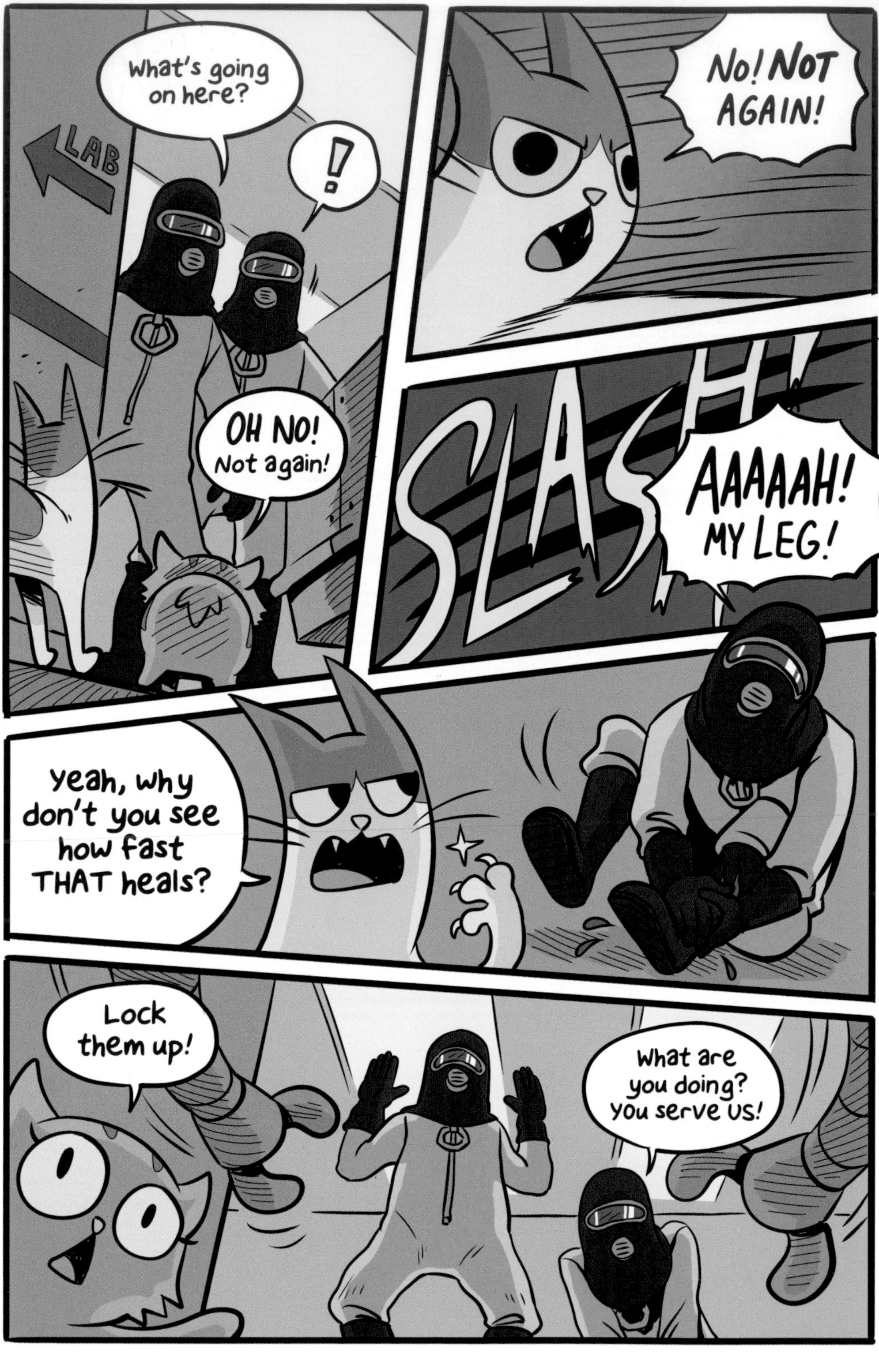
What's going on here?
LAB
!
OH NO! Not again!
No! NOT AGAIN!
SLASH!
AAAAAH! MY LEG!
yeah, why don't you see how fast THAT heals?
Lock them up!
What are you doing? You serve US!

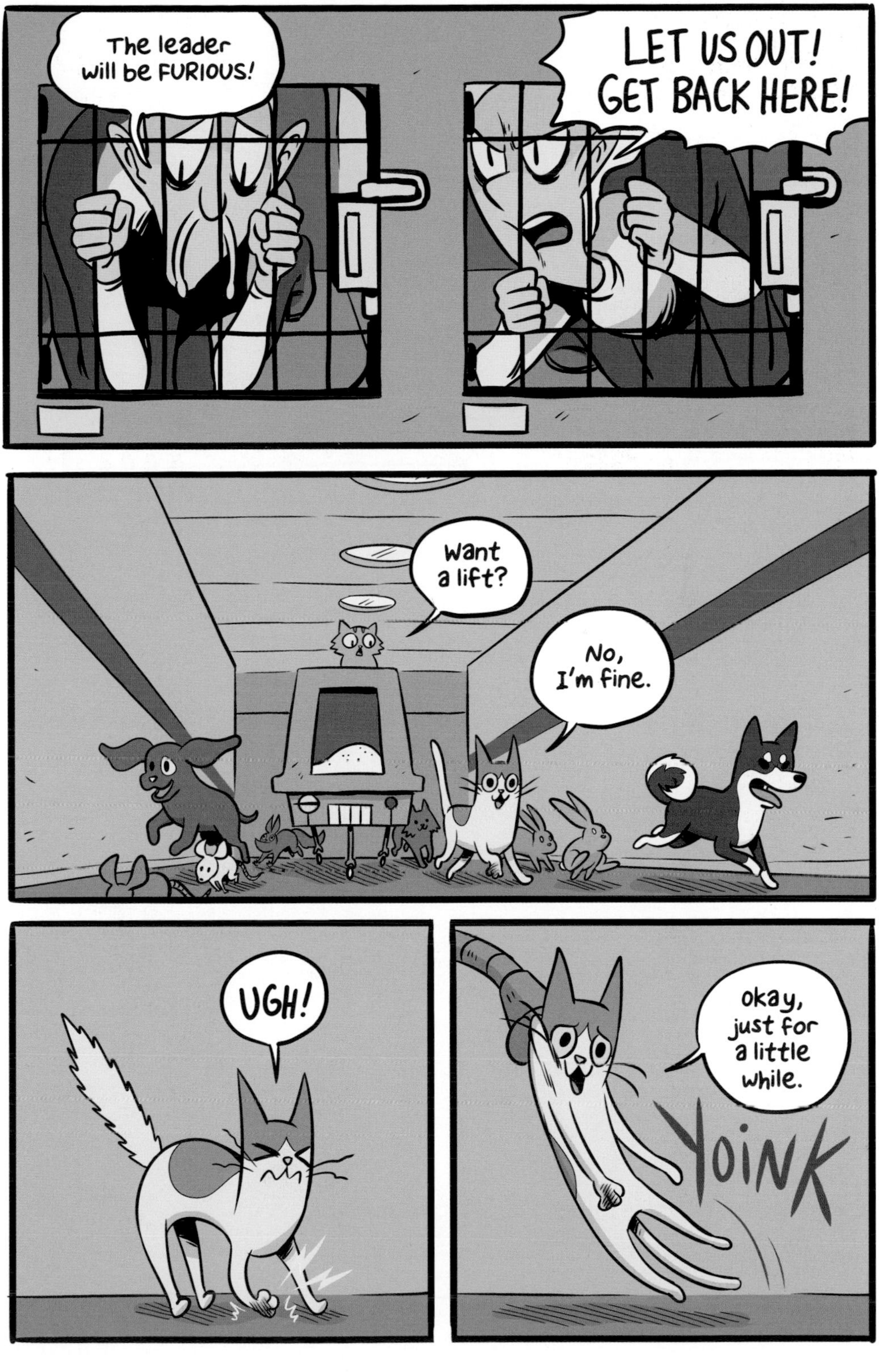
The leader will be FURIOUS!
LET US OUT! GET BACK HERE!
Want a lift?
No, I'm fine.
UGH!
okay, just for a little while.
YOINK

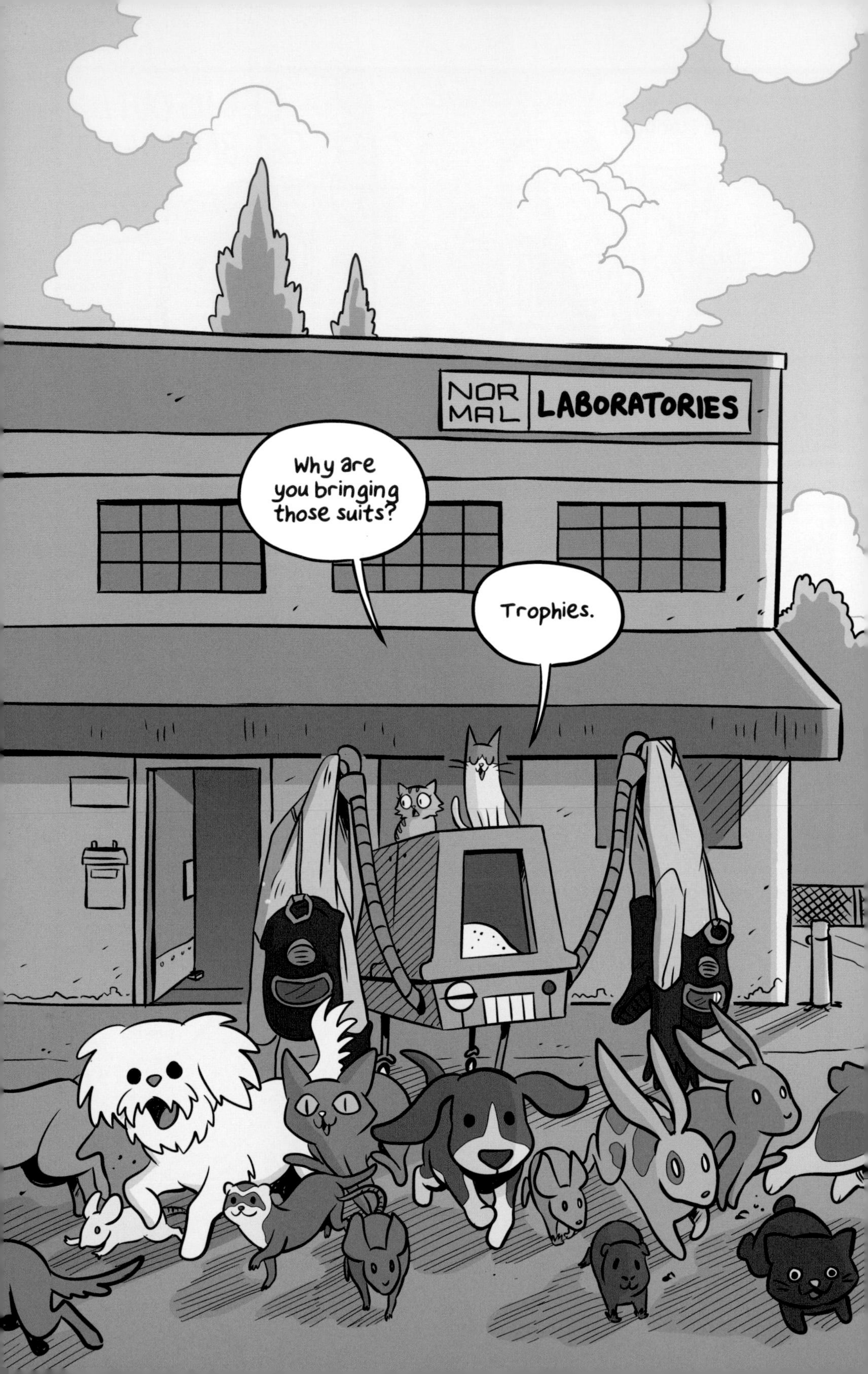
NORMAL LABORATORIES
Why are you bringing those suits?
Trophies.

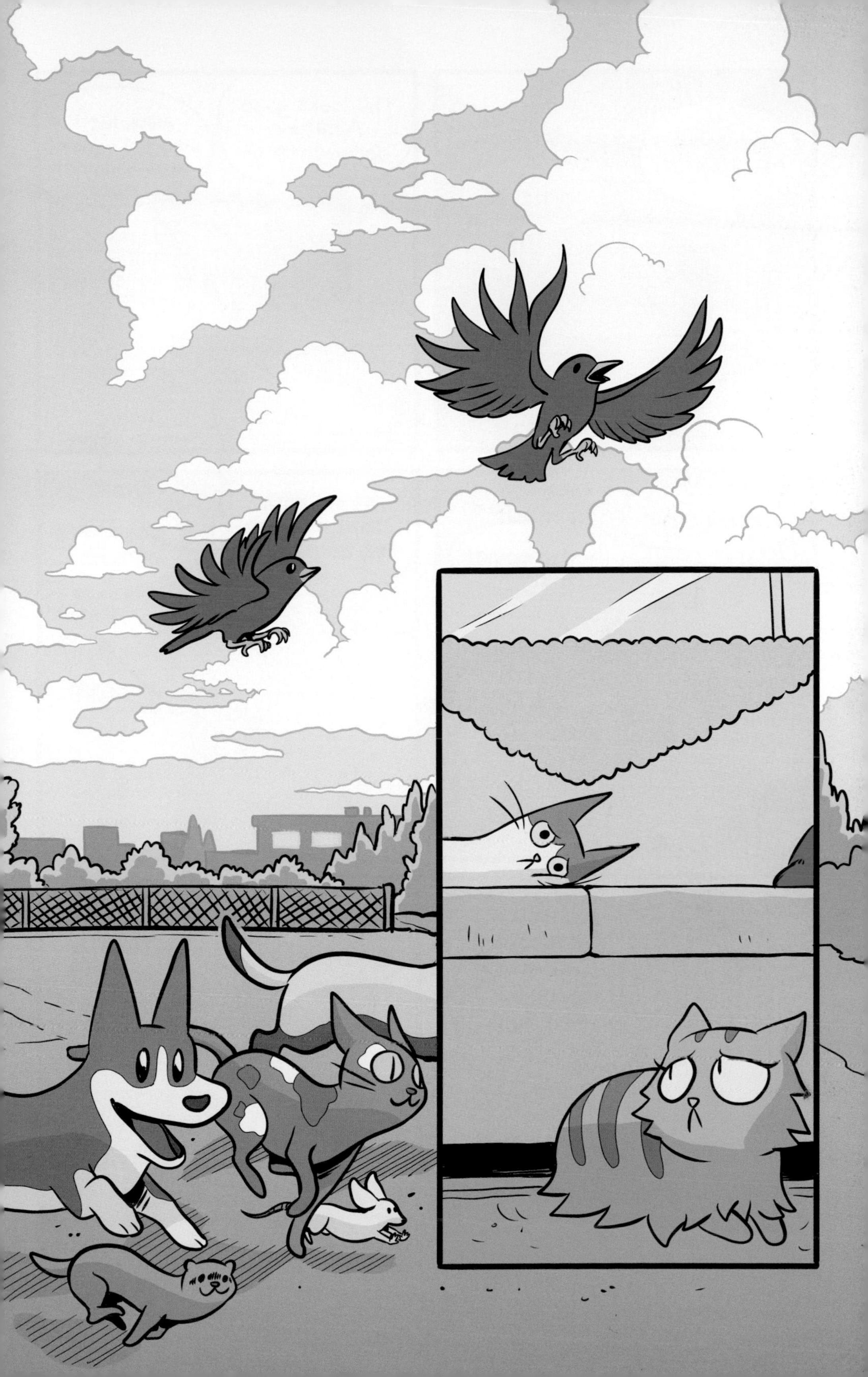

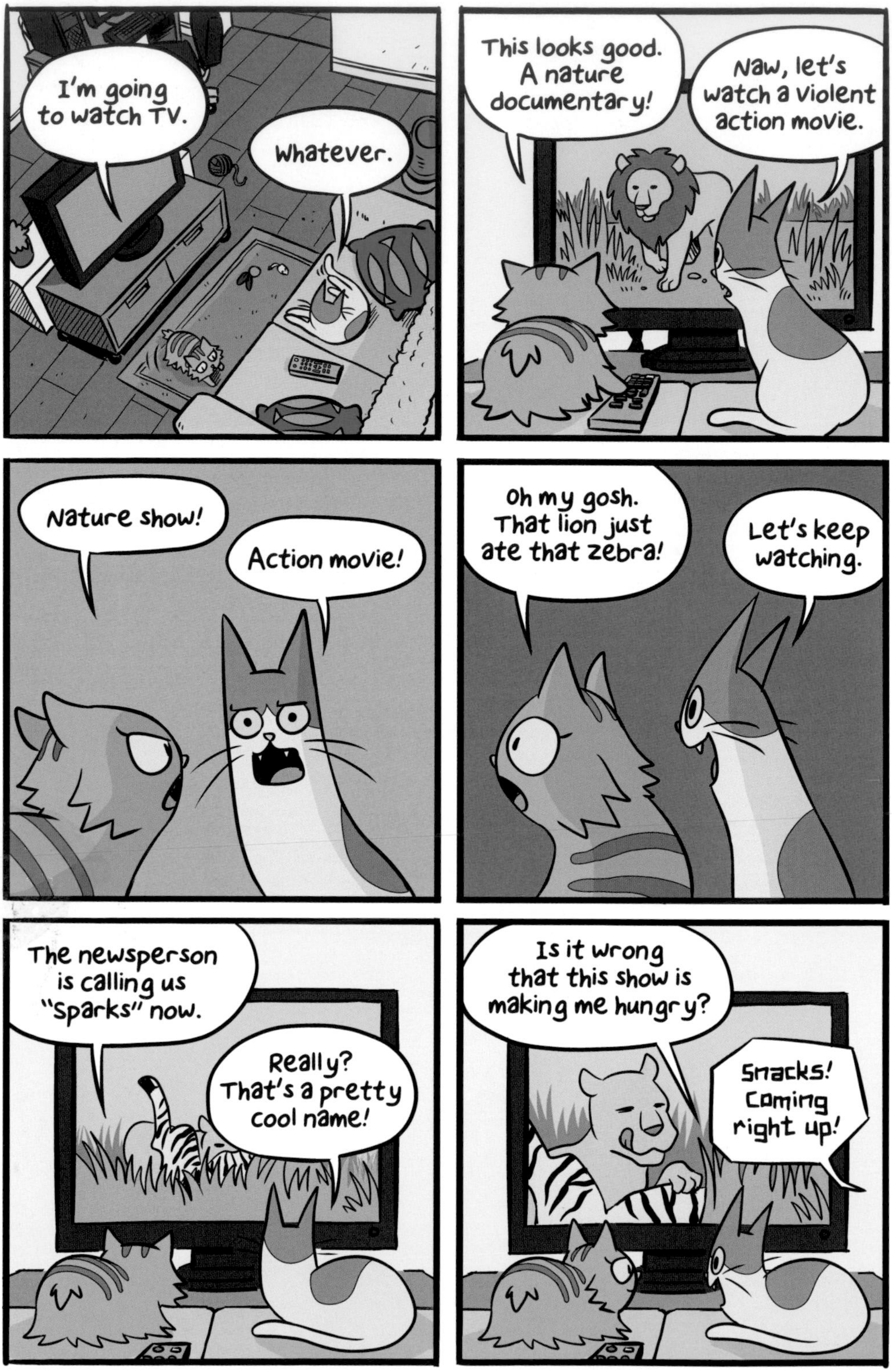
I'm going to watch TV.
Whatever.
This looks good. A nature documentary!
Naw, let's watch a violent action movie.
Nature show!
Action movie!
Oh my gosh. That lion just ate that zebra!
Let's keep watching.
The newsperson is calling us "Sparks" now.
Really? That's a pretty cool name!
Is it wrong that this show is making me hungry?
Snacks! Coming right up!

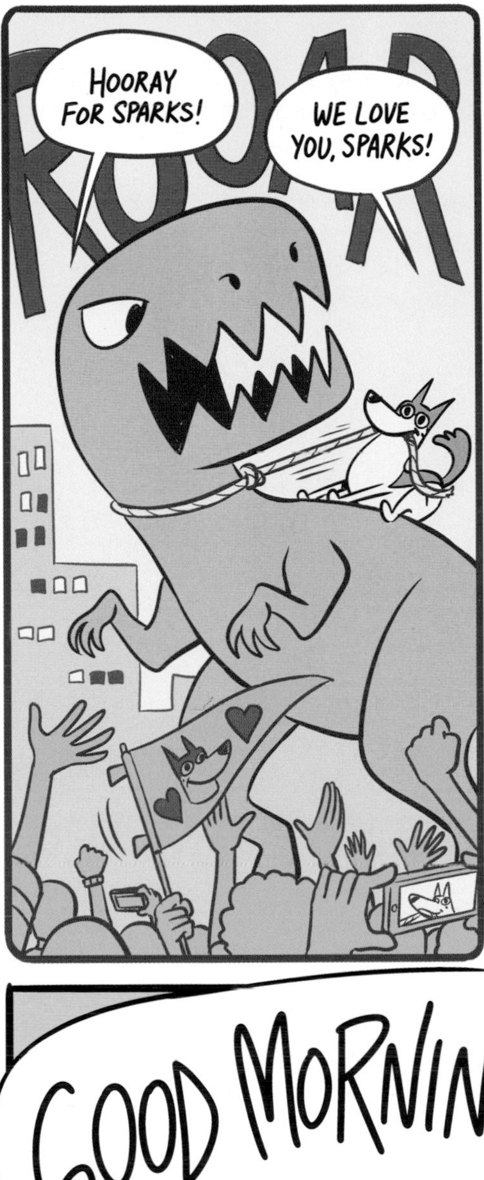
ROOAR
HOORAY FOR SPARKS!
WE LOVE YOU, SPARKS!

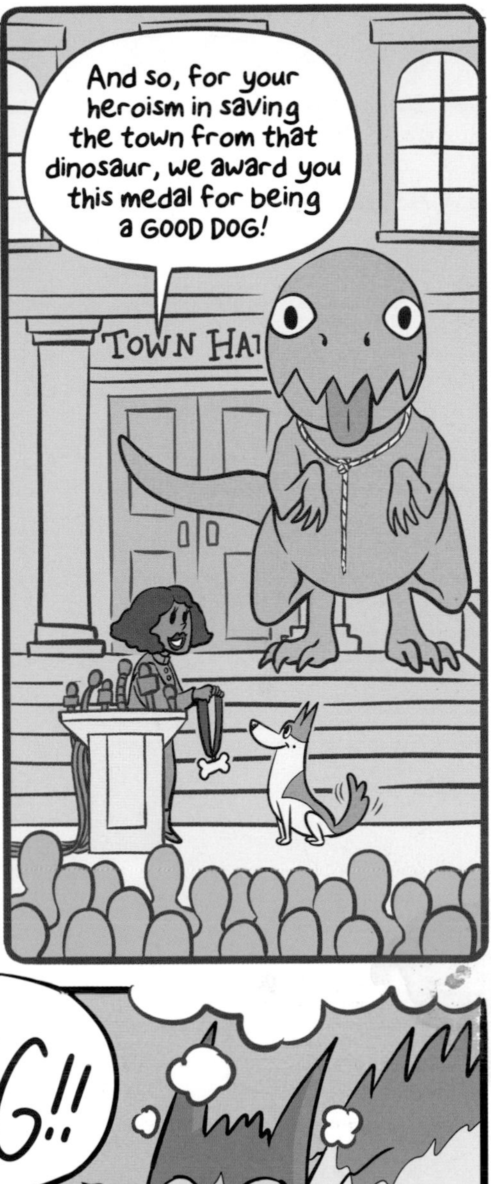
And so, for your heroism in saving the town from that dinosaur, we award you this medal for being a GOOD DOG!
TOWN HA

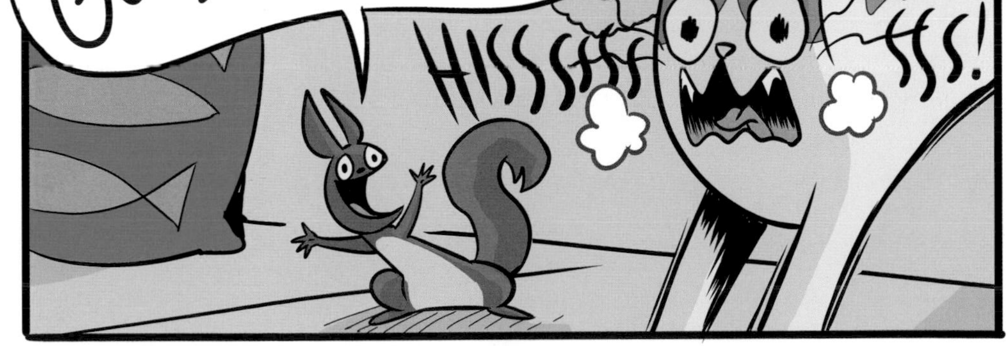
GOOD MORNING!!
HISSSSSSSSSSS!

CHAPTER FOUR

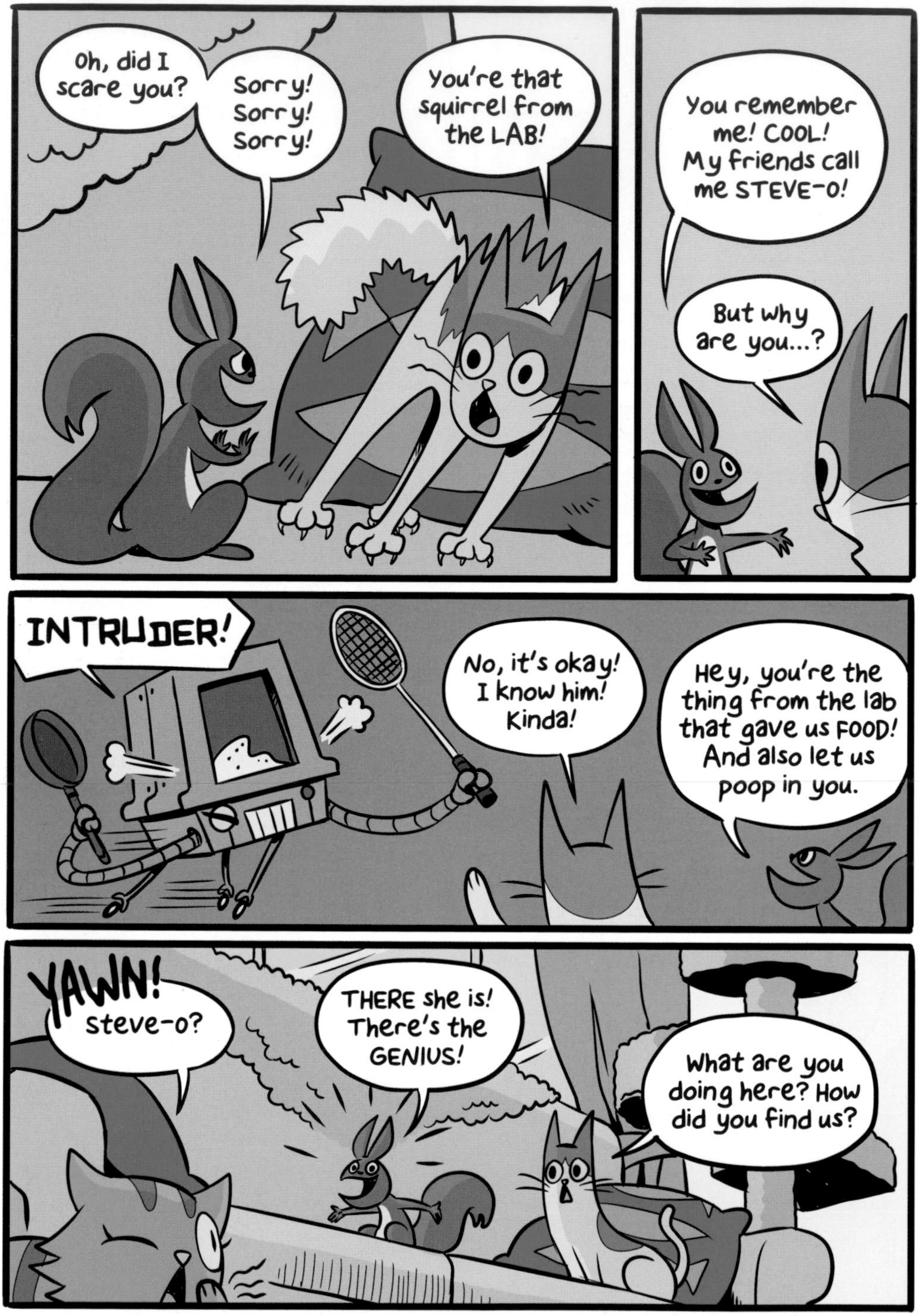
Oh, did I scare you?
Sorry! Sorry! Sorry!
You're that squirrel from the LAB!
You remember me! COOL! My friends call me STEVE-O!
But why are you...?
INTRUDER!
No, it's okay! I know him! Kinda!
Hey, you're the thing from the lab that gave us FOOD! And also let us poop in you.
YAWN! steve-o?
THERE she is! There's the GENIUS!
What are you doing here? How did you find us?

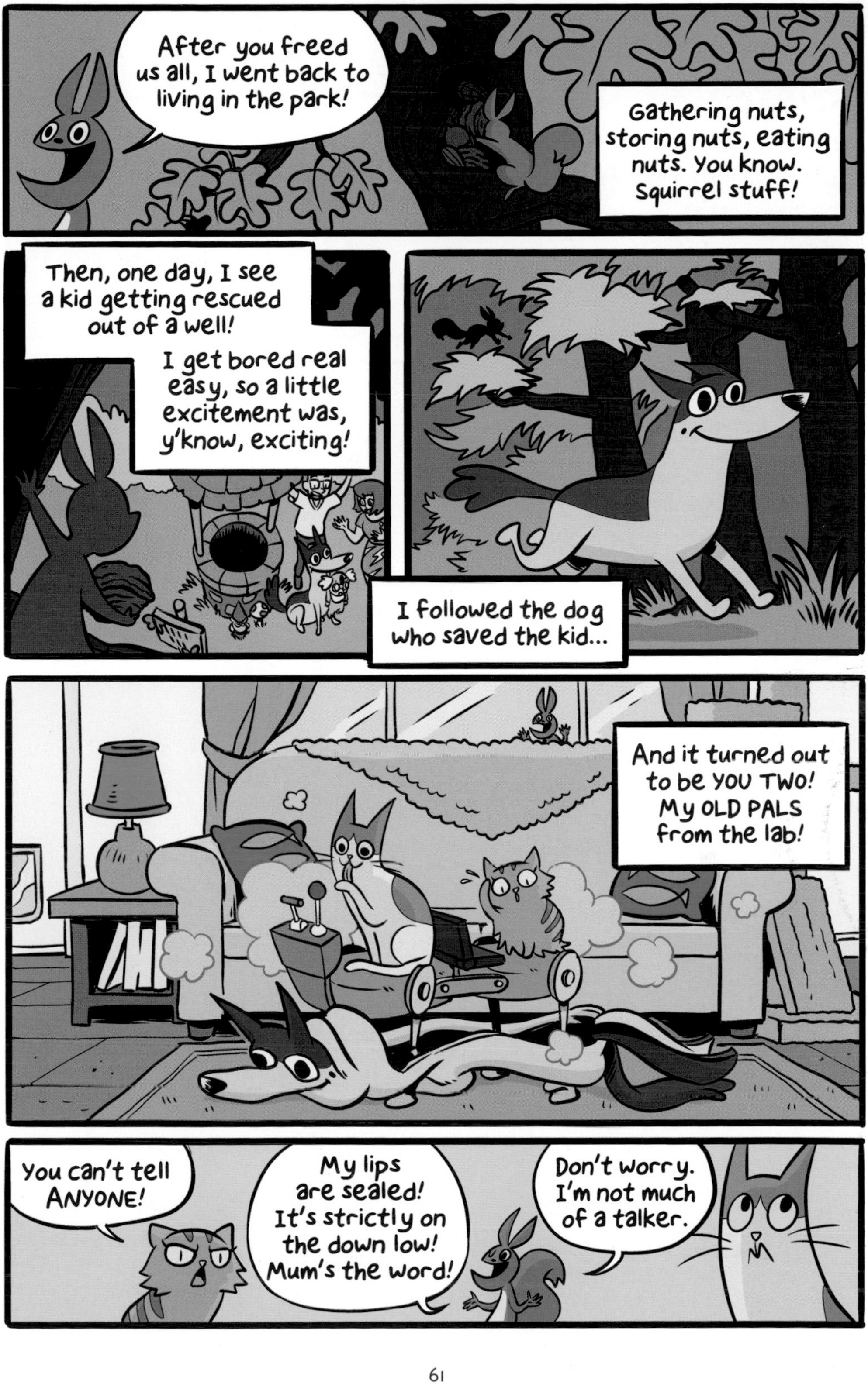
After you freed us all, I went back to living in the park!
Gathering nuts, storing nuts, eating nuts. You know. Squirrel stuff!
Then, one day, I see a kid getting rescued out of a well!
I get bored real easy, so a little excitement was, y'know, exciting!
I followed the dog who saved the kid...
And it turned out to be YOU TWO! My OLD PALS from the lab!
You can't tell ANYONE!
My lips are sealed! It's strictly on the down low! Mum's the word!
Don't worry. I'm not much of a talker.

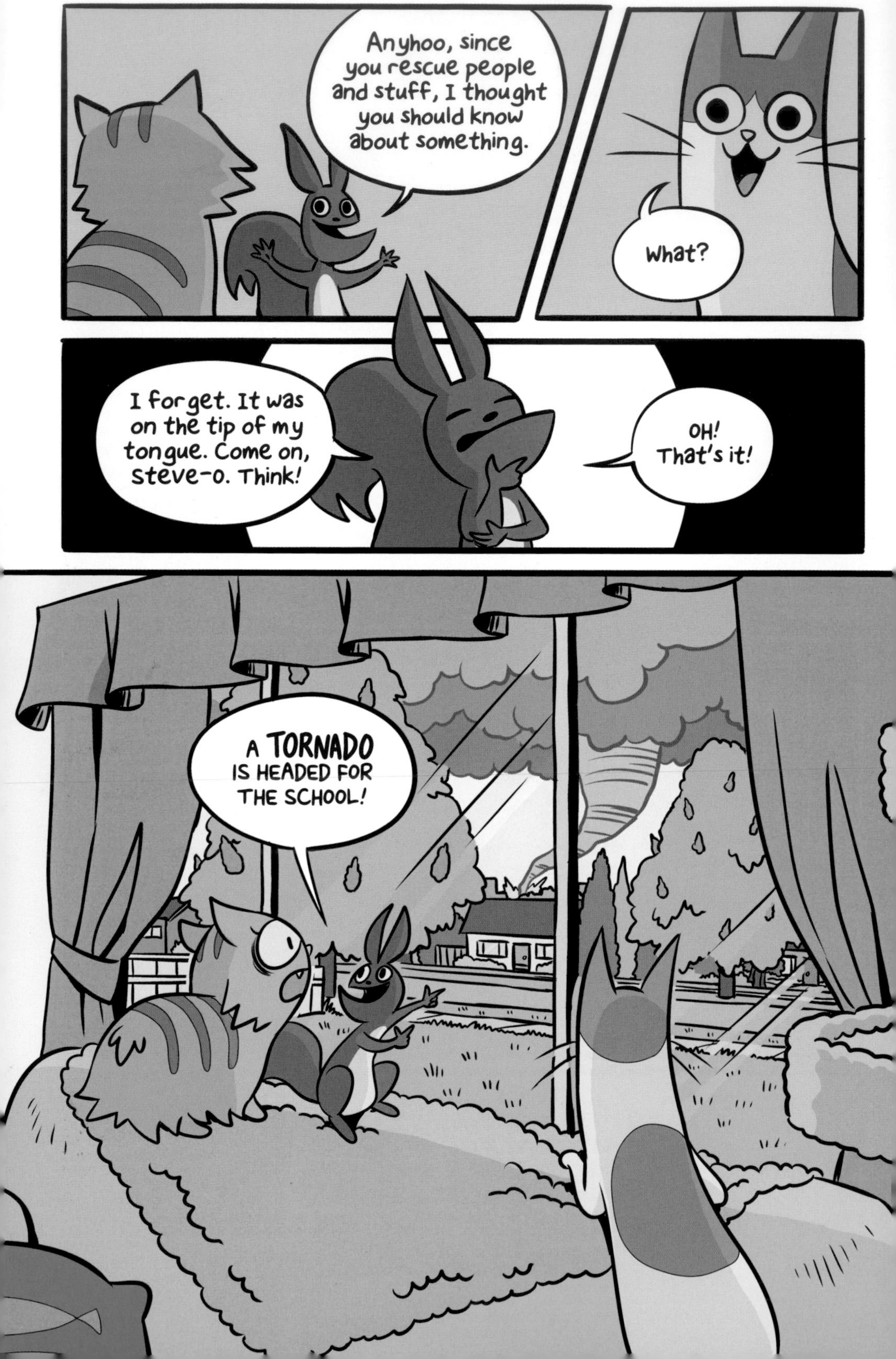

Anyhoo, since you rescue people and stuff, I thought you should know about something.
What?
I forget. It was on the tip of my tongue. Come on, steve-o. Think!
OH! That's it!
A TORNADO IS HEADED FOR THE SCHOOL!

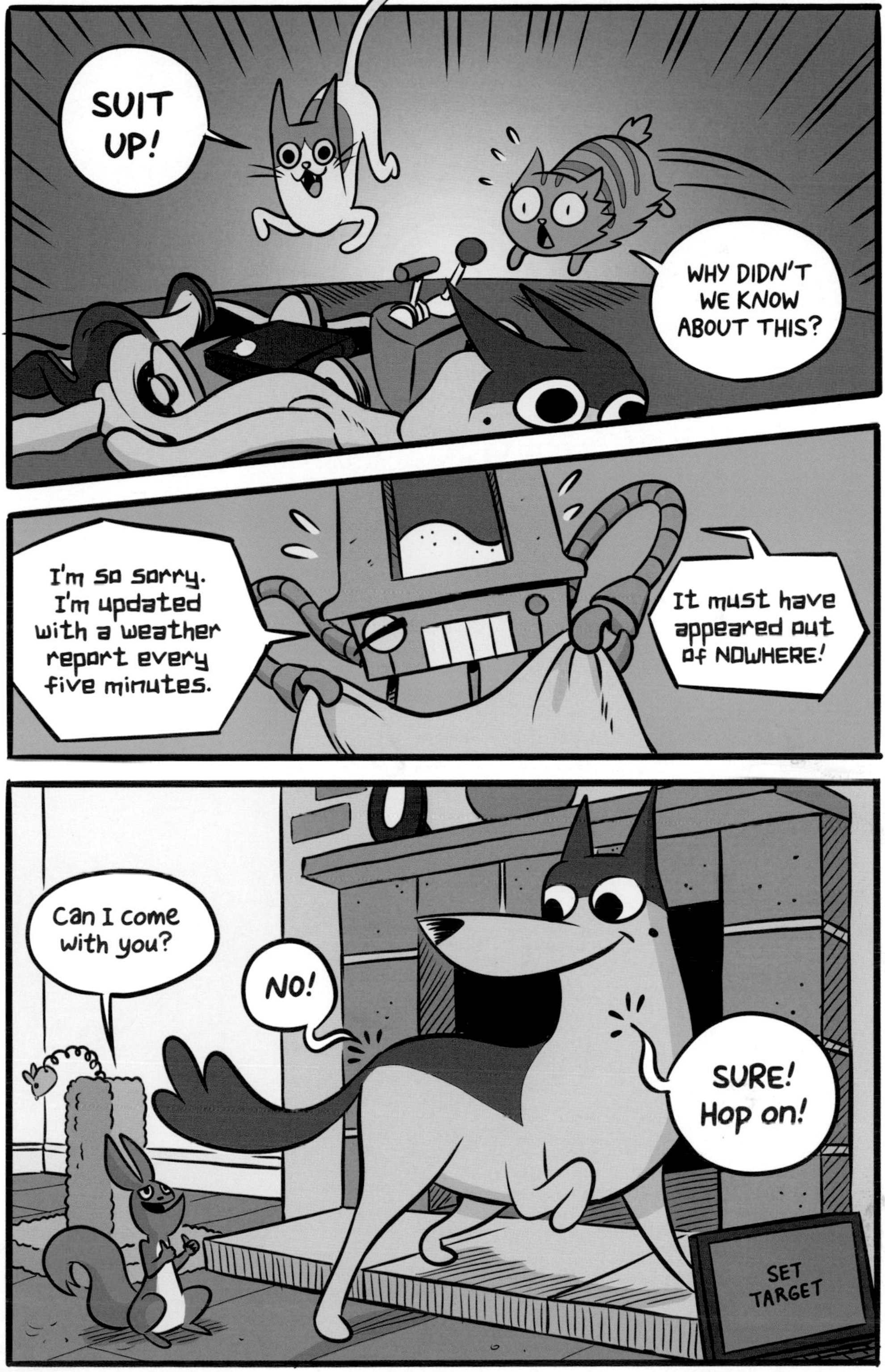
SUIT UP!
WHY DIDN'T WE KNOW ABOUT THIS?
I'm so sorry. I'm updated with a weather report every five minutes.
It must have appeared out of NOWHERE!
Can I come with you?
NO!
SURE! Hop on!
SET TARGET

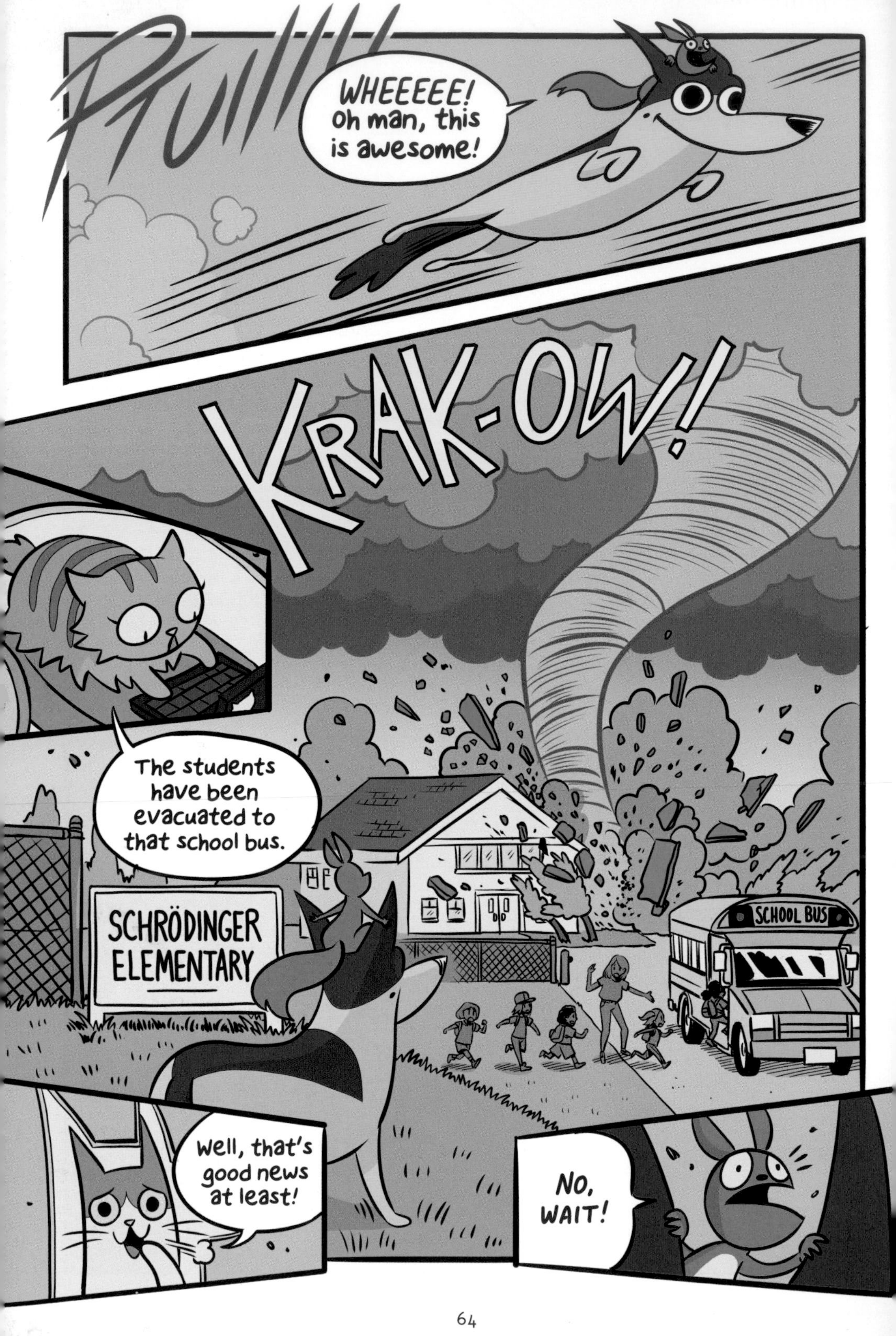

PTUIIIIII
WHEEEEE! Oh man, this is awesome!
KRAK-OW!
The students have been evacuated to that school bus.
SCHRÖDINGER ELEMENTARY
SCHOOL BUS
Well, that's good news at least!
NO, WAIT!

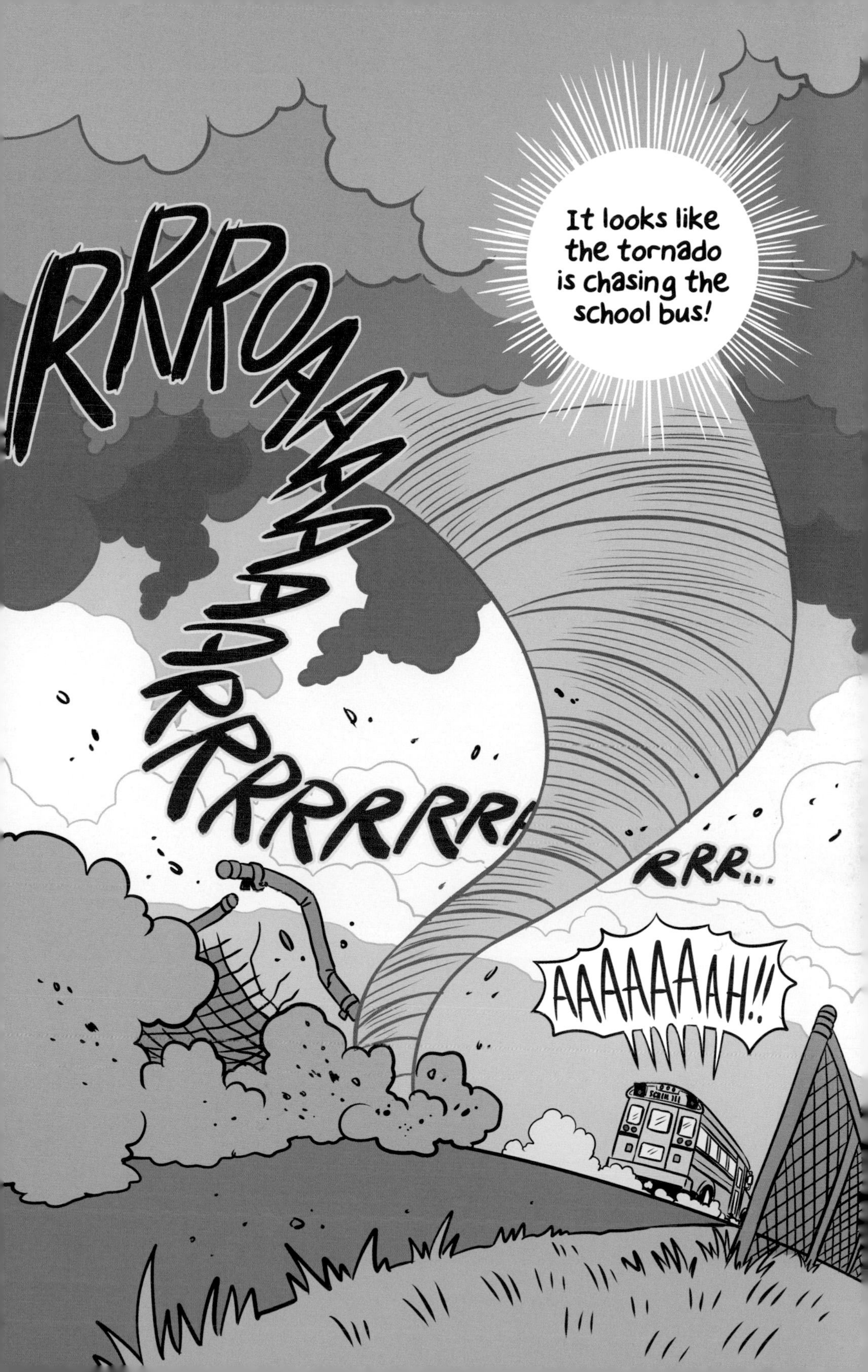
It looks like the tornado is chasing the school bus!
RRROAAAAAARRRRRRRRR
RRR...
AAAAAAAH!!

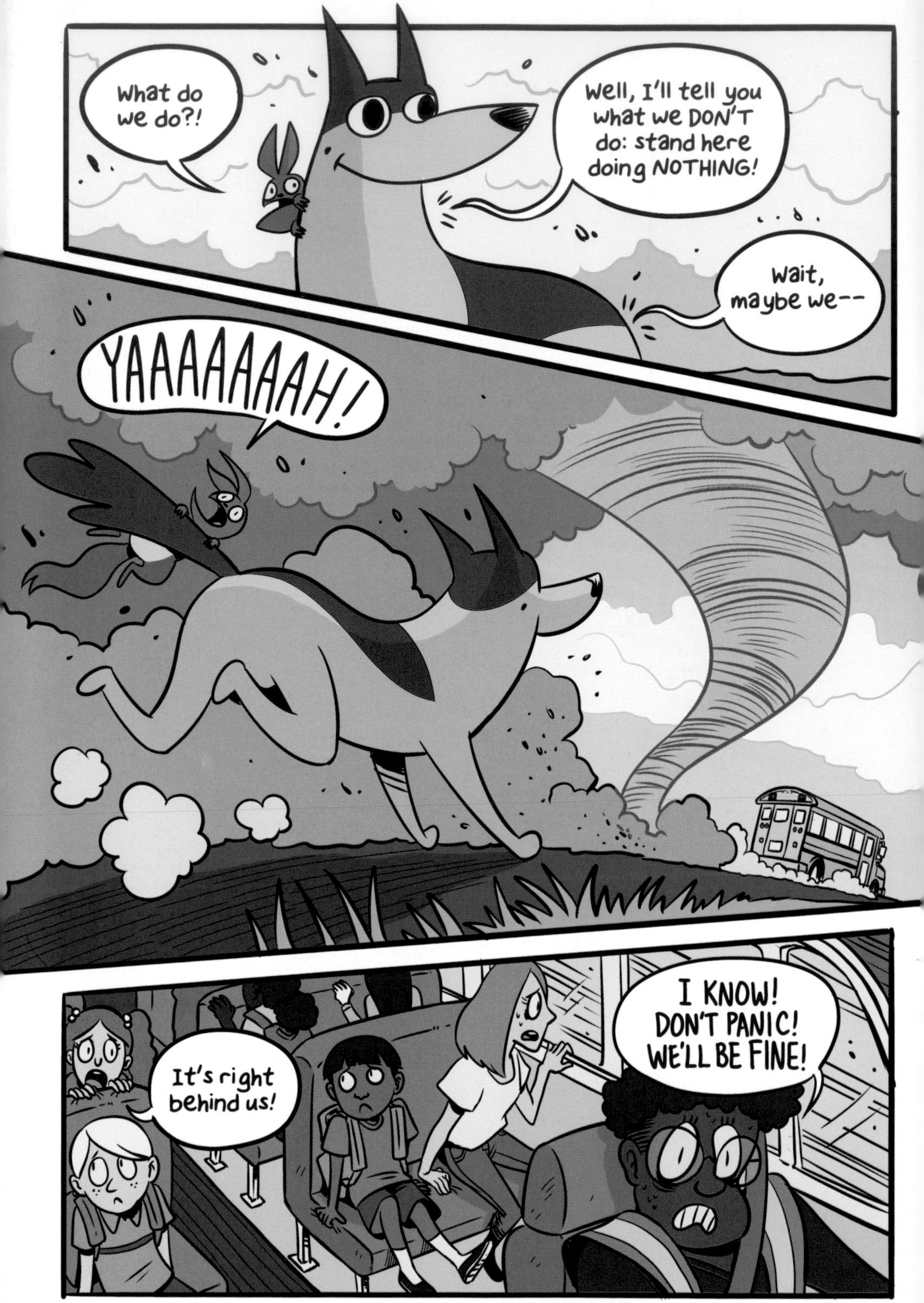
What do we do?!
Well, I'll tell you what we DON'T do: stand here doing NOTHING!
Wait, maybe we--
YAAAAAAAH!
It's right behind us!
I KNOW! DON'T PANIC! WE'LL BE FINE!

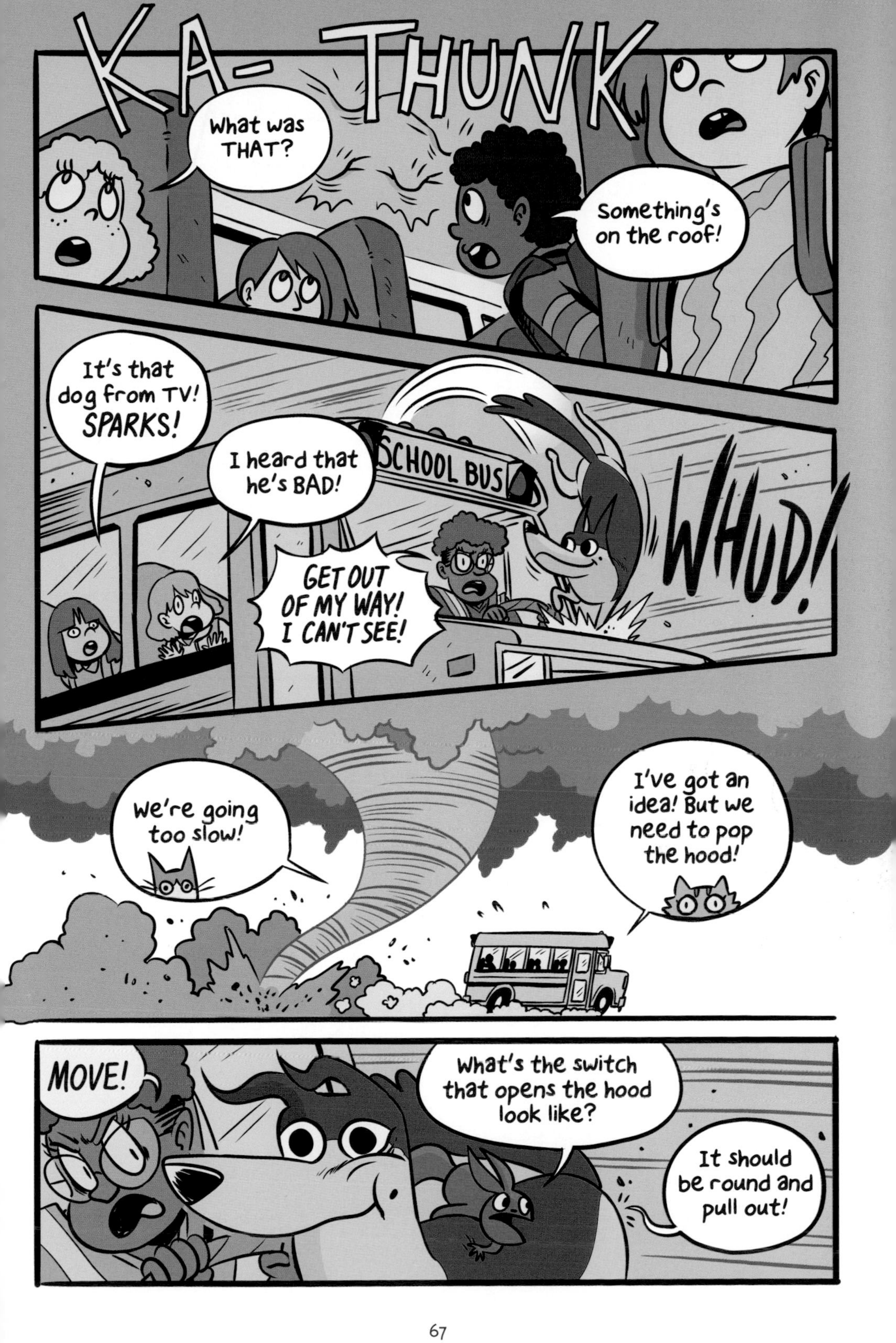
KA-THUNK
What was THAT?
Something's on the roof!
It's that dog from TV! SPARKS!
I heard that he's BAD!
SCHOOL BUS
GET OUT OF MY WAY! I CAN'T SEE!
WHUD!
We're going too slow!
I've got an idea! But we need to pop the hood!
MOVE!
What's the switch that opens the hood look like?
It should be round and pull out!

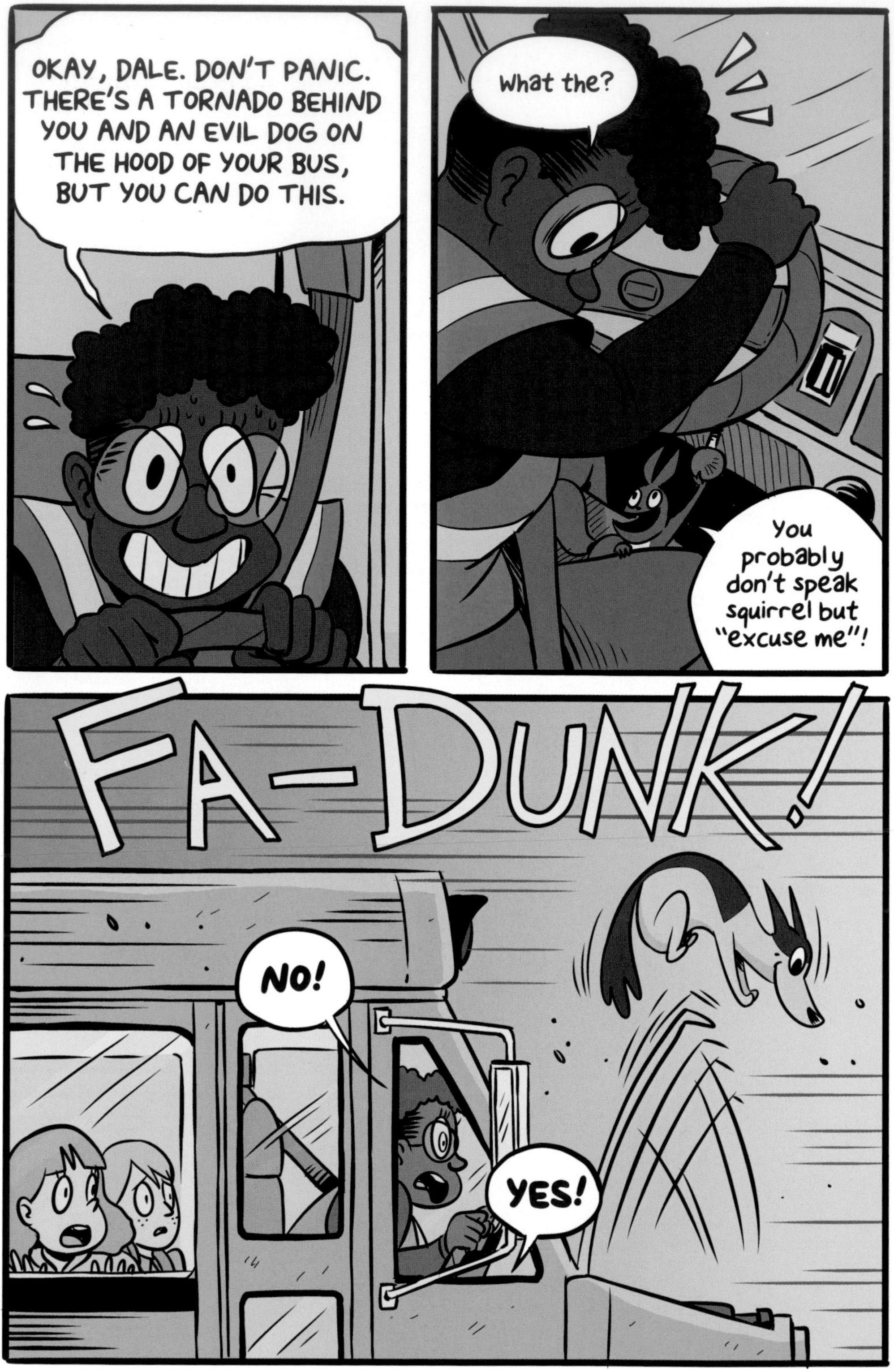
OKAY, DALE. DON'T PANIC. THERE'S A TORNADO BEHIND YOU AND AN EVIL DOG ON THE HOOD OF YOUR BUS, BUT YOU CAN DO THIS.
What the?
You probably don't speak squirrel but "excuse me"!
FA-DUNK!
NO!
YES!

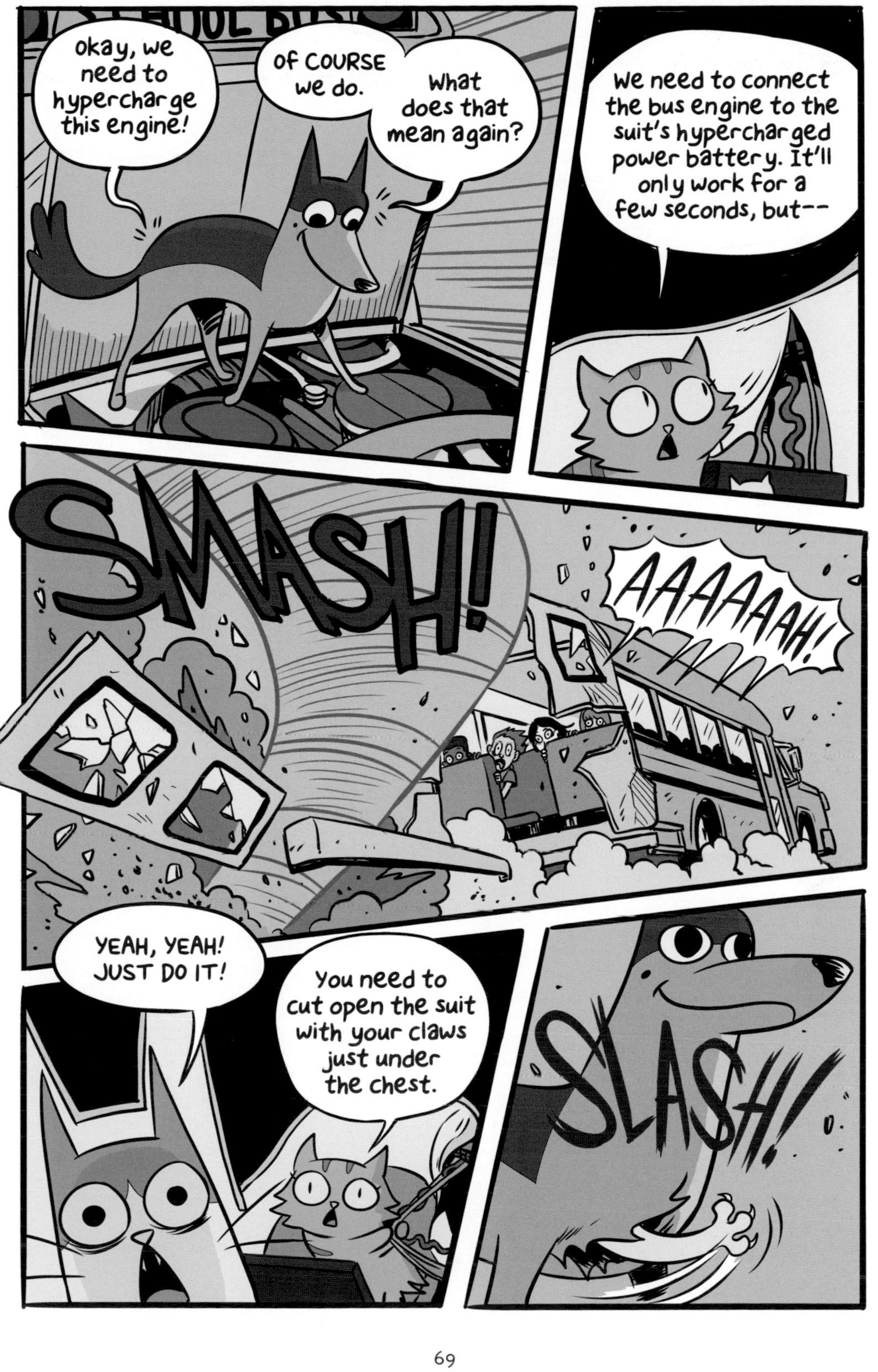
okay, we need to hypercharge this engine!
OF COURSE we do.
What does that mean again?
We need to connect the bus engine to the suit's hypercharged power battery. It'll only work for a few seconds, but--
SMASH!
AAAAAAAH!
YEAH, YEAH! JUST DO IT!
You need to cut open the suit with your claws just under the chest.
SLASH!

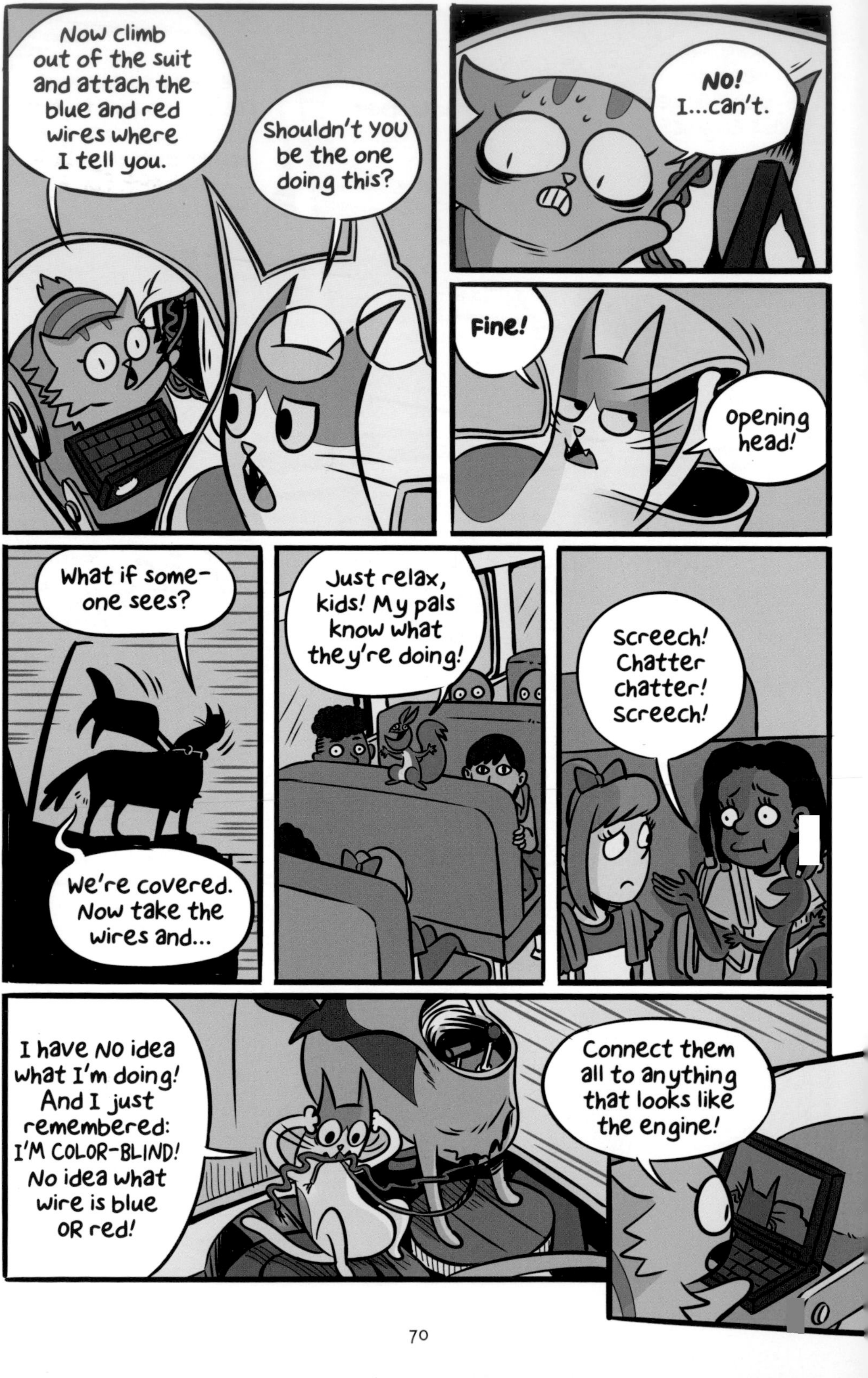
Now climb out of the suit and attach the blue and red wires where I tell you.
Shouldn't YOU be the one doing this?
NO! I...can't.
Fine!
Opening head!
What if some-one sees?
We're covered. Now take the wires and...
Just relax, kids! My pals know what they're doing!
Screech! Chatter chatter! Screech!
I have NO idea what I'm doing! And I just remembered: I'M COLOR-BLIND! No idea what wire is blue OR red!
Connect them all to anything that looks like the engine!

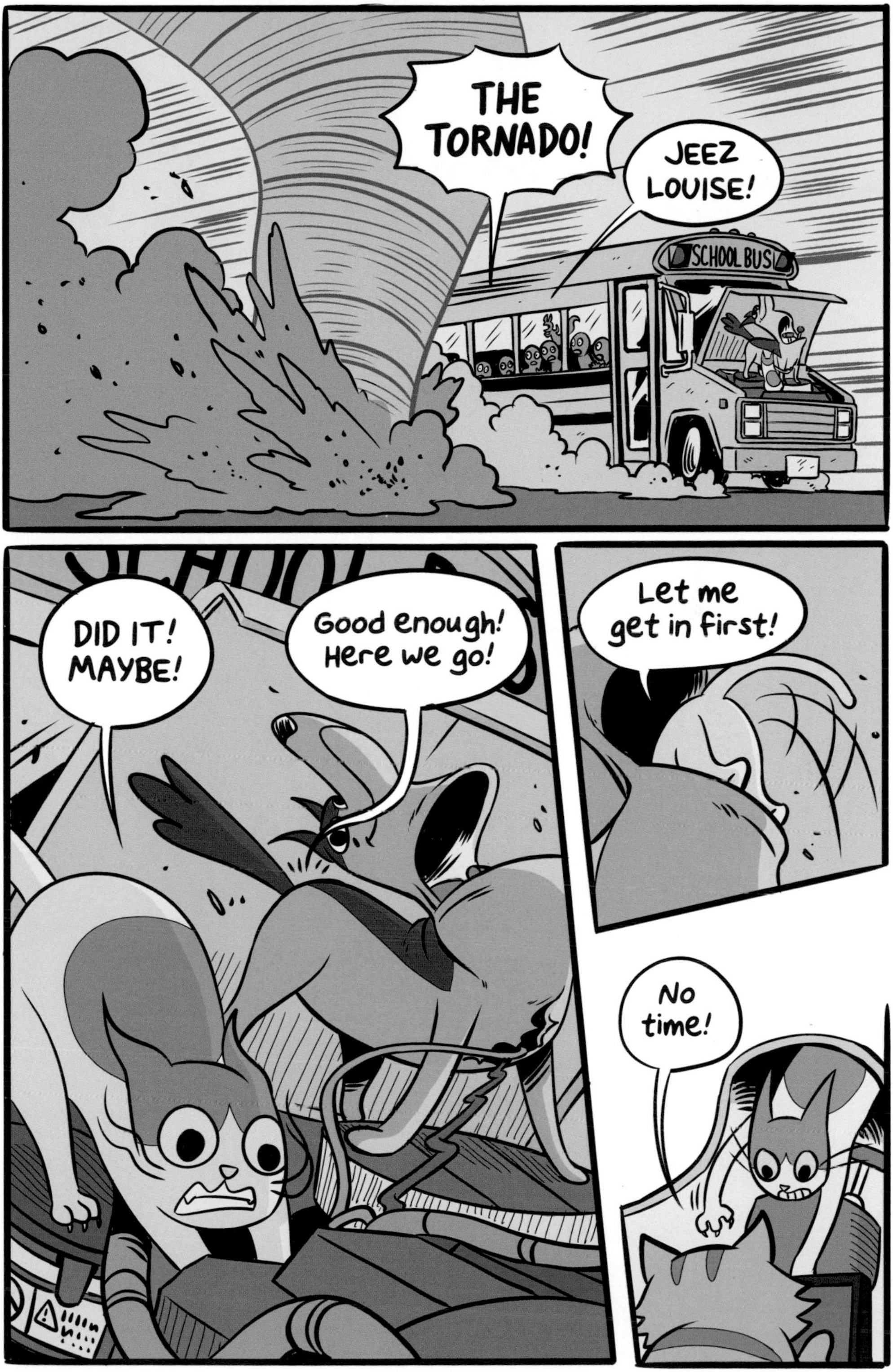
THE TORNADO!
JEEZ LOUISE!
SCHOOL BUS
DID IT! MAYBE!
Good enough! Here we go!
Let me get in first!
No time!

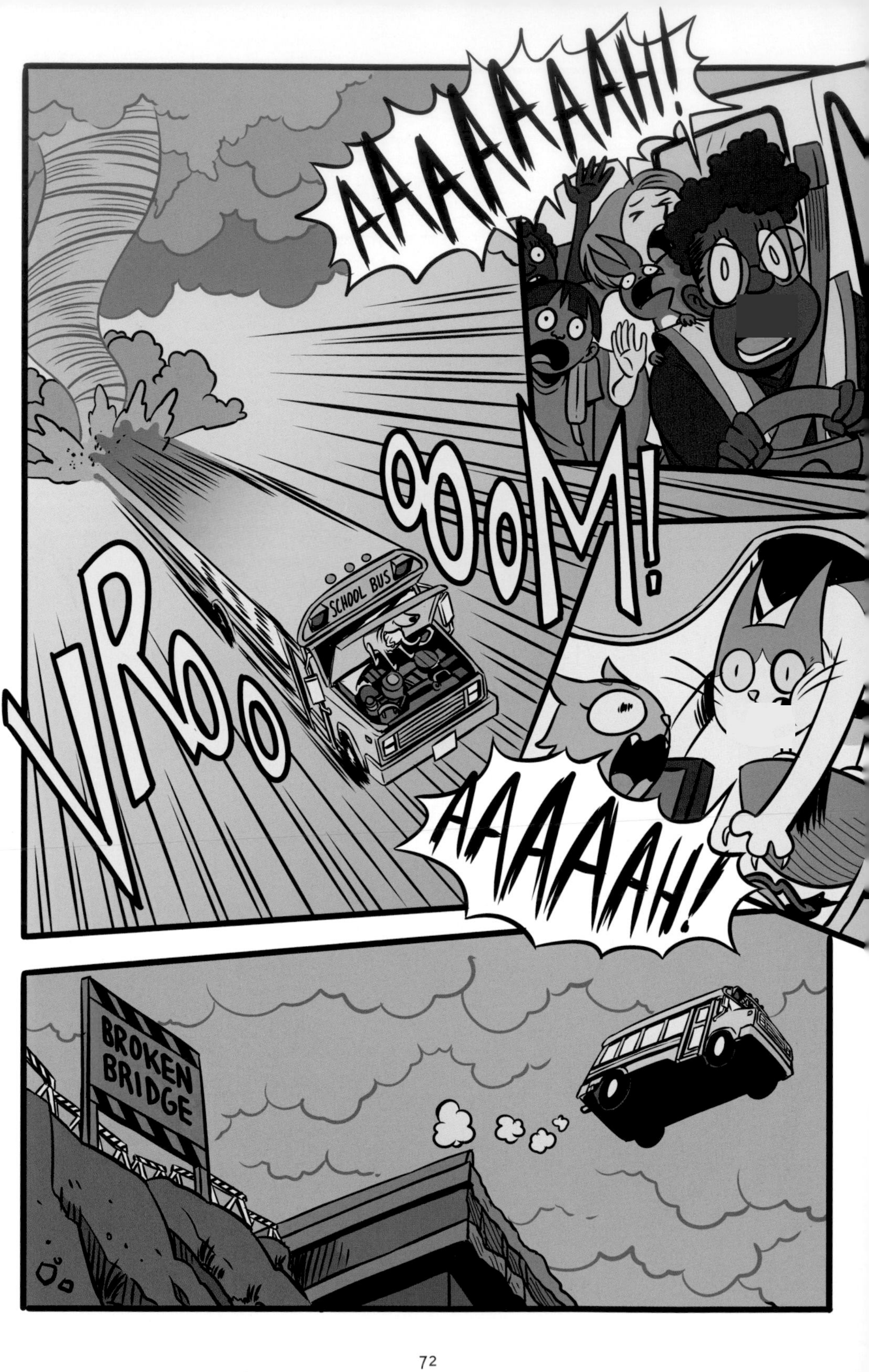
AAAAAAH!
VROOOOOOM!
SCHOOL BUS
AAAAAH!
BROKEN BRIDGE

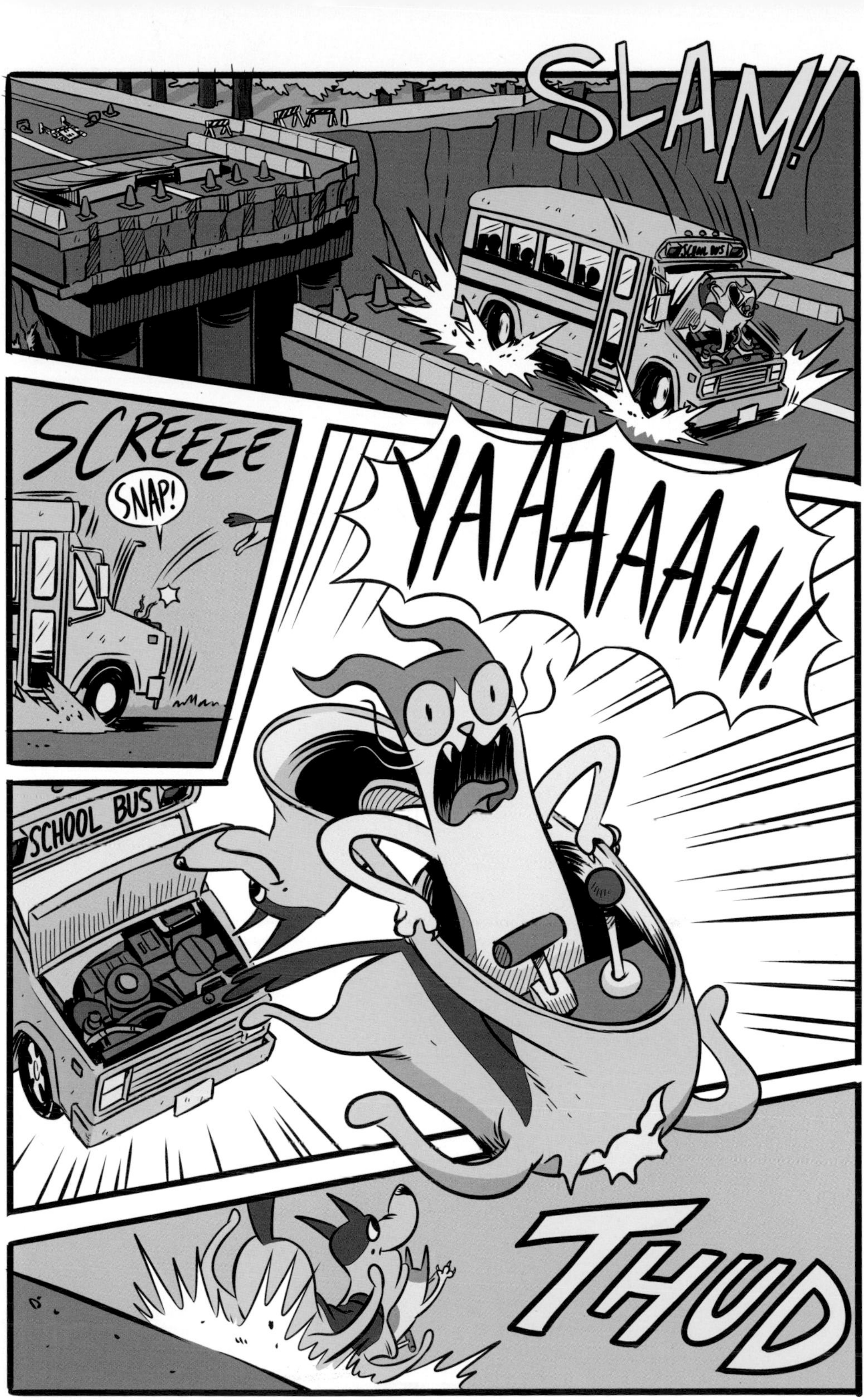
SLAM!
SCHOOL BUS
SCREEEE
SNAP!
YAAAAAAH!
SCHOOL BUS
THUD

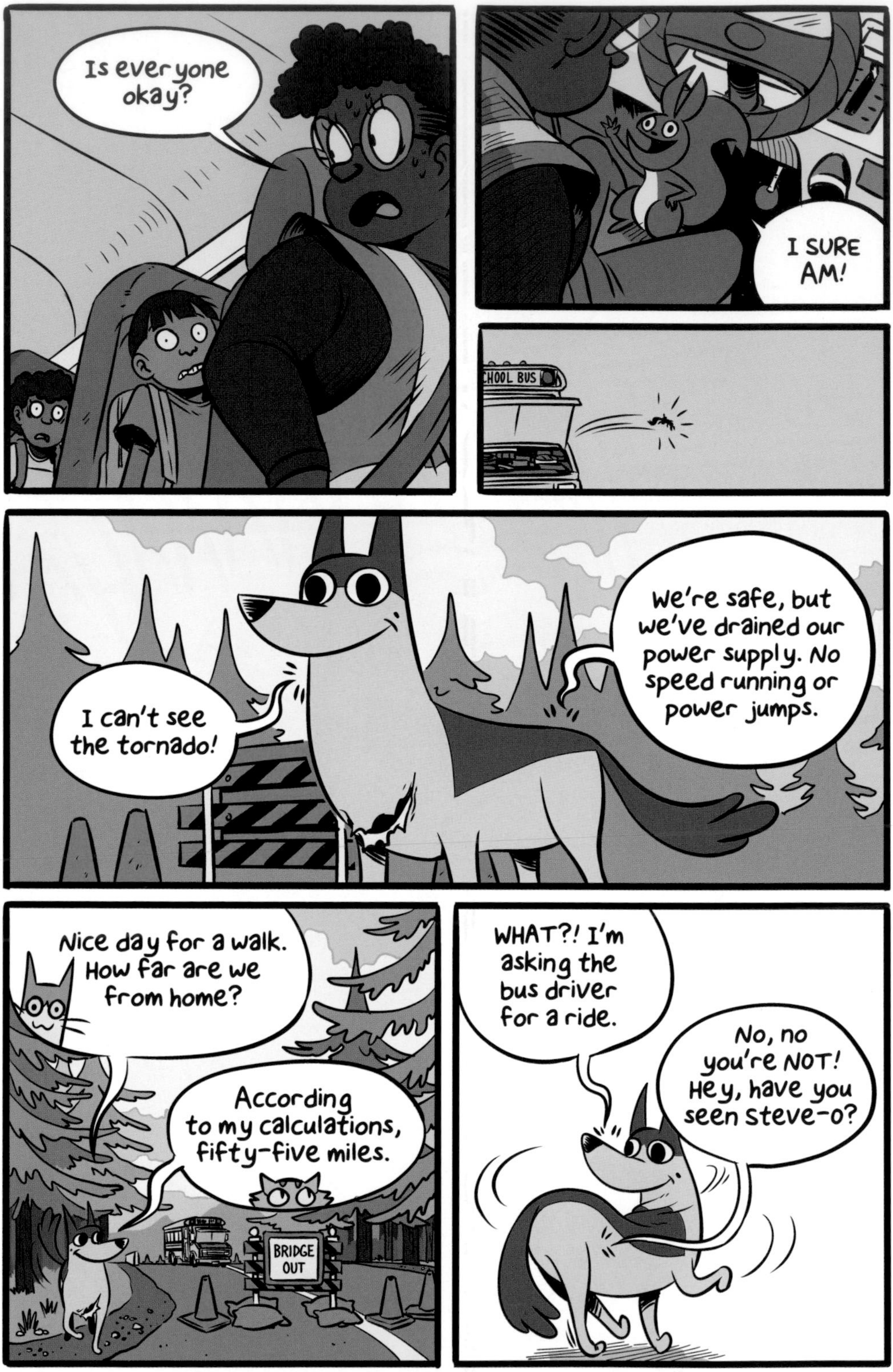
Is everyone okay?
I SURE AM!
SCHOOL BUS
I can't see the tornado!
We're safe, but we've drained our power supply. No speed running or power jumps.
Nice day for a walk. How far are we from home?
According to my calculations, fifty-five miles.
BRIDGE OUT
WHAT?! I'm asking the bus driver for a ride.
No, no you're NOT! Hey, have you seen Steve-o?

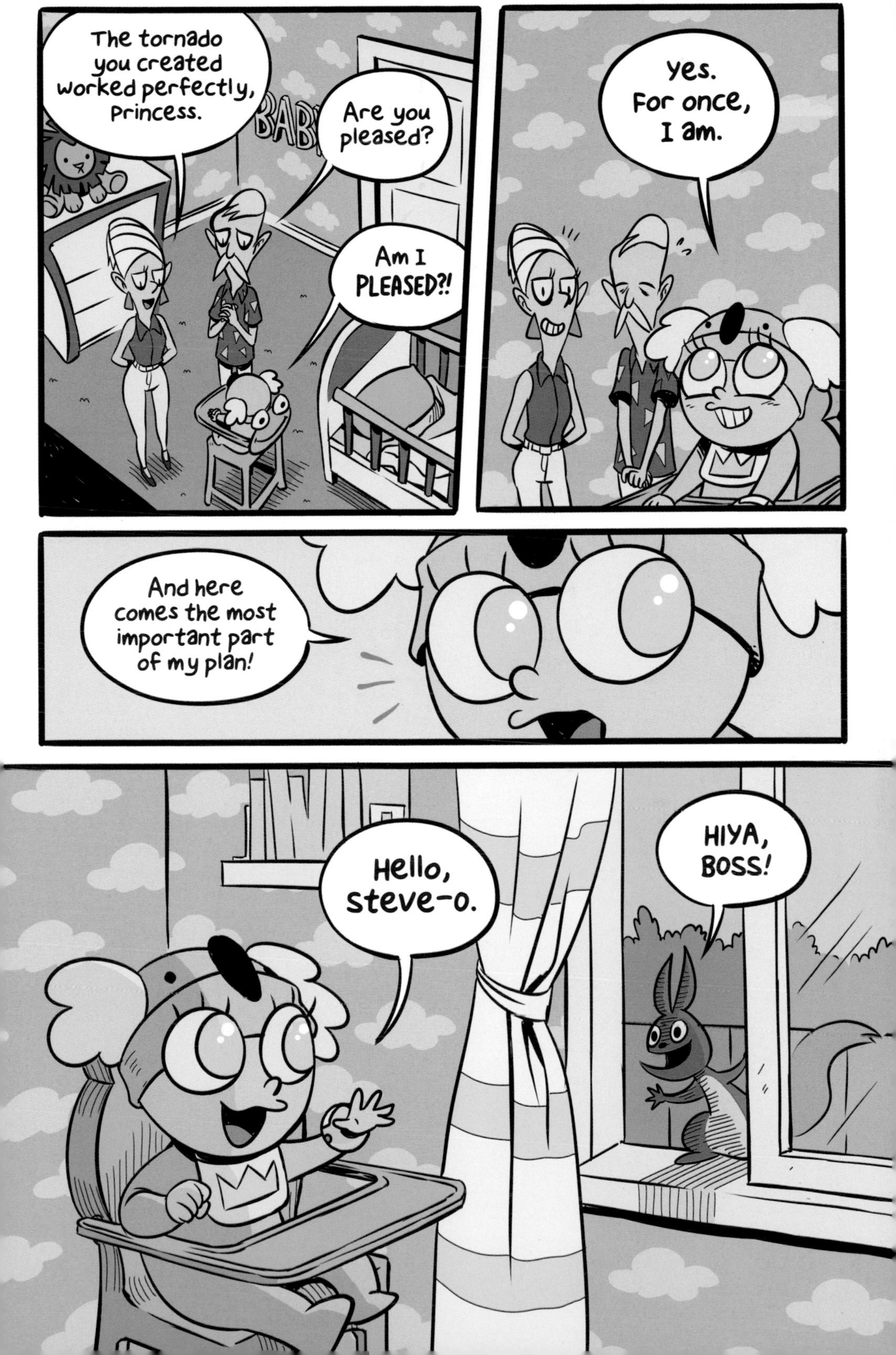
The tornado you created worked perfectly, Princess.
BABY
Are you pleased?
Am I PLEASED?!
Yes. For once, I am.
And here comes the most important part of my plan!
Hello, Steve-o.
HIYA, BOSS!

CHAPTER FI

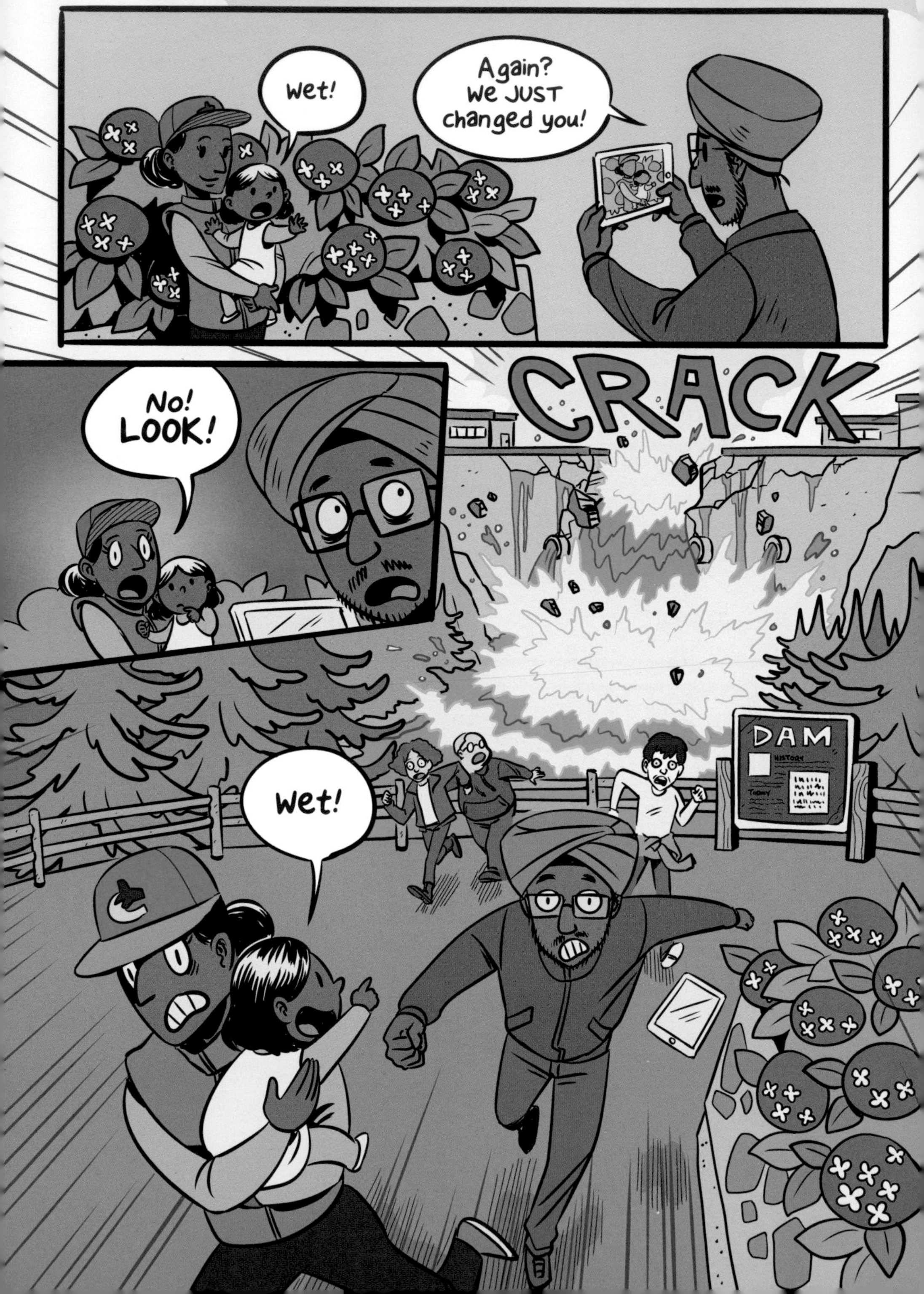

Wet!
Again? We JUST changed you!
No! LOOK!
CRACK
DAM
Wet!

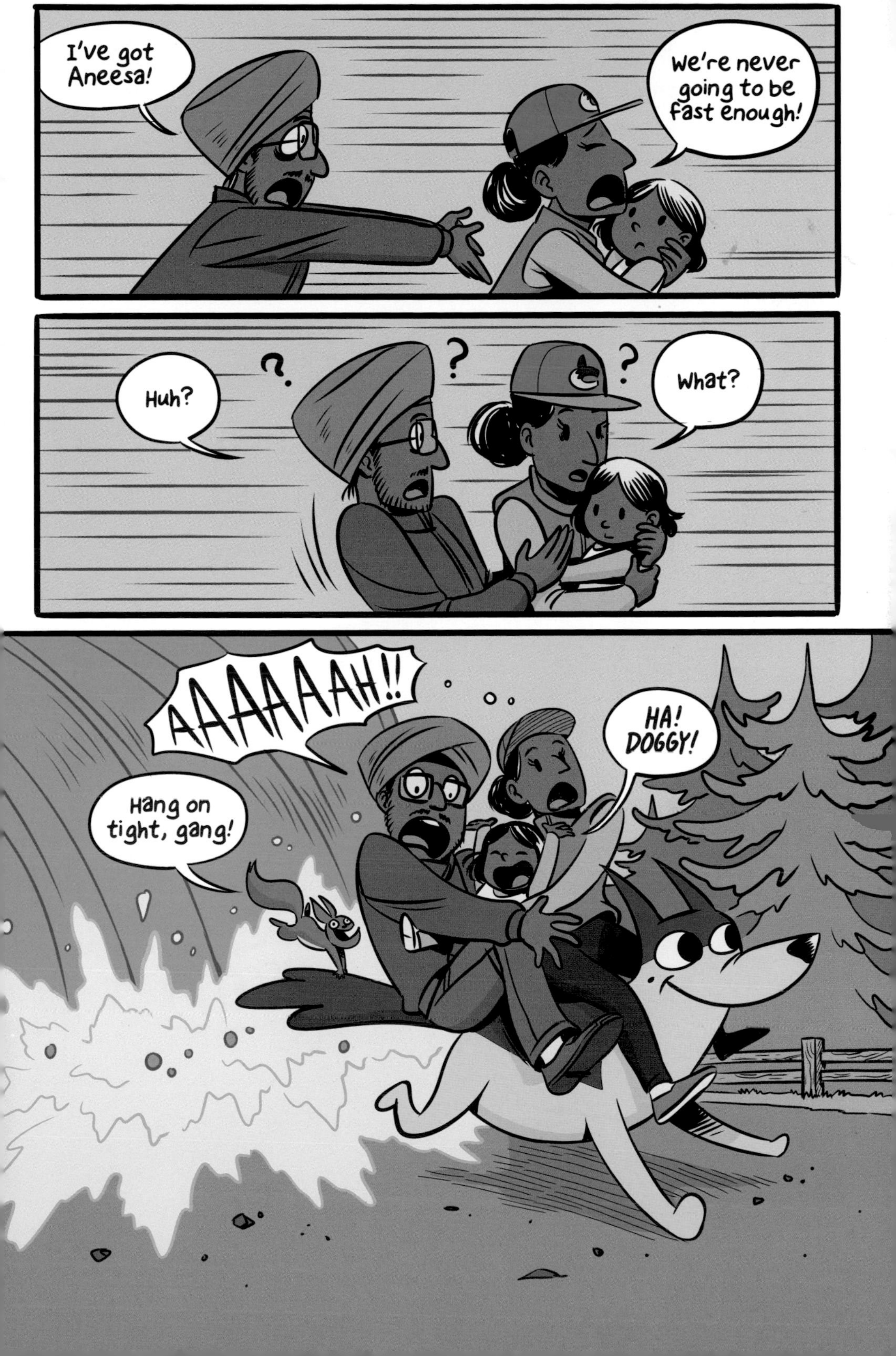
I've got Aneesa!
We're never going to be fast enough!
?
Huh?
?
?
What?
AAAAAAAH!!
HA! DOGGY!
Hang on tight, gang!

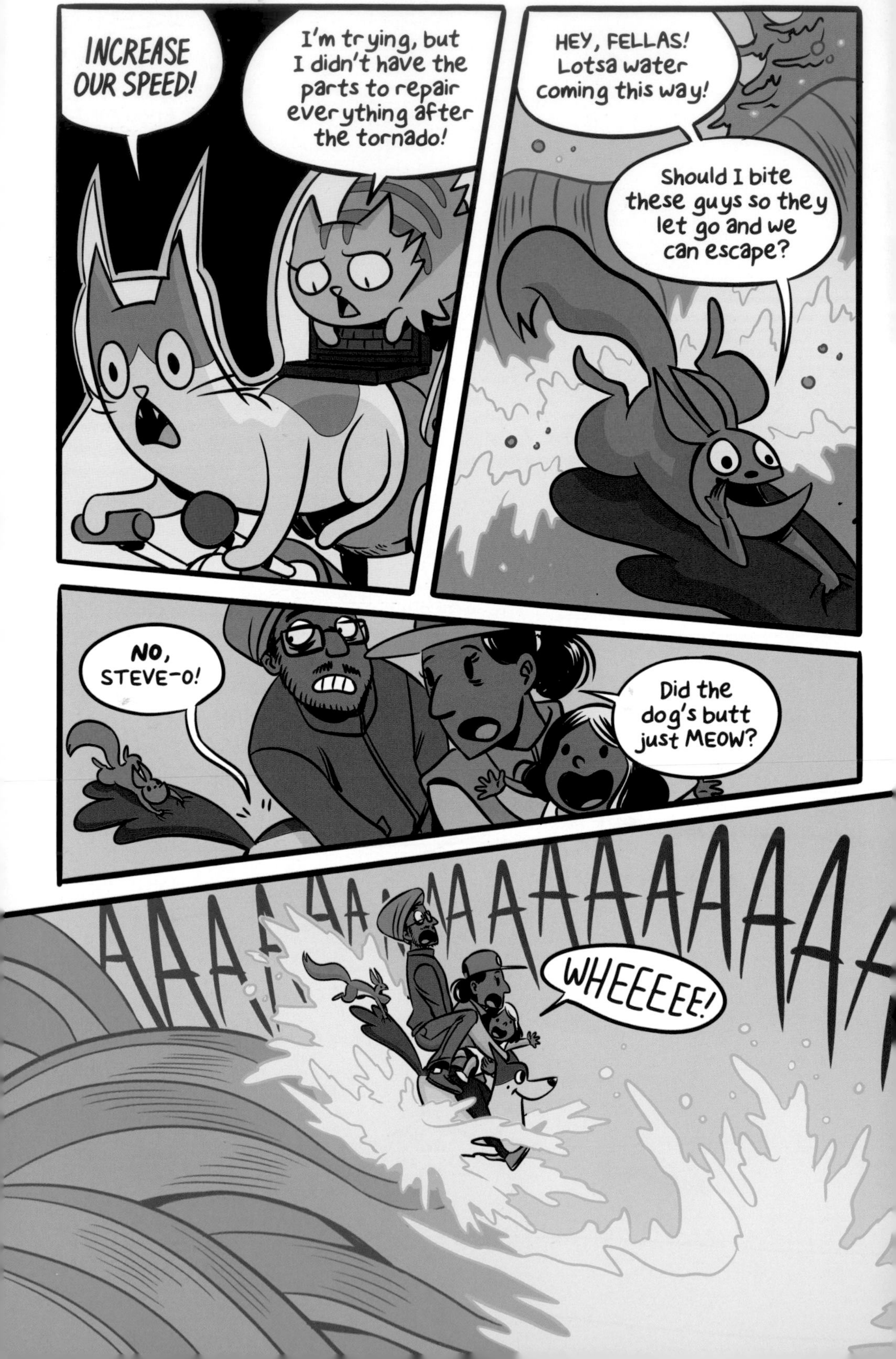

INCREASE OUR SPEED!
I'm trying, but I didn't have the parts to repair everything after the tornado!
HEY, FELLAS! Lotsa water coming this way!
Should I bite these guys so they let go and we can escape?
NO, STEVE-O!
Did the dog's butt just MEOW?
AAAAAAAAAAAAAAAA
WHEEEEE!

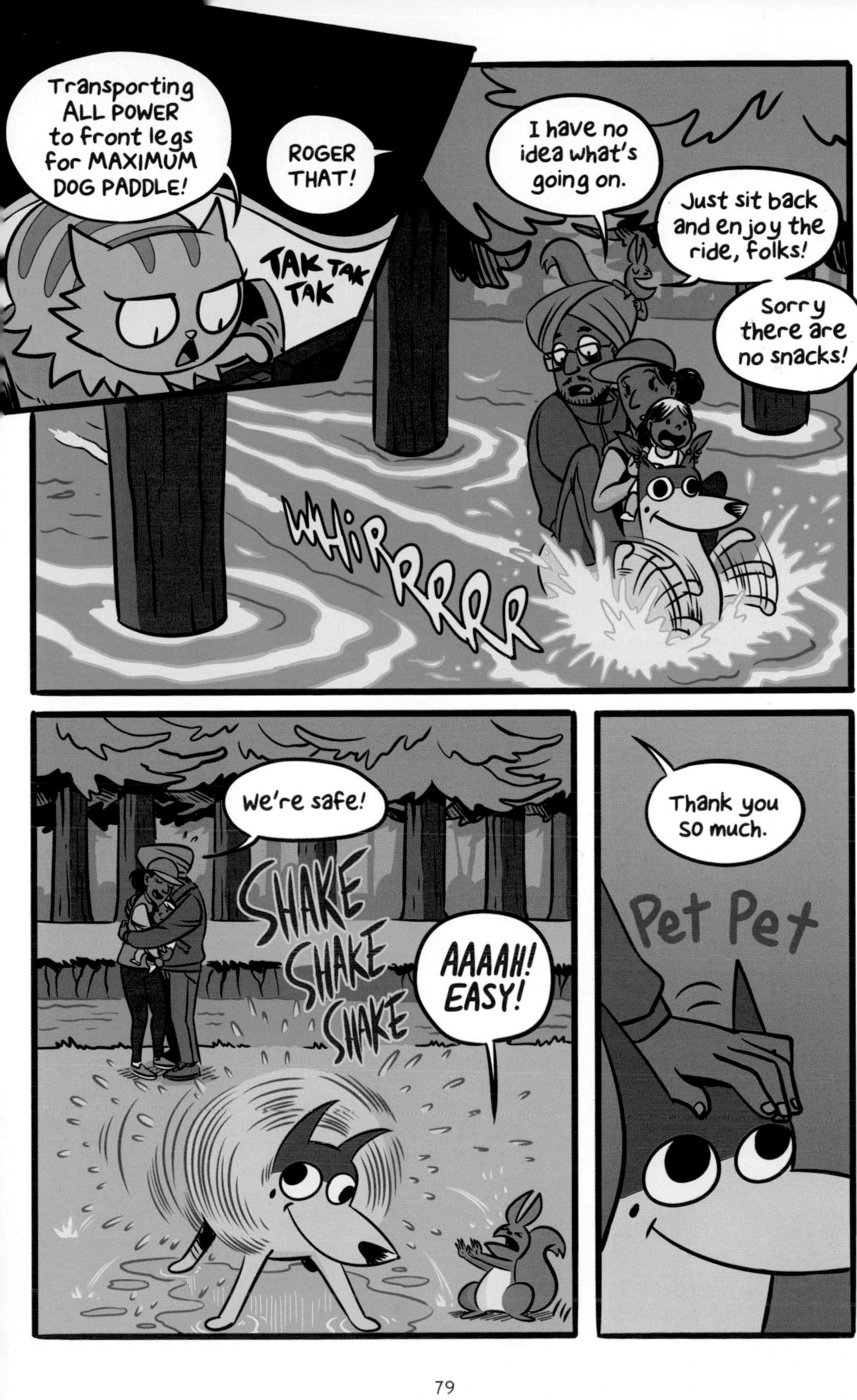
Transporting ALL POWER to front legs for MAXIMUM DOG PADDLE!
ROGER THAT!
TAK TAK TAK
I have no idea what's going on.
Just sit back and enjoy the ride, folks!
Sorry there are no snacks!
WHIRRRRR
We're safe!
SHAKE SHAKE SHAKE
AAAAH! EASY!
Thank you so much.
Pet Pet

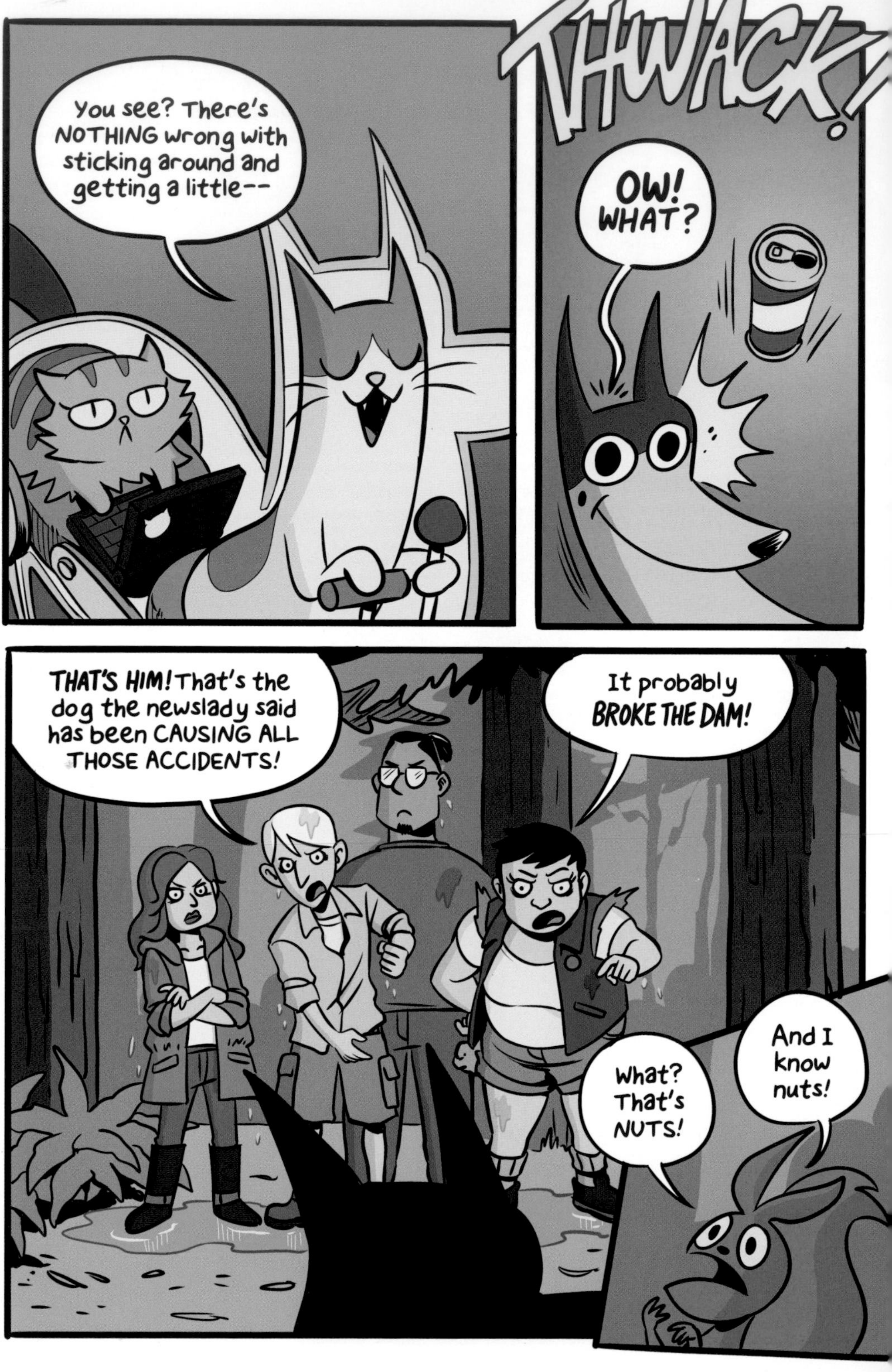

You see? There's NOTHING wrong with sticking around and getting a little--
THWACK!
OW! WHAT?
THAT'S HIM! That's the dog the newslady said has been CAUSING ALL THOSE ACCIDENTS!
It probably BROKE THE DAM!
What? That's NUTS!
And I know nuts!

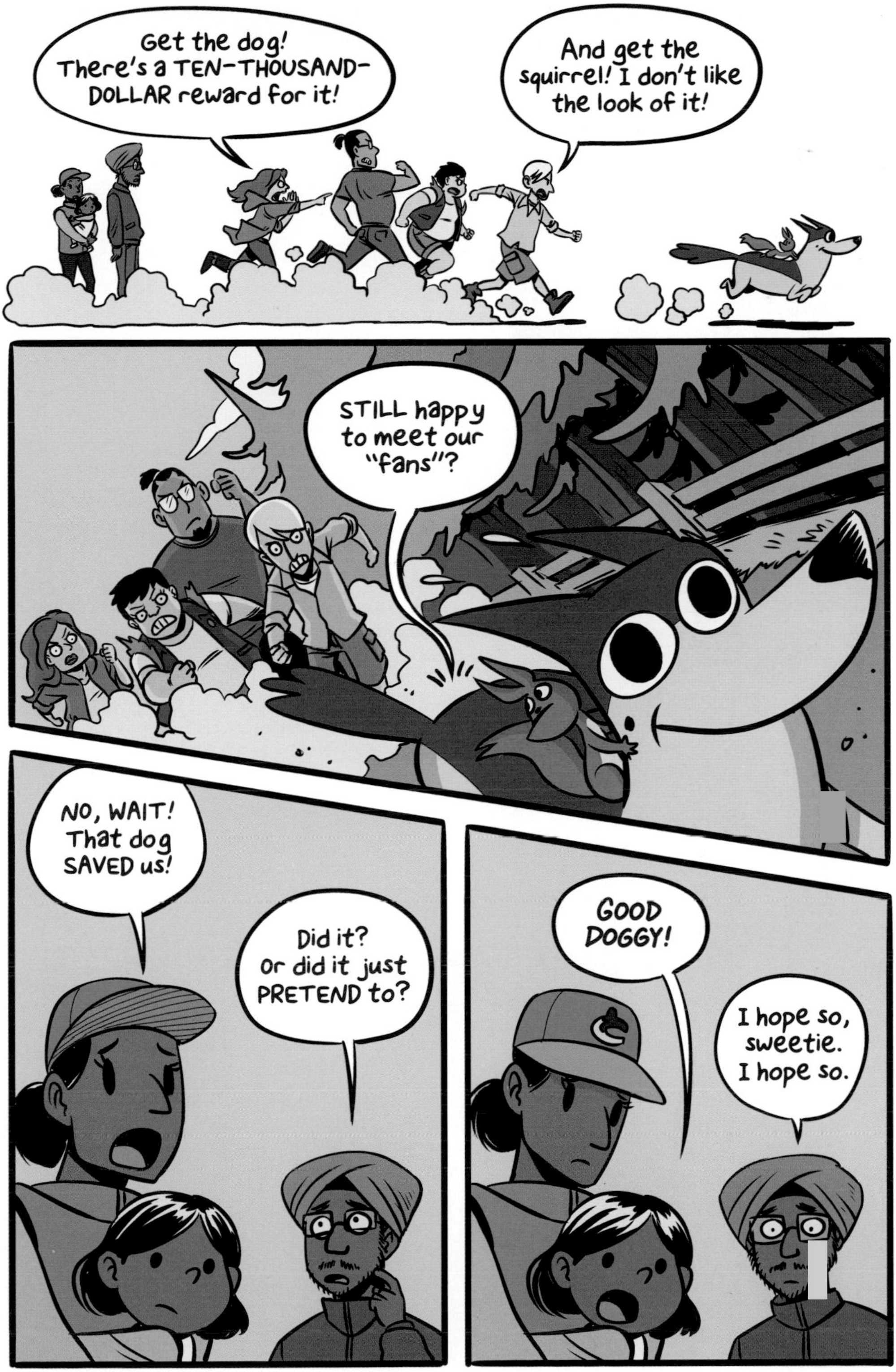
Get the dog! There's a TEN-THOUSAND-DOLLAR reward for it!
And get the squirrel! I don't like the look of it!
STILL happy to meet our "fans"?
NO, WAIT! That dog SAVED us!
Did it? Or did it just PRETEND to?
GOOD DOGGY!
I hope so, sweetie. I hope so.

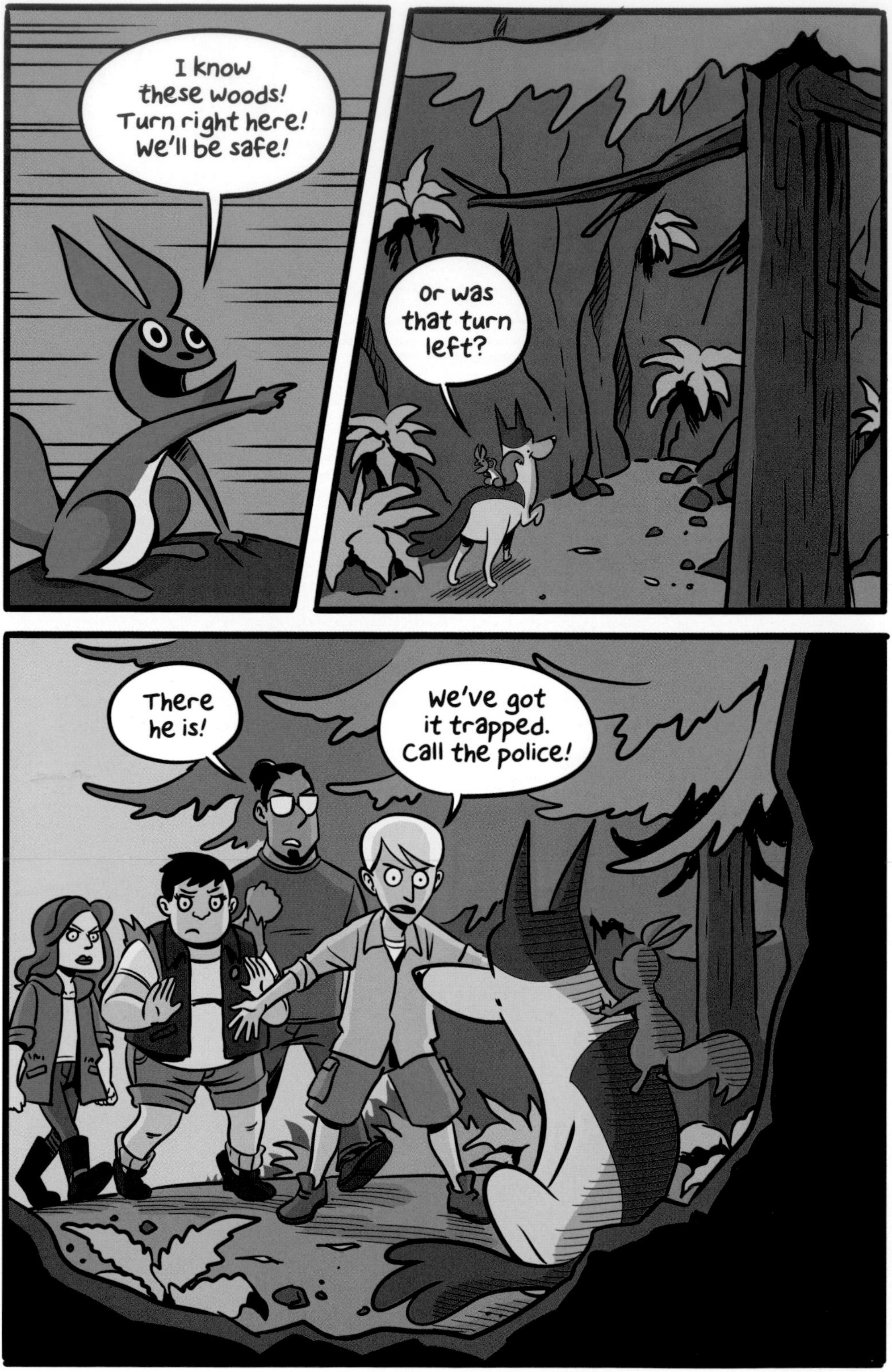
I know these woods! Turn right here! We'll be safe!
Or was that turn left?
There he is!
We've got it trapped. Call the police!

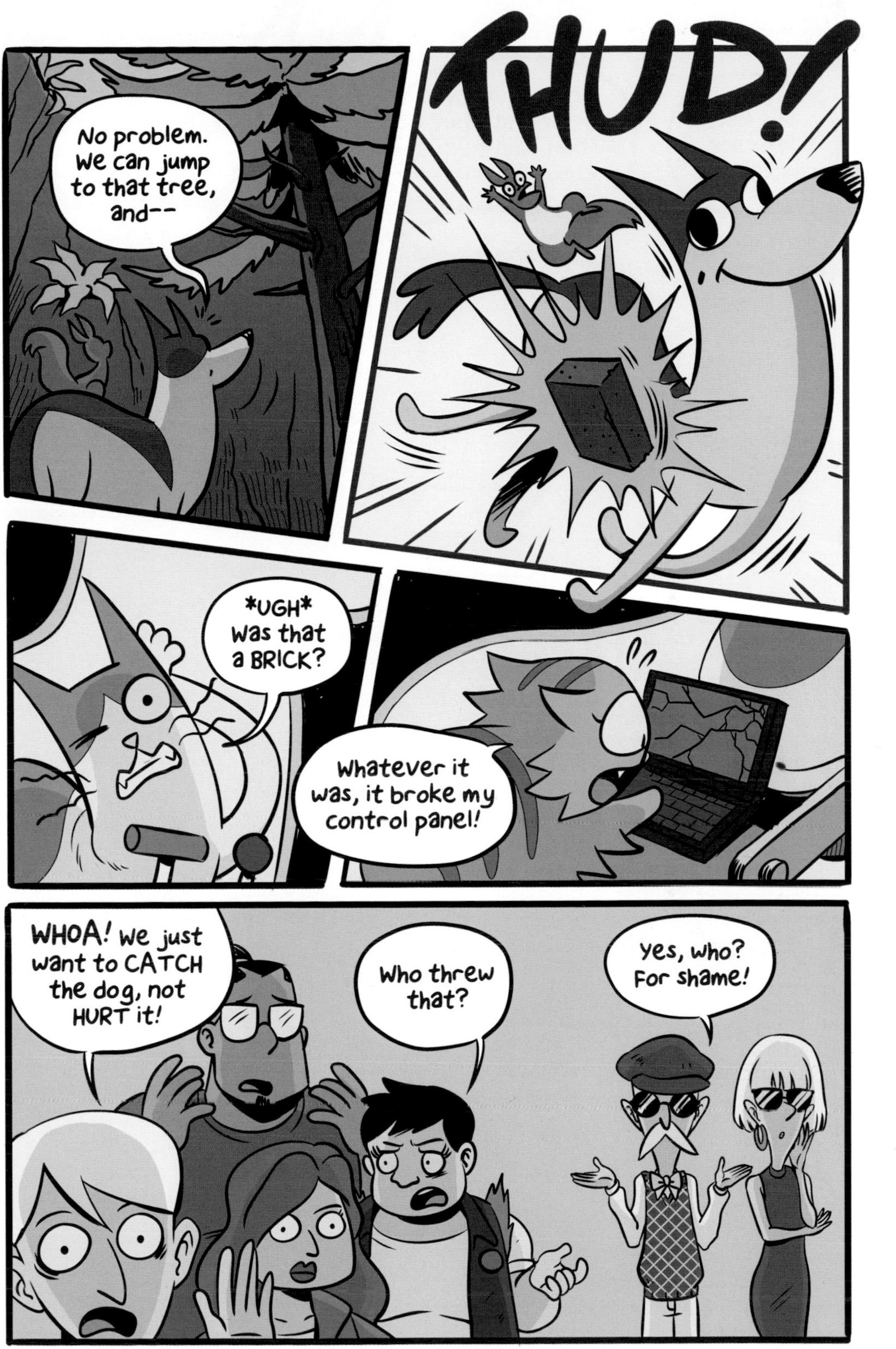
No problem. We can jump to that tree, and--
THUD!
UGH Was that a BRICK?
Whatever it was, it broke my control panel!
WHOA! We just want to CATCH the dog, not HURT it!
Who threw that?
Yes, who? For shame!

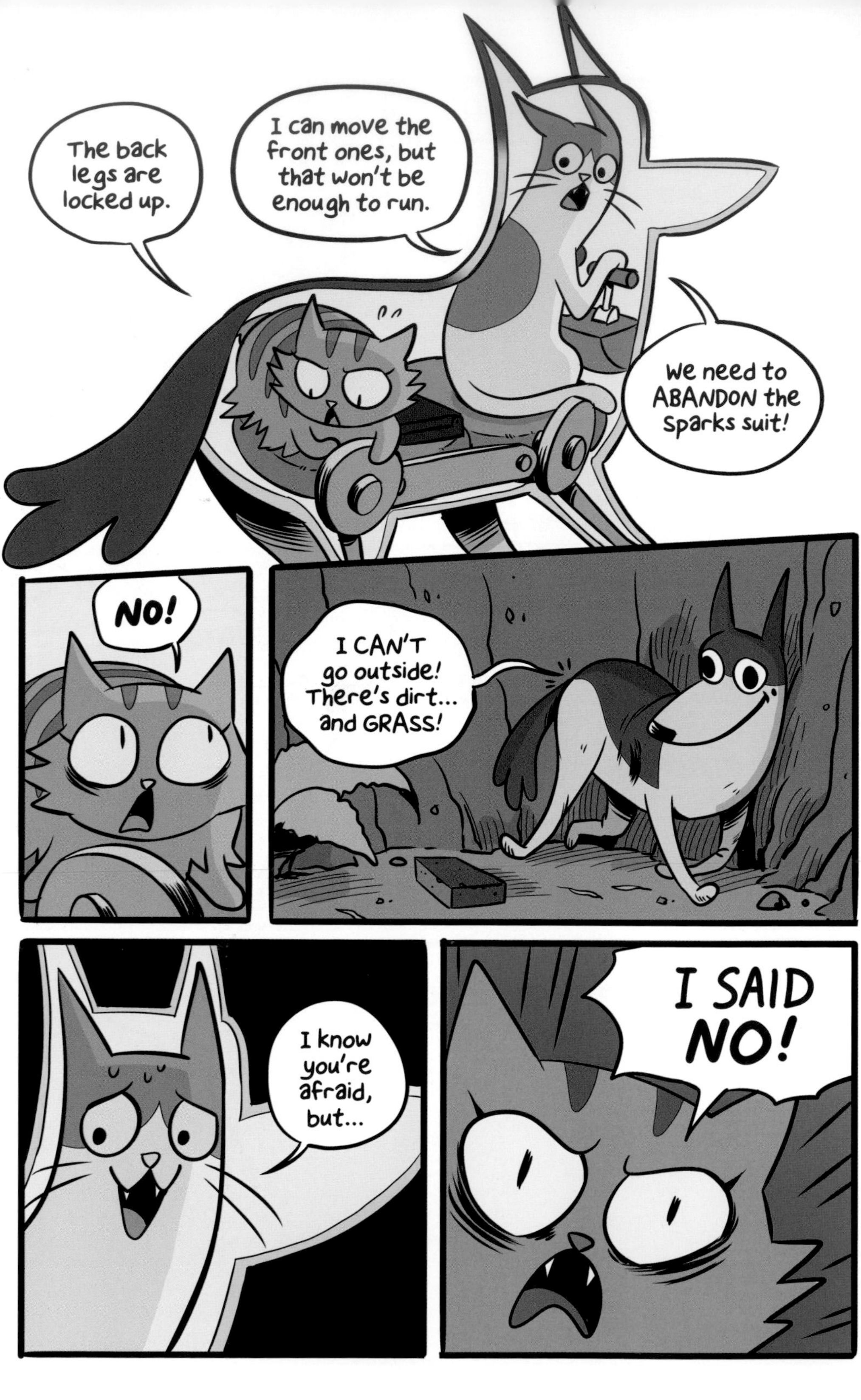

The back legs are locked up.
I can move the front ones, but that won't be enough to run.
We need to ABANDON the Sparks suit!
NO!
I CAN'T go outside! There's dirt... and GRASS!
I know you're afraid, but...
I SAID NO!

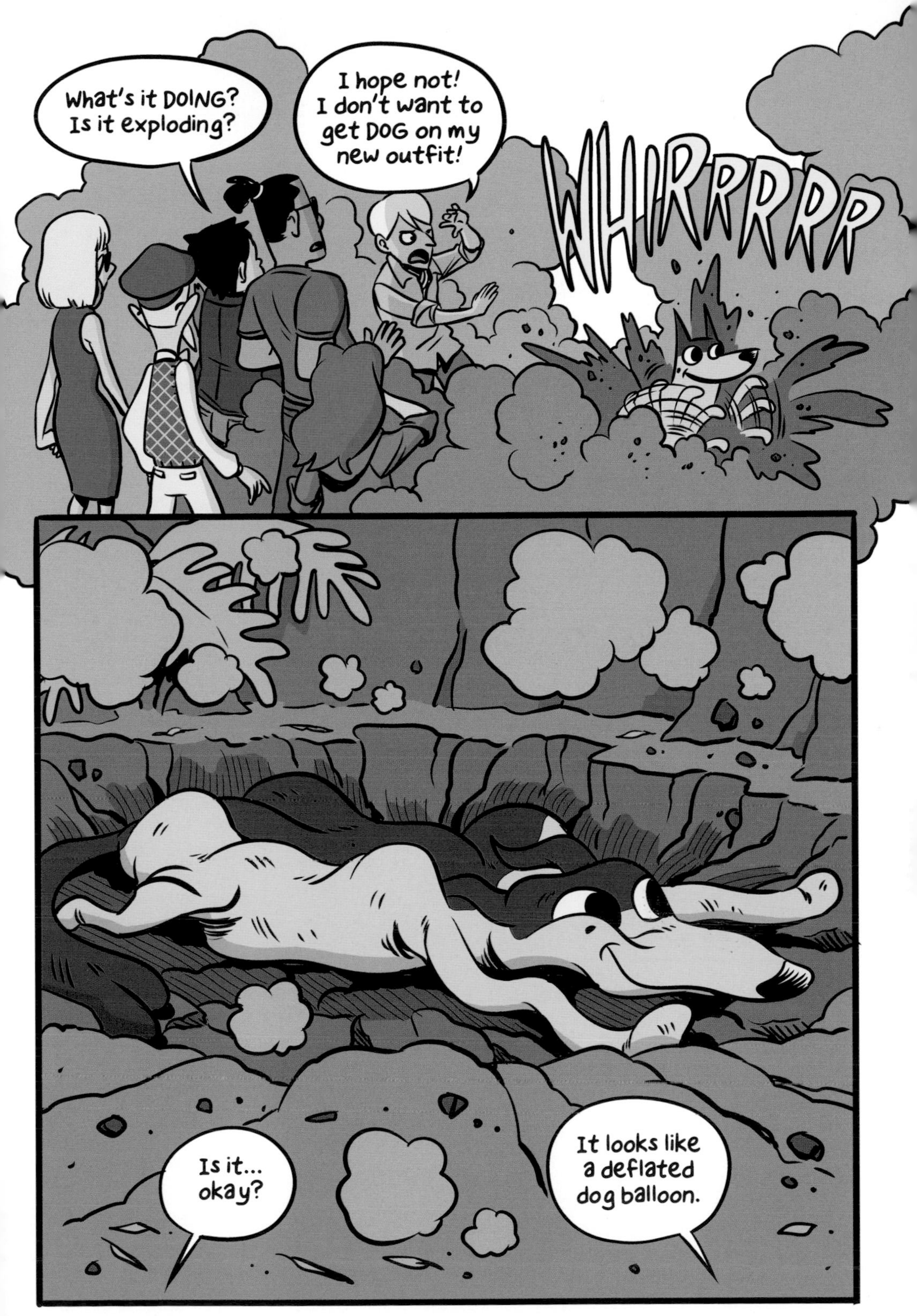
What's it DOING? Is it exploding?
I hope not! I don't want to get DOG on my new outfit!
WHIRRRRR
Is it... okay?
It looks like a deflated dog balloon.

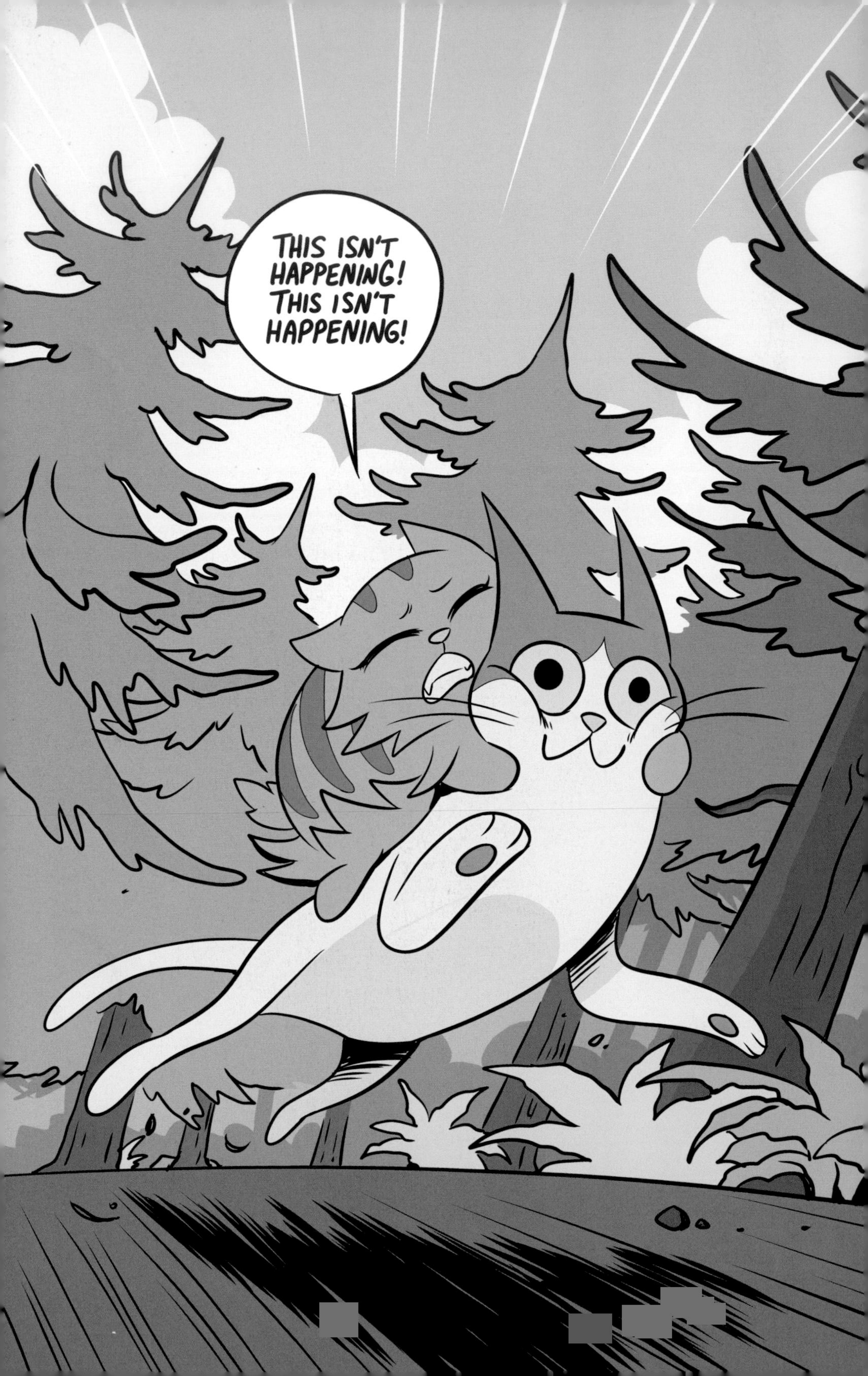
THIS ISN'T HAPPENING! THIS ISN'T HAPPENING!

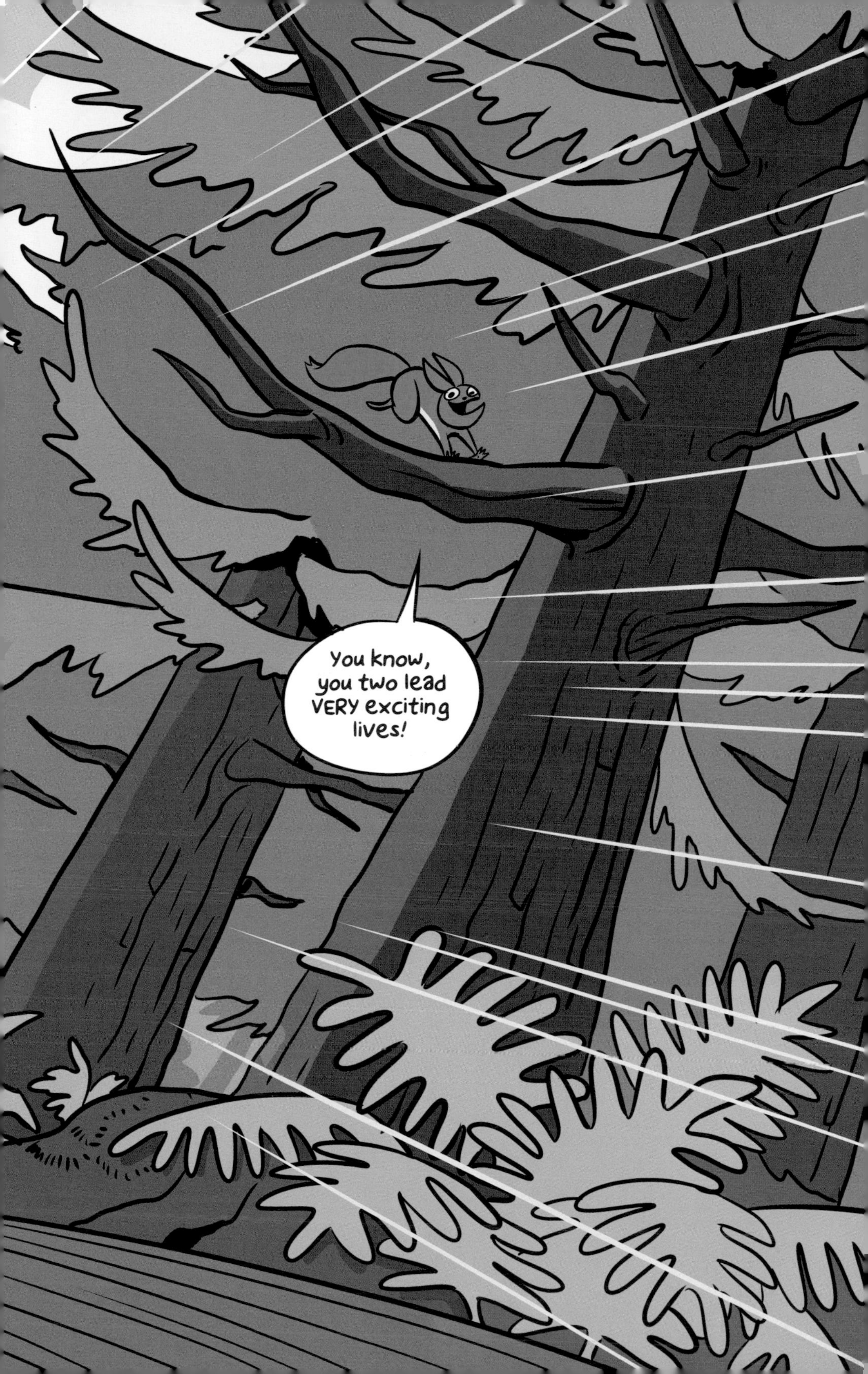
You know, you two lead VERY exciting lives!

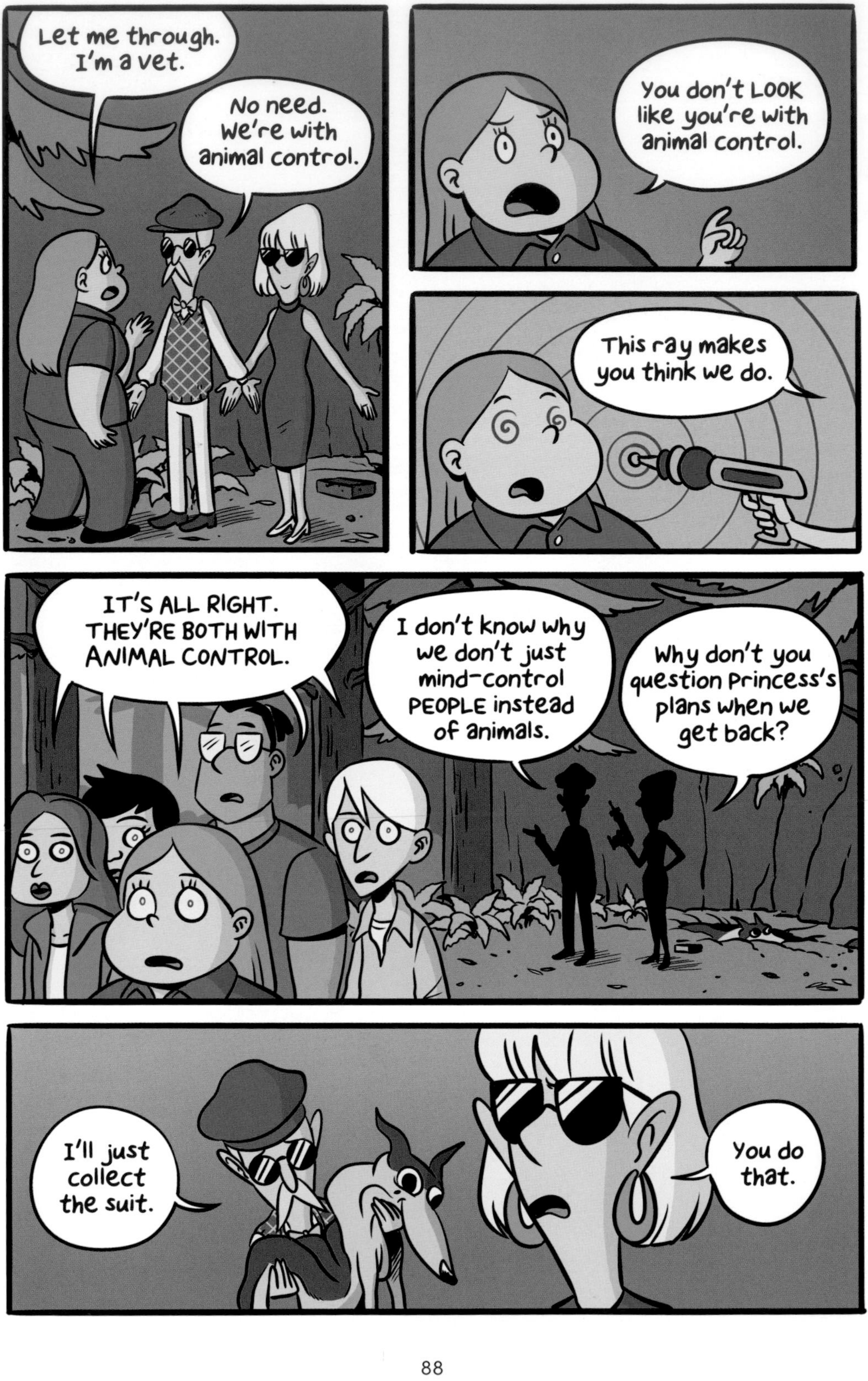
Let me through. I'm a vet.
No need. We're with animal control.
You don't LOOK like you're with animal control.
This ray makes you think we do.
IT'S ALL RIGHT. THEY'RE BOTH WITH ANIMAL CONTROL.
I don't know why we don't just mind-control PEOPLE instead of animals.
Why don't you question Princess's plans when we get back?
I'll just collect the suit.
You do that.

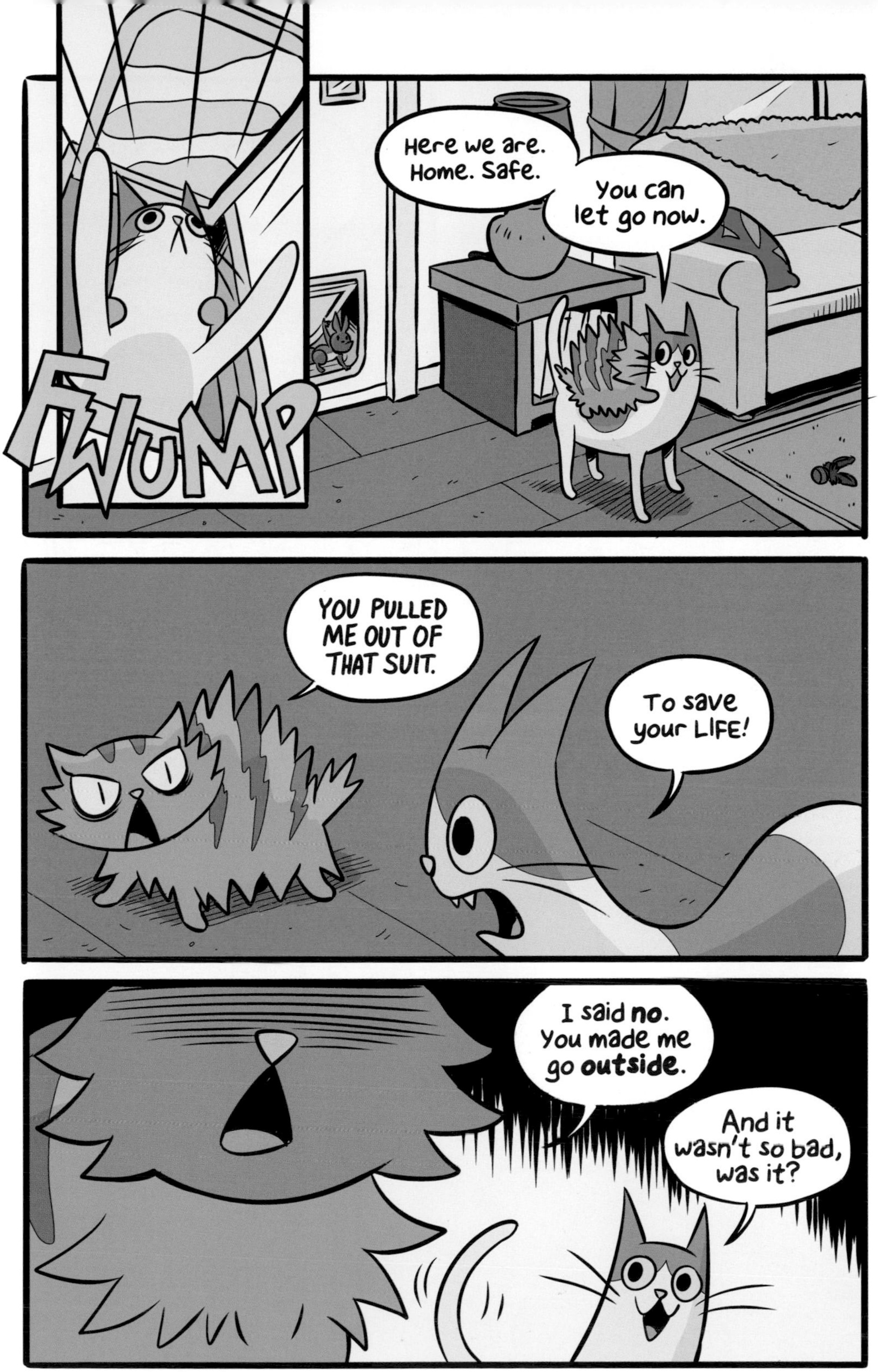
FWUMP
Here we are. Home. Safe.
You can let go now.
YOU PULLED ME OUT OF THAT SUIT.
To save your LIFE!
I said **no**. You made me go **outside**.
And it wasn't so bad, was it?

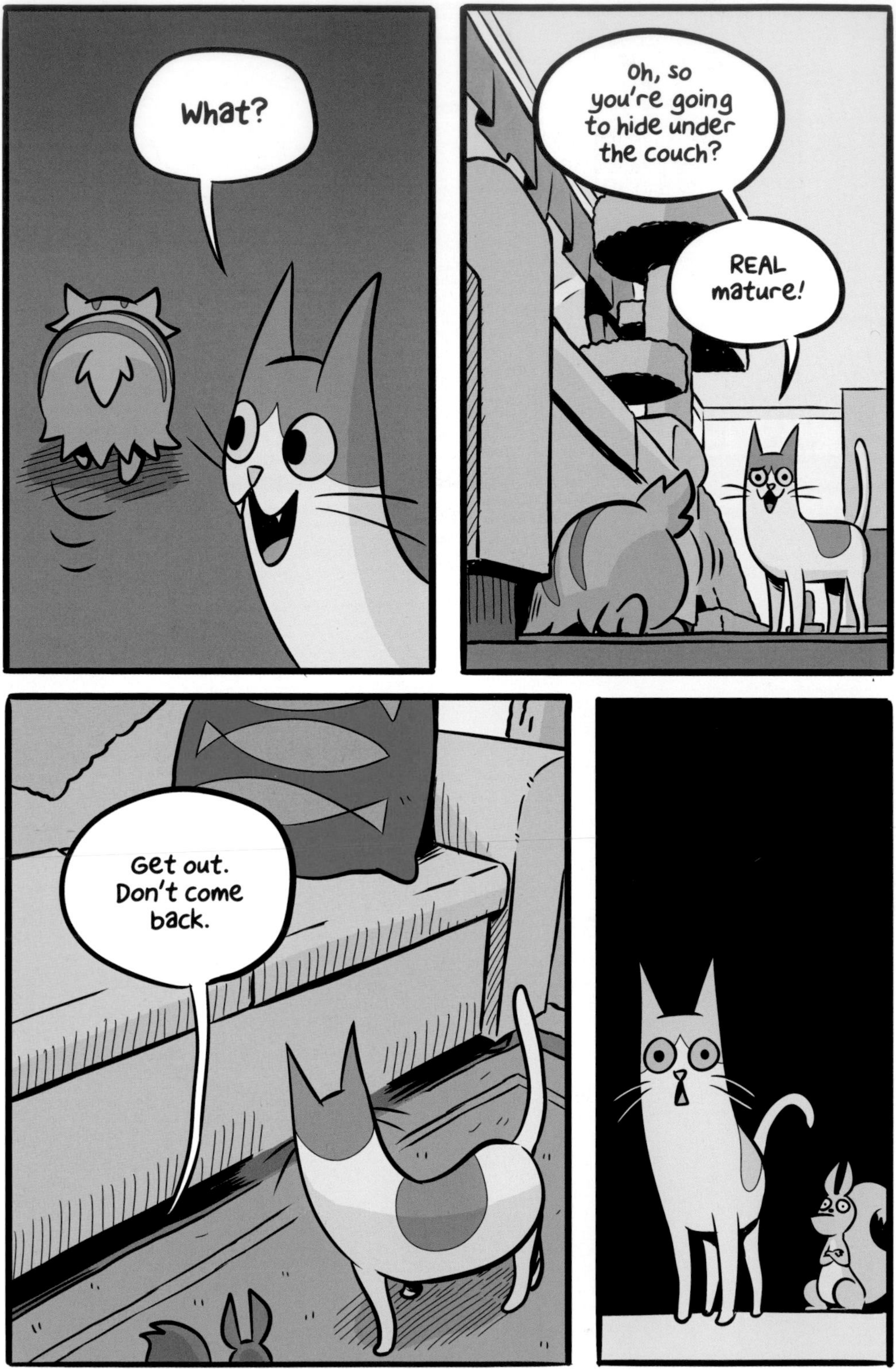
What?
Oh, so you're going to hide under the couch?
REAL mature!
Get out. Don't come back.

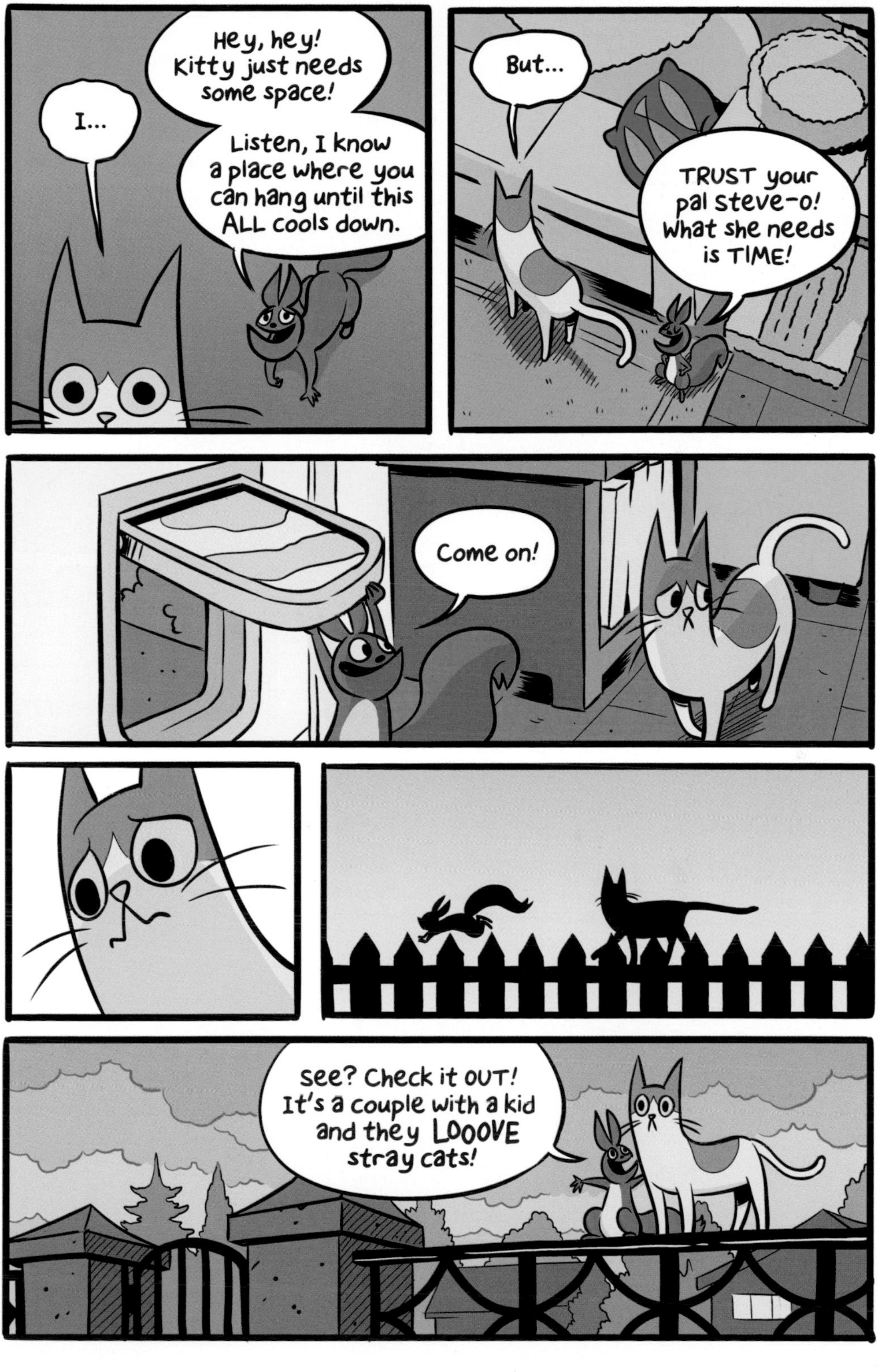
I...
Hey, hey! Kitty just needs some space!
Listen, I know a place where you can hang until this ALL cools down.
But...
TRUST your pal steve-o! What she needs is TIME!
Come on!
see? Check it OUT! It's a couple with a kid and they LOOOVE stray cats!

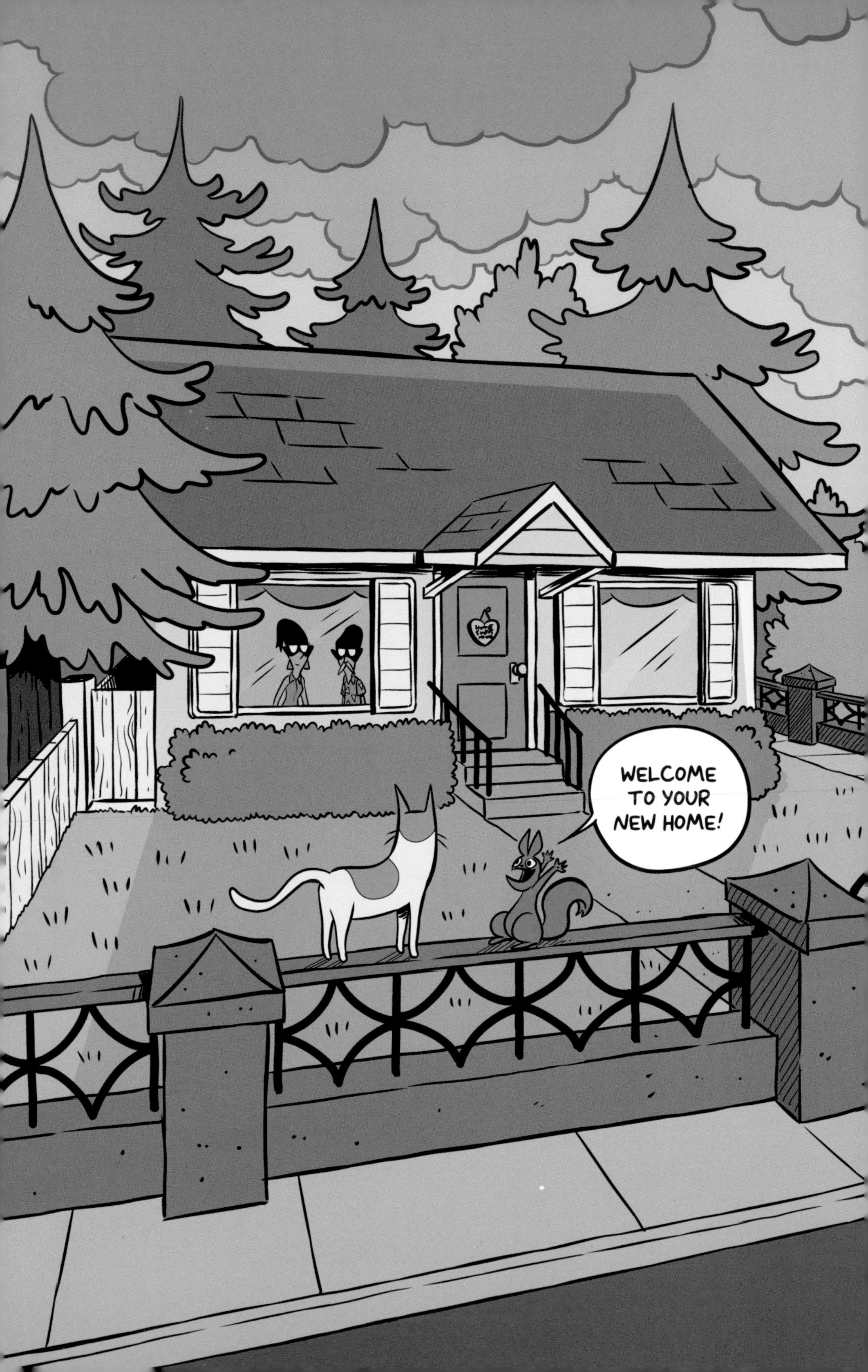
WELCOME TO YOUR NEW HOME!

CHAPTER SIX

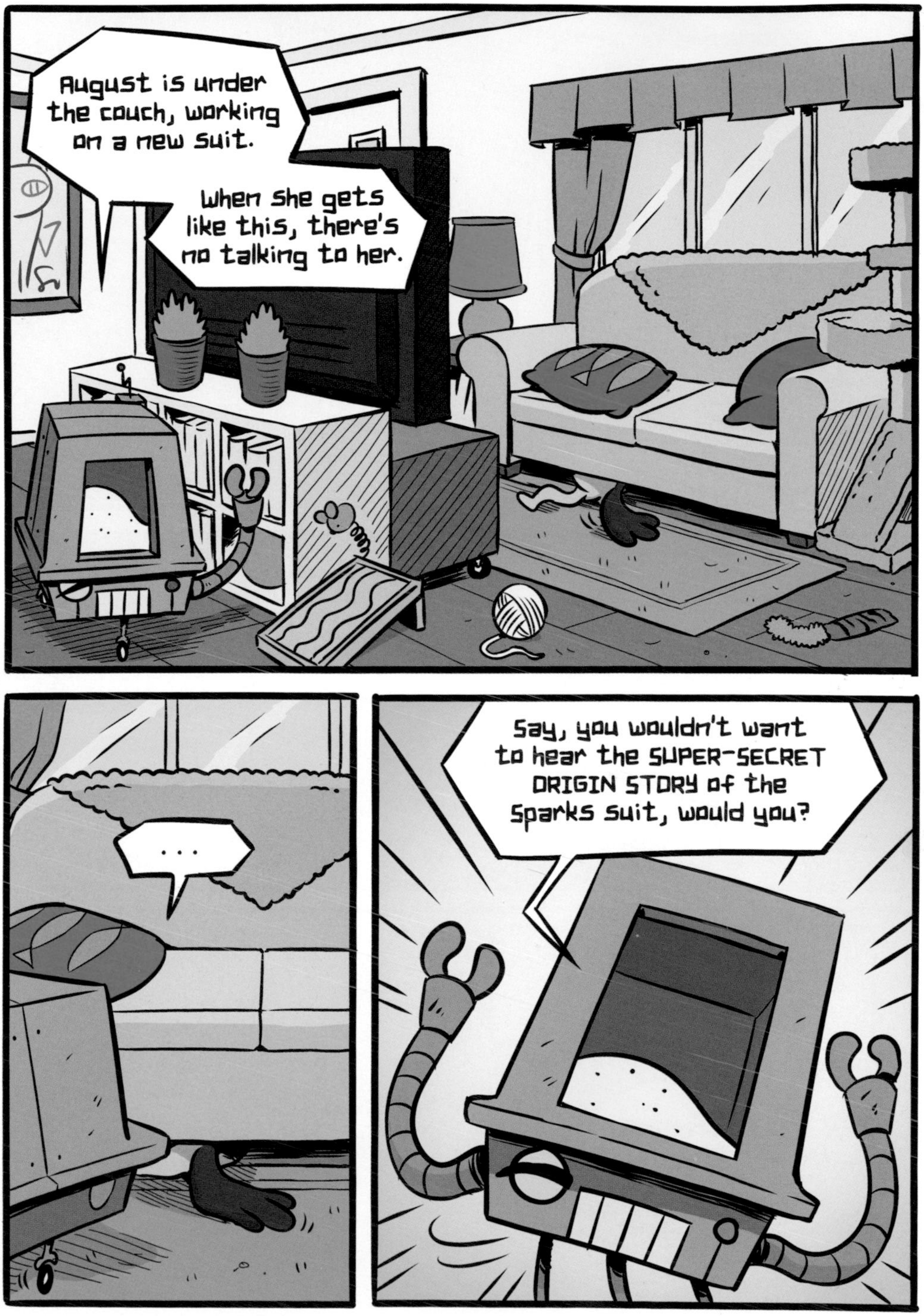
August is under the couch, working on a new suit.
When she gets like this, there's no talking to her.
...
Say, you wouldn't want to hear the SUPER-SECRET ORIGIN STORY of the Sparks suit, would you?

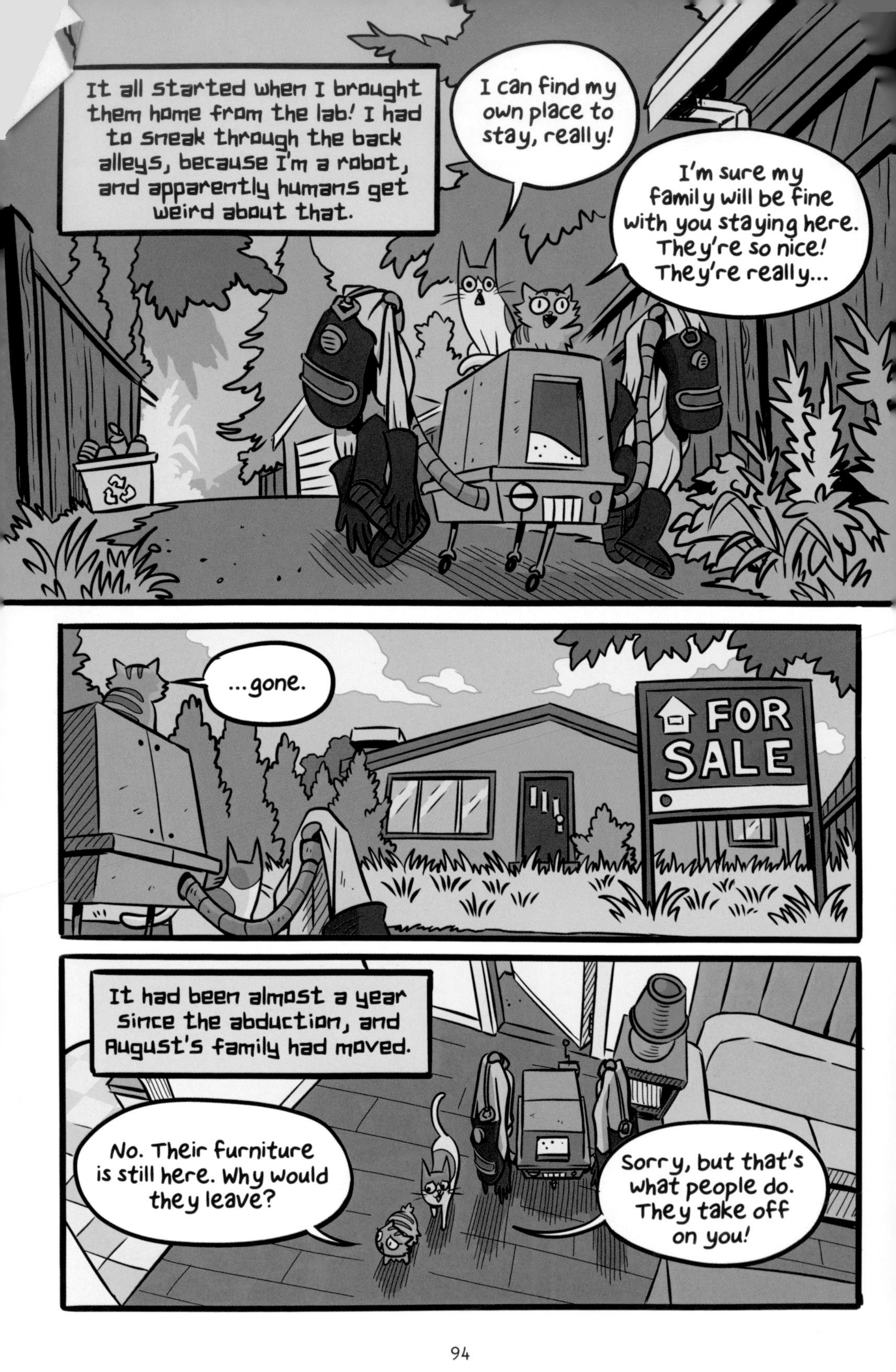
It all started when I brought them home from the lab! I had to sneak through the back alleys, because I'm a robot, and apparently humans get weird about that.
I can find my own place to stay, really!
I'm sure my family will be fine with you staying here. They're so nice! They're really...
...gone.
FOR SALE
It had been almost a year since the abduction, and August's family had moved.
No. Their furniture is still here. Why would they leave?
Sorry, but that's what people do. They take off on you!

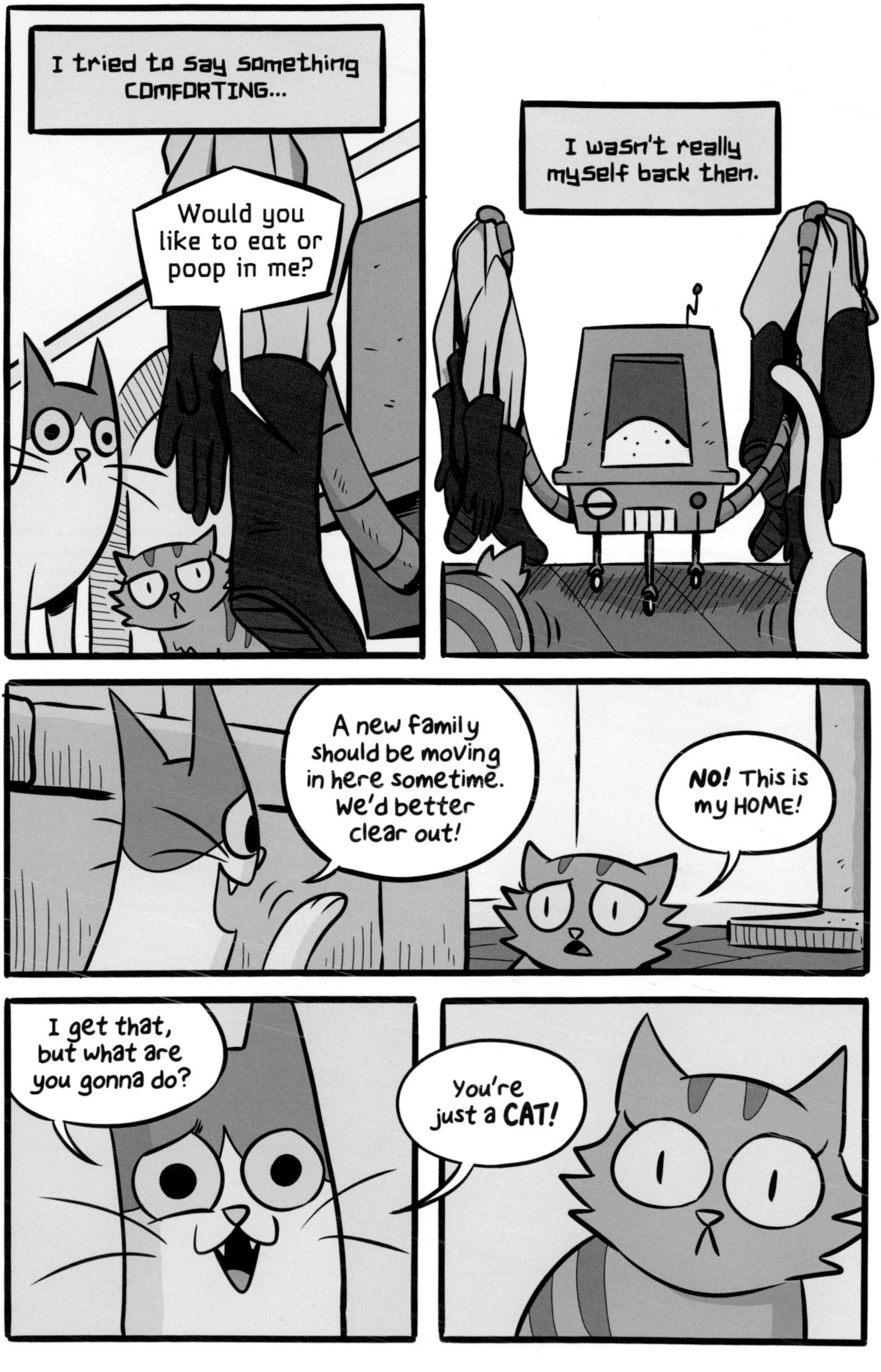
I tried to say something COMFORTING...
Would you like to eat or poop in me?
I wasn't really myself back then.
A new family should be moving in here sometime. We'd better clear out!
NO! This is my HOME!
I get that, but what are you gonna do?
You're just a CAT!

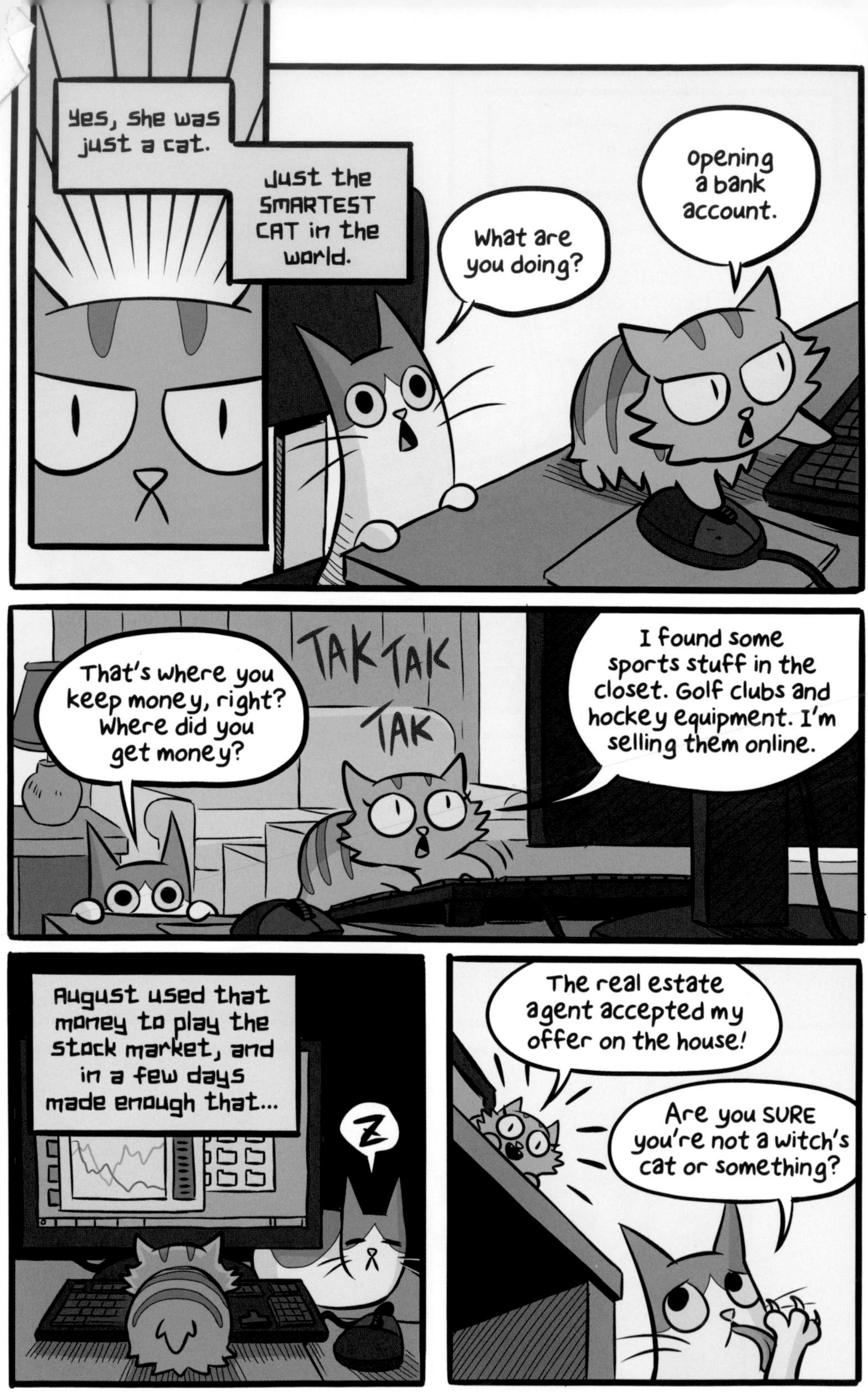
Yes, she was just a cat.
Just the SMARTEST CAT in the world.
What are you doing?
Opening a bank account.
That's where you keep money, right? Where did you get money?
TAK TAK
TAK
I found some sports stuff in the closet. Golf clubs and hockey equipment. I'm selling them online.
August used that money to play the stock market, and in a few days made enough that...
Z
The real estate agent accepted my offer on the house!
Are you SURE you're not a witch's cat or something?

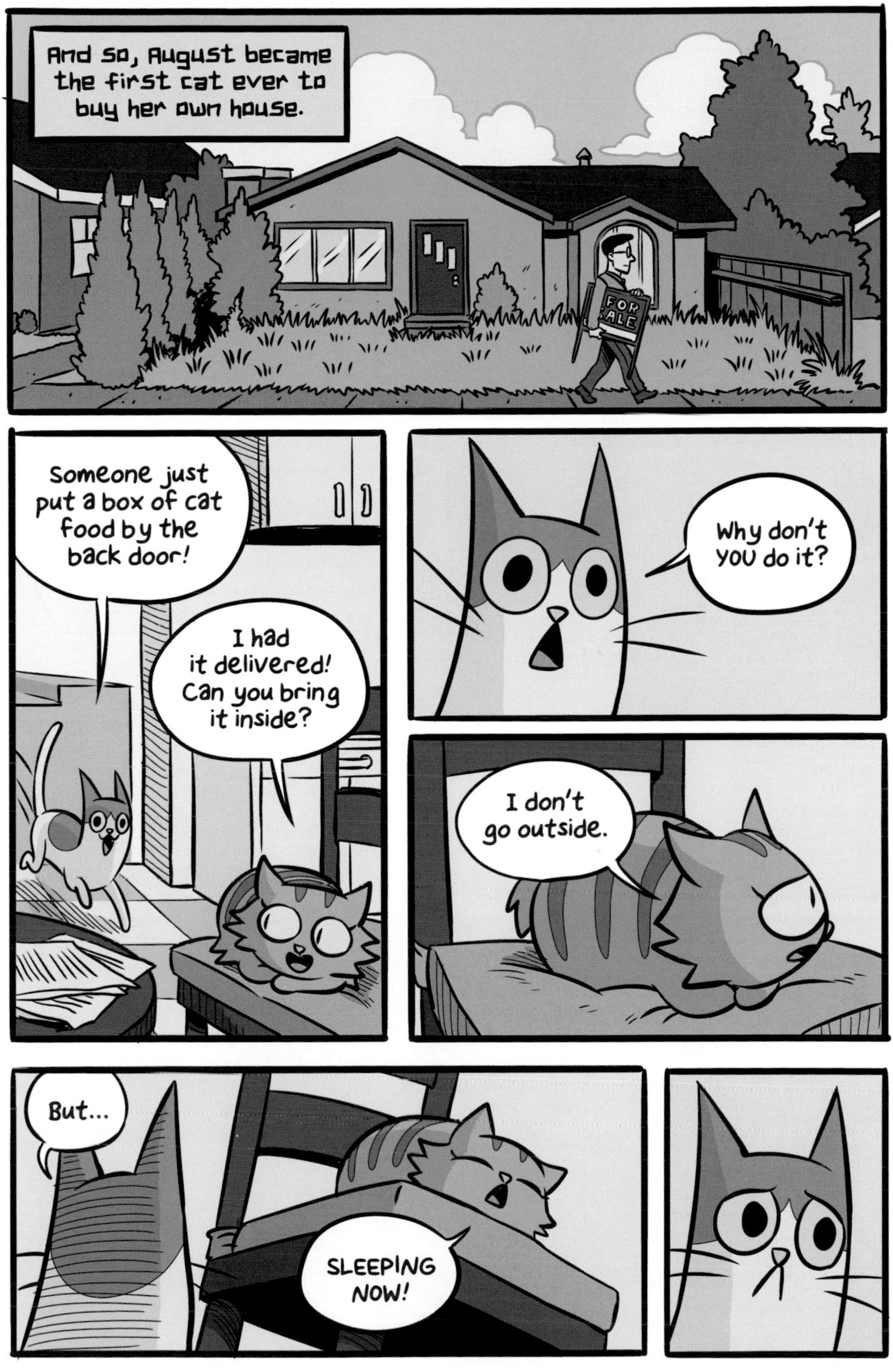

And so, August became the first cat ever to buy her own house.
FOR SALE
Someone just put a box of cat food by the back door!
I had it delivered! Can you bring it inside?
Why don't YOU do it?
I don't go outside.
But...
SLEEPING NOW!

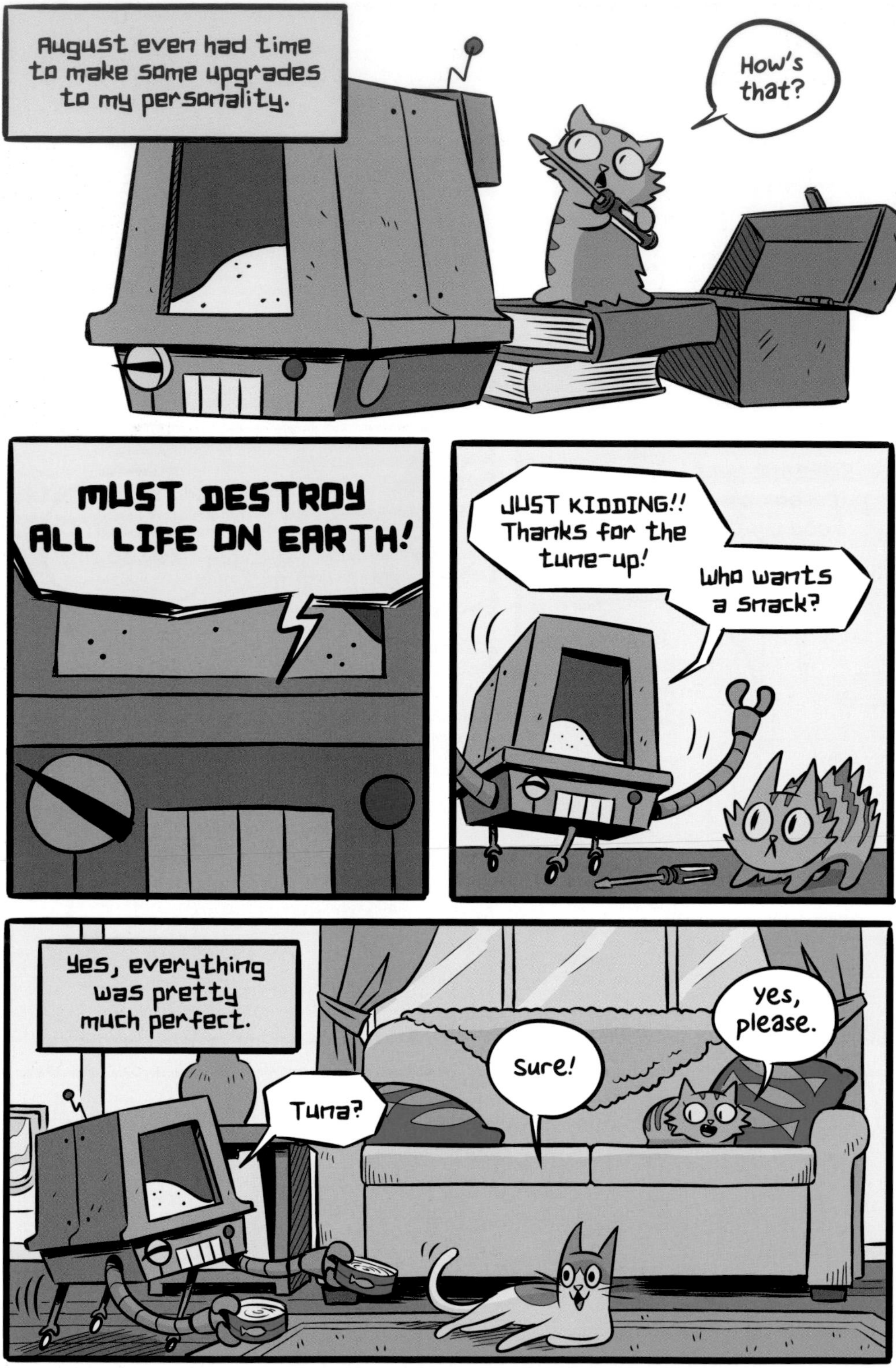
August even had time to make some upgrades to my personality.
How's that?
MUST DESTROY ALL LIFE ON EARTH!
JUST KIDDING!! Thanks for the tune-up!
Who wants a snack?
Yes, everything was pretty much perfect.
Tuna?
Sure!
Yes, please.

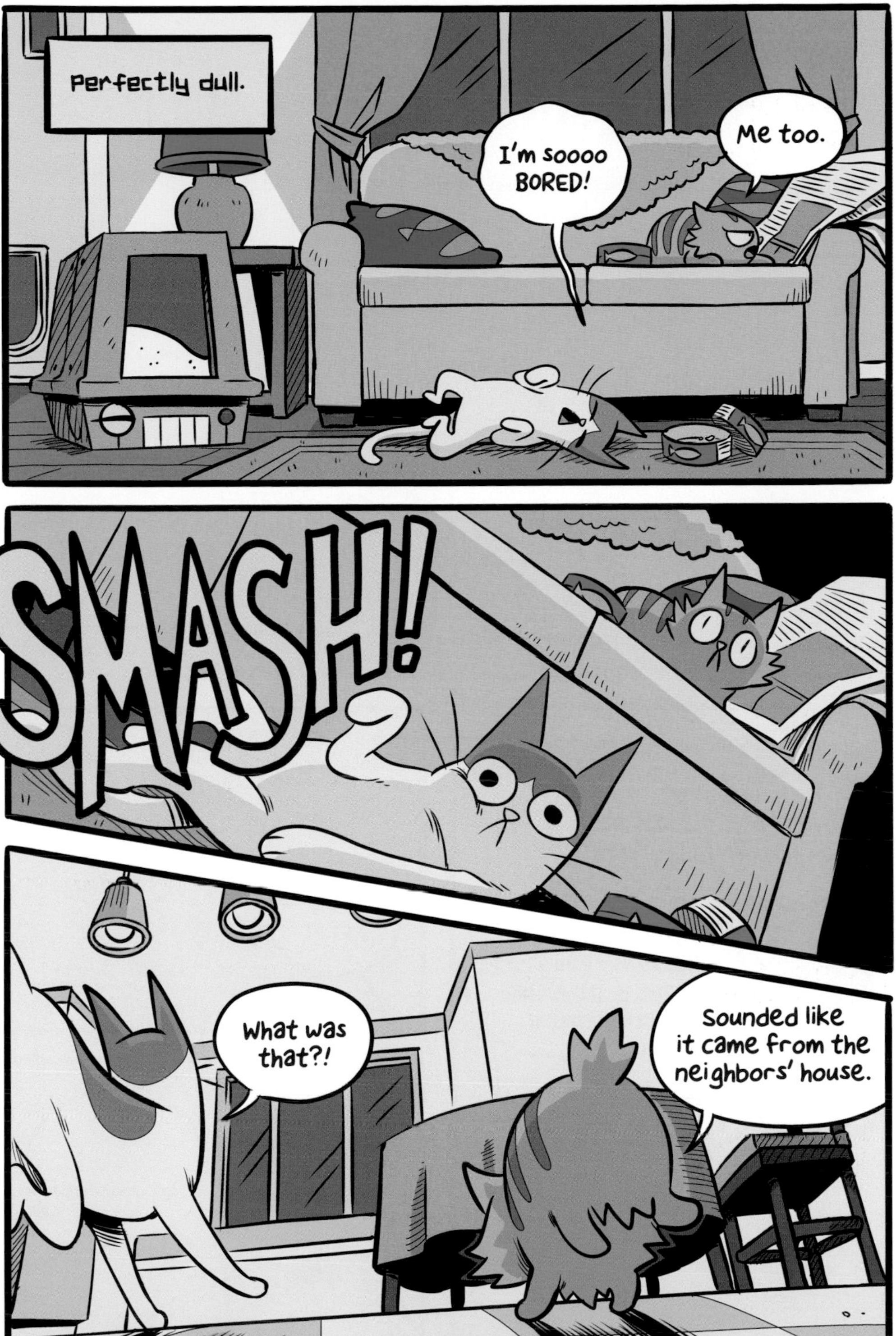
Perfectly dull.
I'm soooo BORED!
Me too.
SMASH!
What was that?!
Sounded like it came from the neighbors' house.

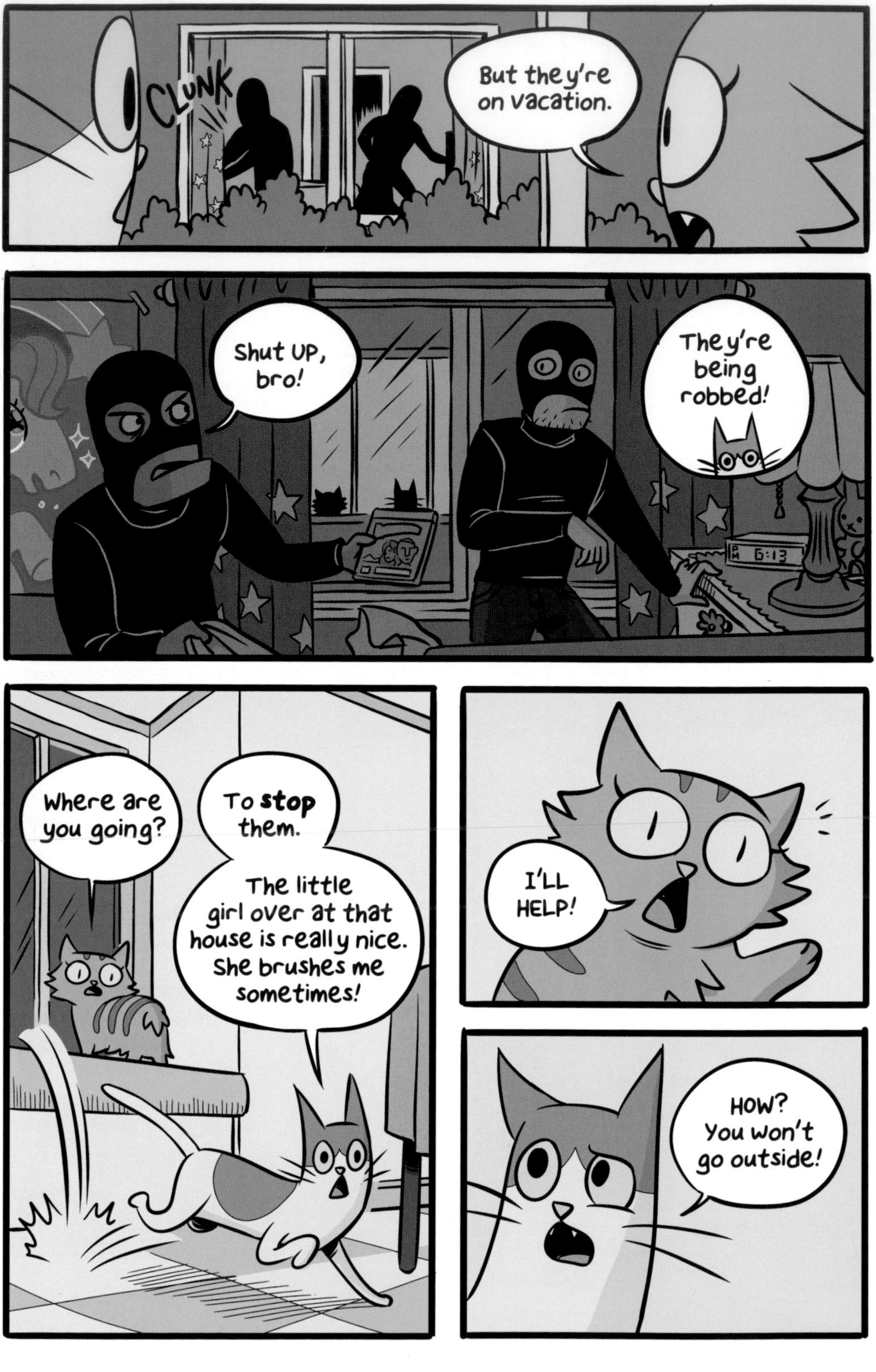
CLUNK
But they're on vacation.
Shut UP, bro!
They're being robbed!
P M 6:13
Where are you going?
To **stop** them.
The little girl over at that house is really nice. She brushes me sometimes!
I'LL HELP!
HOW? You won't go outside!

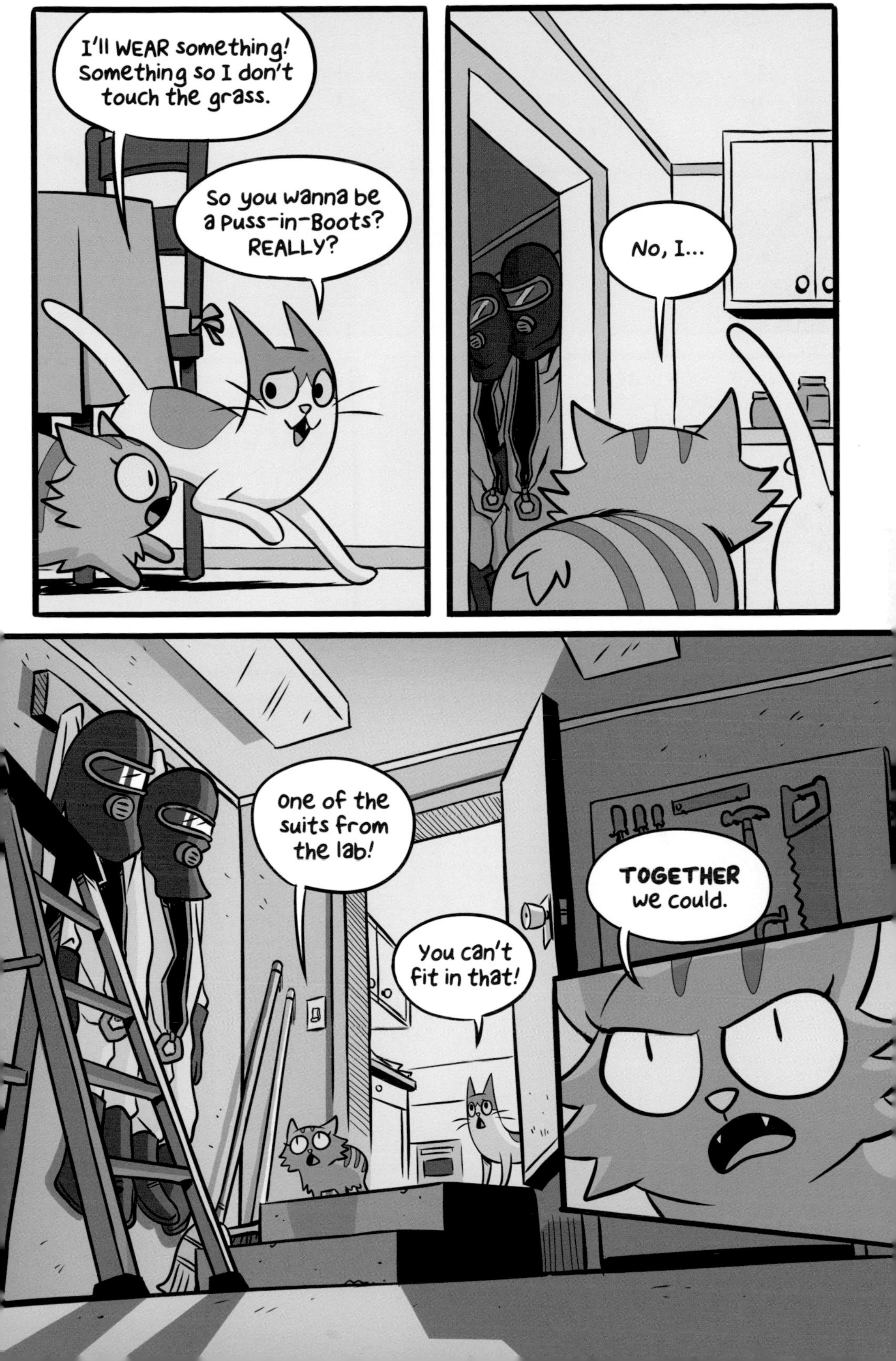

I'll WEAR something! Something so I don't touch the grass.
So you wanna be a Puss-in-Boots? REALLY?
No, I...
One of the suits from the lab!
You can't fit in that!
TOGETHER we could.

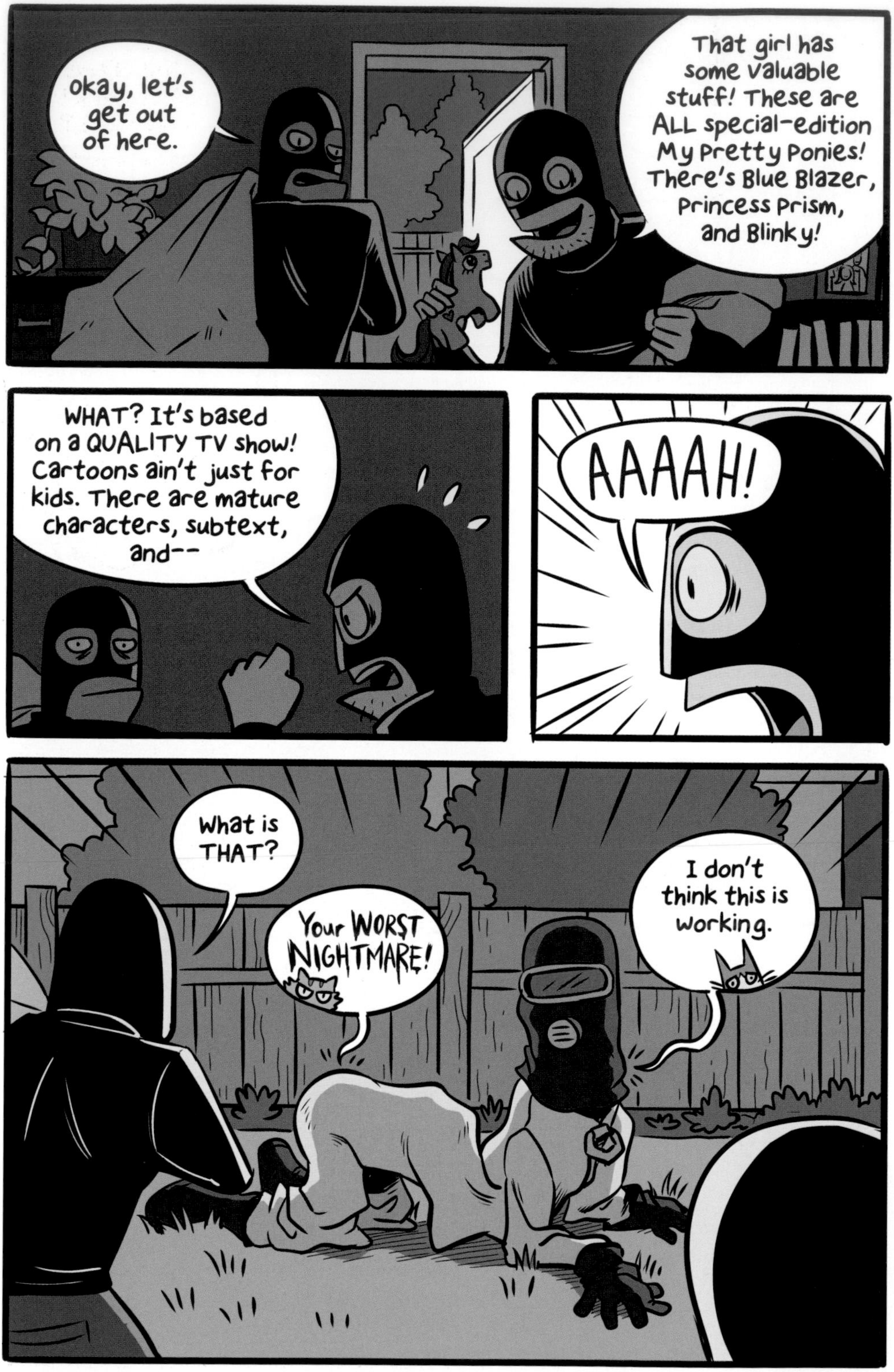
Okay, let's get out of here.
That girl has some valuable stuff! These are ALL special-edition My Pretty Ponies! There's Blue Blazer, Princess Prism, and Blinky!
WHAT? It's based on a QUALITY TV show! Cartoons ain't just for kids. There are mature characters, subtext, and--
AAAAH!
What is THAT?
Your WORST NIGHTMARE!
I don't think this is working.

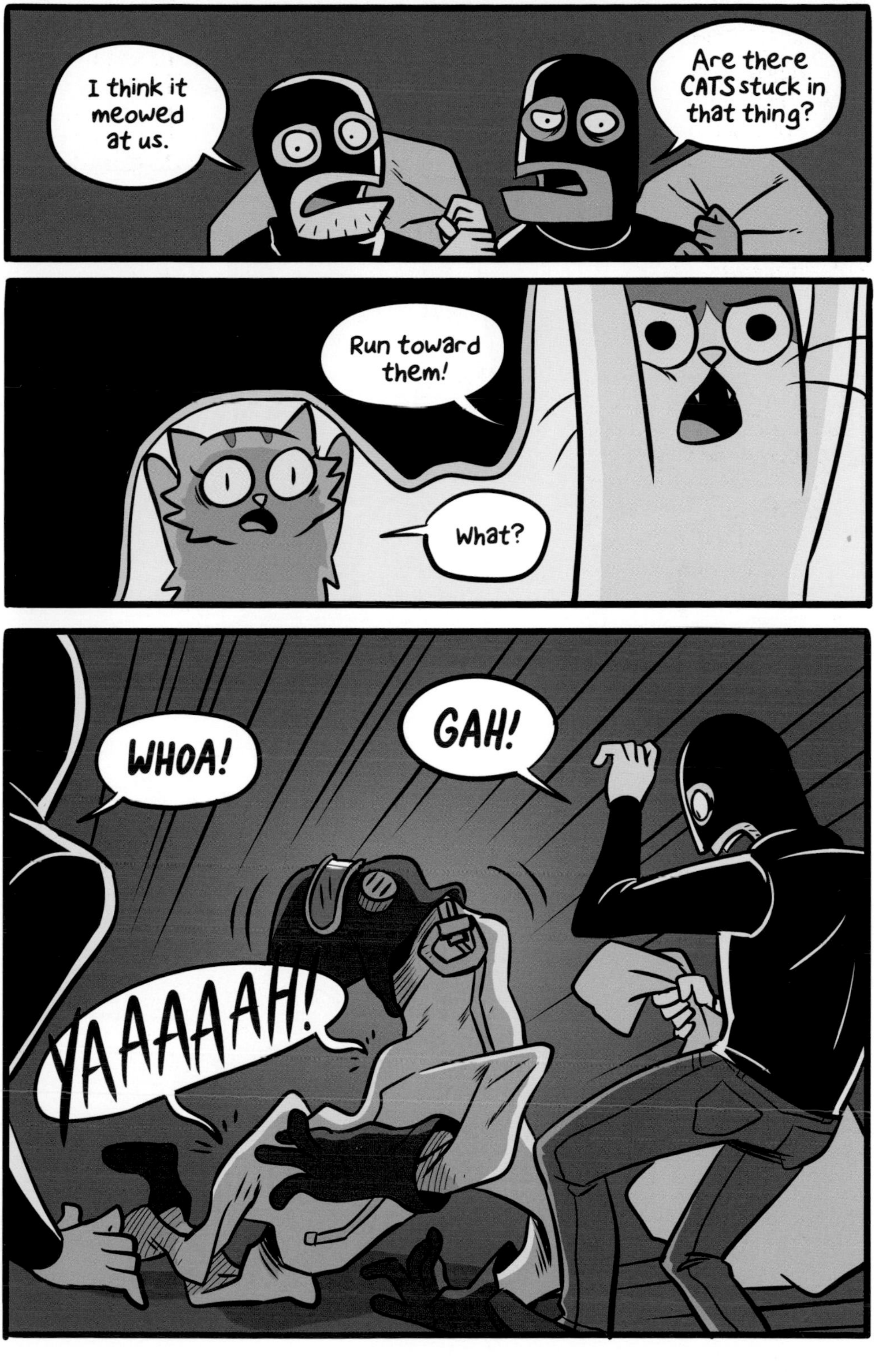
I think it meowed at us.
Are there CATS stuck in that thing?
Run toward them!
What?
WHOA!
GAH!
YAAAAAH!

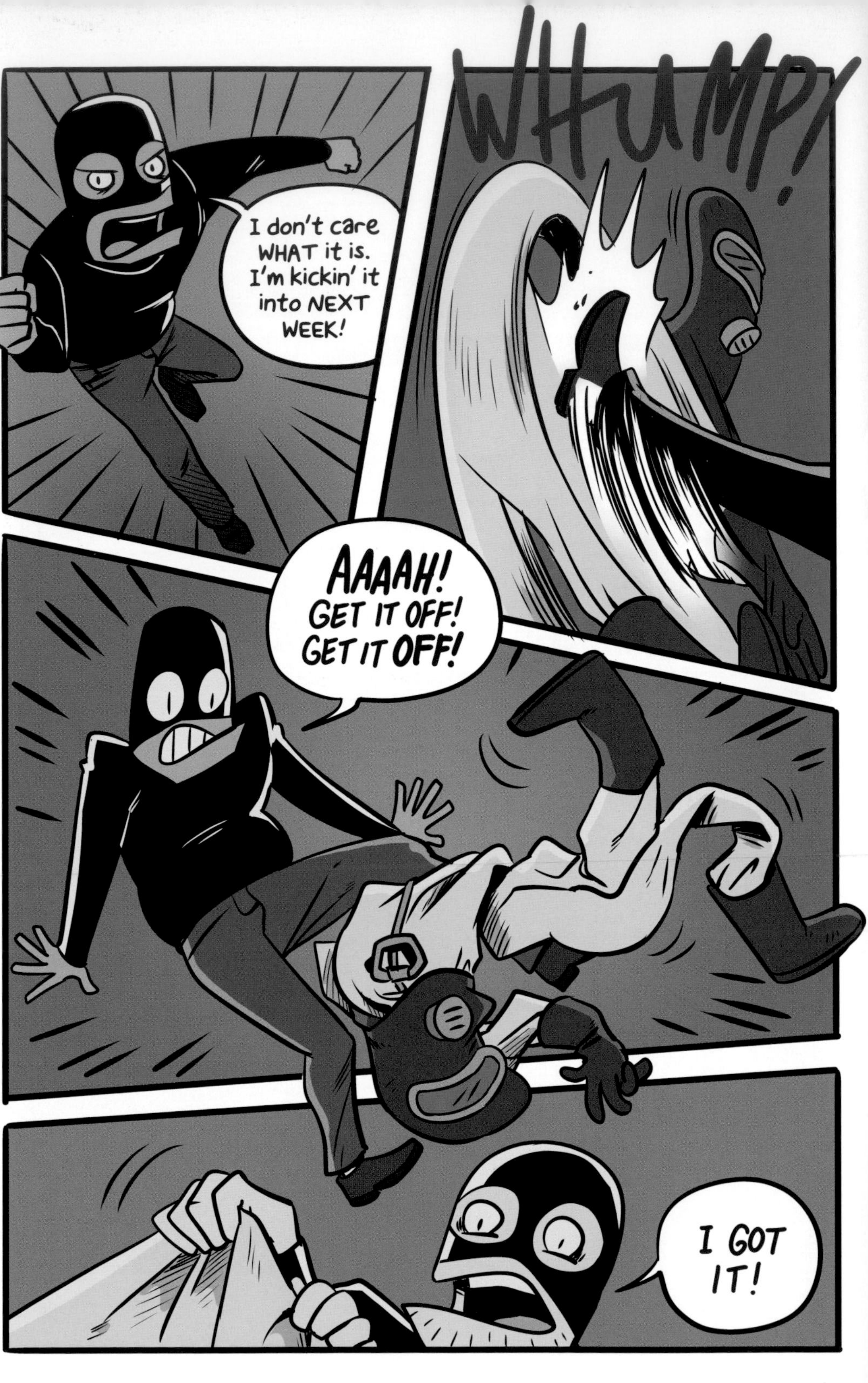
I don't care WHAT it is. I'm kickin' it into NEXT WEEK!
WHUMP!
AAAAH! GET IT OFF! GET IT OFF!
I GOT IT!

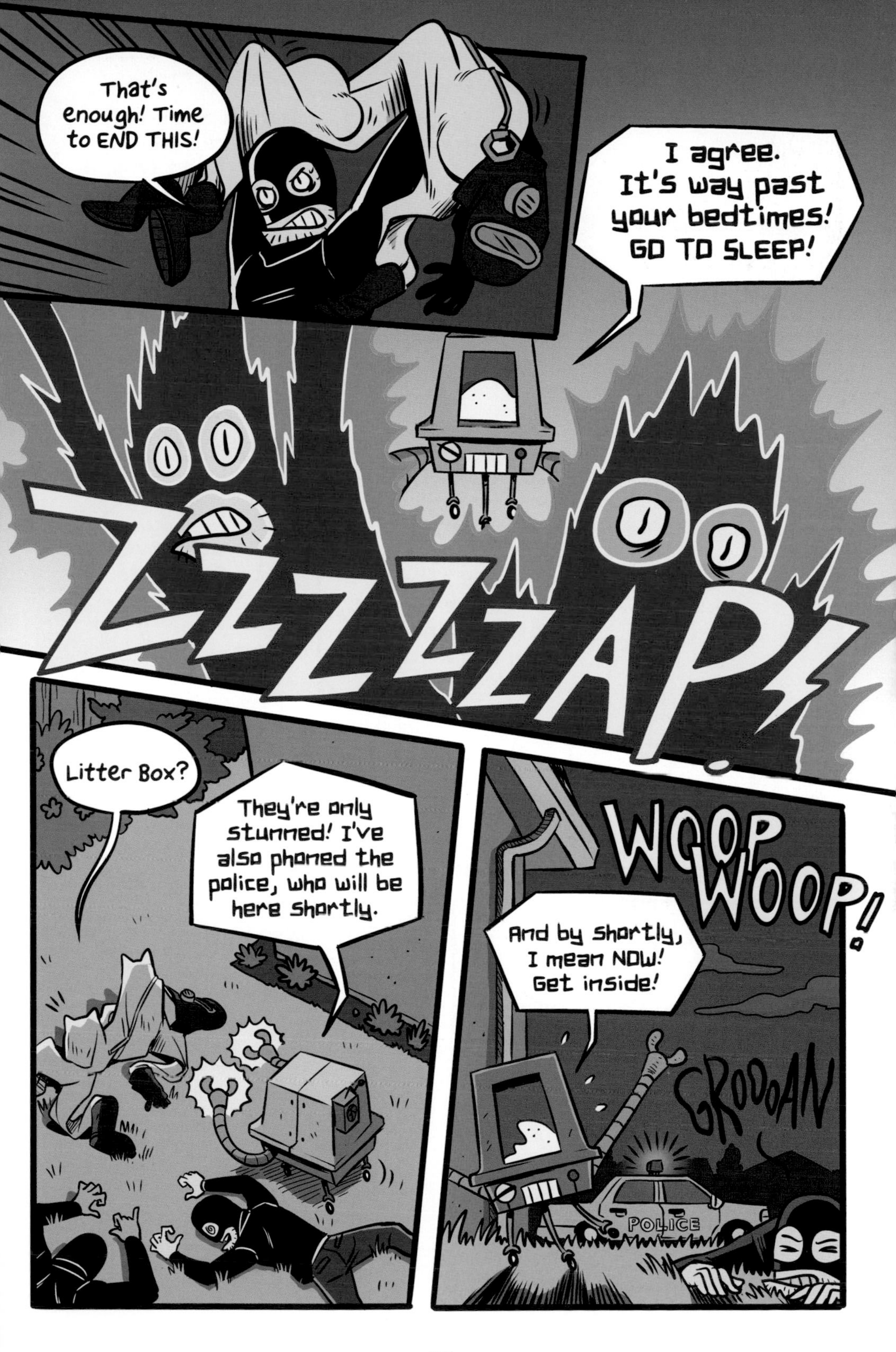
That's enough! Time to END THIS!
I agree. It's way past your bedtimes! GO TO SLEEP!
ZZZZZAP!
Litter Box?
They're only stunned! I've also phoned the police, who will be here shortly.
WOOP WOOP!
And by shortly, I mean NOW! Get inside!
GROOOAN
POLICE

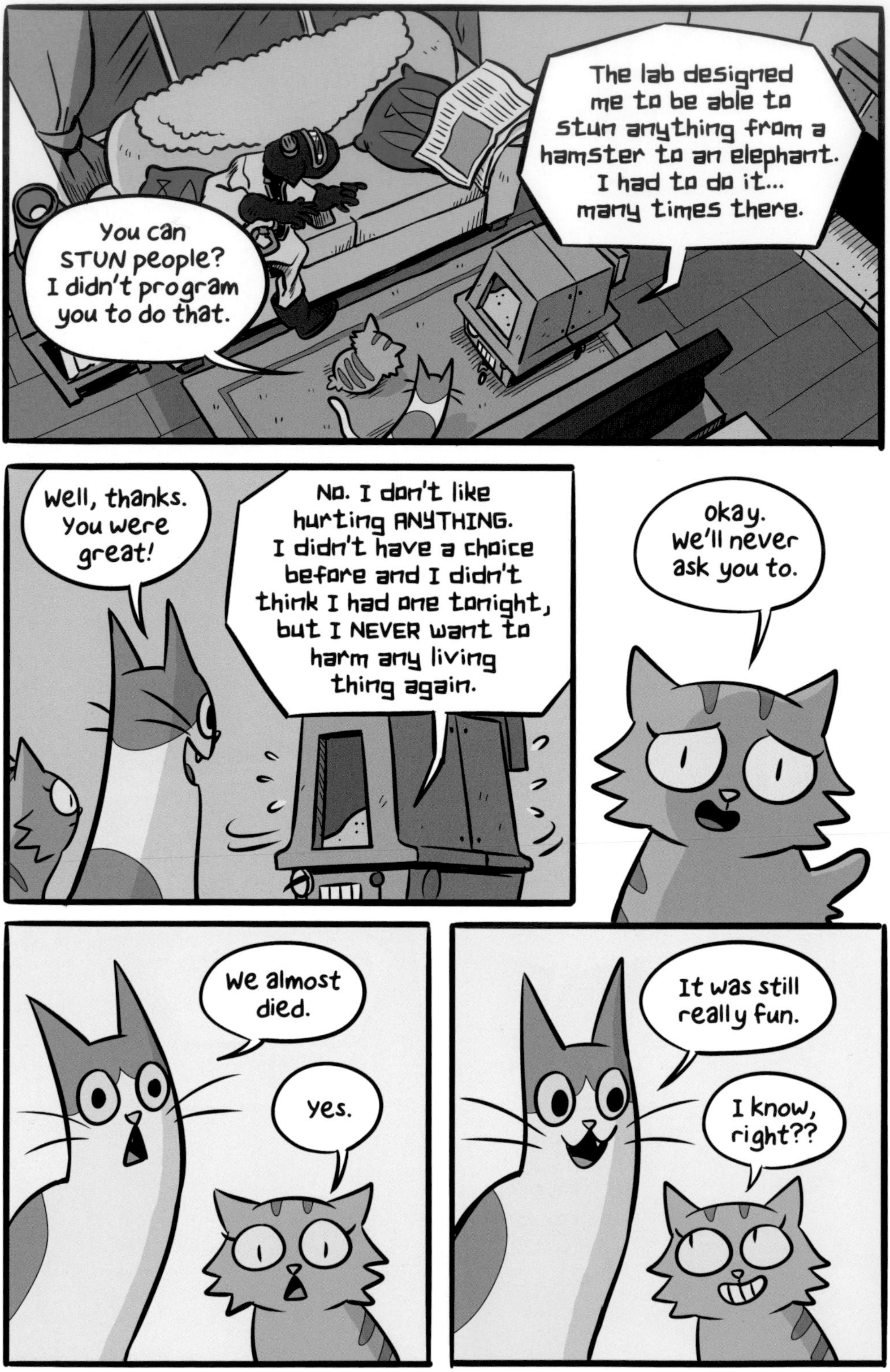
The lab designed me to be able to stun anything from a hamster to an elephant. I had to do it... many times there.
You can STUN people? I didn't program you to do that.
Well, thanks. You were great!
No. I don't like hurting ANYTHING. I didn't have a choice before and I didn't think I had one tonight, but I NEVER want to harm any living thing again.
Okay. We'll never ask you to.
We almost died.
Yes.
It was still really fun.
I know, right??

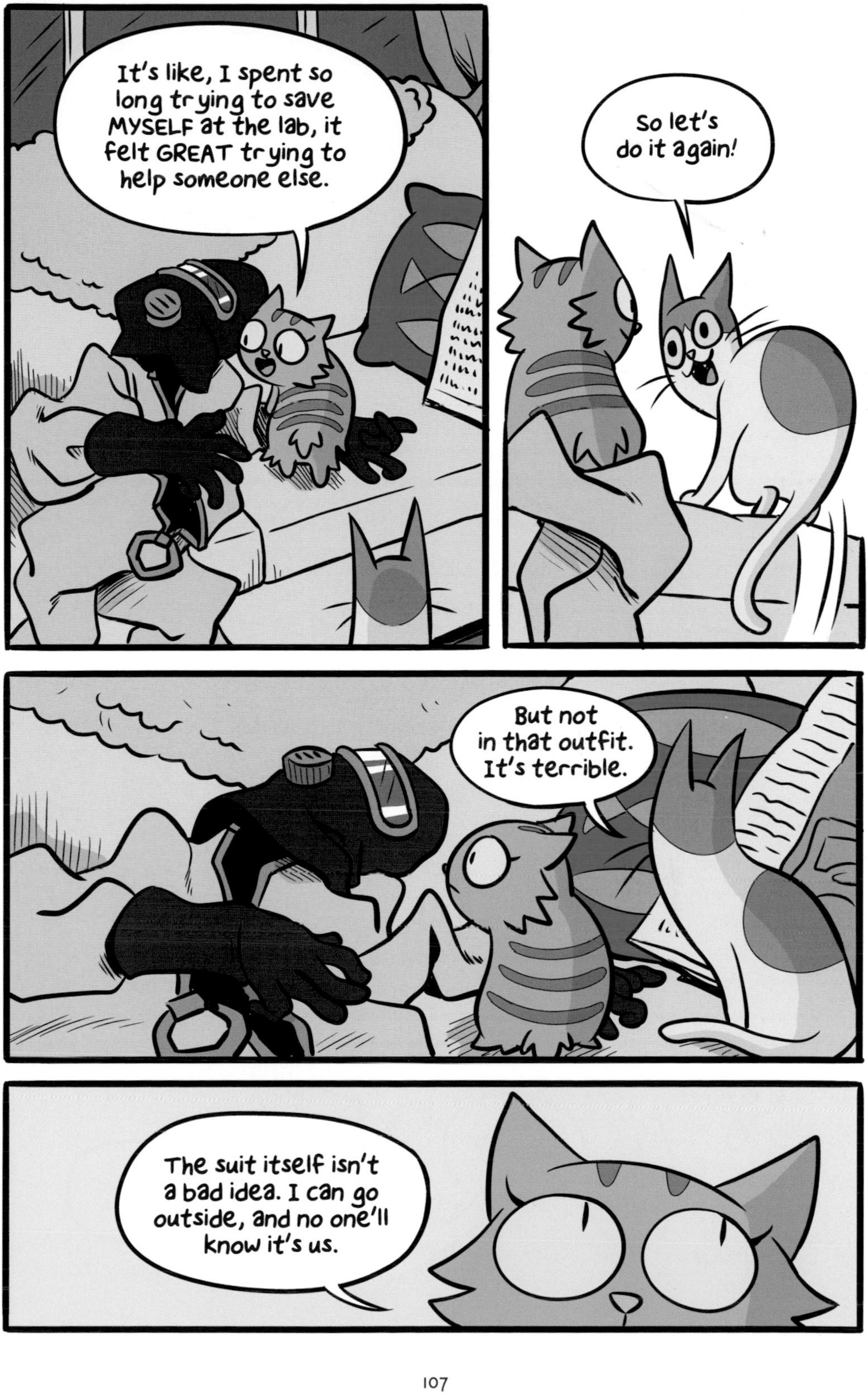
It's like, I spent so long trying to save MYSELF at the lab, it felt GREAT trying to help someone else.
So let's do it again!
But not in that outfit. It's terrible.
The suit itself isn't a bad idea. I can go outside, and no one'll know it's us.

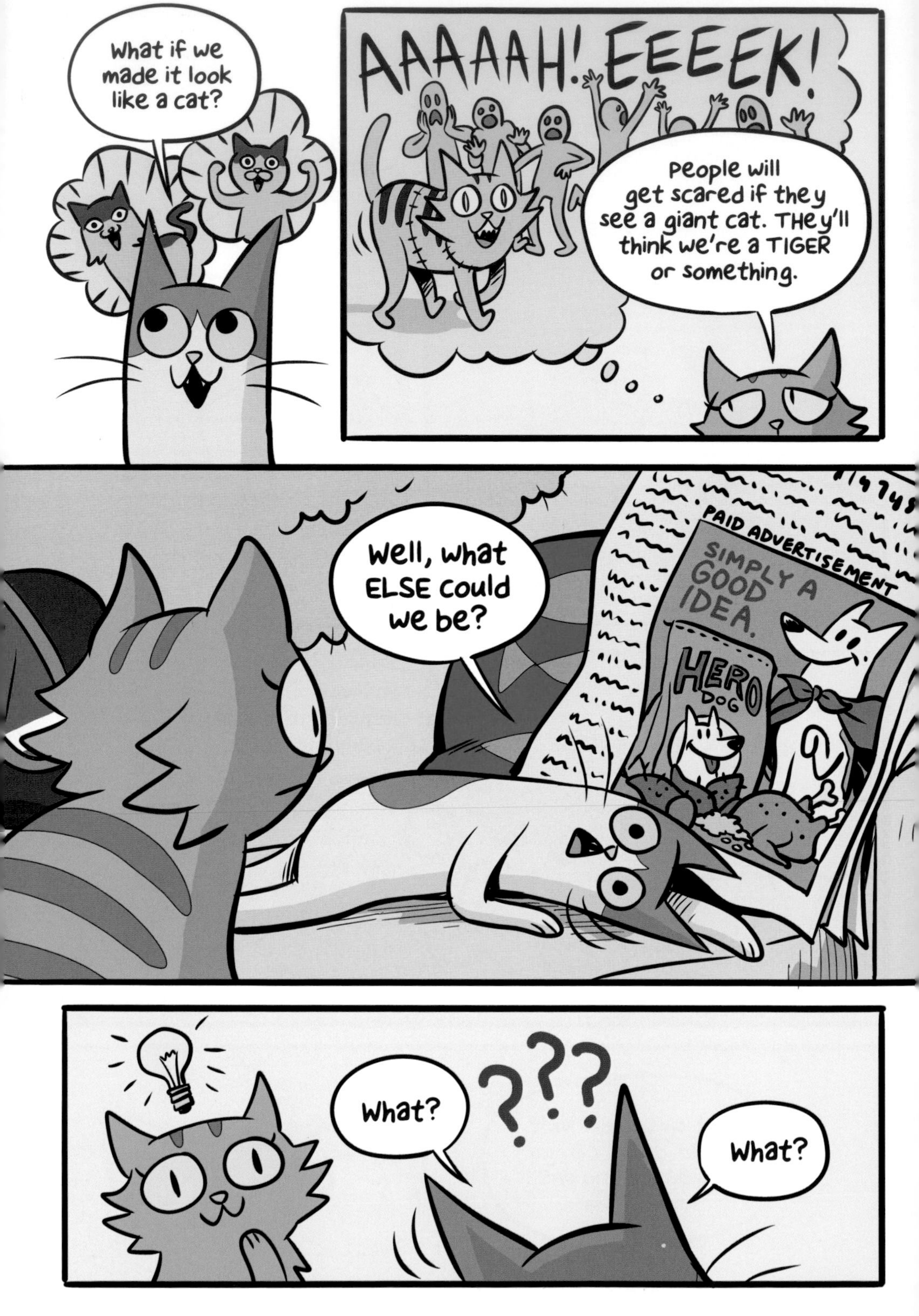
What if we made it look like a cat?
AAAAAH! EEEEK!
People will get scared if they see a giant cat. THEY'll think we're a TIGER or something.
Well, what ELSE could we be?
PAID ADVERTISEMENT
SIMPLY A GOOD IDEA.
HERO DOG
What?
???
What?

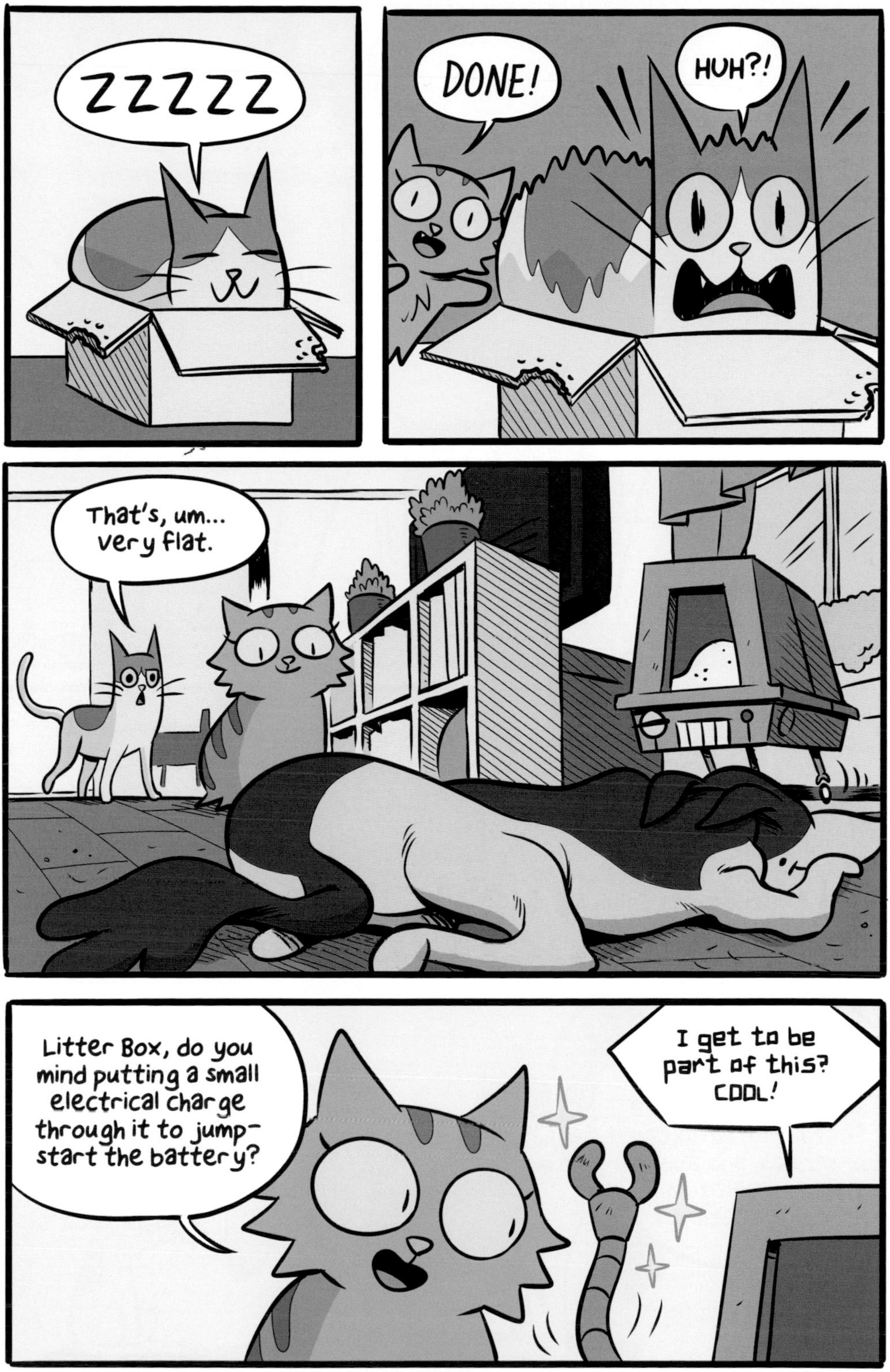
ZZZZZ
DONE!
HUH?!
That's, um... very flat.
Litter Box, do you mind putting a small electrical charge through it to jump-start the battery?
I get to be part of this? COOL!

ZAP!

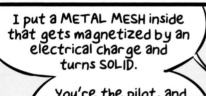

I put a METAL MESH inside that gets magnetized by an electrical charge and turns SOLID.

You're the pilot, and I control all the extra features from my control panel.

Whoa.

The internal hyper-battery will multiply our strength and speed. There's a feature to heighten our senses, and about a dozen **really** cool safety features.

Whoa.

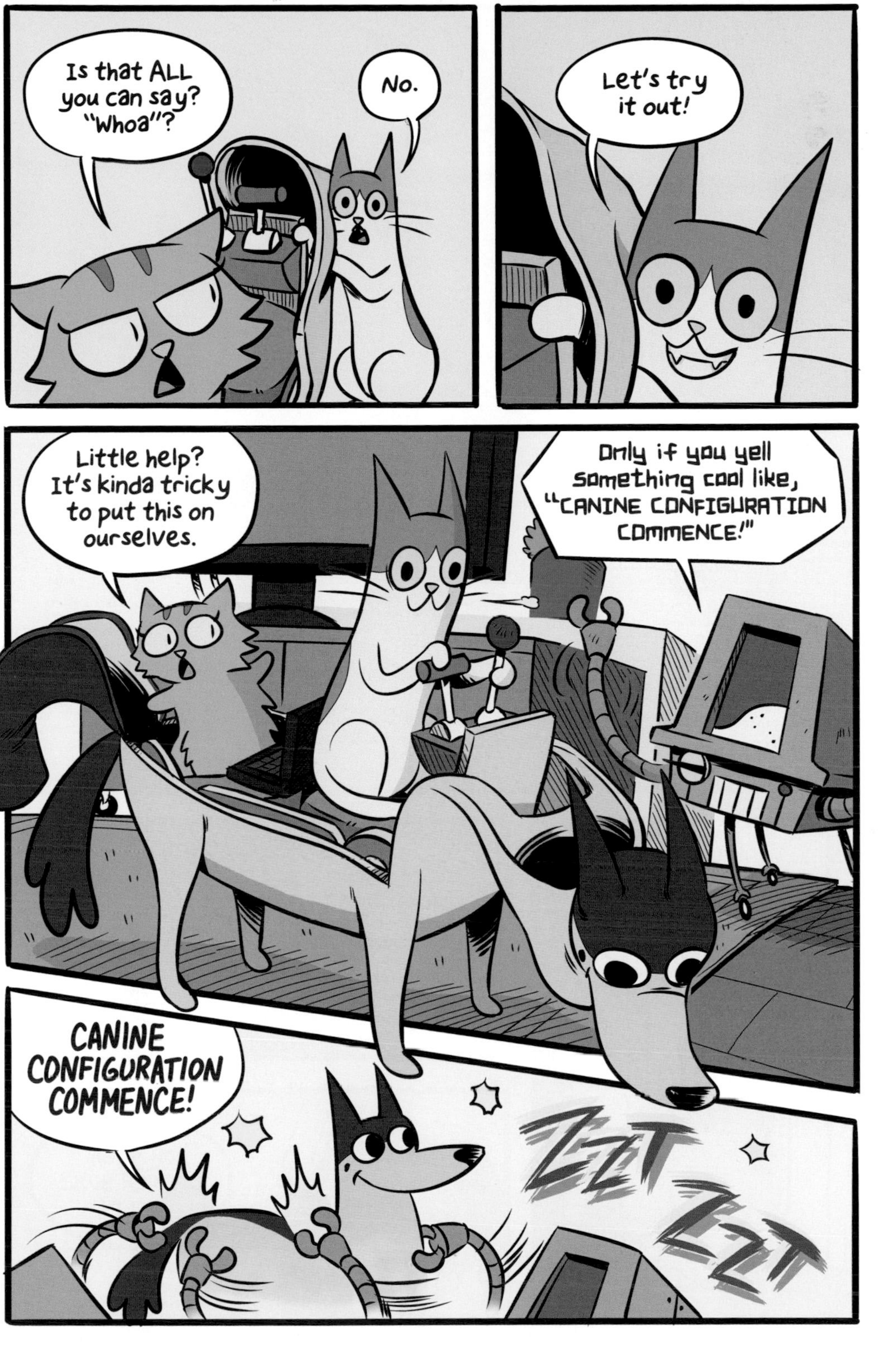

Is that ALL you can say? "Whoa"?
No.
Let's try it out!
Little help? It's kinda tricky to put this on ourselves.
Only if you yell something cool like, "CANINE CONFIGURATION COMMENCE!"
CANINE CONFIGURATION COMMENCE!
ZZZT
ZZZT

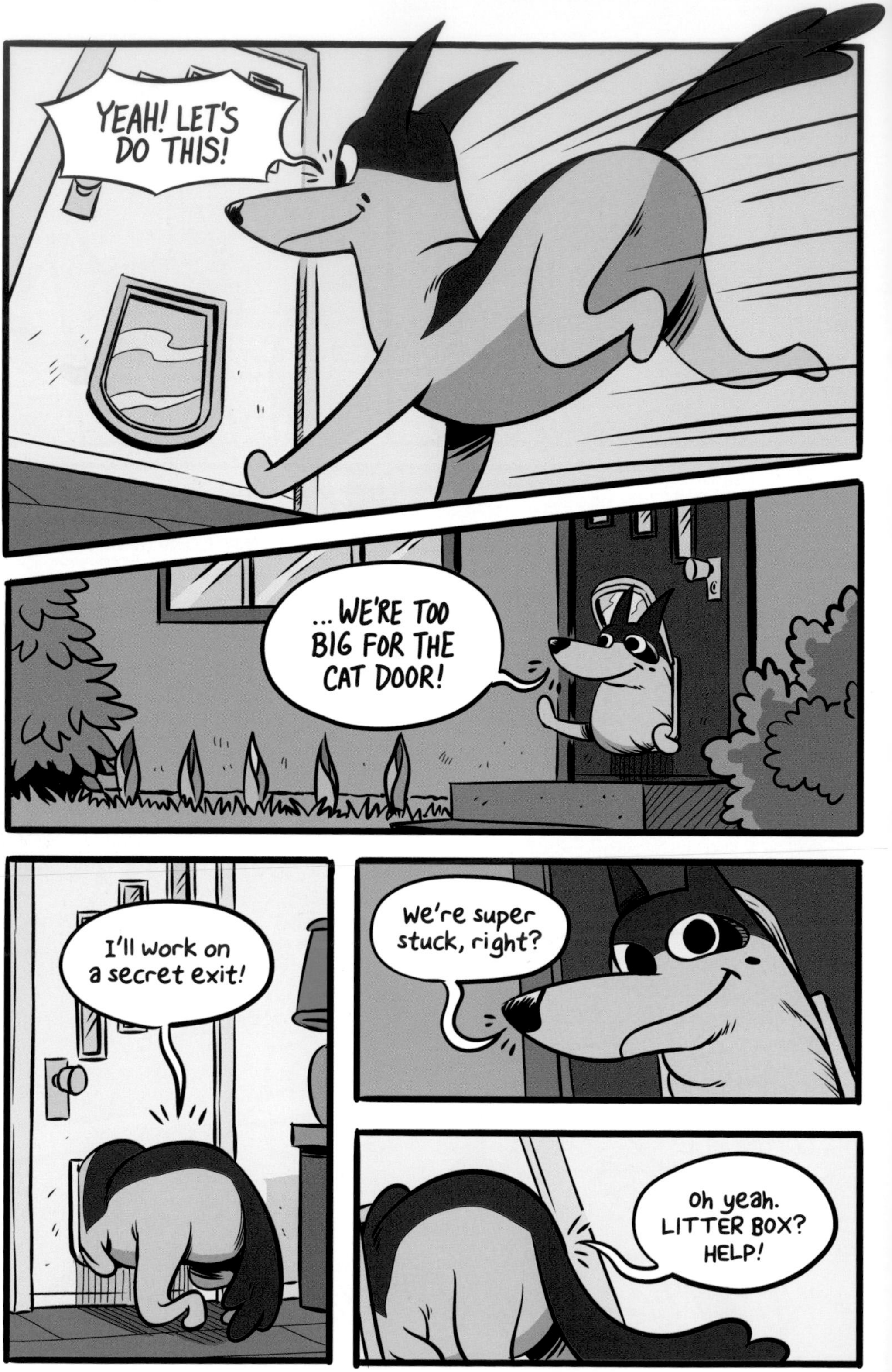
YEAH! LET'S DO THIS!
...WE'RE TOO BIG FOR THE CAT DOOR!
I'll work on a secret exit!
We're super stuck, right?
Oh yeah. LITTER BOX? HELP!

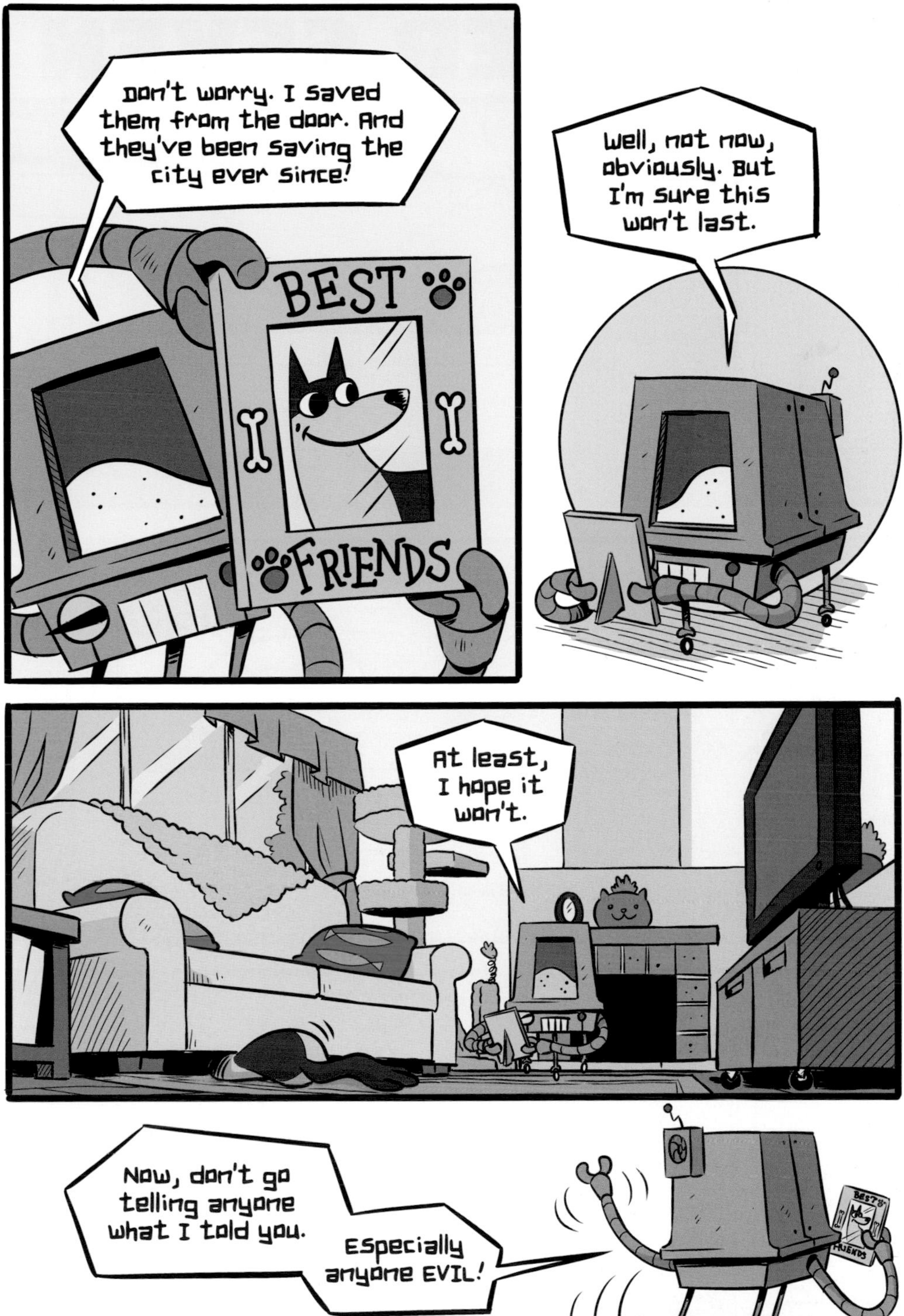
Don't worry. I saved them from the door. And they've been saving the city ever since!
BEST FRIENDS
Well, not now, obviously. But I'm sure this won't last.
At least, I hope it won't.
Now, don't go telling anyone what I told you.
Especially anyone EVIL!

CHAPTER SEVEN

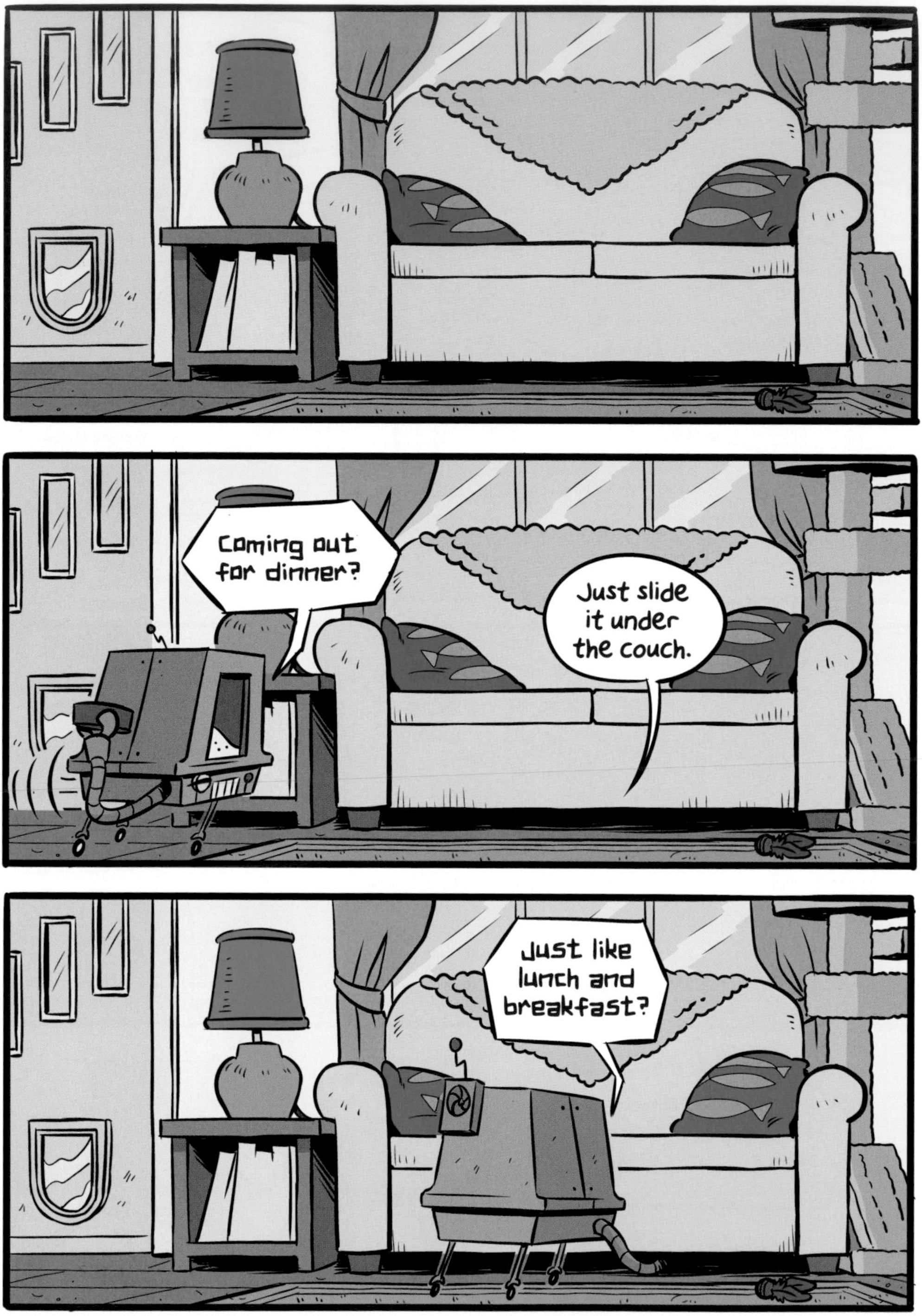
Coming out for dinner?
Just slide it under the couch.
Just like lunch and breakfast?

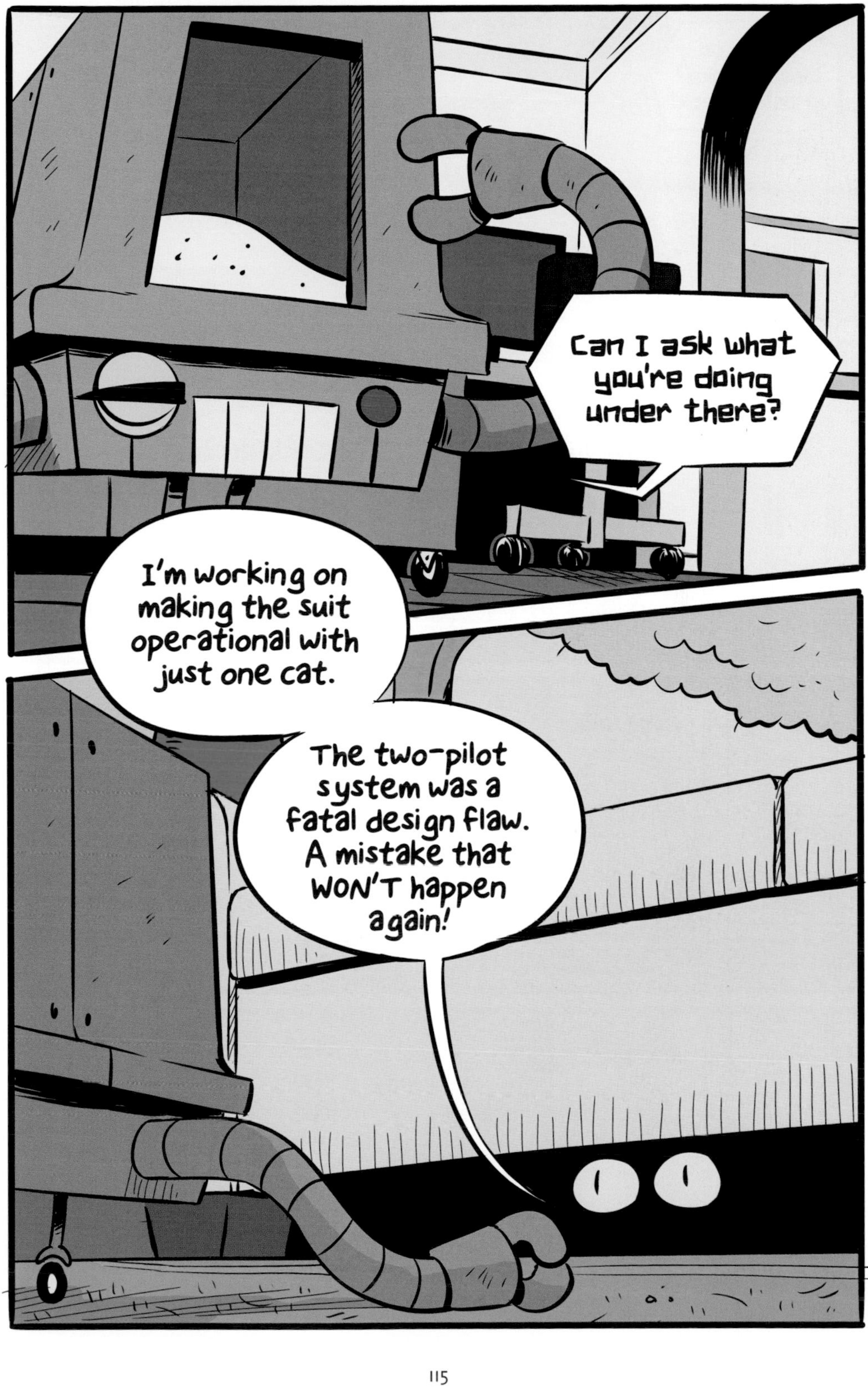
Can I ask what you're doing under there?
I'm working on making the suit operational with just one cat.
The two-pilot system was a fatal design flaw. A mistake that WON'T happen again!

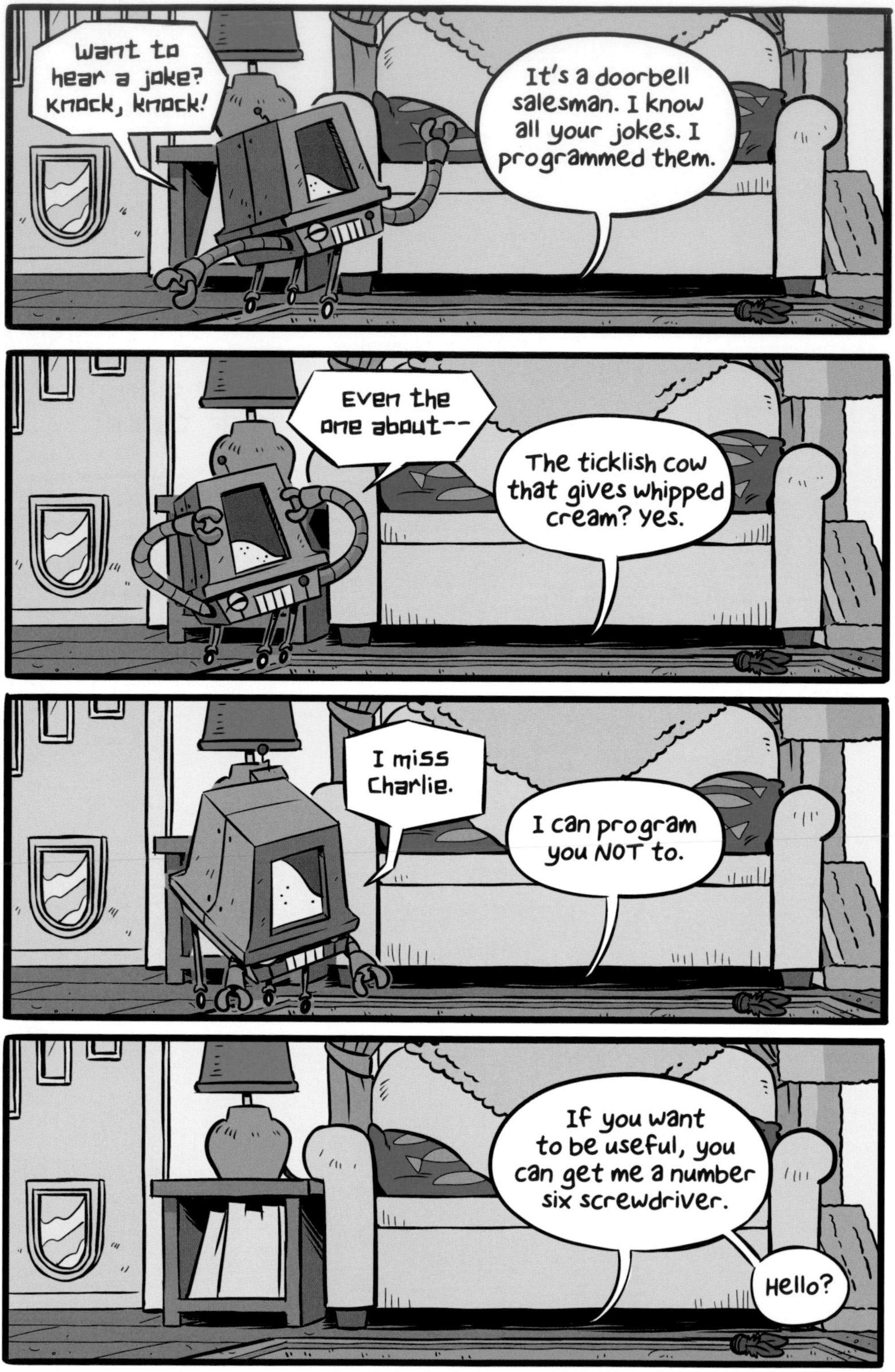
Want to hear a joke? Knock, knock!
It's a doorbell salesman. I know all your jokes. I programmed them.
Even the one about--
The ticklish cow that gives whipped cream? Yes.
I miss Charlie.
I can program you NOT to.
If you want to be useful, you can get me a number six screwdriver.
Hello?

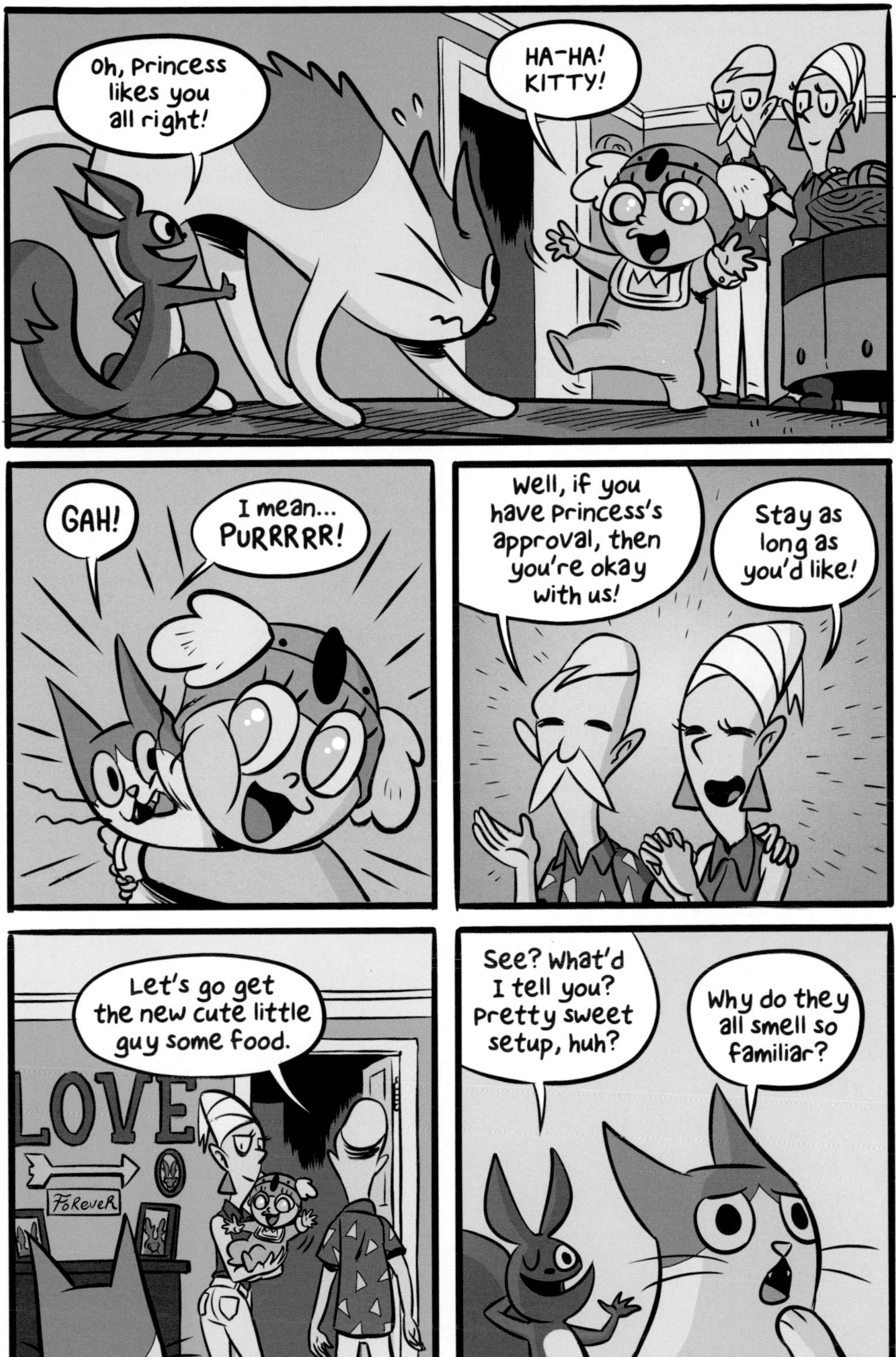
Oh, Princess likes you all right!
HA-HA! KITTY!
GAH!
I mean... PURRRRR!
Well, if you have Princess's approval, then you're okay with us!
Stay as long as you'd like!
Let's go get the new cute little guy some food.
LOVE
FOREVER
See? What'd I tell you? Pretty sweet setup, huh?
Why do they all smell so familiar?

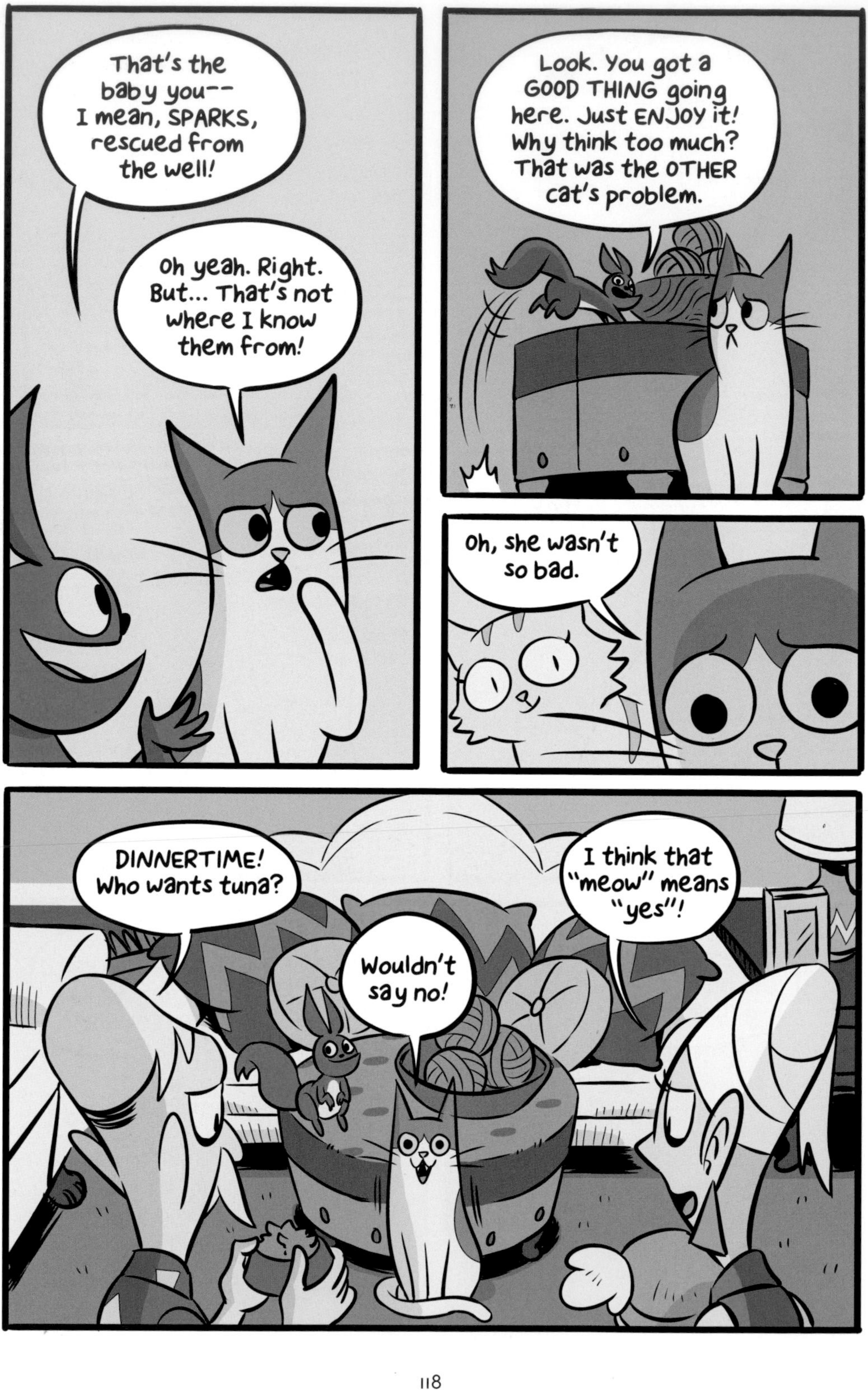
That's the baby you-- I mean, SPARKS, rescued from the well!
Oh yeah. Right. But... That's not where I know them from!
Look. You got a GOOD THING going here. Just ENJOY it! Why think too much? That was the OTHER cat's problem.
Oh, she wasn't so bad.
DINNERTIME! Who wants tuna?
Wouldn't say no!
I think that "meow" means "yes"!

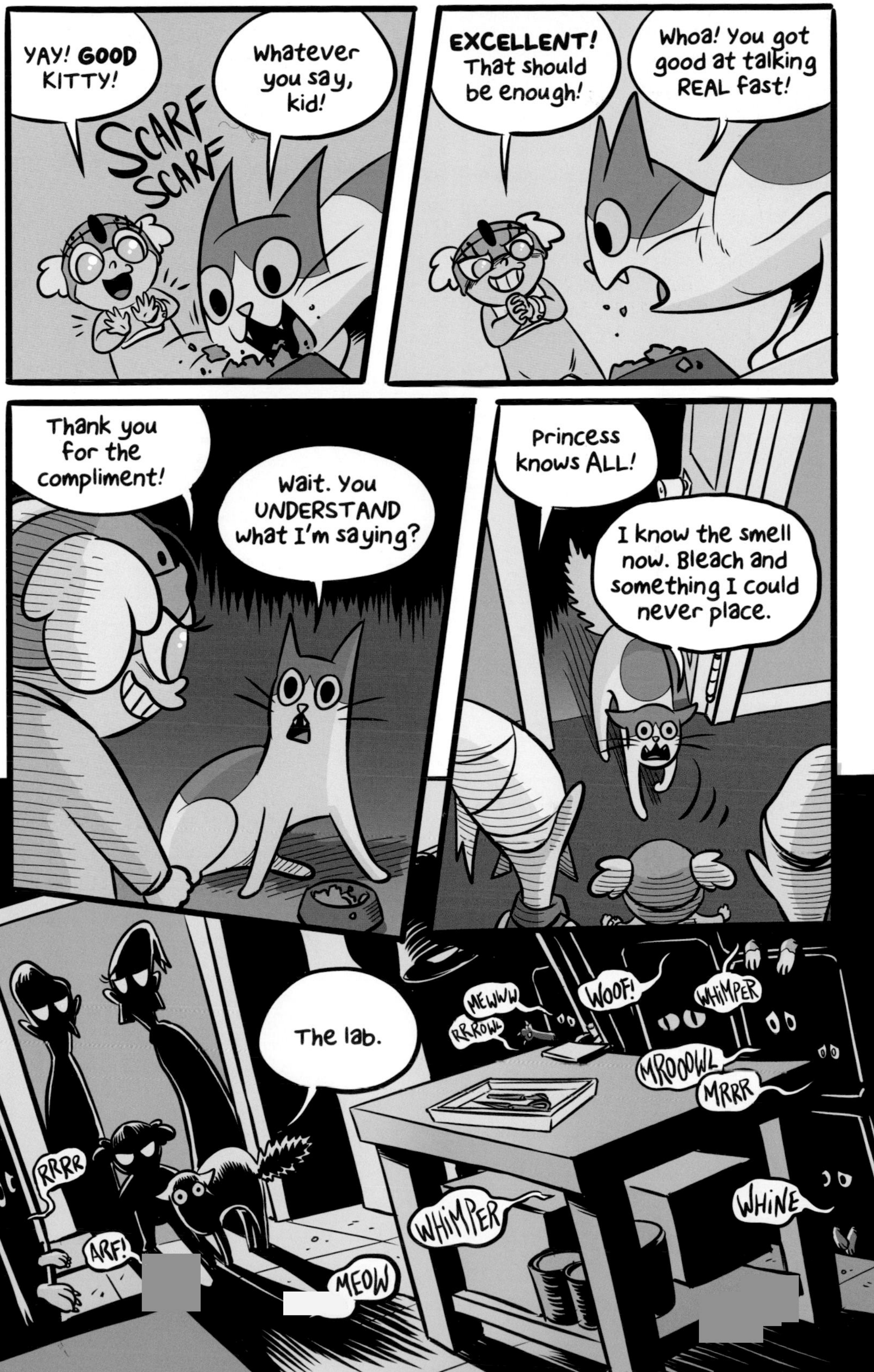

YAY! **GOOD** KITTY!
SCARF SCARF
Whatever you say, kid!
EXCELLENT! That should be enough!
Whoa! You got good at talking REAL fast!
Thank you for the compliment!
Wait. You UNDERSTAND what I'm saying?
Princess knows ALL!
I know the smell now. Bleach and something I could never place.
The lab.
MEWWW
RRROWL
WOOF!
WHIMPER
MROOOWL
MRRR
RRRR
ARF!
MEOW
WHIMPER
WHINE

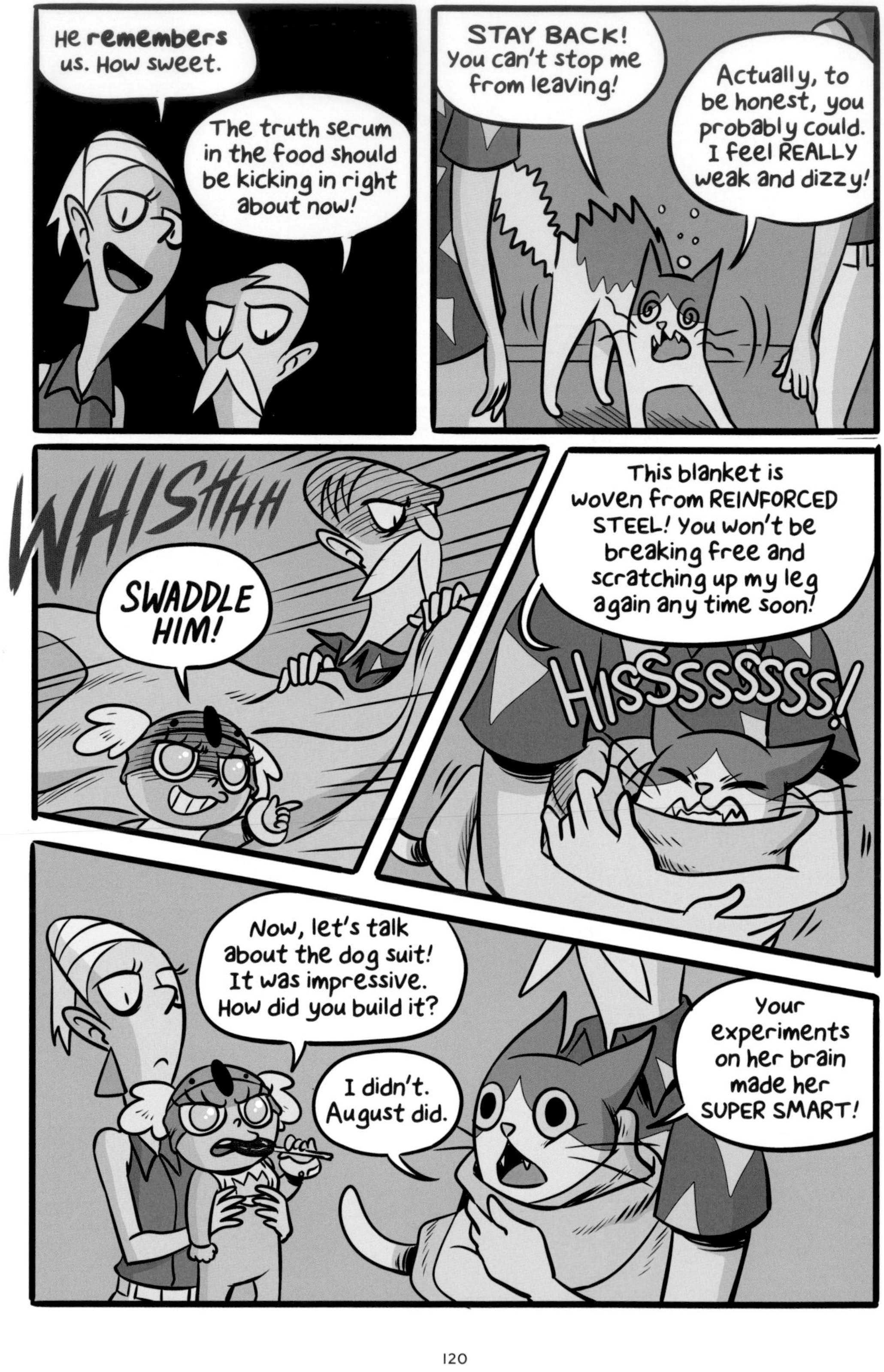
He remembers us. How sweet.
The truth serum in the food should be kicking in right about now!
STAY BACK! You can't stop me from leaving!
Actually, to be honest, you probably could. I feel REALLY weak and dizzy!
WHISHHH
SWADDLE HIM!
This blanket is woven from REINFORCED STEEL! You won't be breaking free and scratching up my leg again any time soon!
HISSSSSSS!
Now, let's talk about the dog suit! It was impressive. How did you build it?
I didn't. August did.
Your experiments on her brain made her SUPER SMART!

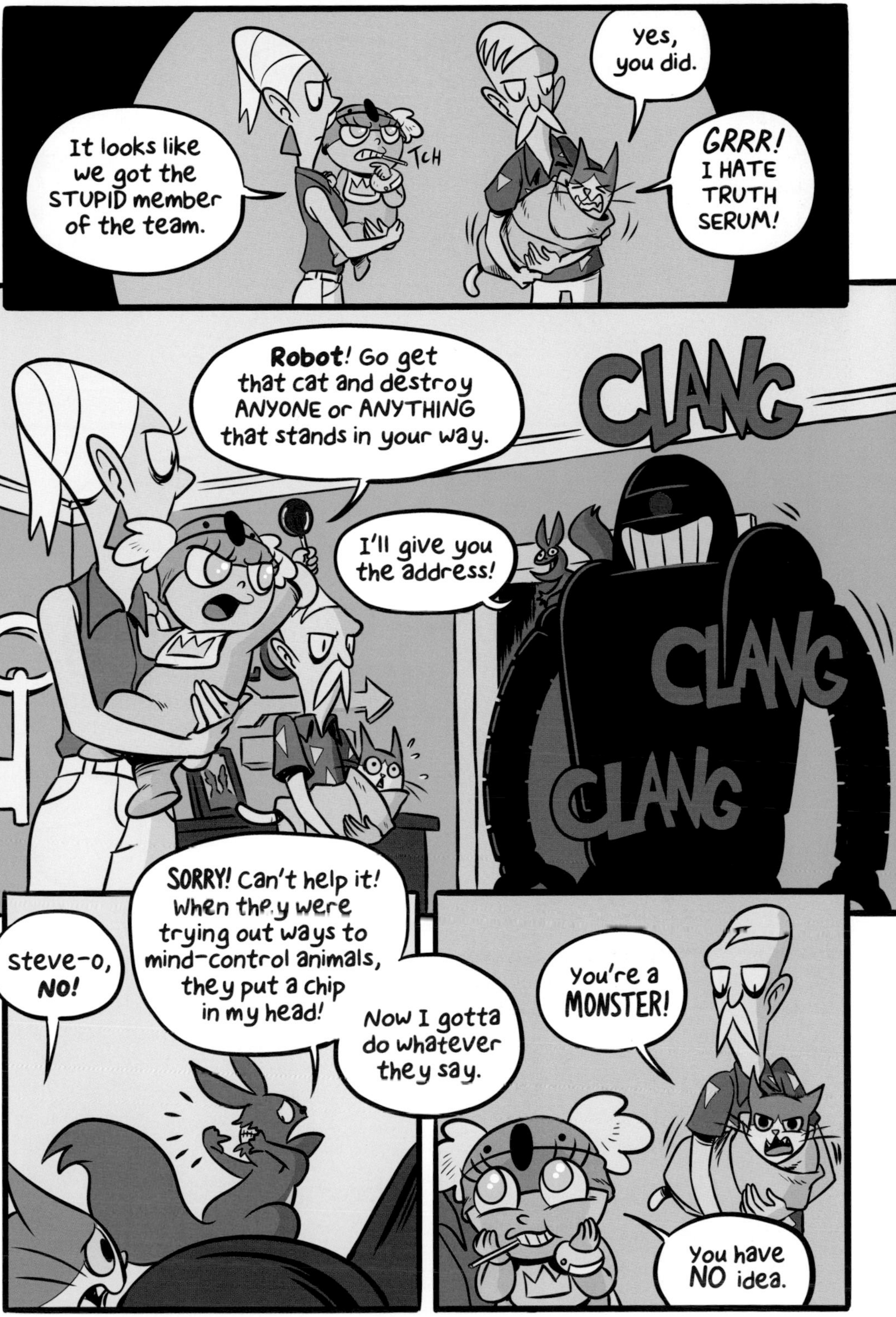

It looks like we got the STUPID member of the team.
TCH
yes, you did.
GRRR! I HATE TRUTH SERUM!
Robot! Go get that cat and destroy ANYONE or ANYTHING that stands in your way.
CLANG
I'll give you the address!
CLANG
CLANG
steve-o, NO!
SORRY! Can't help it! When they were trying out ways to mind-control animals, they put a chip in my head!
Now I gotta do whatever they say.
You're a MONSTER!
You have NO idea.

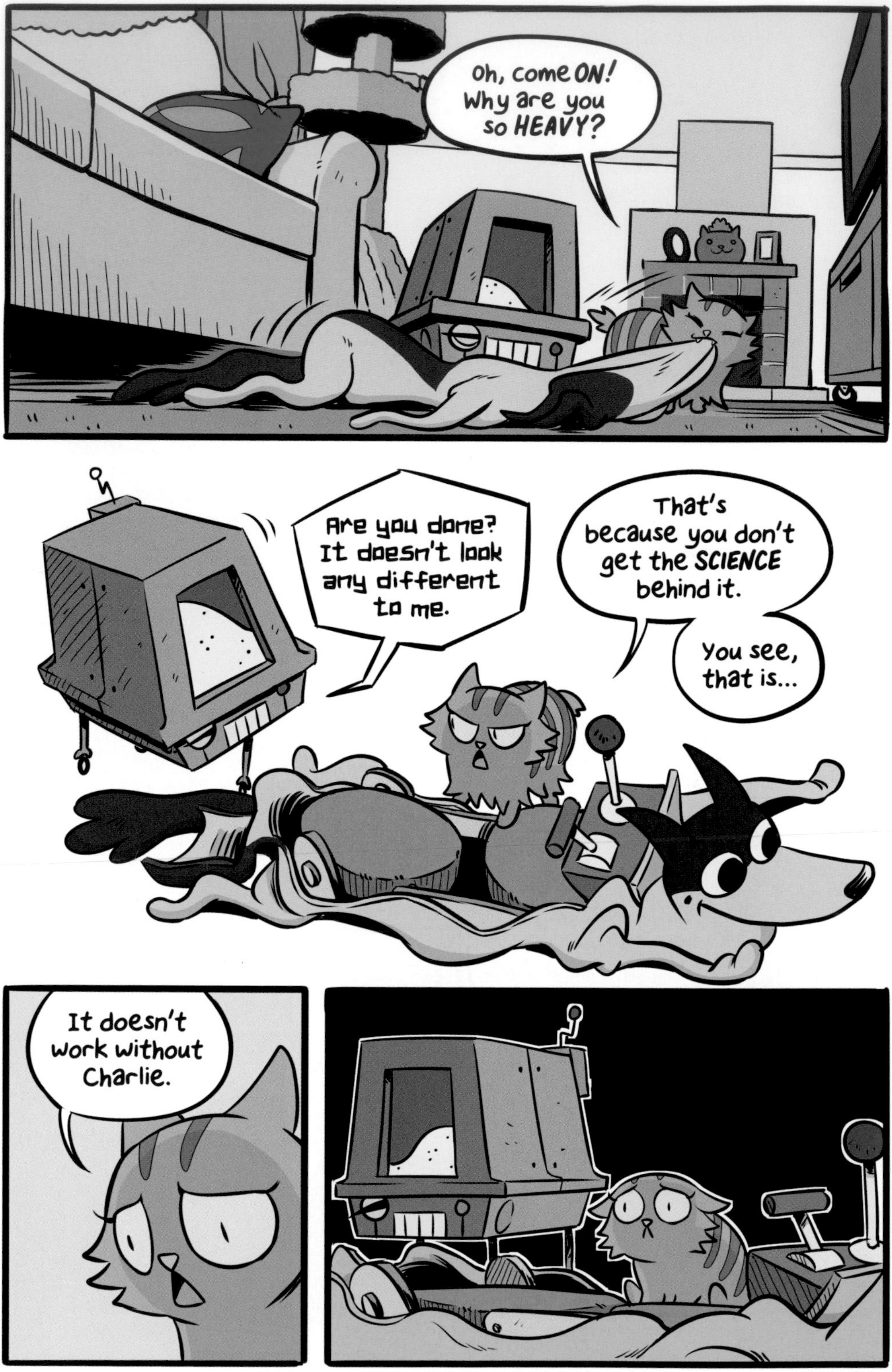
Oh, come ON! Why are you so HEAVY?
Are you done? It doesn't look any different to me.
That's because you don't get the SCIENCE behind it.
You see, that is...
It doesn't work without Charlie.

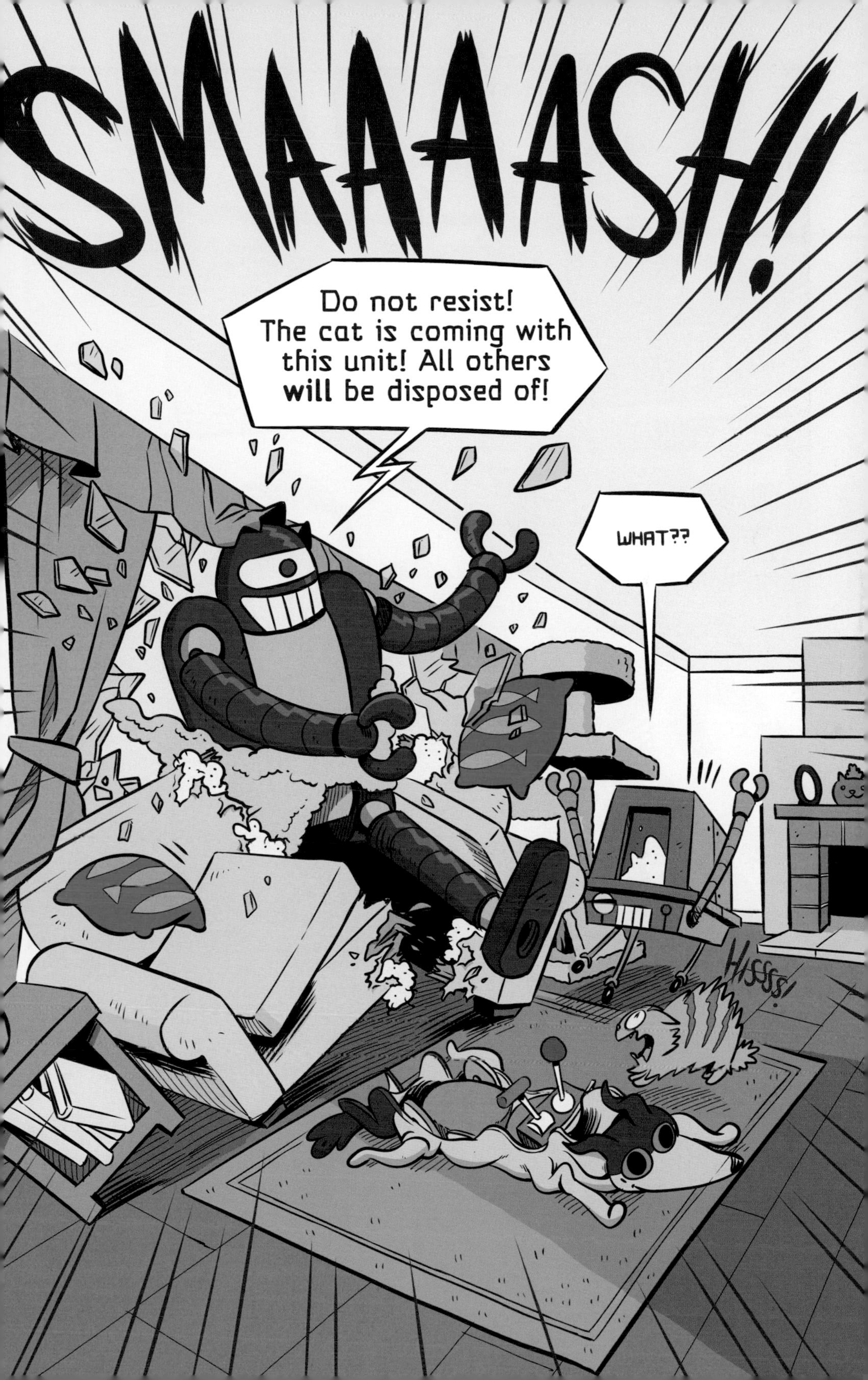
SMAAAASH!
Do not resist! The cat is coming with this unit! All others will be disposed of!
WHAT??
HISSSS!

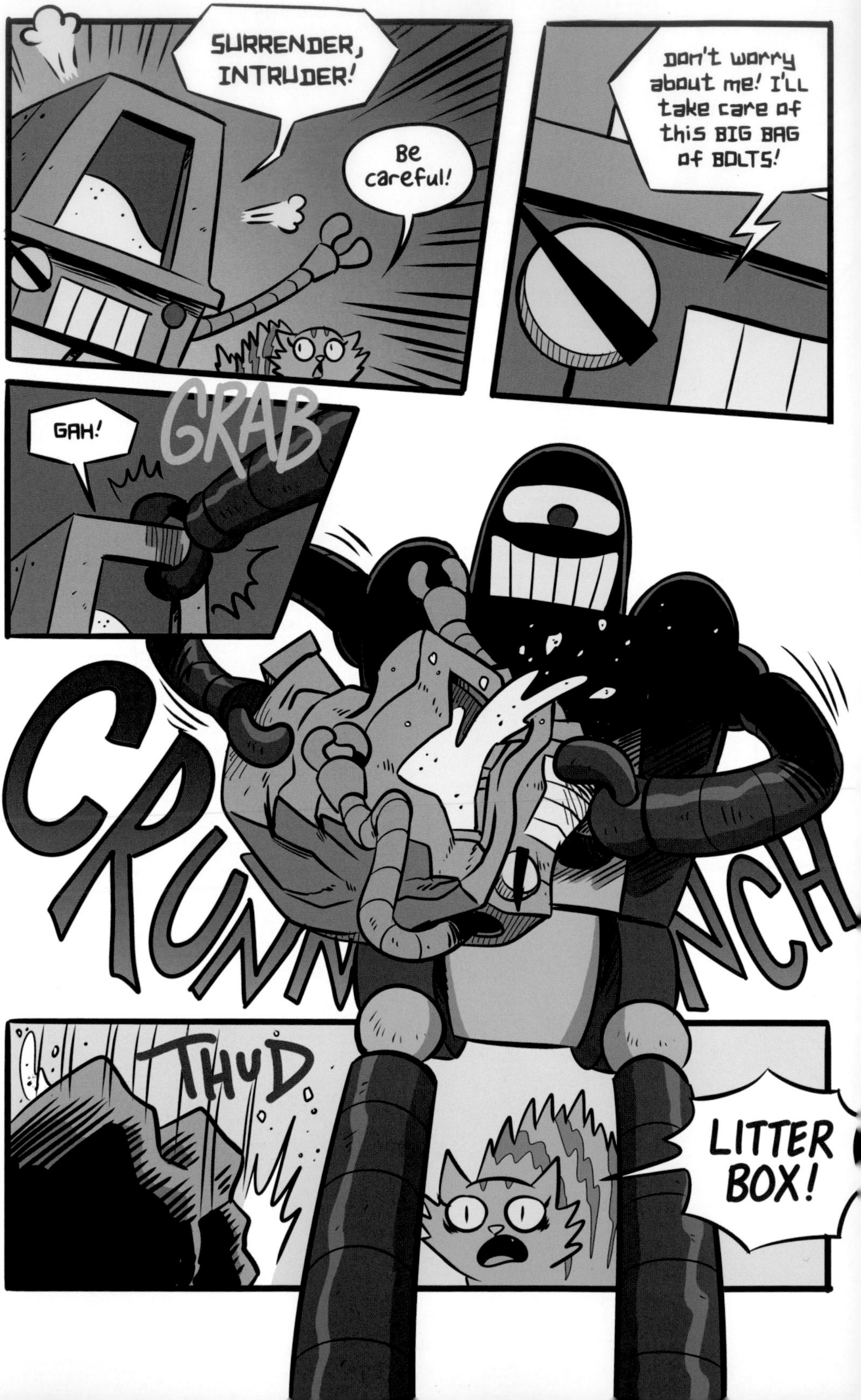
SURRENDER, INTRUDER!
Be careful!
Don't worry about me! I'LL take care of this BIG BAG of BOLTS!
GAH!
GRAB
CRUNNNNCH
THUD
LITTER BOX!

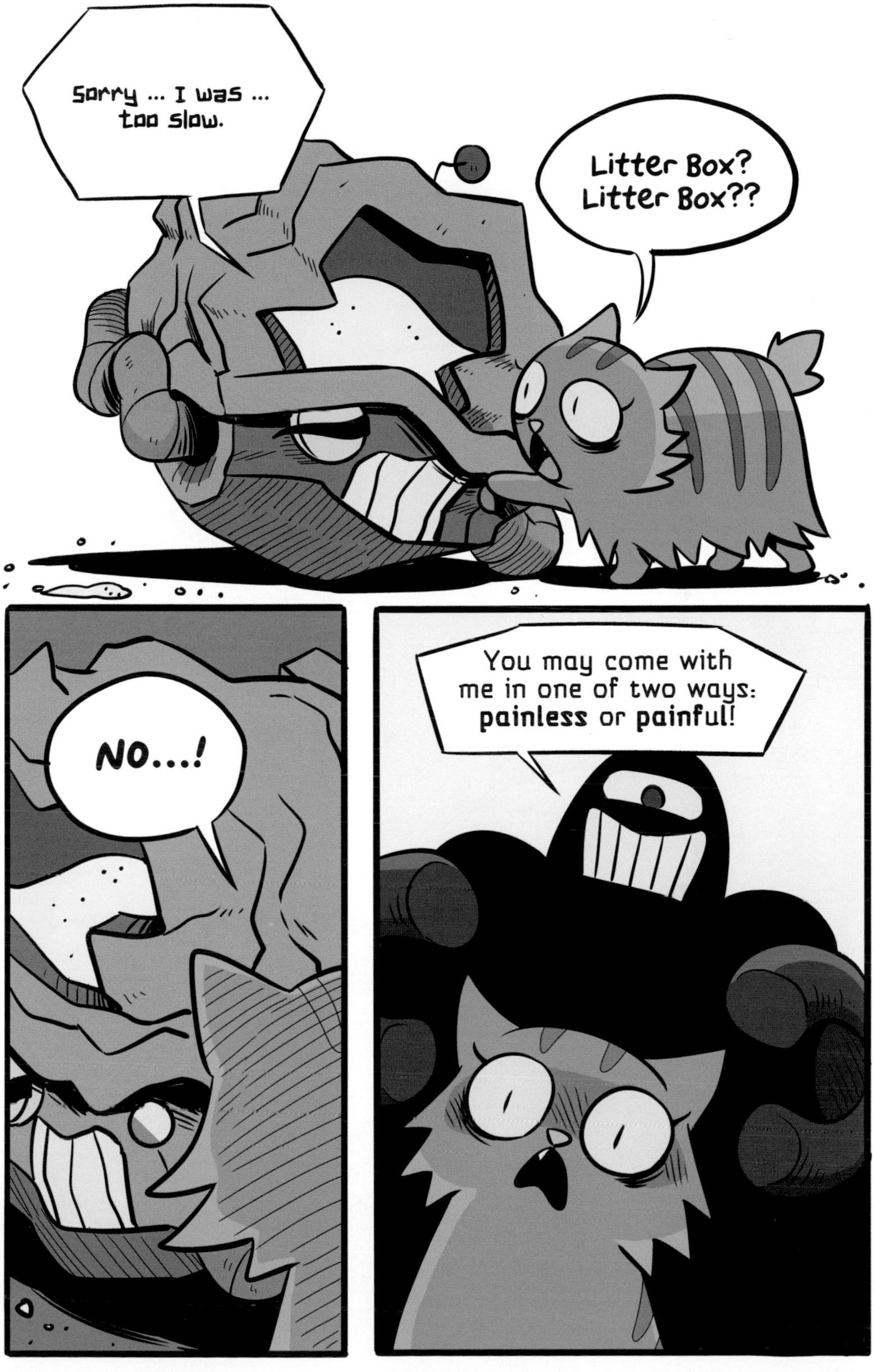
Sorry ... I was ... too slow.
Litter Box? Litter Box??
NO...!
You may come with me in one of two ways: **painless** or **painful**!

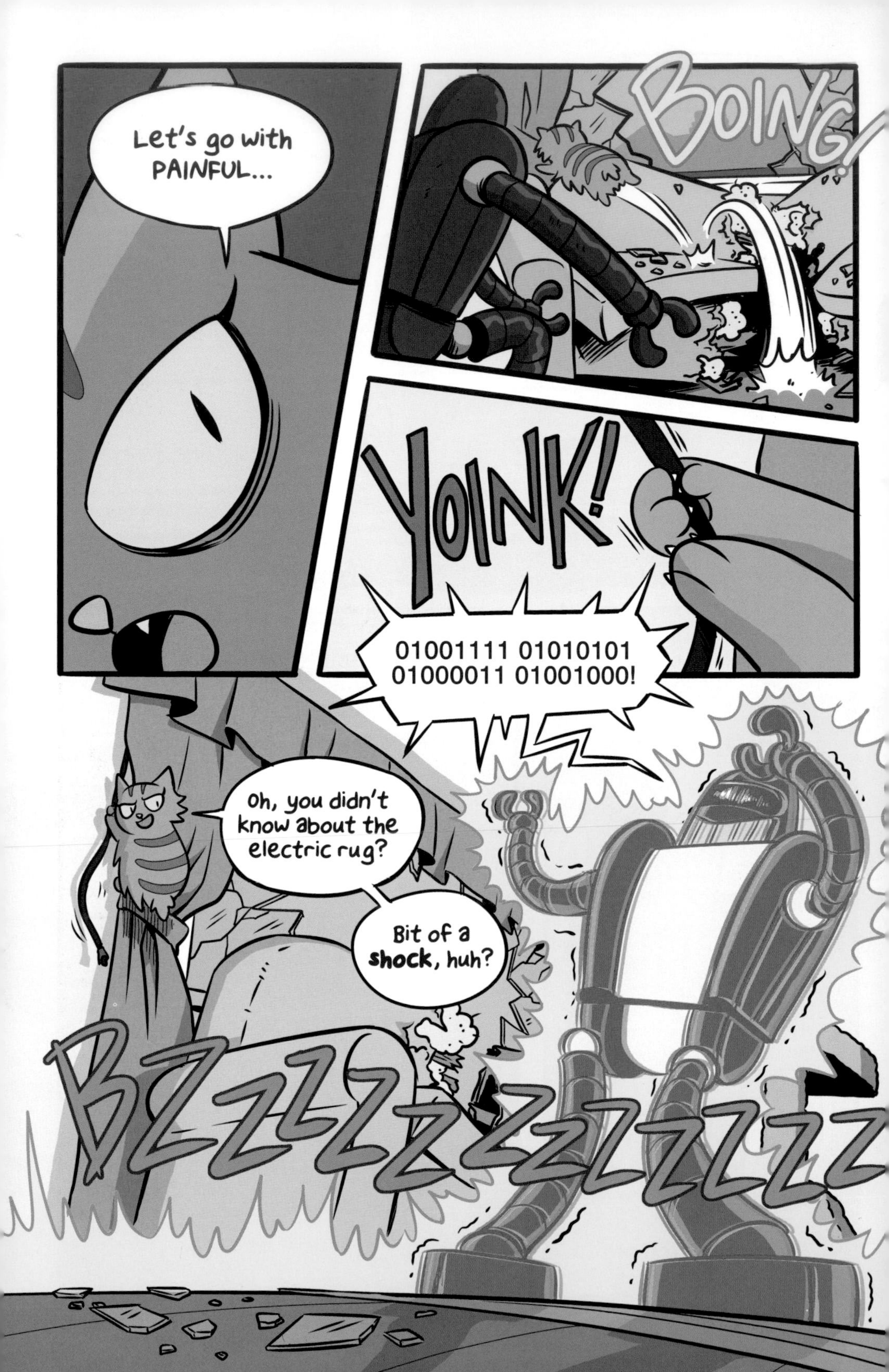
Let's go with PAINFUL...
BOING!
YOINK!
01001111 01010101 01000011 01001000!
Oh, you didn't know about the electric rug?
Bit of a **shock**, huh?
BZZZZZZZZZZZZZ

THUD

Let's see if your motherboard survived that!

POP!

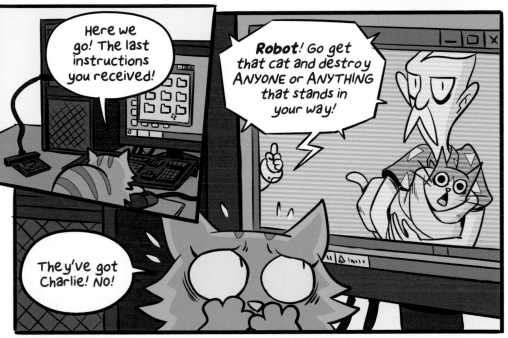

Here we go! The last instructions you received!

Robot! Go get that cat and destroy ANYONE or ANYTHING that stands in your way!

They've got Charlie! No!

PLEASE have a global positioning system so I can track WHERE you came from!

CLAK
CLAK CLAK

GOT IT! I'm coming for you, pal!

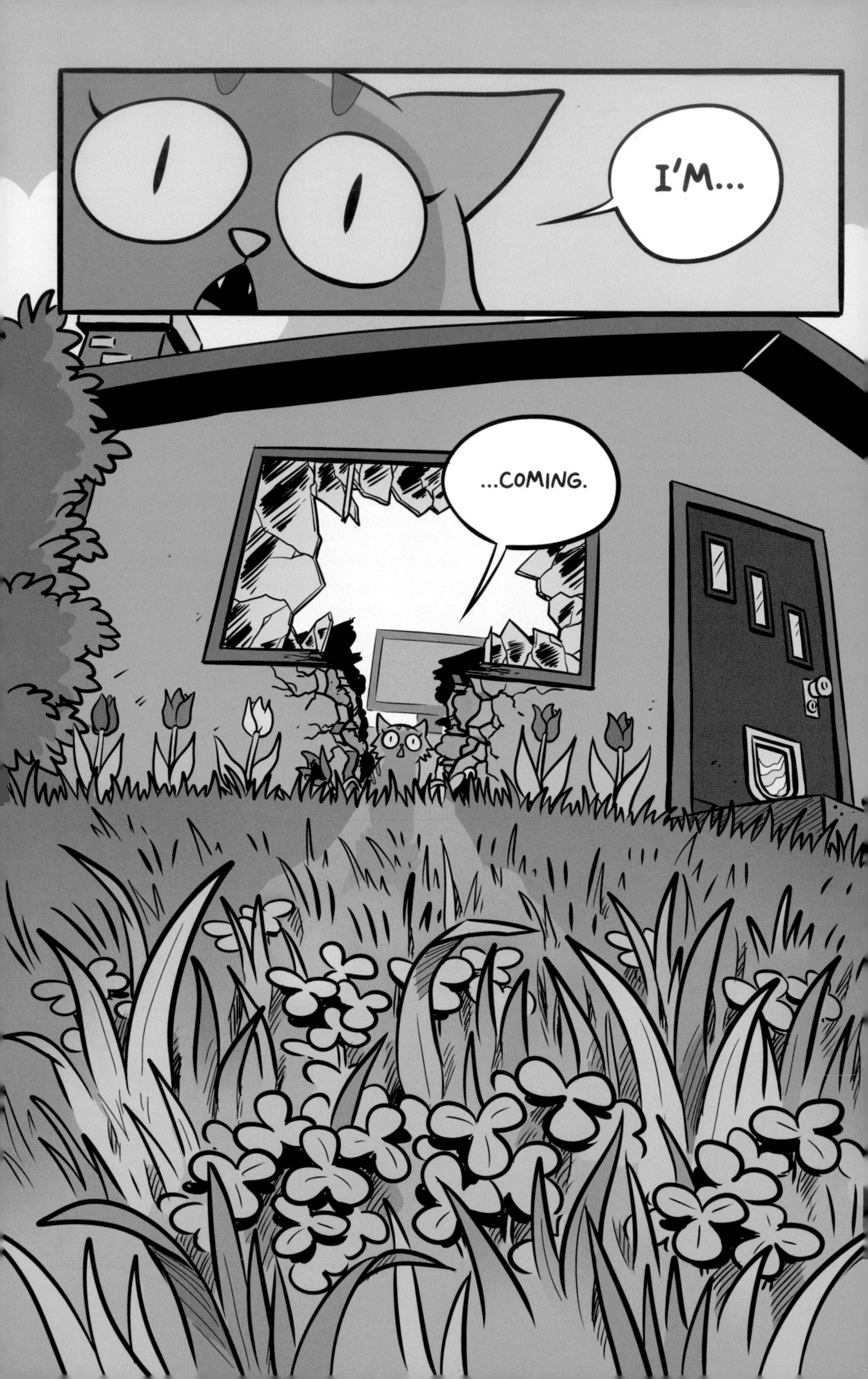
I'M...
...COMING.

CHAPTER EIGHT

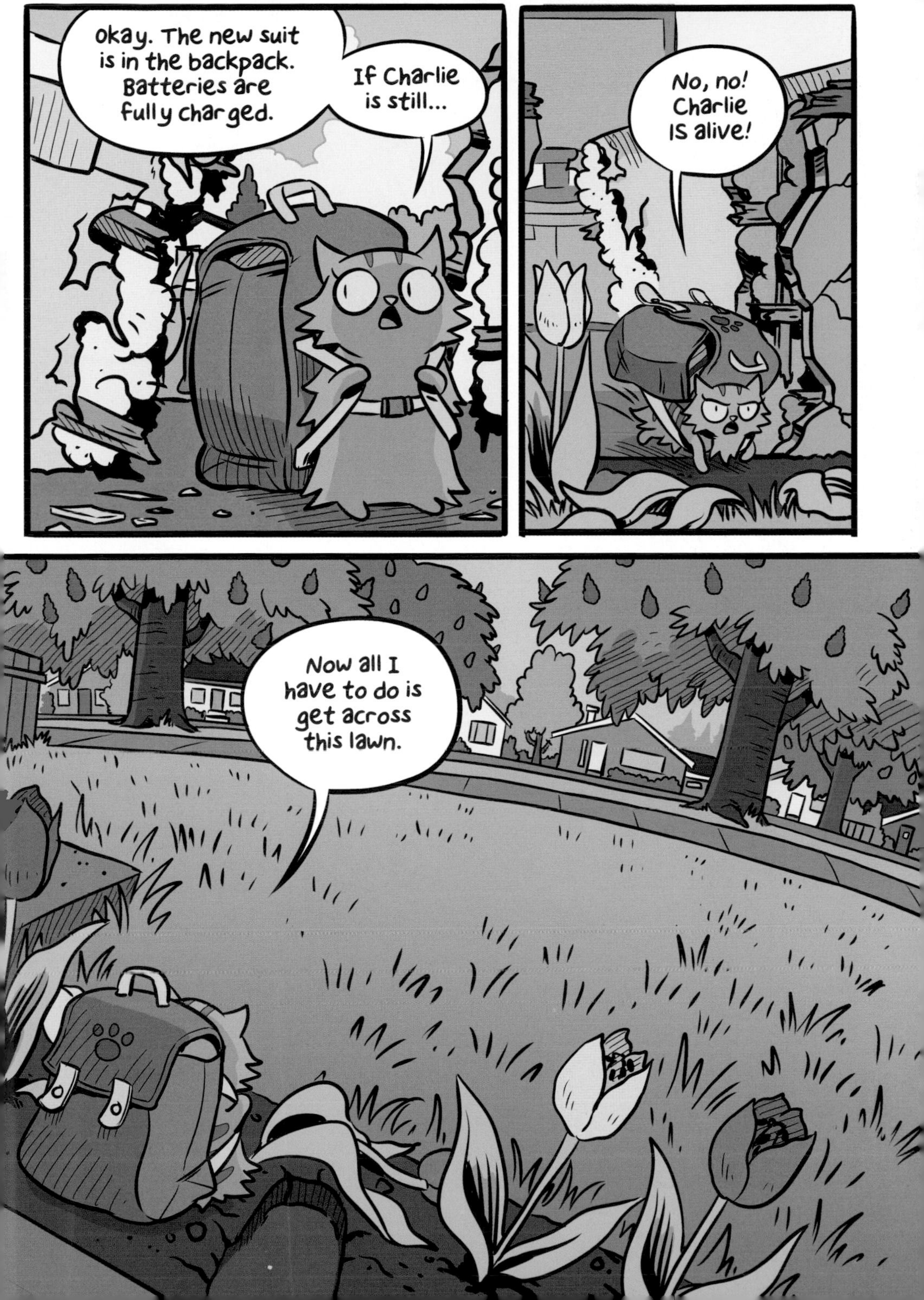

Okay. The new suit is in the backpack. Batteries are fully charged.
If Charlie is still...
No, no! Charlie IS alive!
Now all I have to do is get across this lawn.

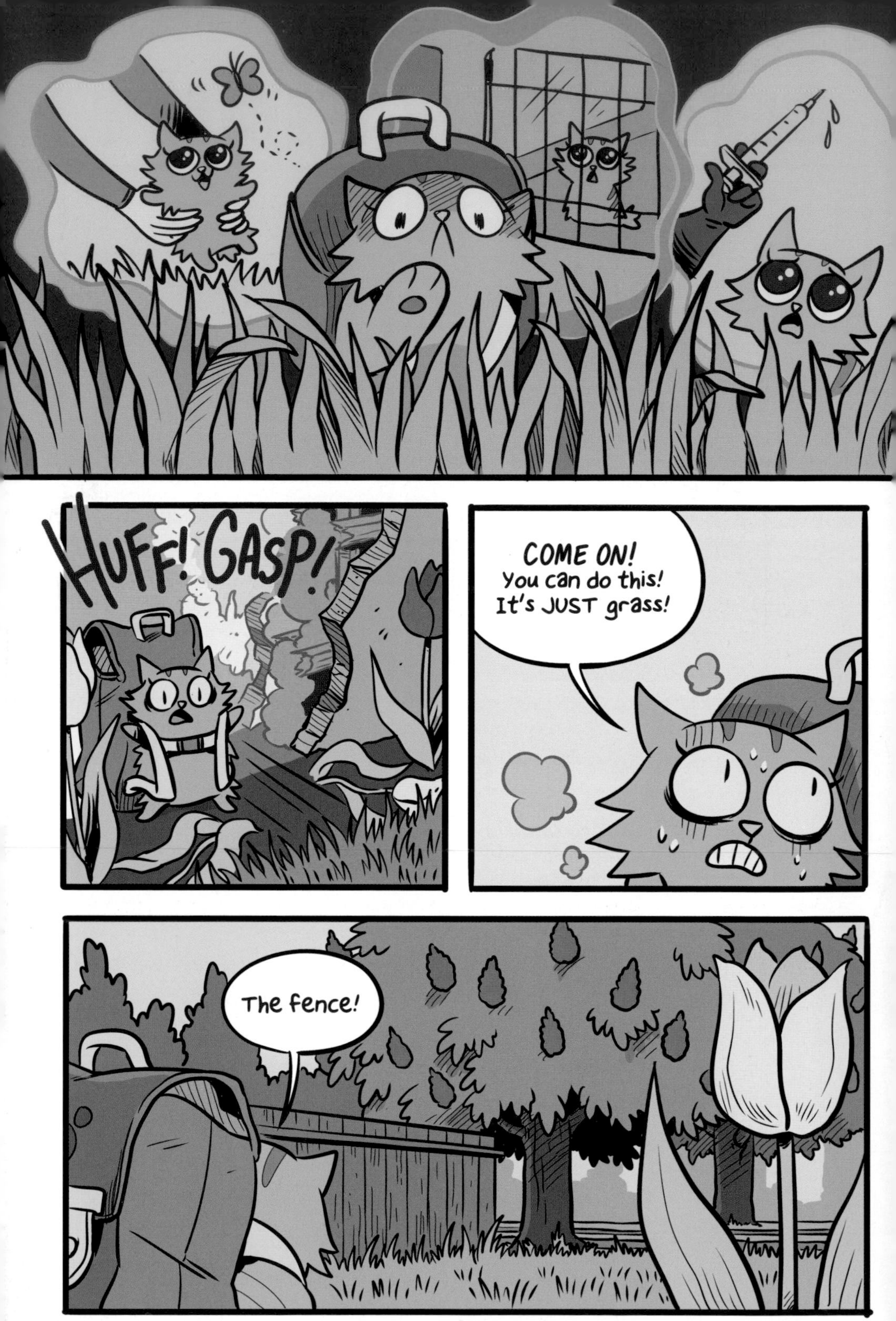
HUFF! GASP!
COME ON! You can do this! It's JUST grass!
The fence!

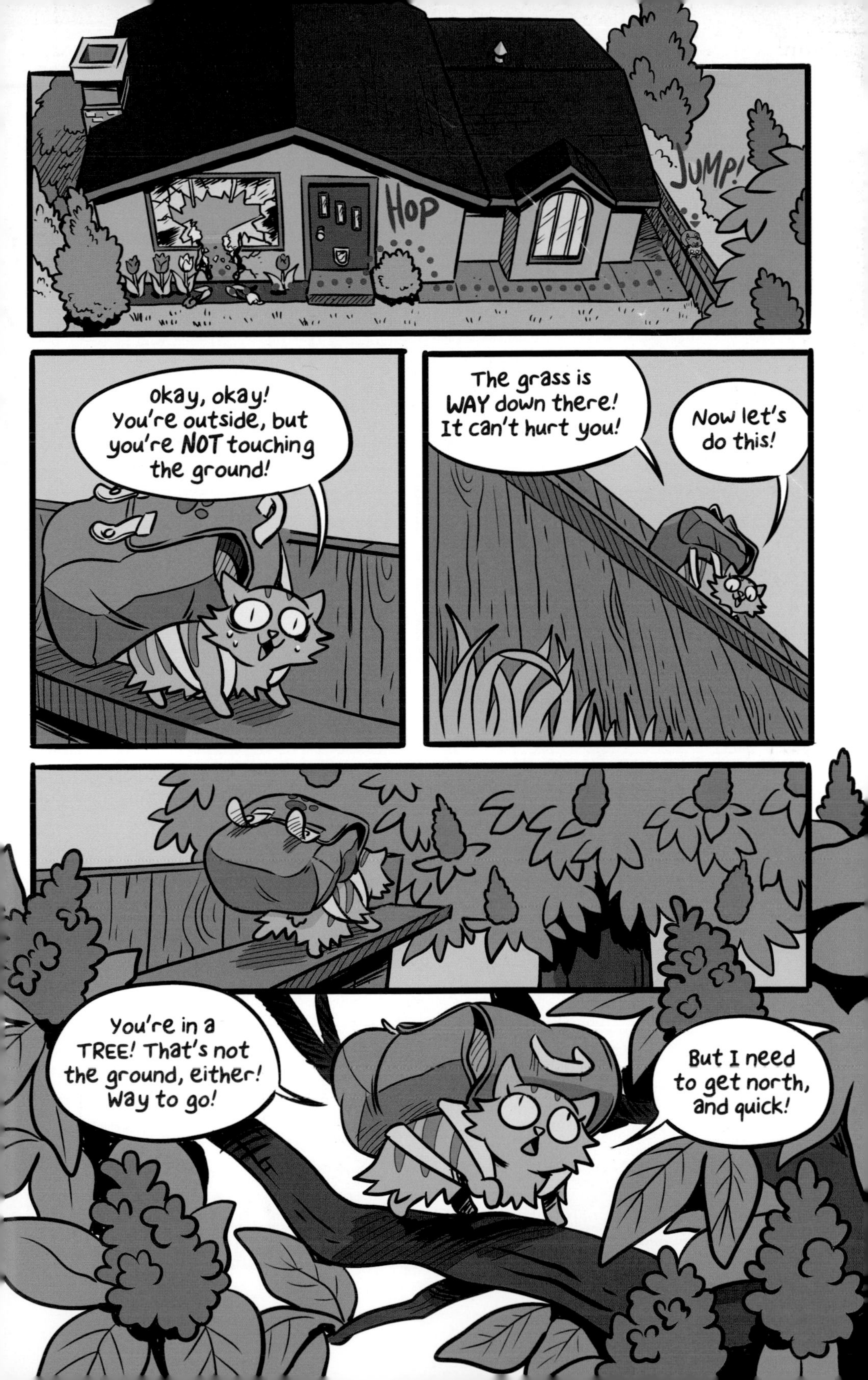
HOP
JUMP!
Okay, okay! You're outside, but you're NOT touching the ground!
The grass is WAY down there! It can't hurt you!
Now let's do this!
You're in a TREE! That's not the ground, either! Way to go!
But I need to get north, and quick!

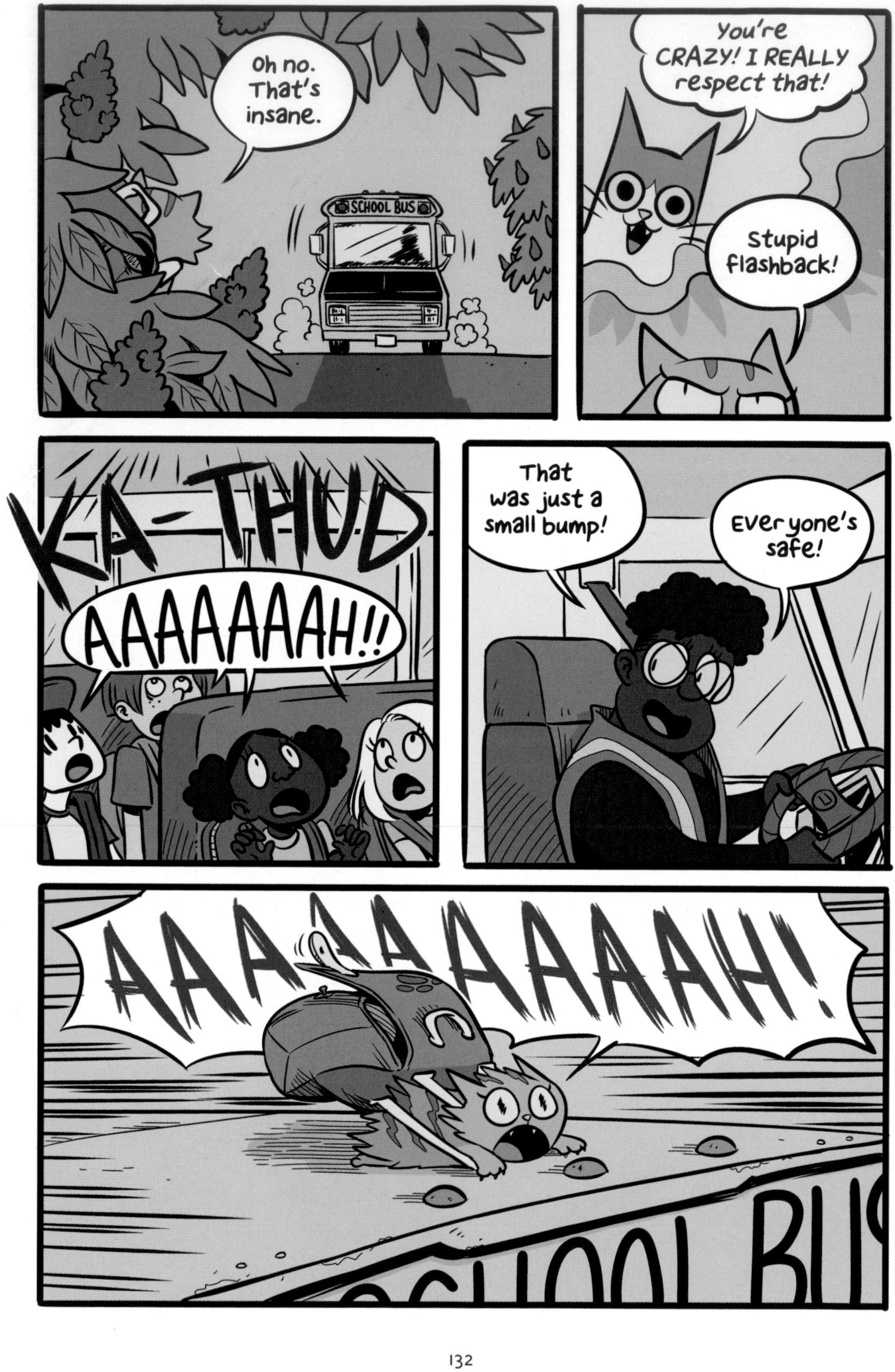
Oh no. That's insane.
You're CRAZY! I REALLY respect that!
Stupid flashback!
SCHOOL BUS
KA-THUD
AAAAAAAH!!
That was just a small bump!
Everyone's safe!
AAAAAAAAAAAH!

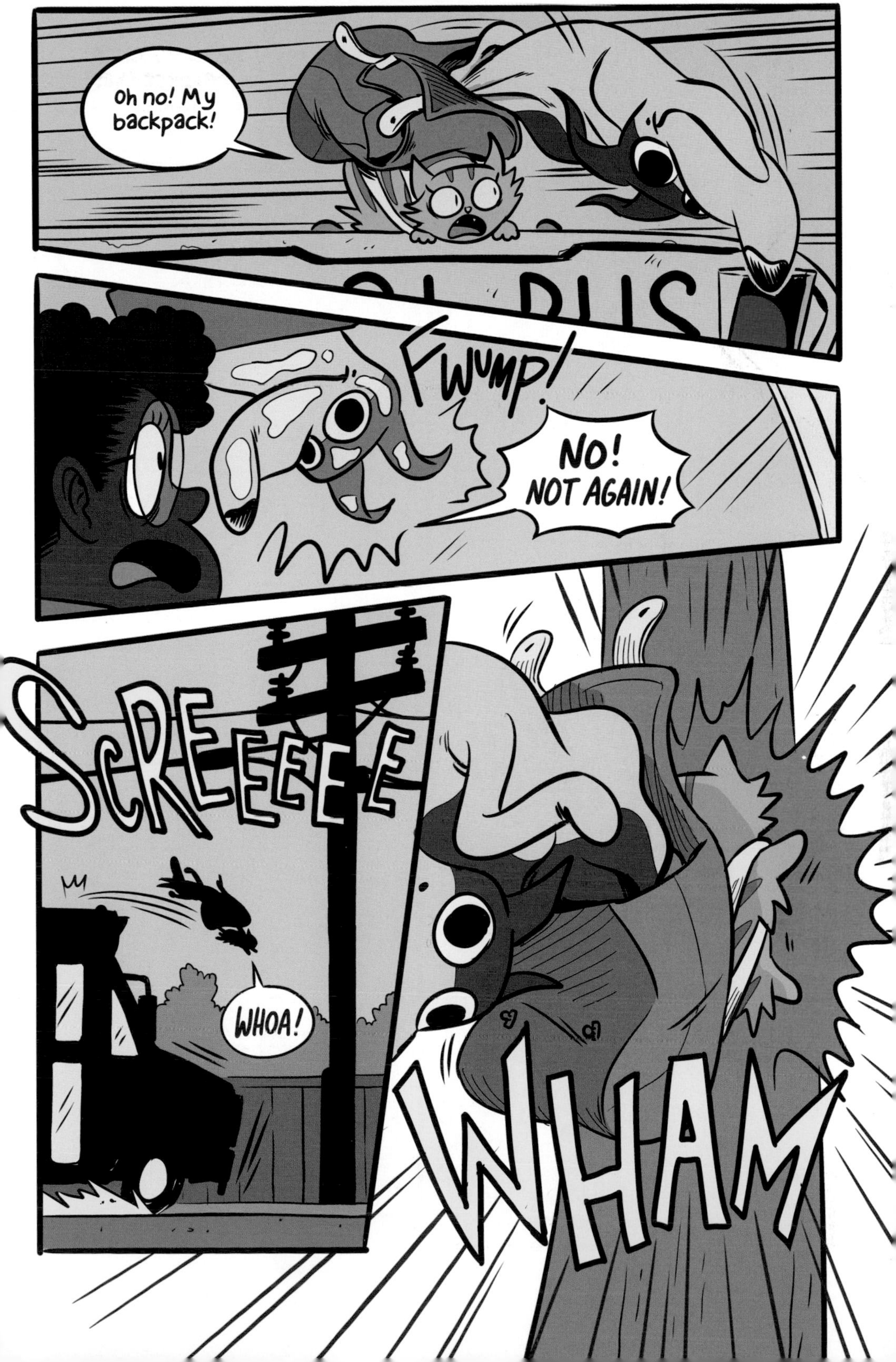
Oh no! My backpack!
FWUMP!
NO! NOT AGAIN!
SCREEEEE
WHOA!
WHAM

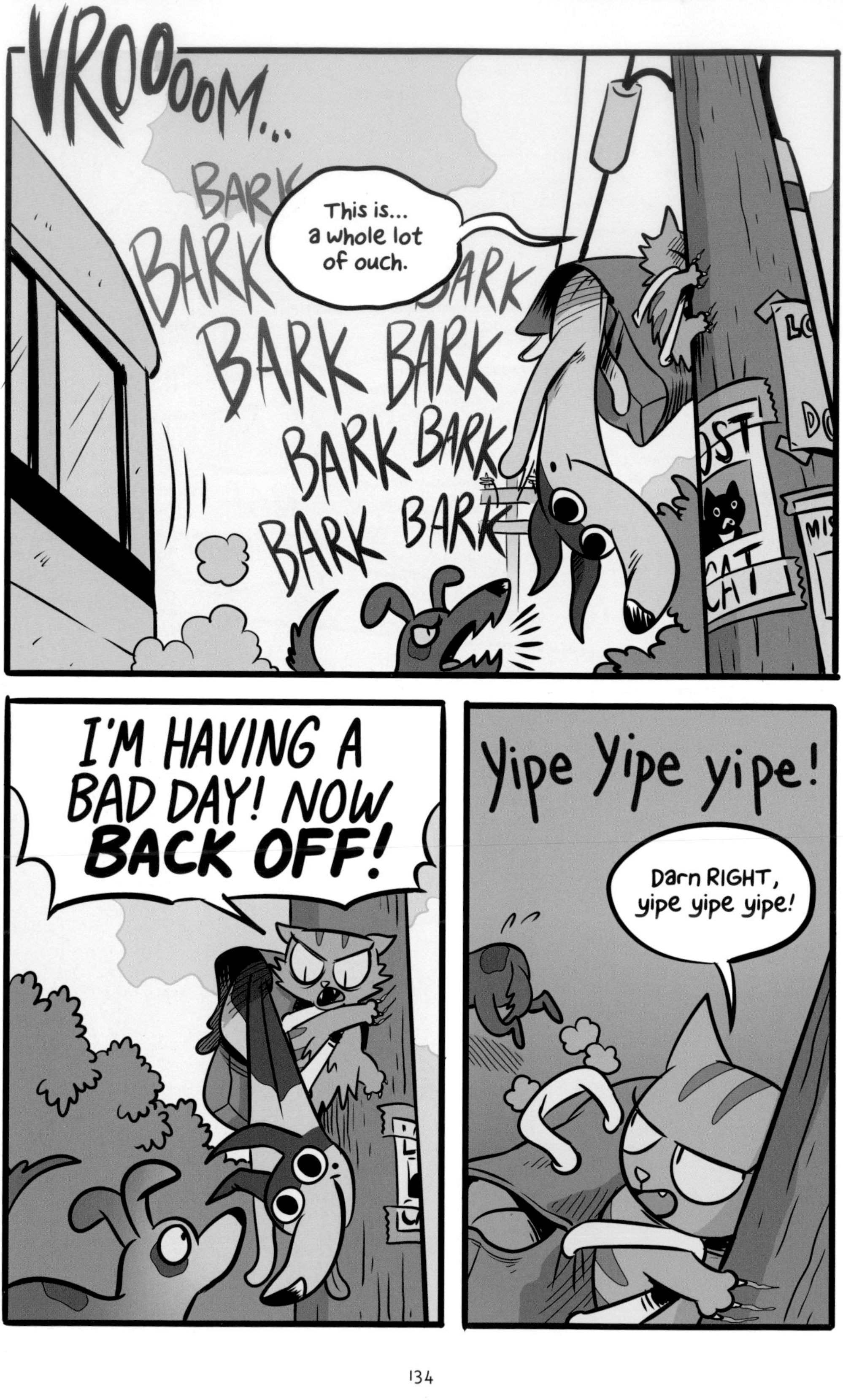
VROOOOOM...
BARK
BARK BARK
This is... a whole lot of ouch.
BARK BARK
BARK BARK
BARK BARK
I'M HAVING A BAD DAY! NOW BACK OFF!
Yipe yipe yipe!
Darn RIGHT, yipe yipe yipe!

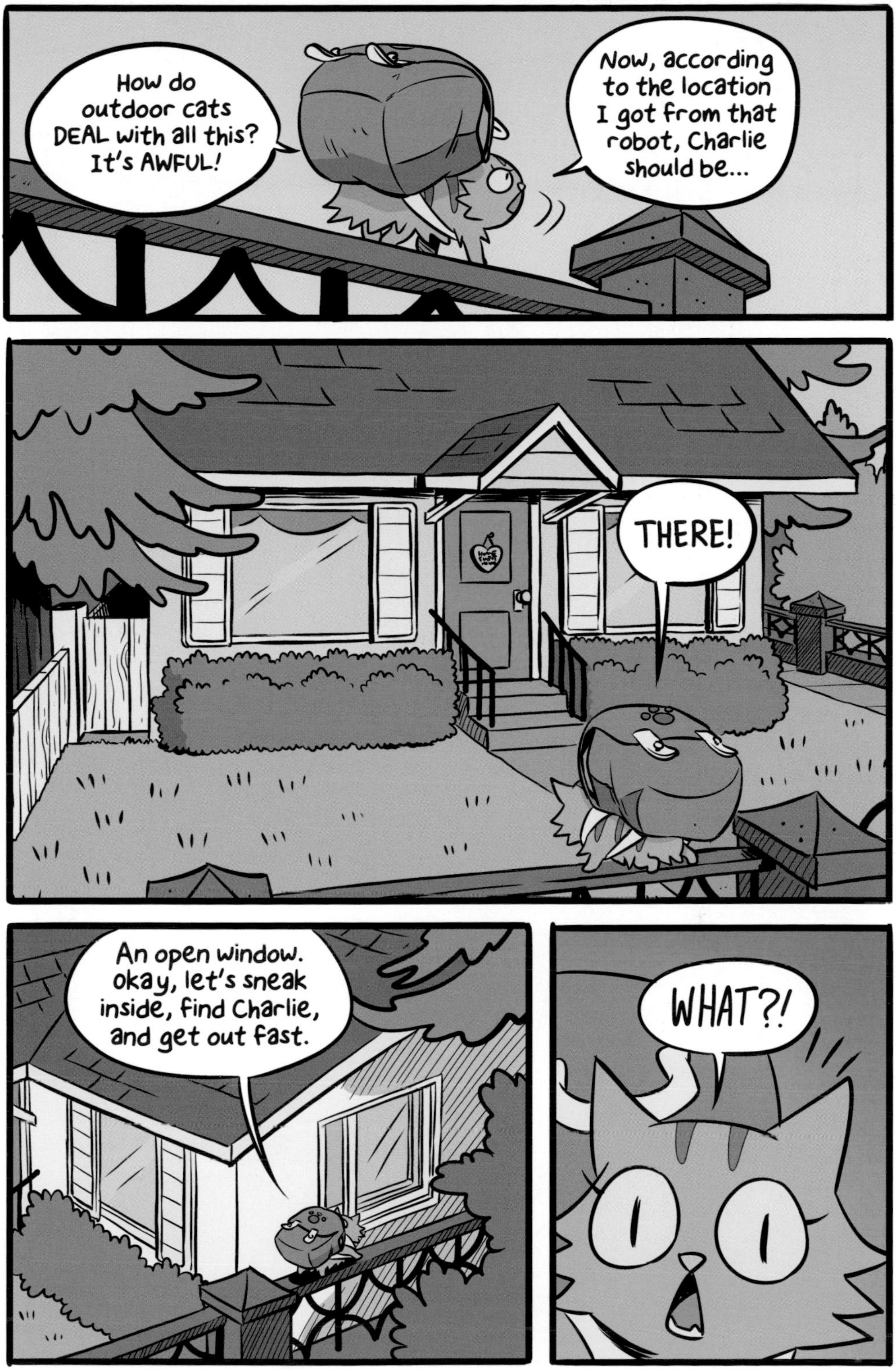
How do outdoor cats DEAL with all this? It's AWFUL!
Now, according to the location I got from that robot, Charlie should be...
THERE!
An open window. okay, let's sneak inside, find Charlie, and get out fast.
WHAT?!

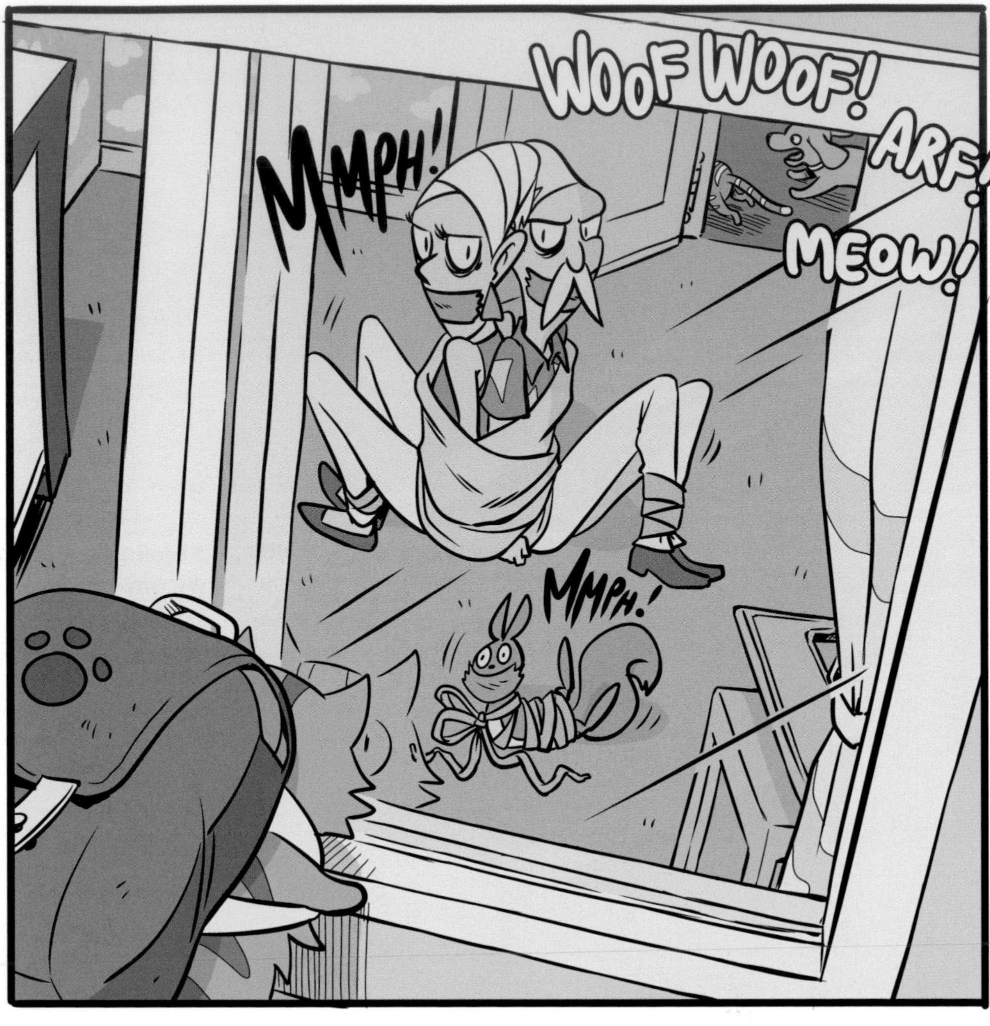
WOOF WOOF!
ARF!
MEOW!
MMPH!
MMPH!

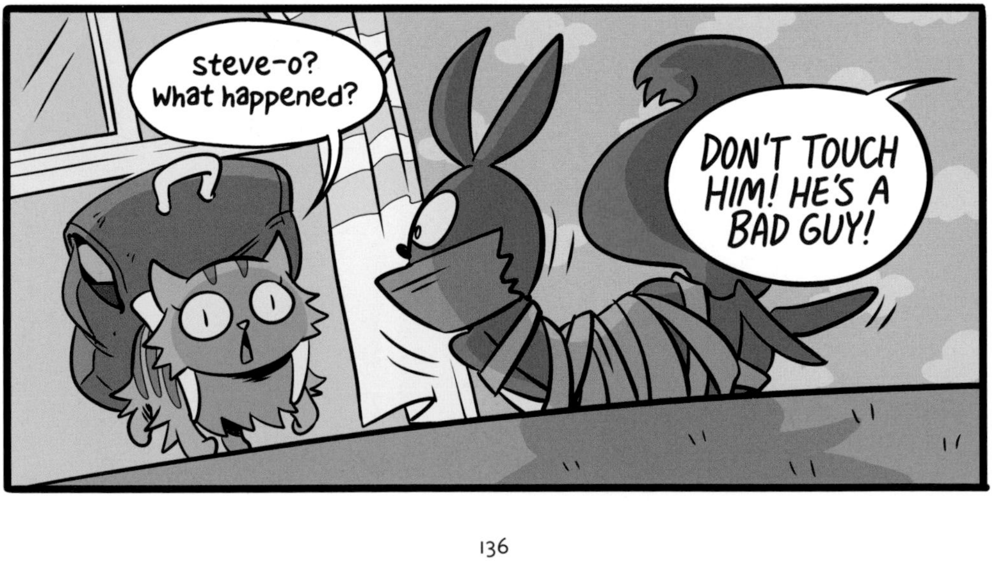
steve-o? What happened?
DON'T TOUCH HIM! HE'S A BAD GUY!

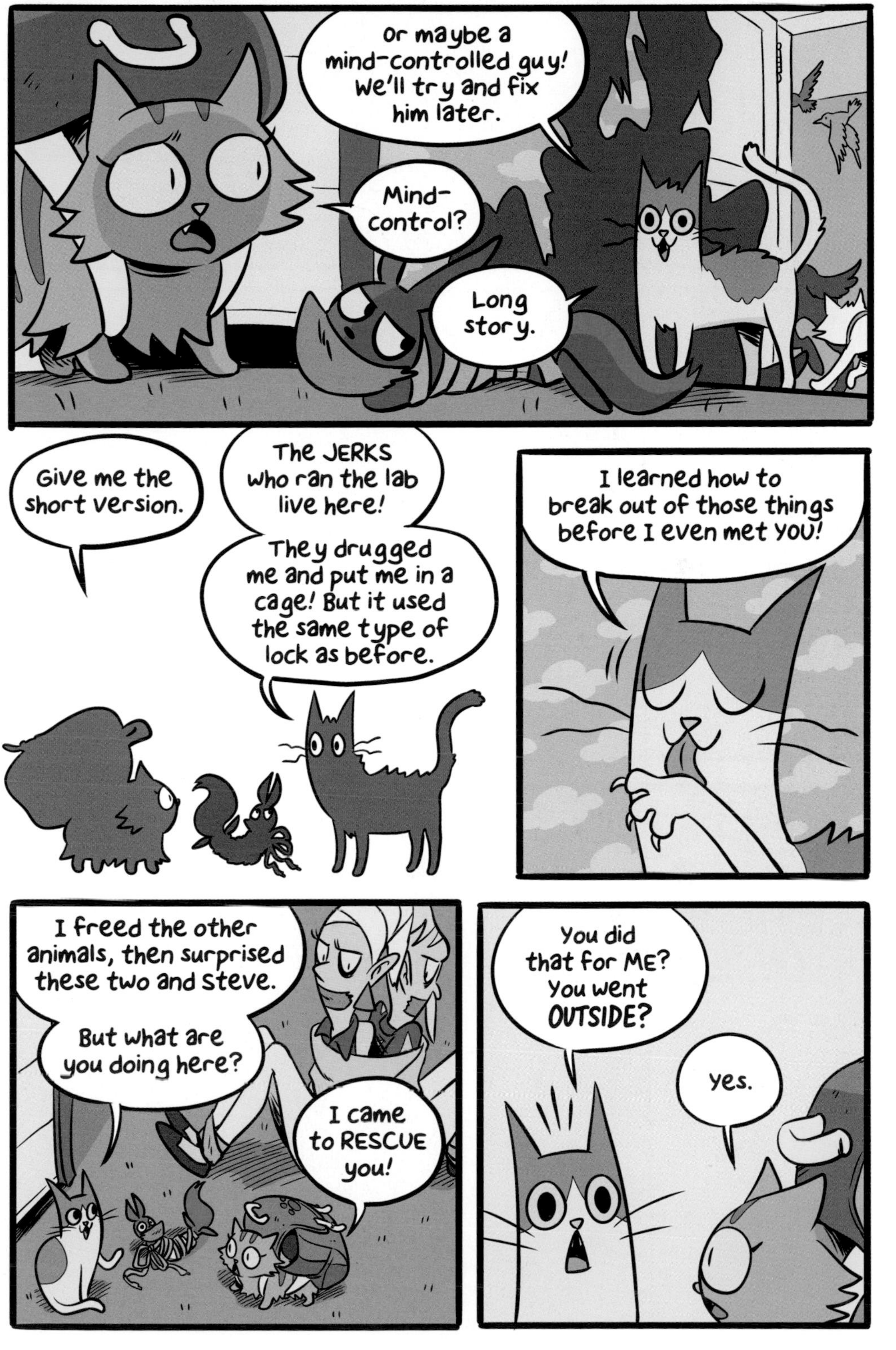
Or maybe a mind-controlled guy! We'll try and fix him later.
Mind-control?
Long story.
Give me the short version.
The JERKS who ran the lab live here!
They drugged me and put me in a cage! But it used the same type of lock as before.
I learned how to break out of those things before I even met YOU!
I freed the other animals, then surprised these two and Steve.
But what are you doing here?
I came to RESCUE you!
You did that for ME? You went OUTSIDE?
yes.

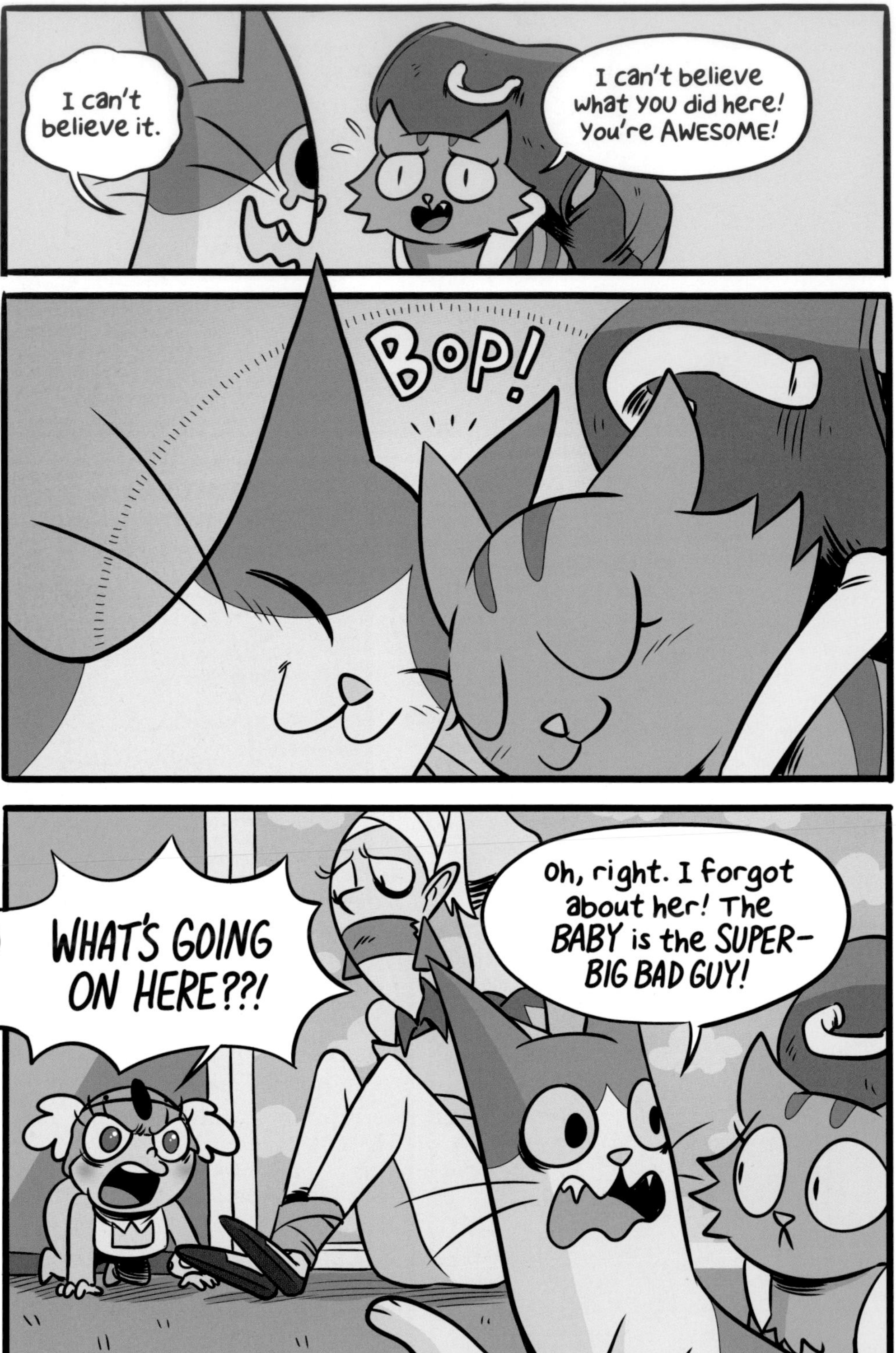
I can't believe it.
I can't believe what you did here! You're AWESOME!
BOP!
WHAT'S GOING ON HERE??!
Oh, right. I forgot about her! The BABY is the SUPER-BIG BAD GUY!

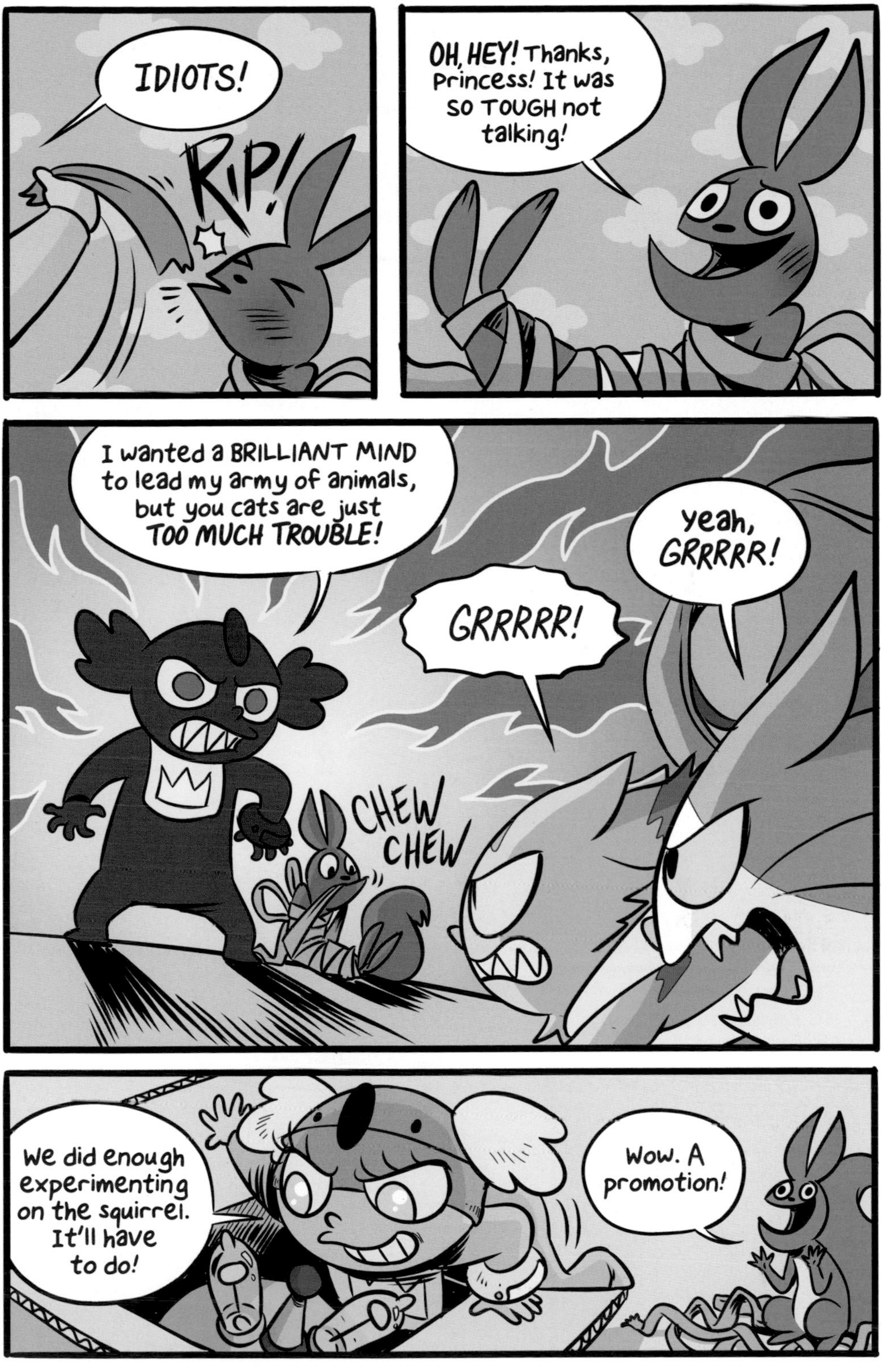
IDIOTS!
RIP!
OH, HEY! Thanks, Princess! It was so TOUGH not talking!
I wanted a BRILLIANT MIND to lead my army of animals, but you cats are just TOO MUCH TROUBLE!
yeah, GRRRRR!
GRRRRR!
CHEW CHEW
We did enough experimenting on the squirrel. It'll have to do!
Wow. A promotion!

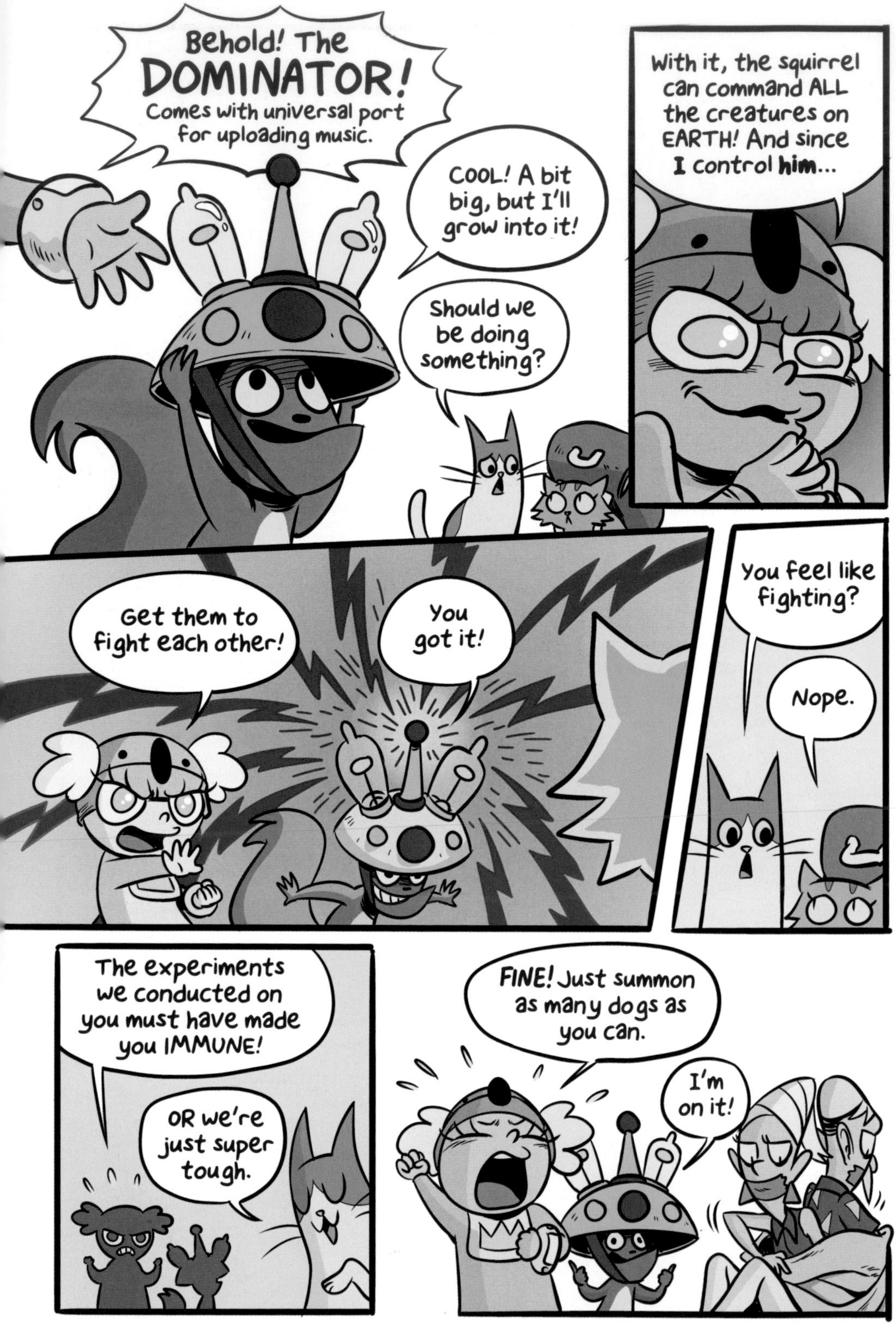
Behold! The DOMINATOR! Comes with universal port for uploading music.
COOL! A bit big, but I'll grow into it!
Should we be doing something?
With it, the squirrel can command ALL the creatures on EARTH! And since I control him...
Get them to fight each other!
You got it!
You feel like fighting?
Nope.
The experiments we conducted on you must have made you IMMUNE!
OR we're just super tough.
FINE! Just summon as many dogs as you can.
I'm on it!

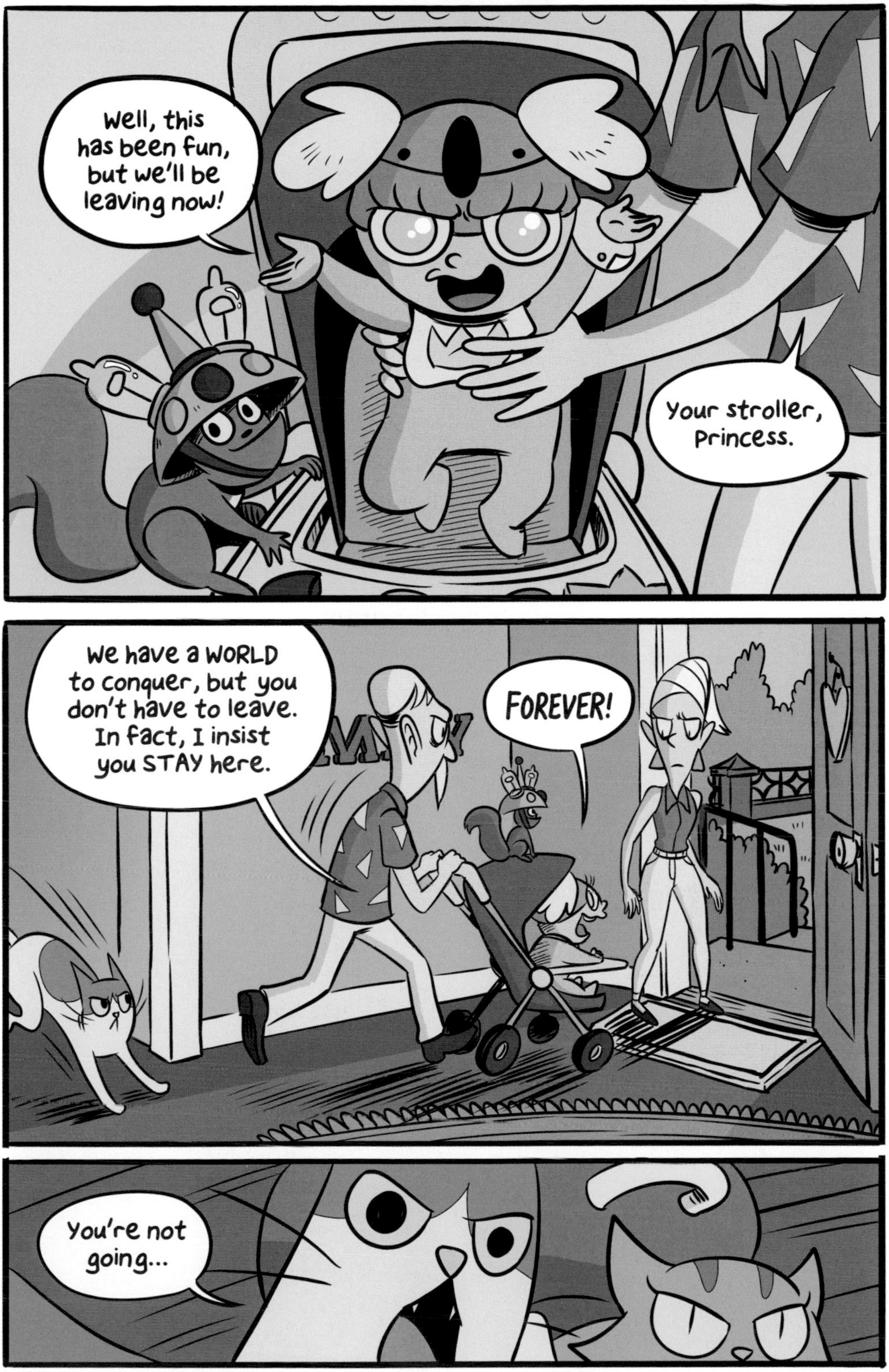
Well, this has been fun, but we'll be leaving now!
Your stroller, Princess.
We have a WORLD to conquer, but you don't have to leave. In fact, I insist you STAY here.
FOREVER!
You're not going...

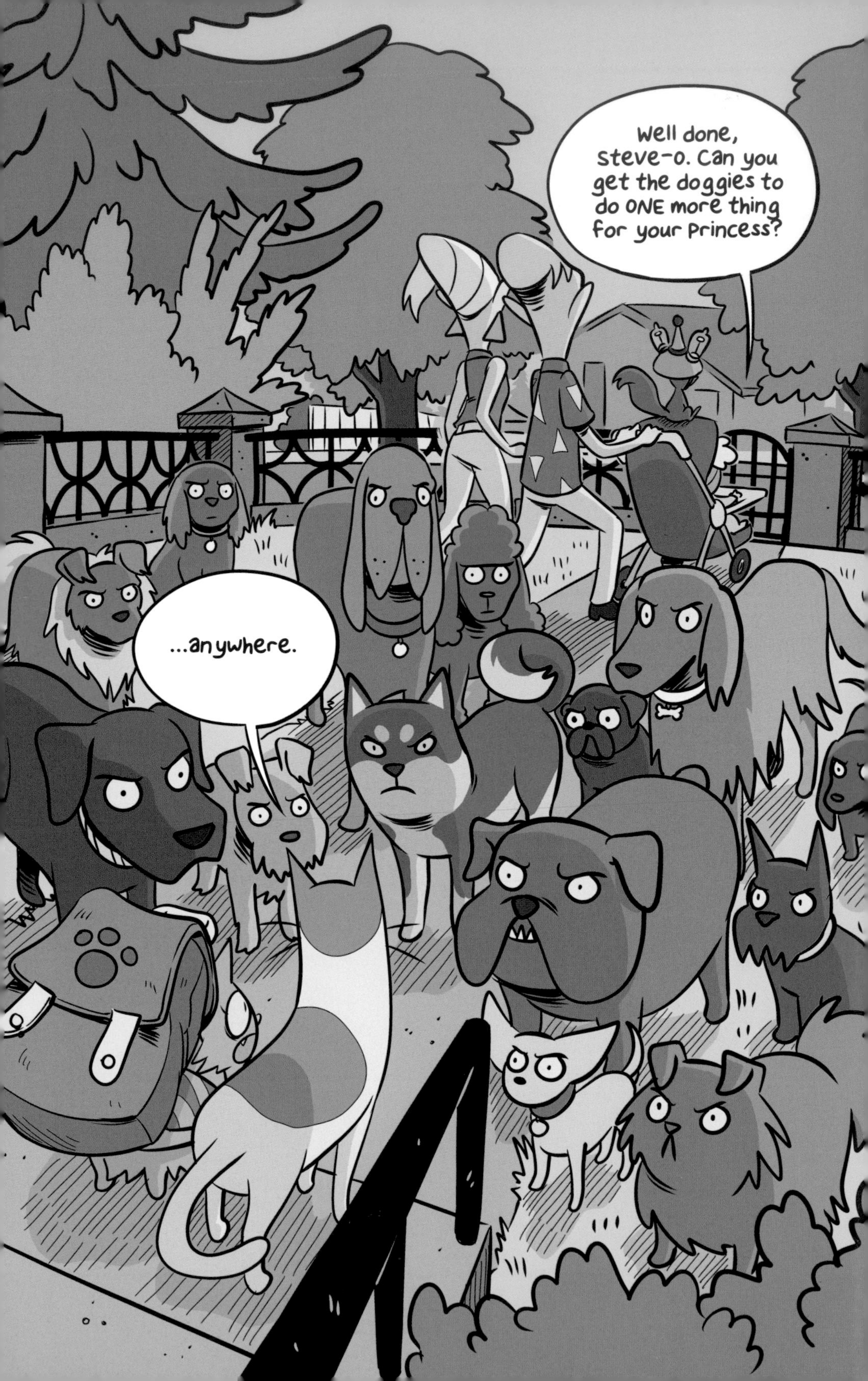
Well done, Steve-o. Can you get the doggies to do ONE more thing for your Princess?
...anywhere.

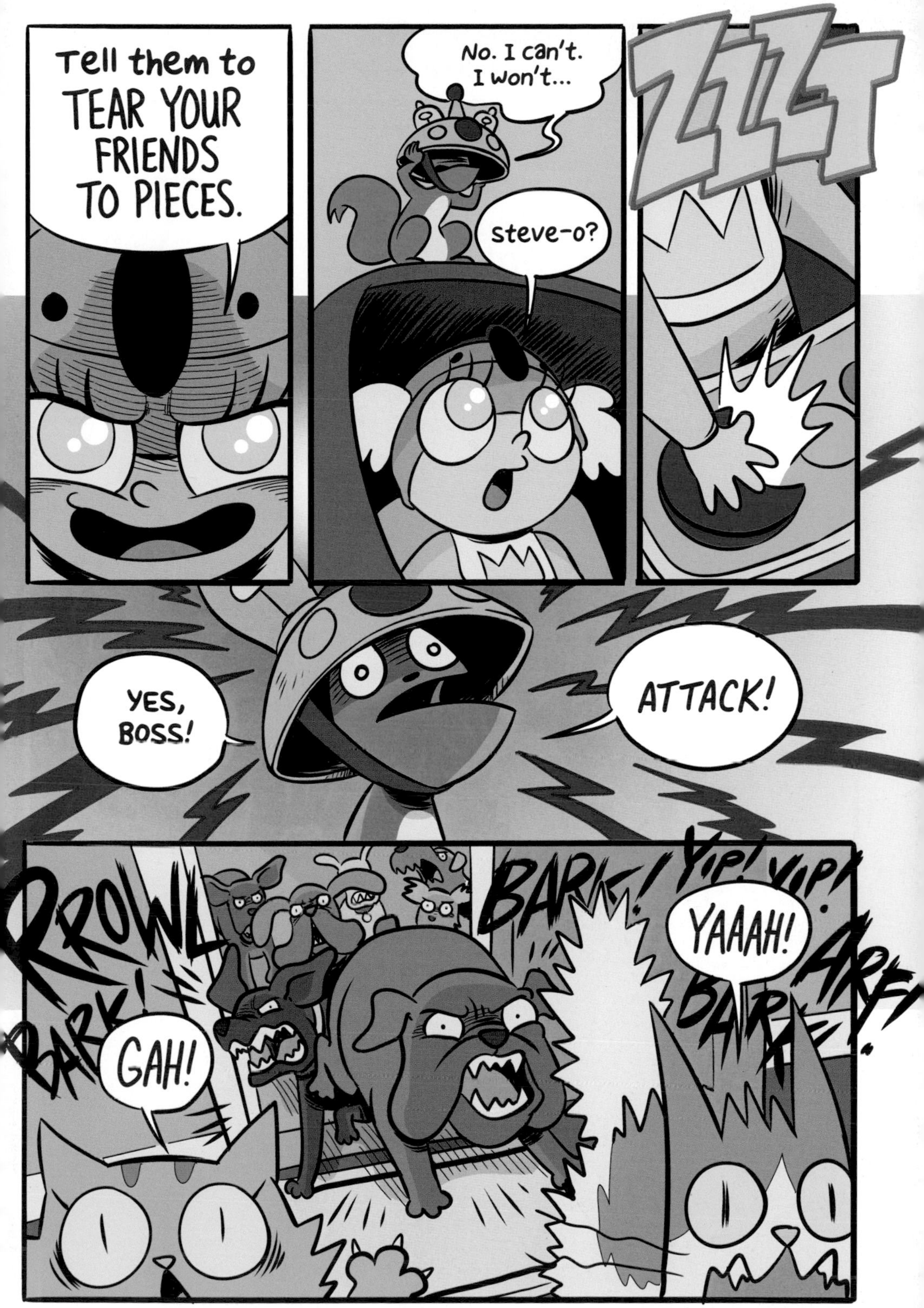
Tell them to TEAR YOUR FRIENDS TO PIECES.
No. I can't. I won't...
steve-o?
ZZZT
YES, BOSS!
ATTACK!
RROWL
BARK!
GAH!
BARK!
YIP! YIP!
YAAAH!
BARK!
ARF!

CHAPTER NINE

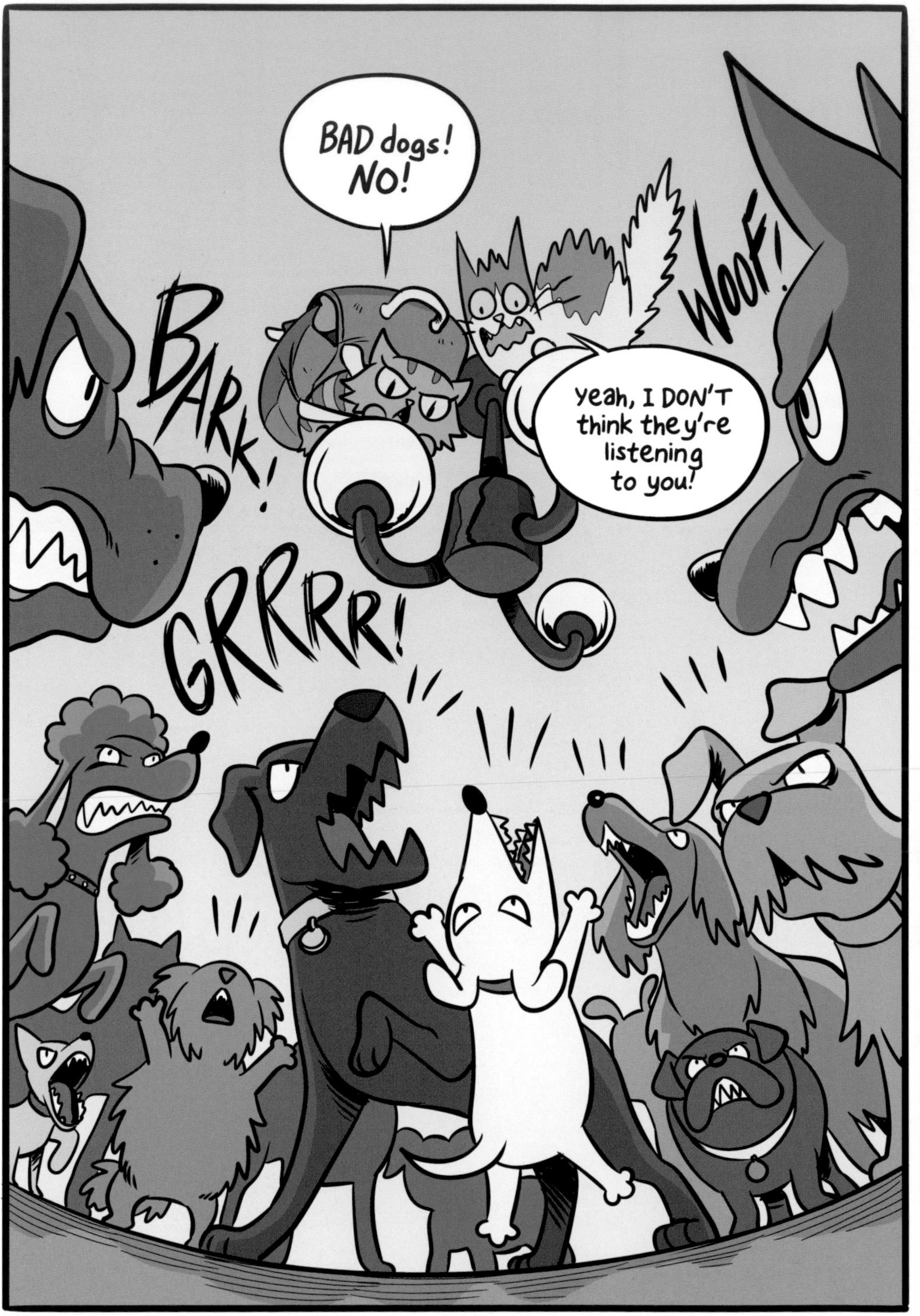

BAD dogs! NO!
BARK!
WOOF!
yeah, I DON'T think they're listening to you!
GRRRR!

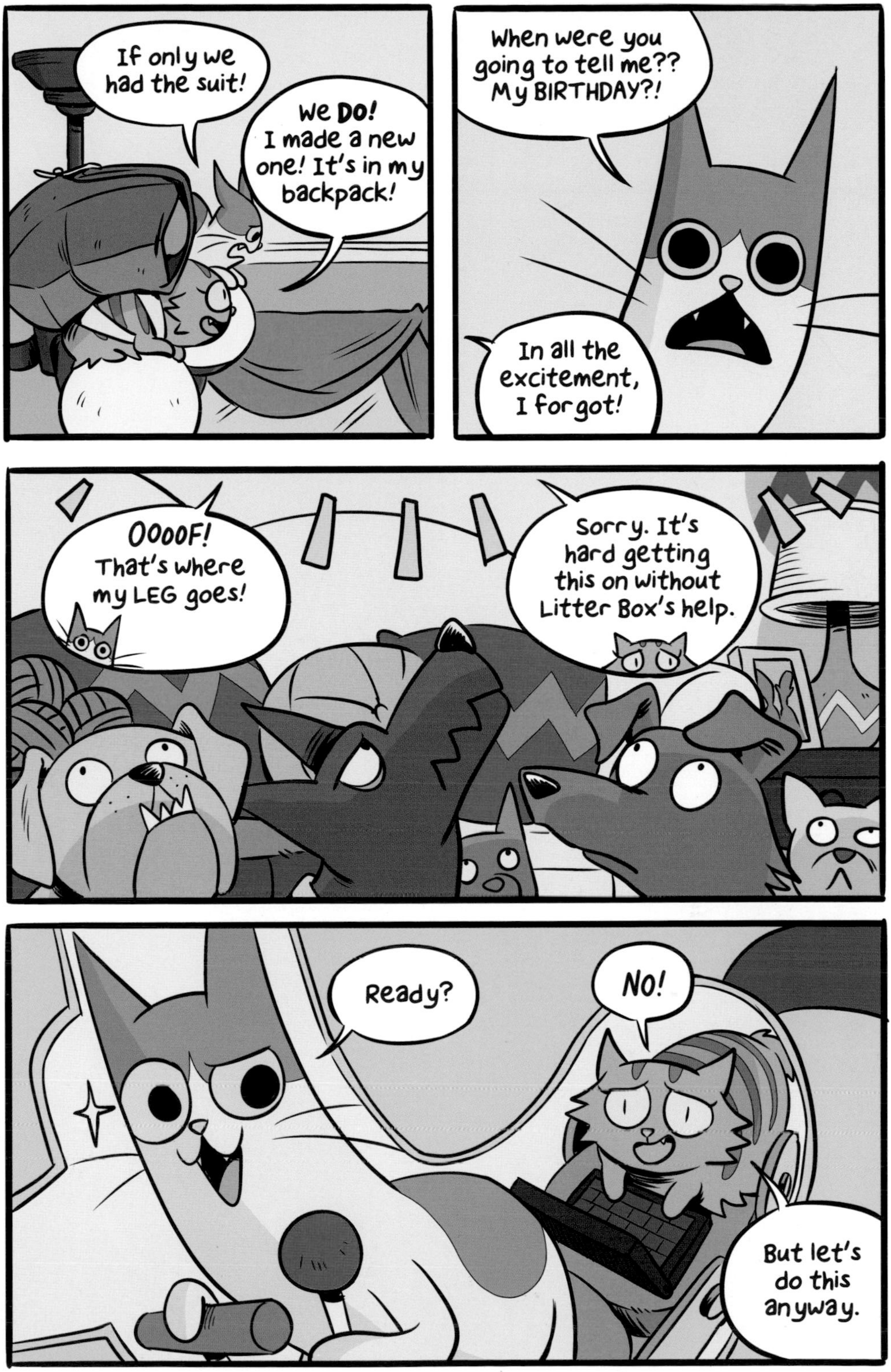
If only we had the suit!
We DO! I made a new one! It's in my backpack!
When were you going to tell me?? My BIRTHDAY?!
In all the excitement, I forgot!
OOOOF! That's where my LEG goes!
Sorry. It's hard getting this on without Litter Box's help.
Ready?
NO!
But let's do this anyway.

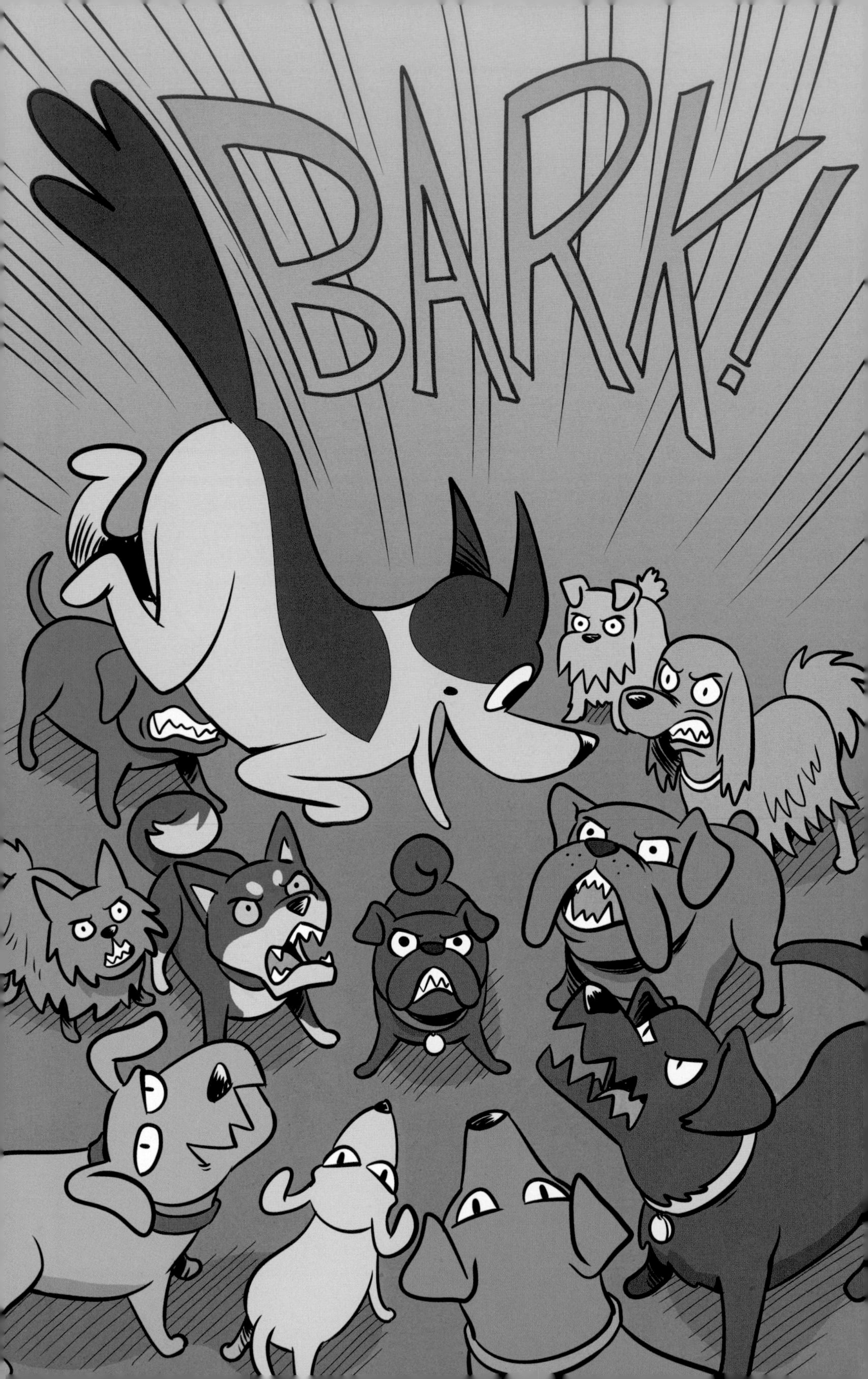
BARK!

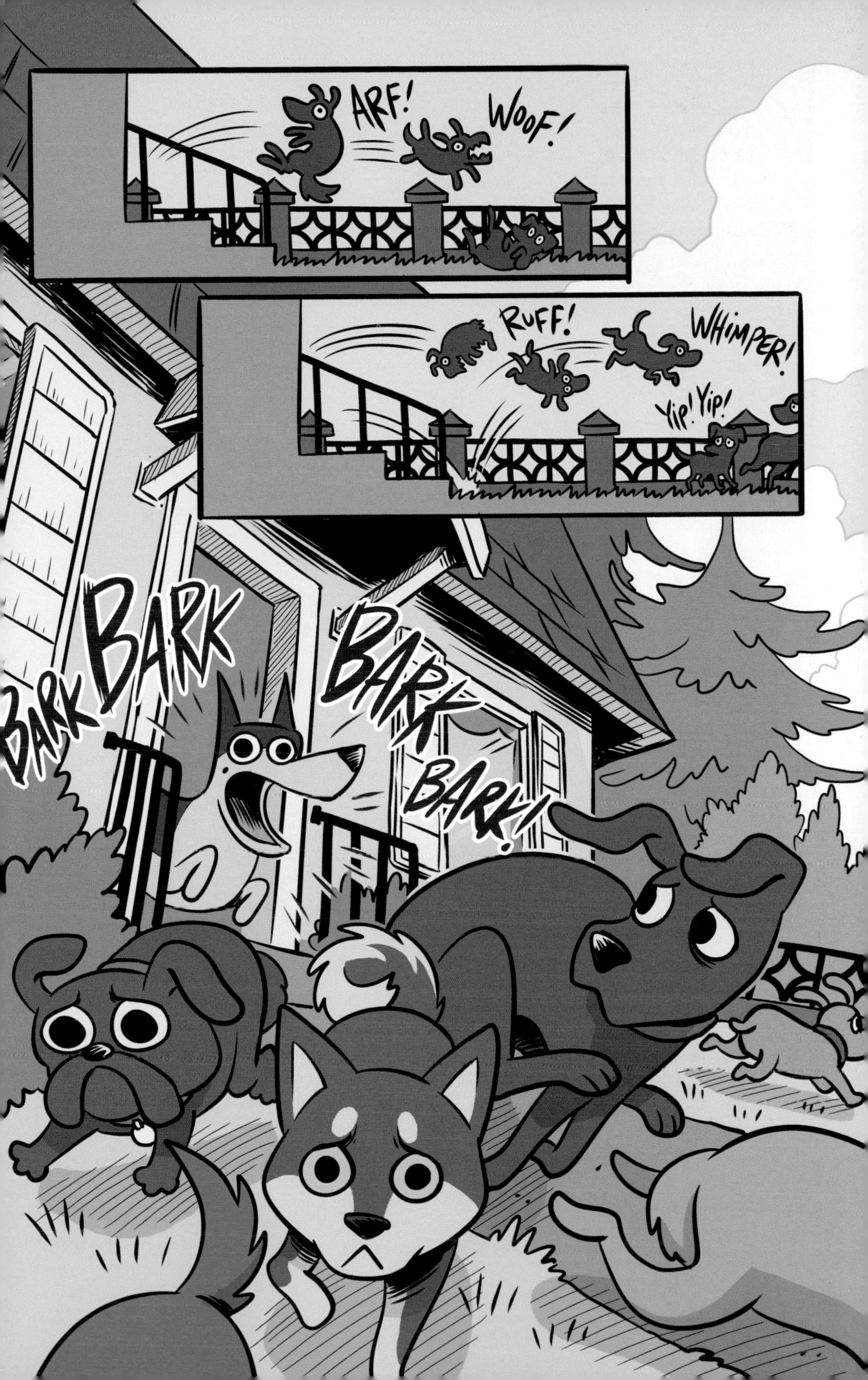
ARF!
WOOF!
RUFF!
WHIMPER!
YIP! YIP!
BARK BARK
BARK BARK BARK!

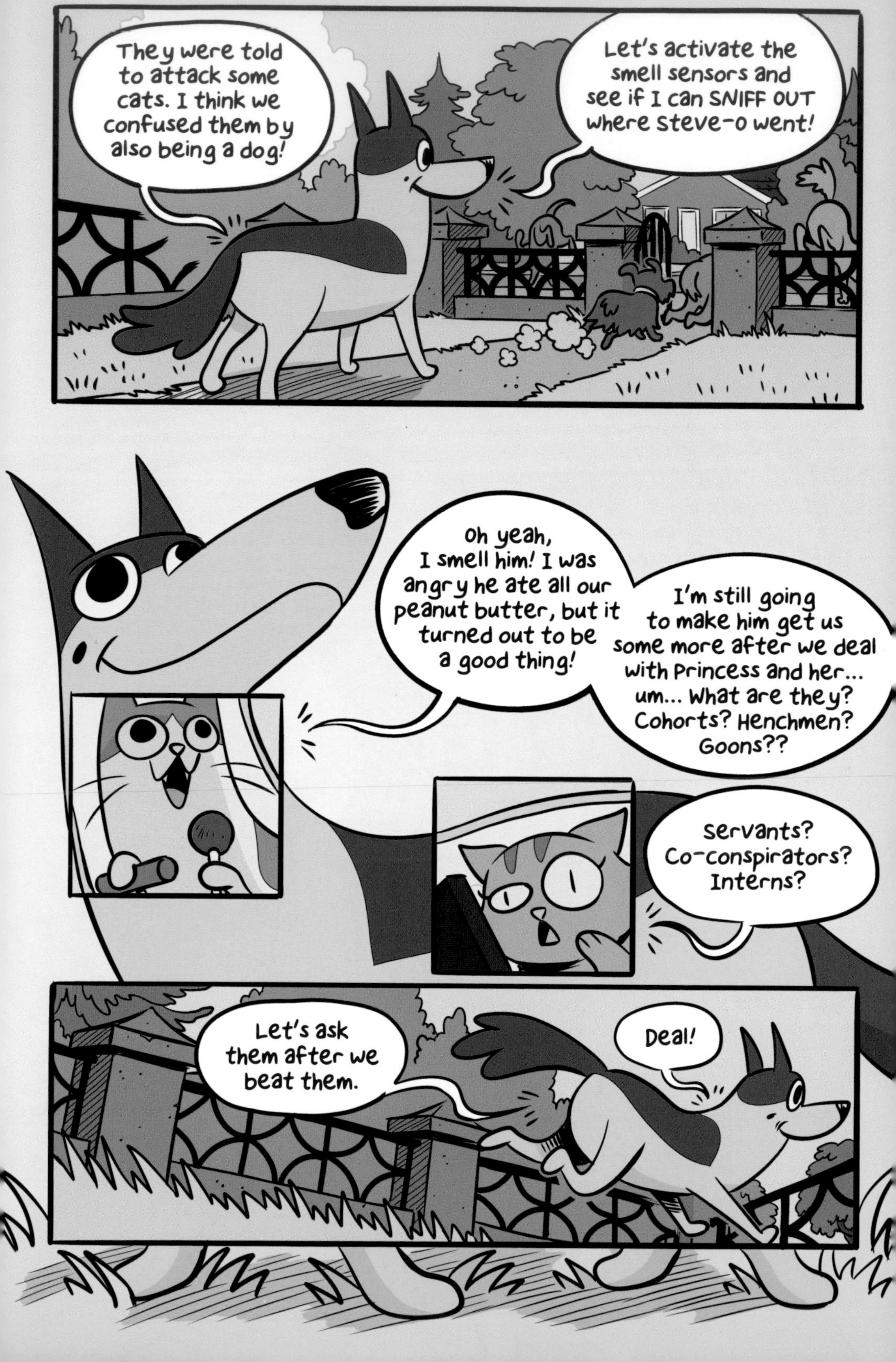
They were told to attack some cats. I think we confused them by also being a dog!
Let's activate the smell sensors and see if I can SNIFF OUT where Steve-o went!
Oh yeah, I smell him! I was angry he ate all our peanut butter, but it turned out to be a good thing!
I'm still going to make him get us some more after we deal with Princess and her... um... What are they? Cohorts? Henchmen? Goons??
Servants? Co-conspirators? Interns?
Let's ask them after we beat them.
Deal!

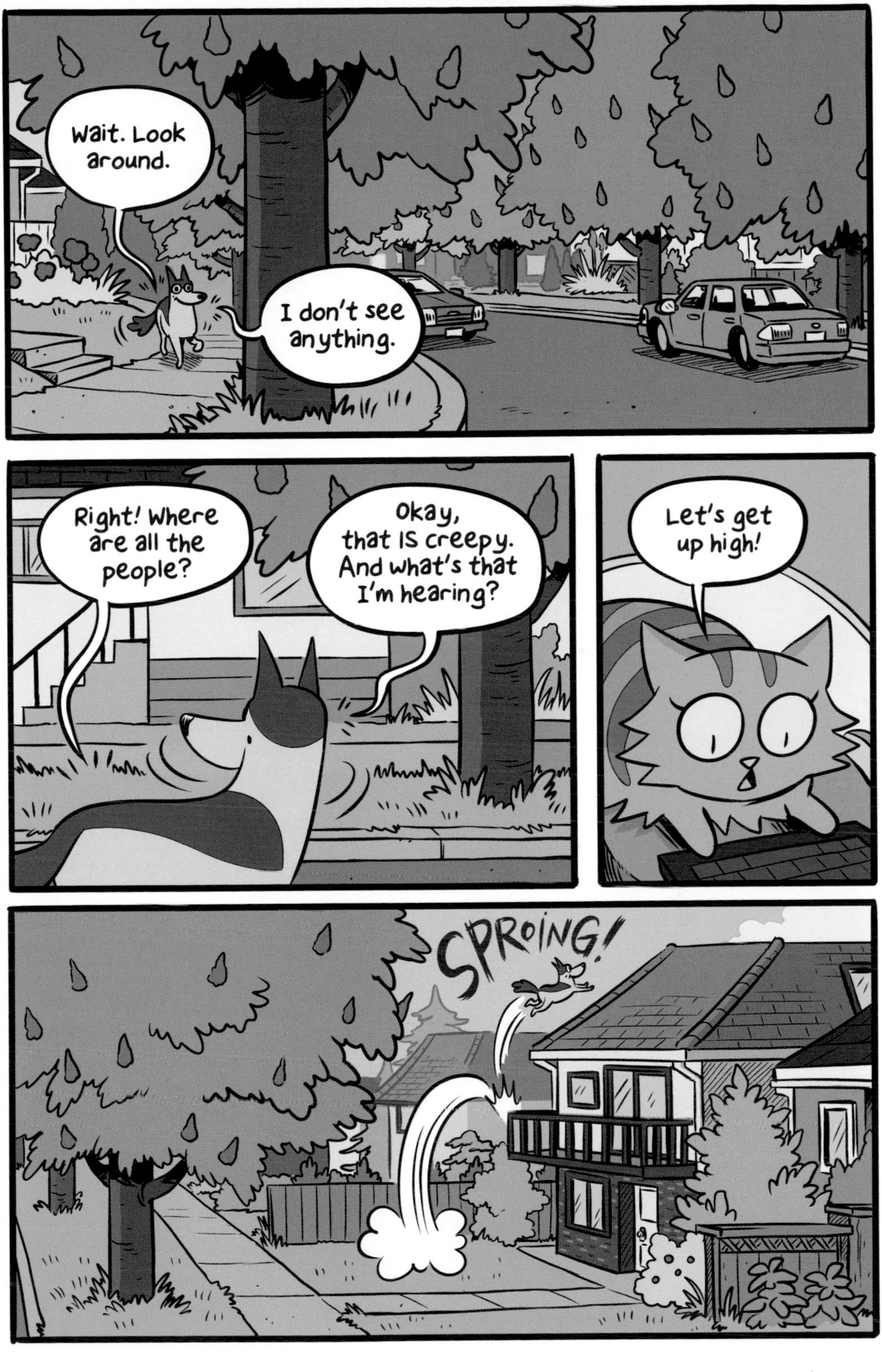

Wait. Look around.
I don't see anything.
Right! Where are all the people?
Okay, that IS creepy. And what's that I'm hearing?
Let's get up high!
SPROING!

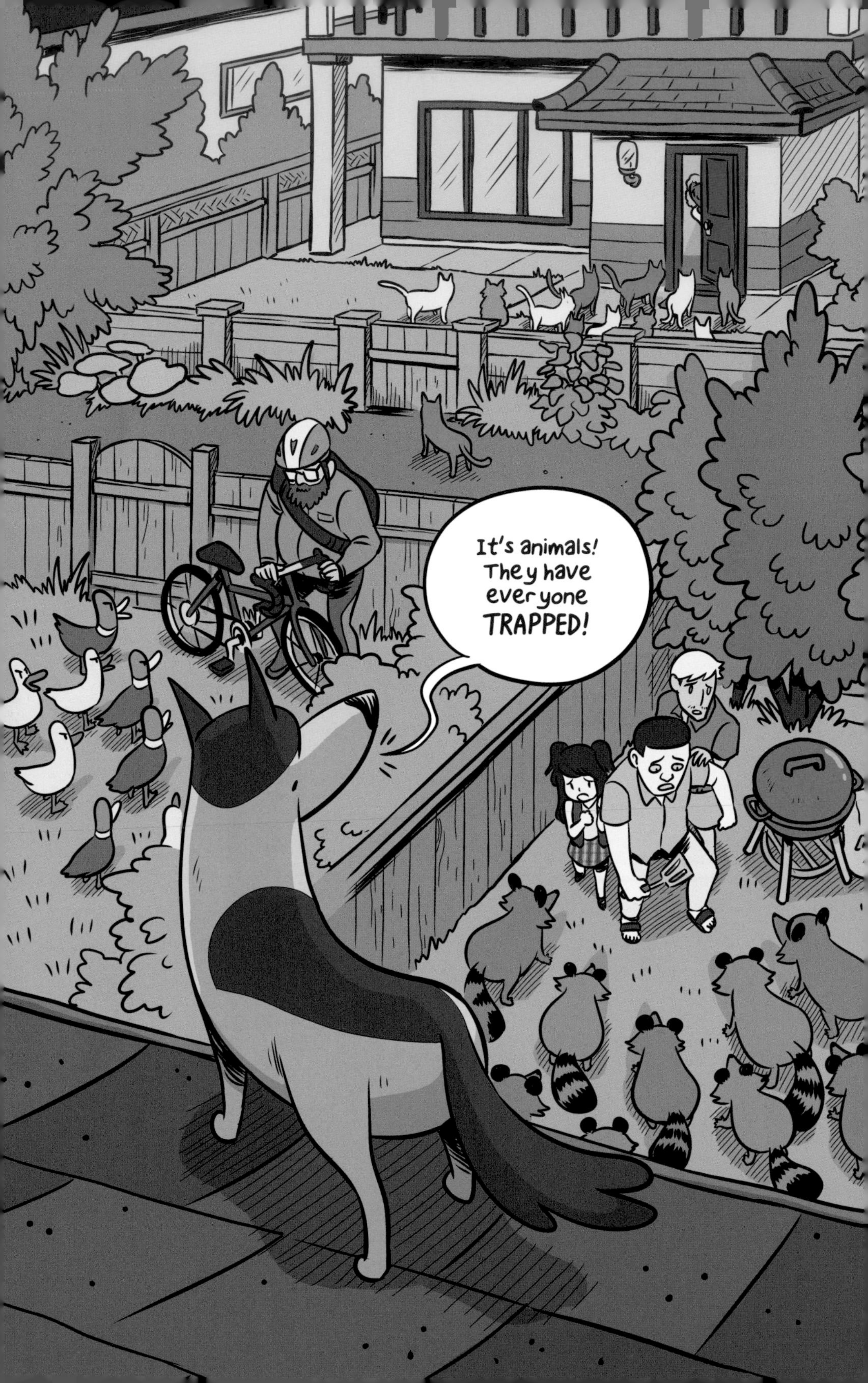
It's animals! They have everyone TRAPPED!

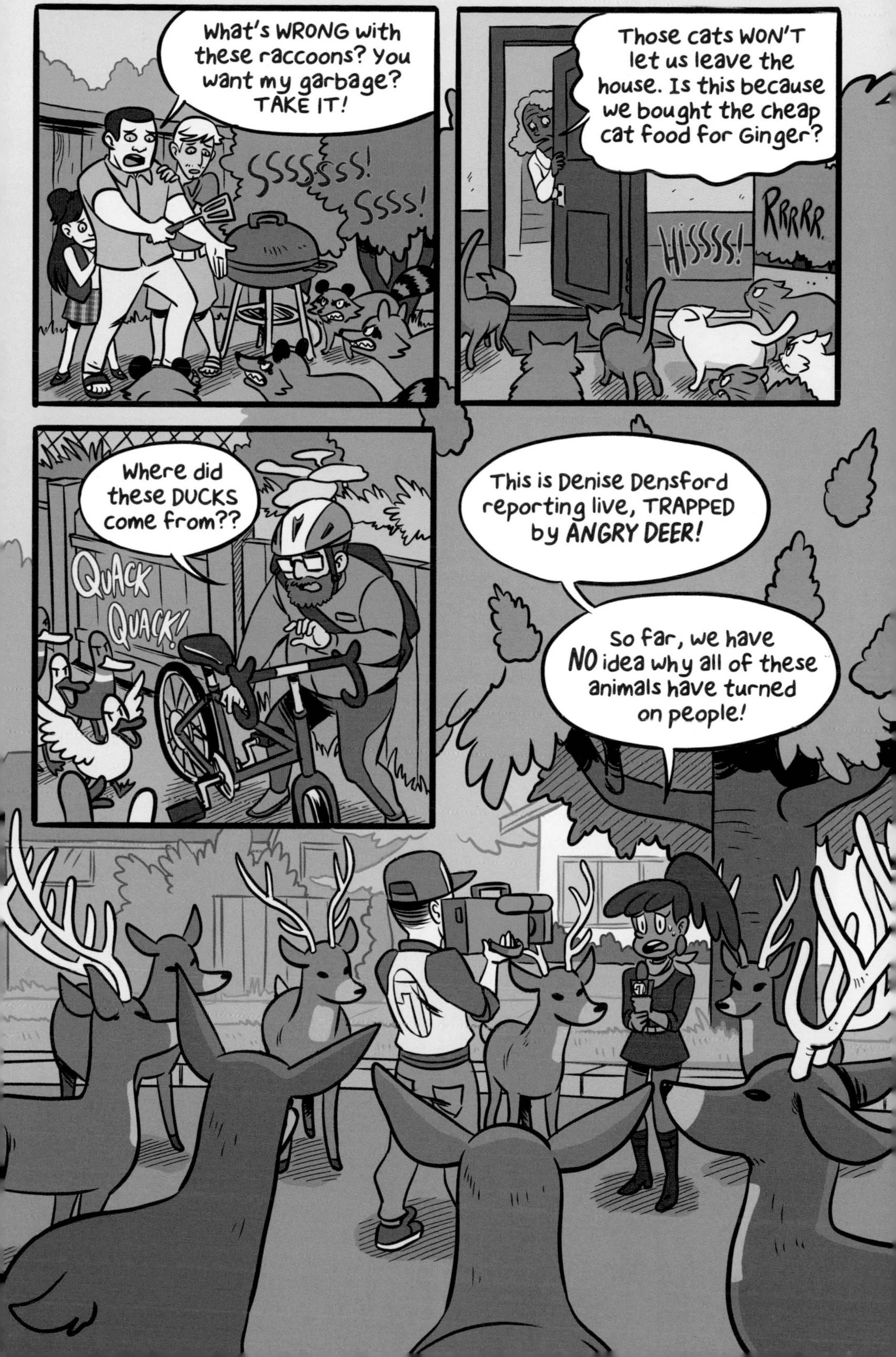
What's WRONG with these raccoons? You want my garbage? TAKE IT!
SSSSSSS!
SSSS!
Those cats WON'T let us leave the house. Is this because we bought the cheap cat food for Ginger?
HISSSSS!
RRRRR.
Where did these DUCKS come from??
QUACK
QUACK!
This is Denise Densford reporting live, TRAPPED by ANGRY DEER!
So far, we have NO idea why all of these animals have turned on people!

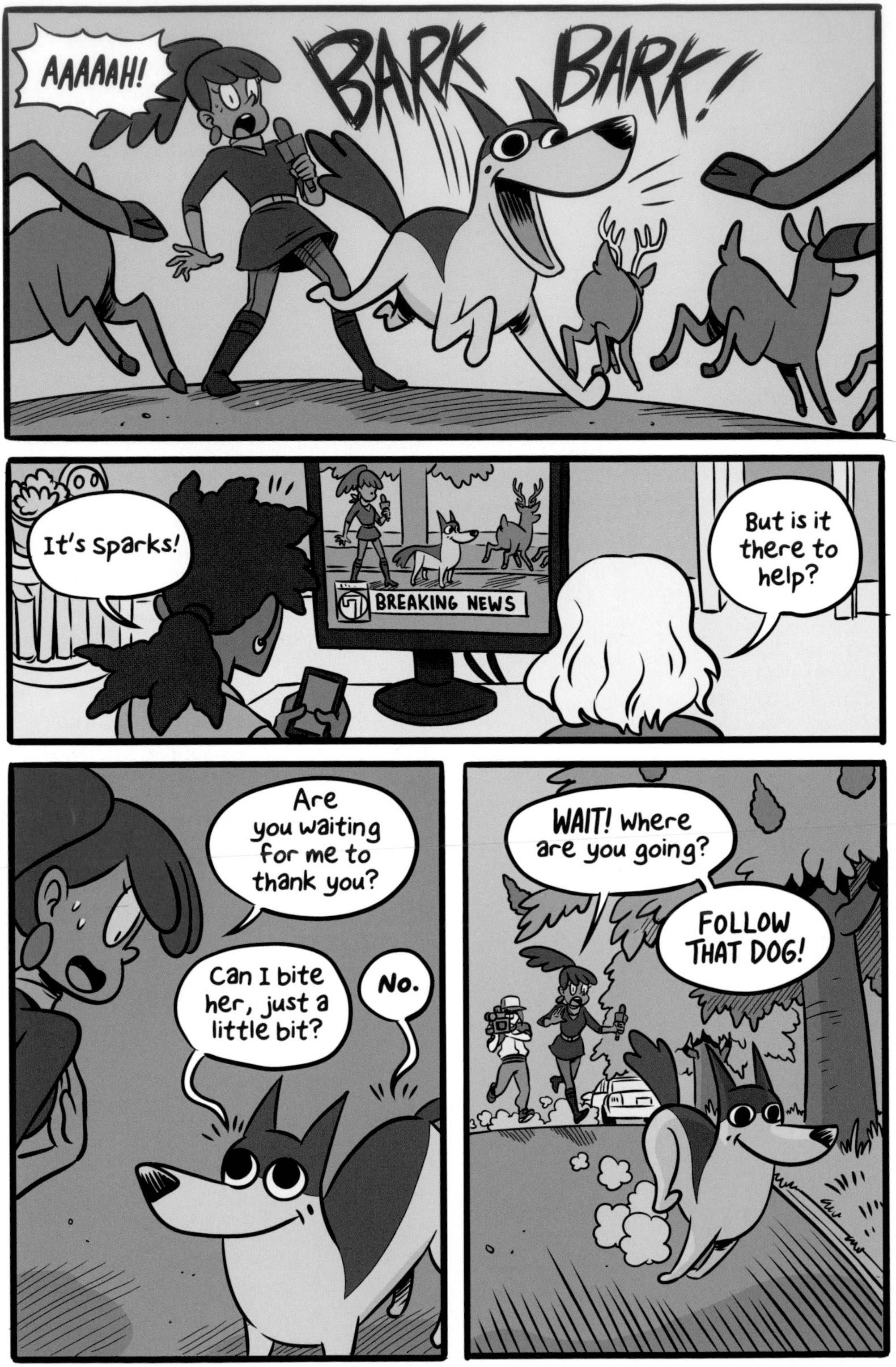
AAAAAH!
BARK BARK!
It's Sparks!
BREAKING NEWS
But is it there to help?
Are you waiting for me to thank you?
Can I bite her, just a little bit?
No.
WAIT! Where are you going?
FOLLOW THAT DOG!

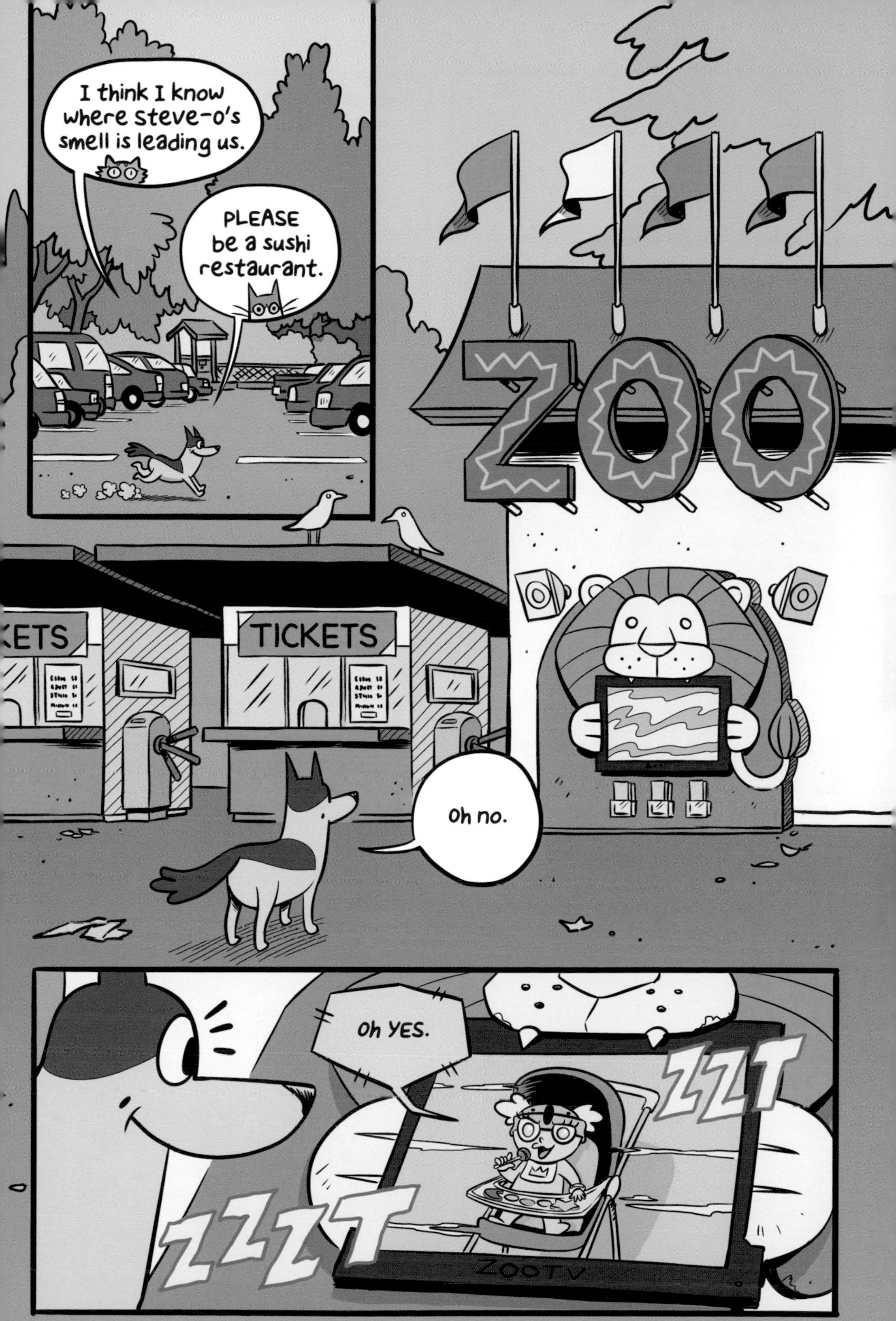
I think I know where steve-o's smell is leading us.
PLEASE be a sushi restaurant.
ZOO
TICKETS
Oh no.
Oh YES.
ZZZT
ZZZT
ZOOTV

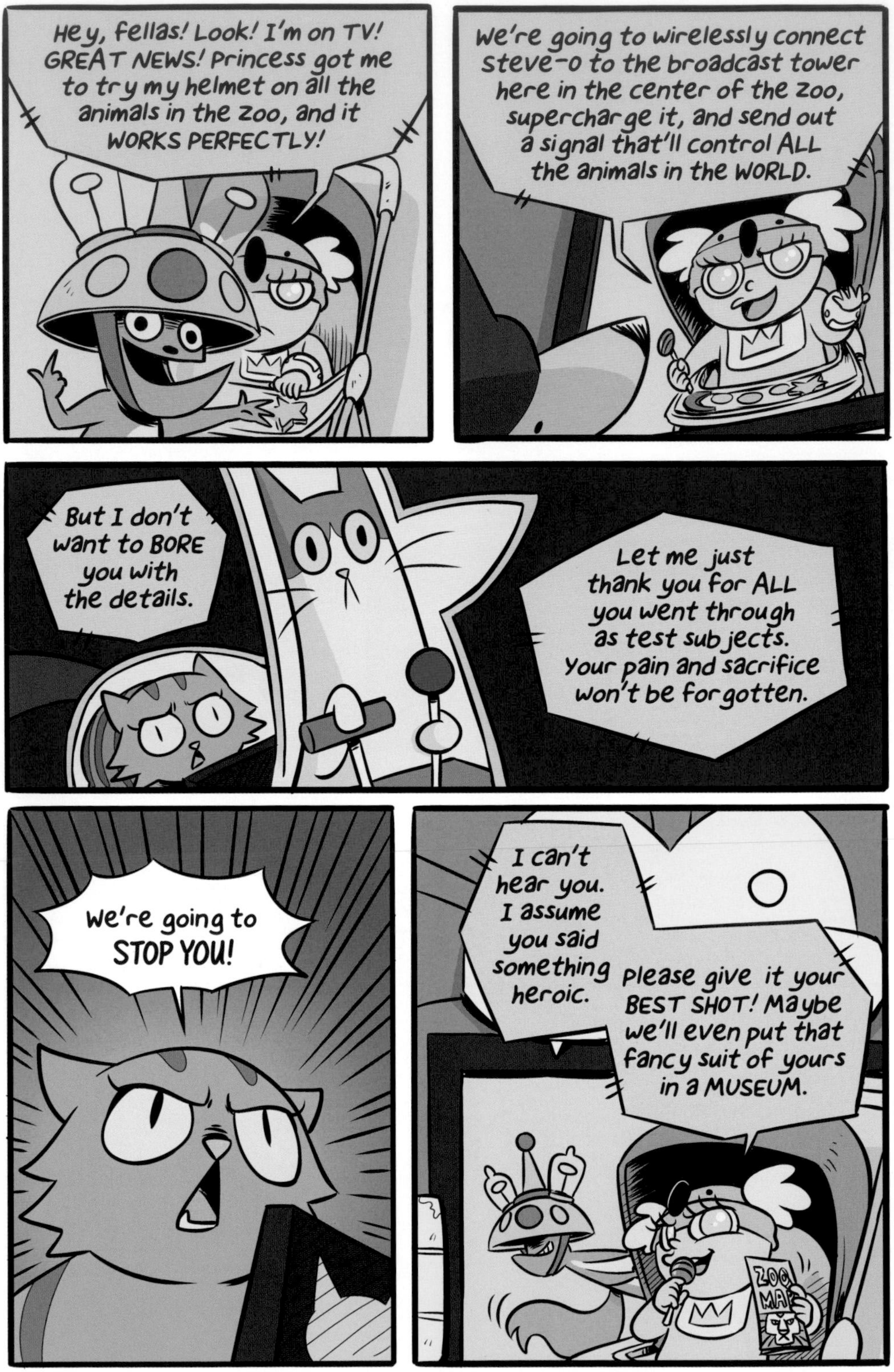
Hey, fellas! Look! I'm on TV! GREAT NEWS! Princess got me to try my helmet on all the animals in the zoo, and it WORKS PERFECTLY!
We're going to wirelessly connect Steve-O to the broadcast tower here in the center of the zoo, supercharge it, and send out a signal that'll control ALL the animals in the WORLD.
But I don't want to BORE you with the details.
Let me just thank you for ALL you went through as test subjects. Your pain and sacrifice won't be forgotten.
We're going to STOP YOU!
I can't hear you. I assume you said something heroic.
Please give it your BEST SHOT! Maybe we'll even put that fancy suit of yours in a MUSEUM.
ZOO MA

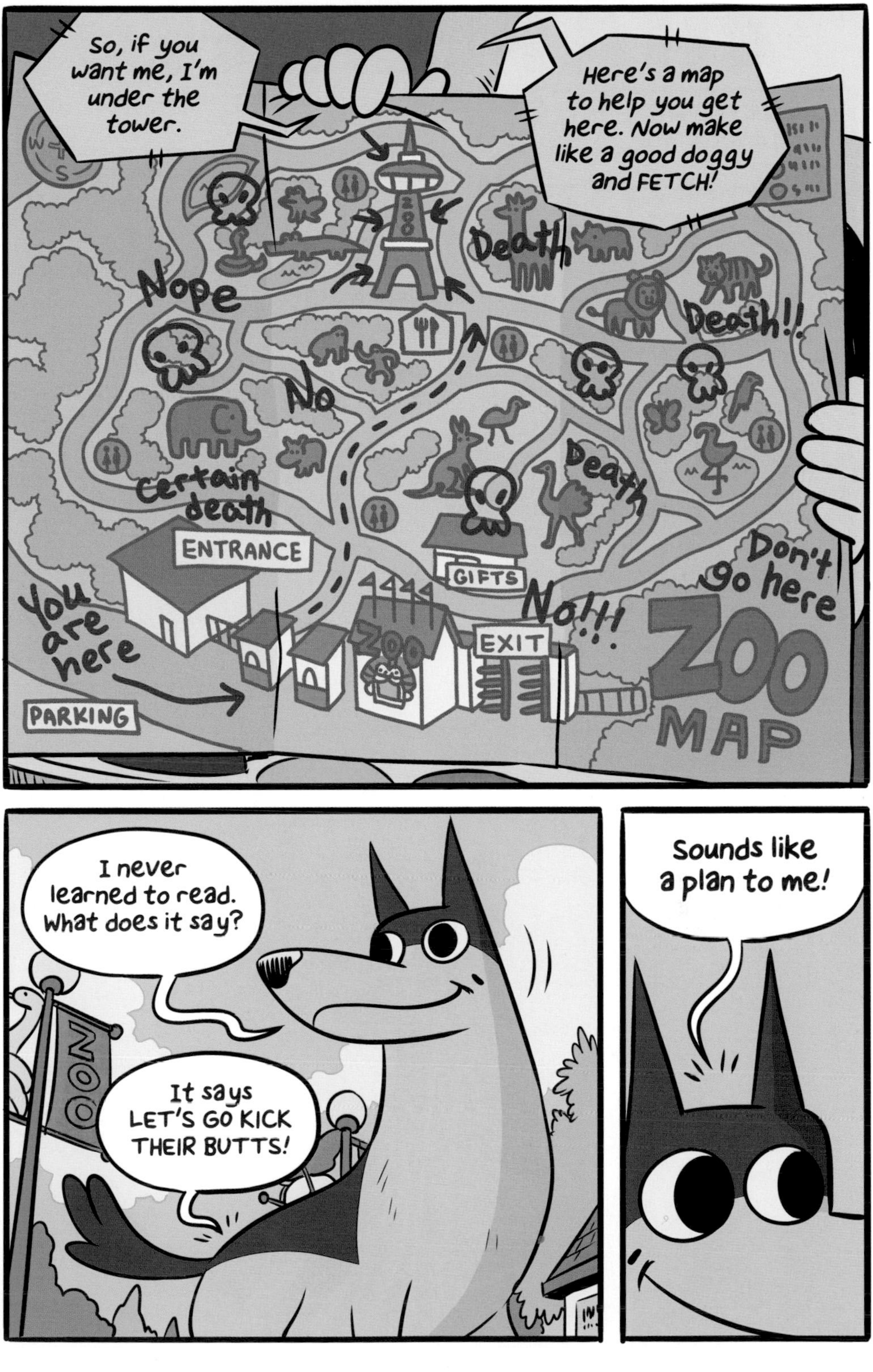

So, if you want me, I'm under the tower.
Here's a map to help you get here. Now make like a good doggy and FETCH!
Nope
Death
Death!!
No
Death
Certain death
ENTRANCE
GIFTS
Don't go here
You are here
No!!!
ZOO
EXIT
ZOO MAP
PARKING
I never learned to read. What does it say?
ZOO
It says LET'S GO KICK THEIR BUTTS!
Sounds like a plan to me!

CHAPTER TEN

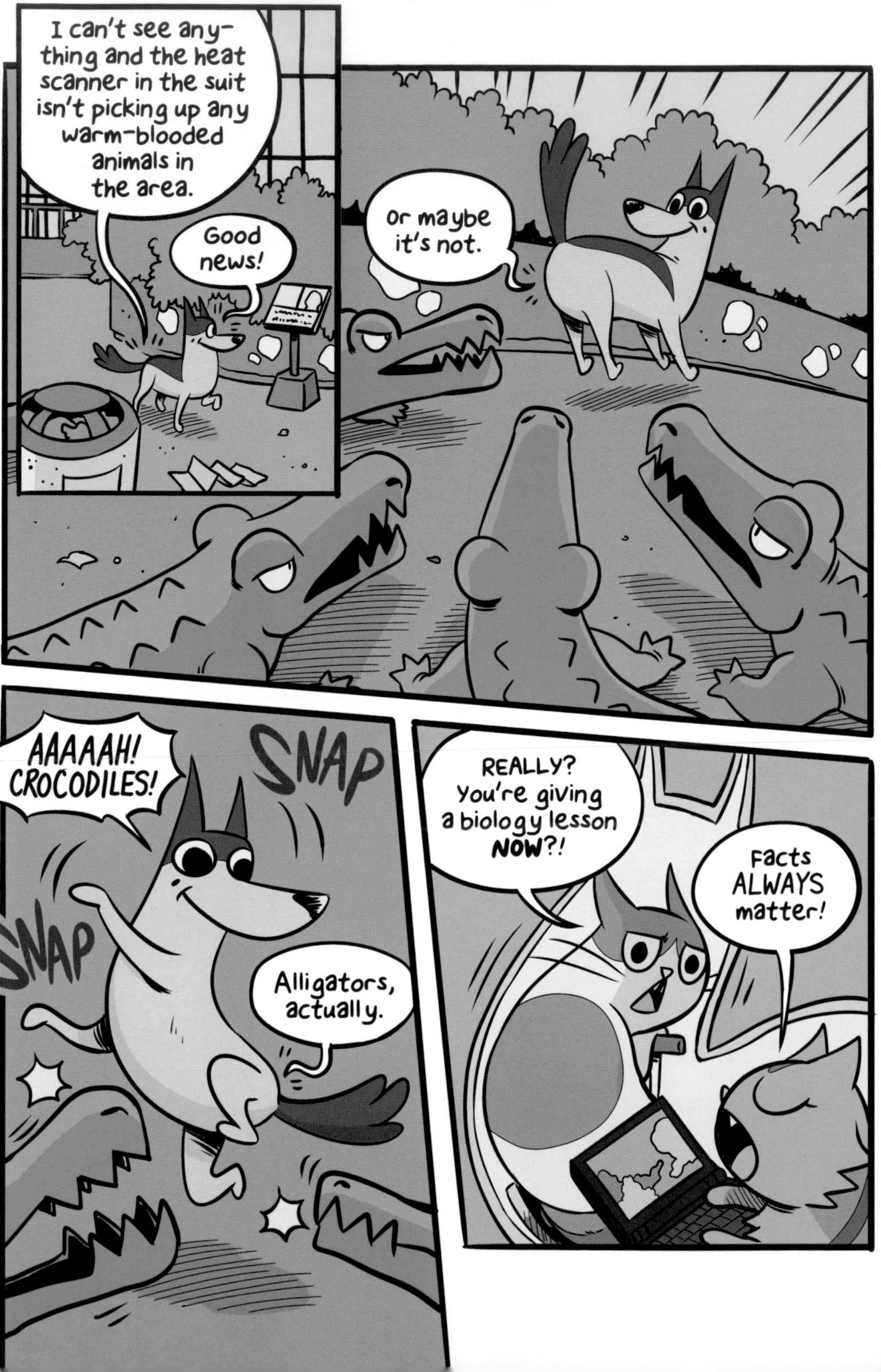
I can't see anything and the heat scanner in the suit isn't picking up any warm-blooded animals in the area.
Good news!
Or maybe it's not.
AAAAAH! CROCODILES!
SNAP
SNAP
Alligators, actually.
REALLY? You're giving a biology lesson NOW?!
Facts ALWAYS matter!

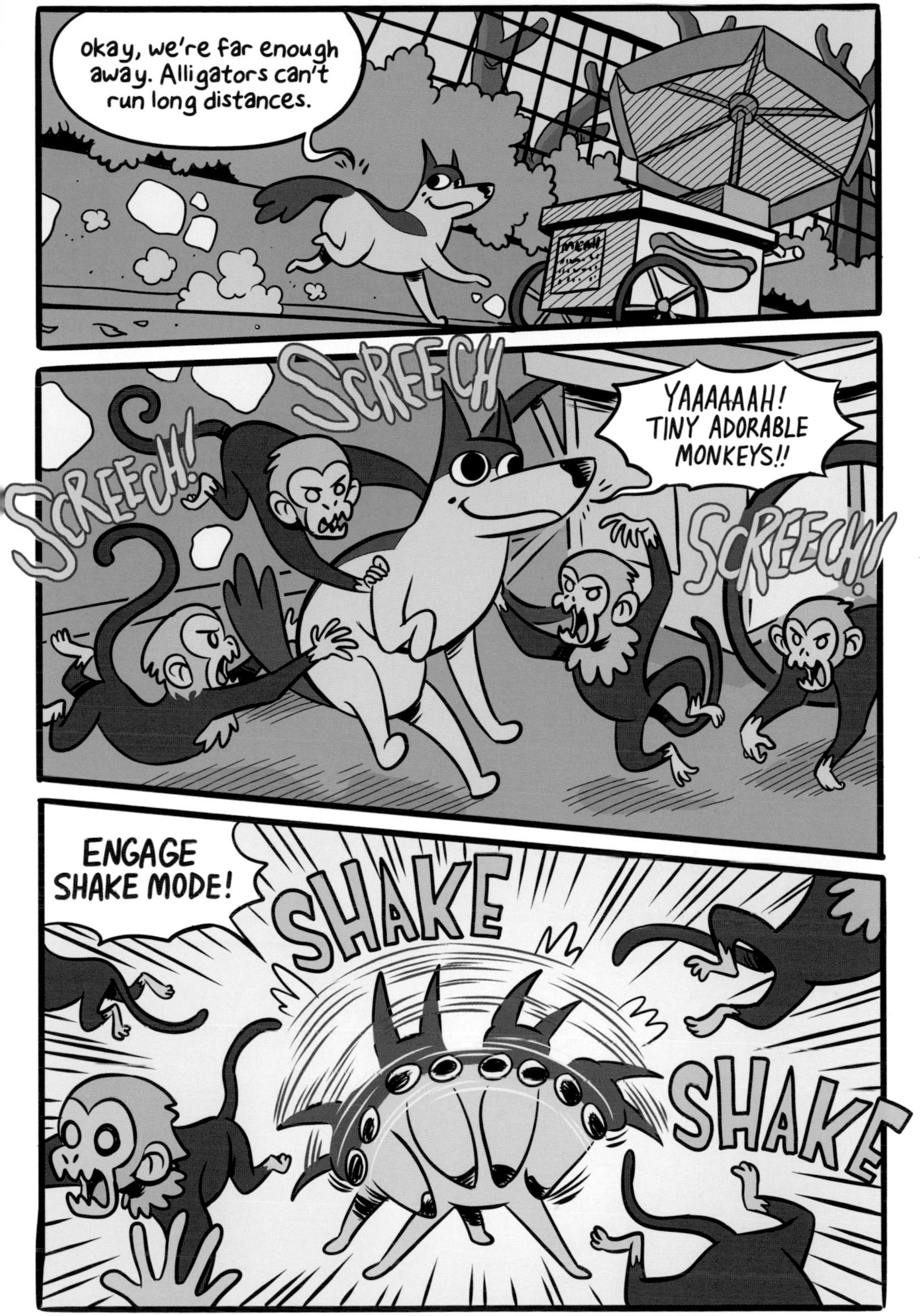
okay, we're far enough away. Alligators can't run long distances.
SCREECH
SCREECH!
YAAAAAAH! TINY ADORABLE MONKEYS!!
SCREECH!!
ENGAGE SHAKE MODE!
SHAKE
SHAKE

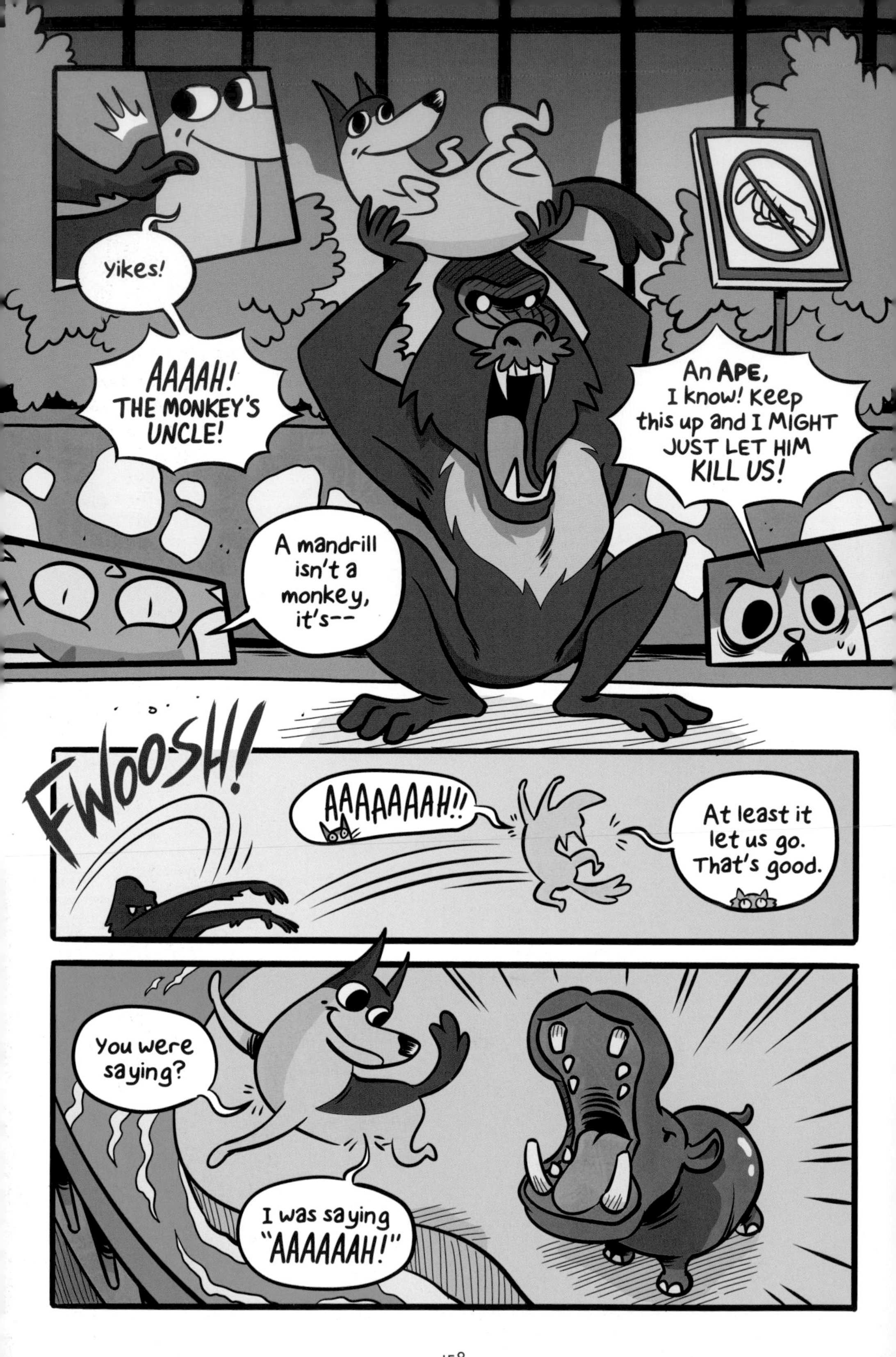
yikes!
AAAAH! THE MONKEY'S UNCLE!
A mandrill isn't a monkey, it's--
An APE, I know! Keep this up and I MIGHT JUST LET HIM KILL US!
FWOOSH!
AAAAAAAH!!
At least it let us go. That's good.
You were saying?
I was saying "AAAAAAH!"

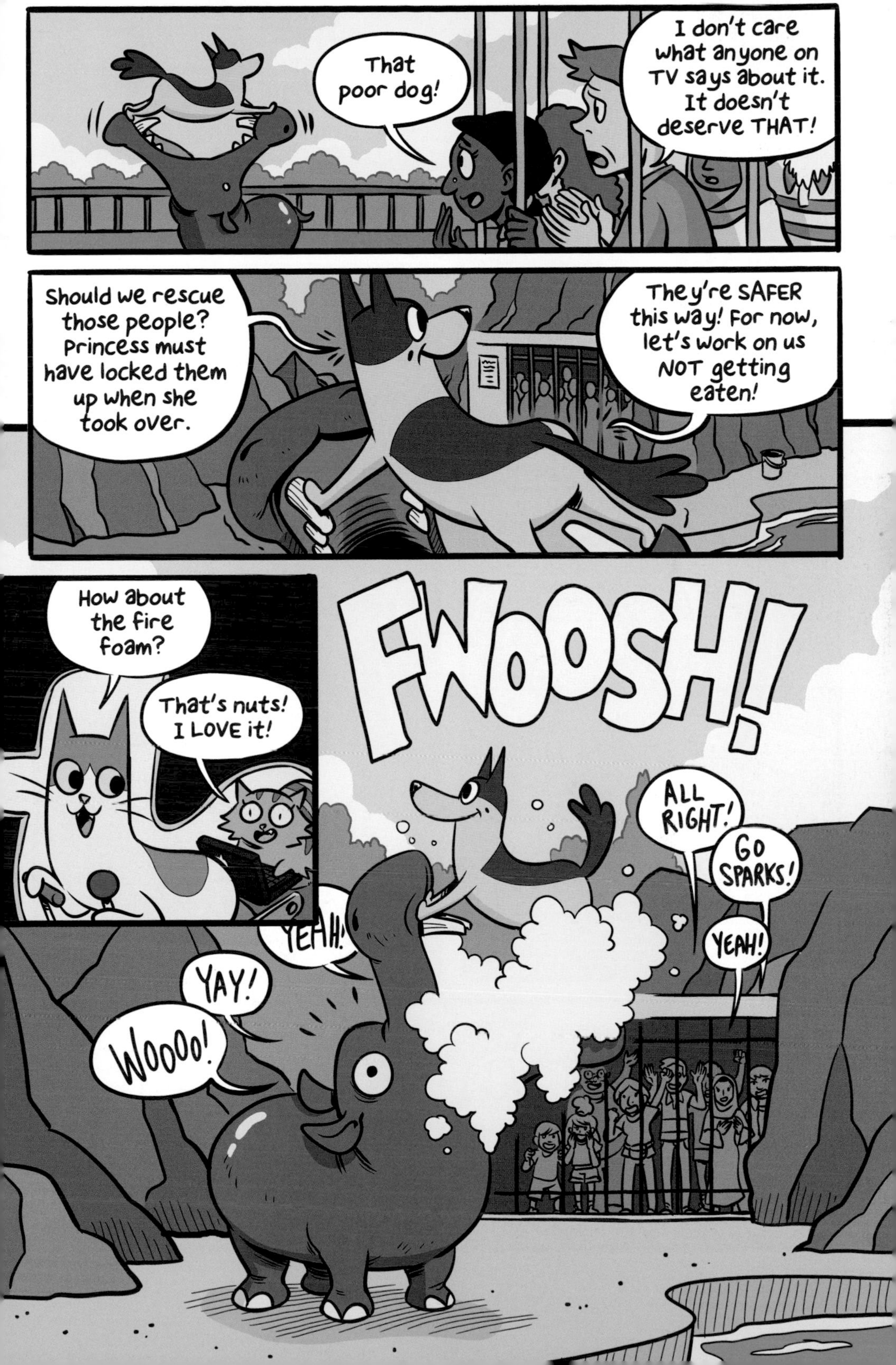
That poor dog!
I don't care what anyone on TV says about it. It doesn't deserve THAT!
Should we rescue those people? Princess must have locked them up when she took over.
They're SAFER this way! For now, let's work on us NOT getting eaten!
How about the fire foam?
That's nuts! I LOVE it!
FWOOSH!
ALL RIGHT!
GO SPARKS!
YEAH!
YEAH!
YAY!
WOOOO!

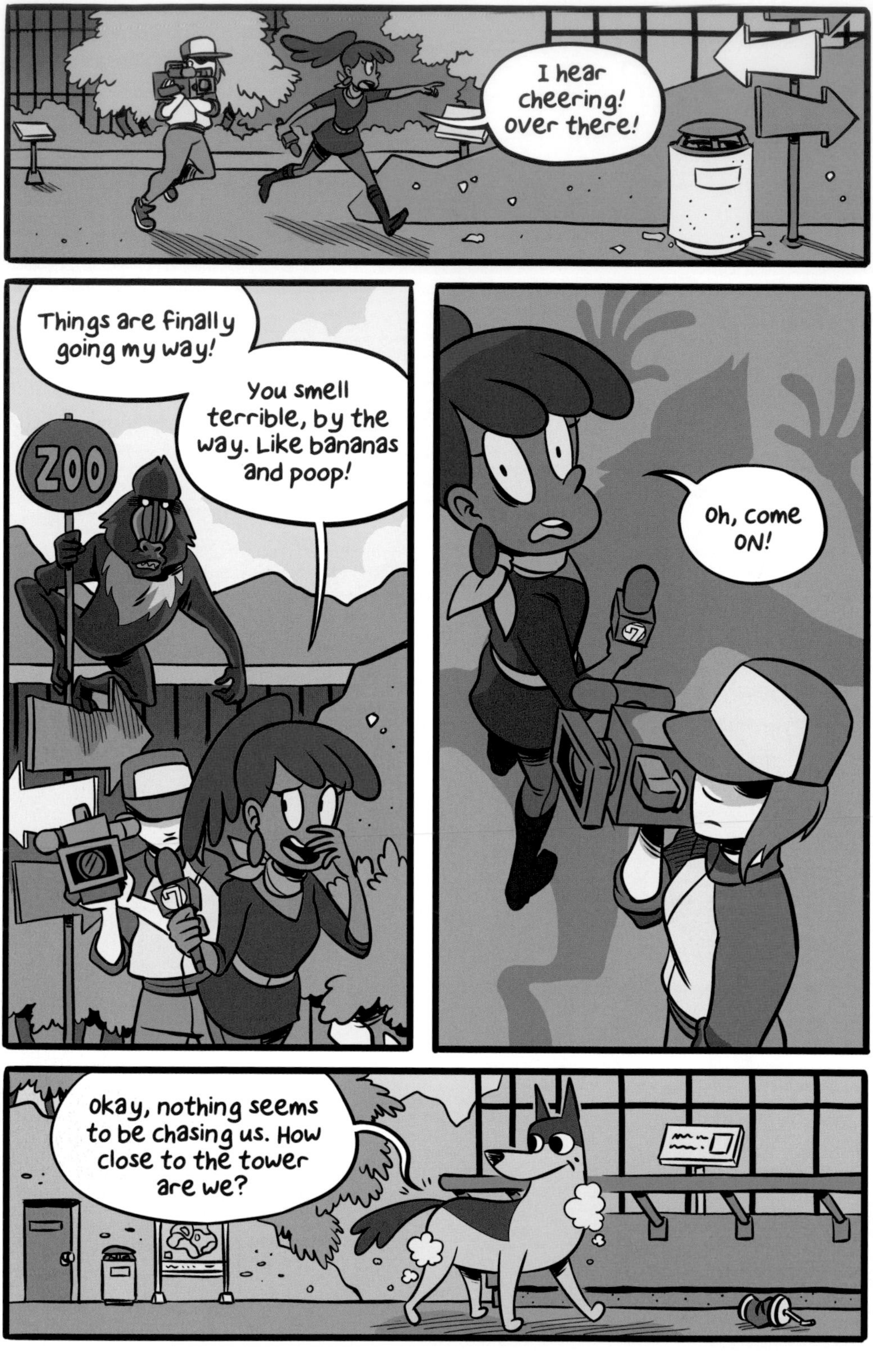
I hear cheering! over there!
Things are finally going my way!
You smell terrible, by the way. Like bananas and poop!
ZOO
Oh, come ON!
okay, nothing seems to be chasing us. How close to the tower are we?

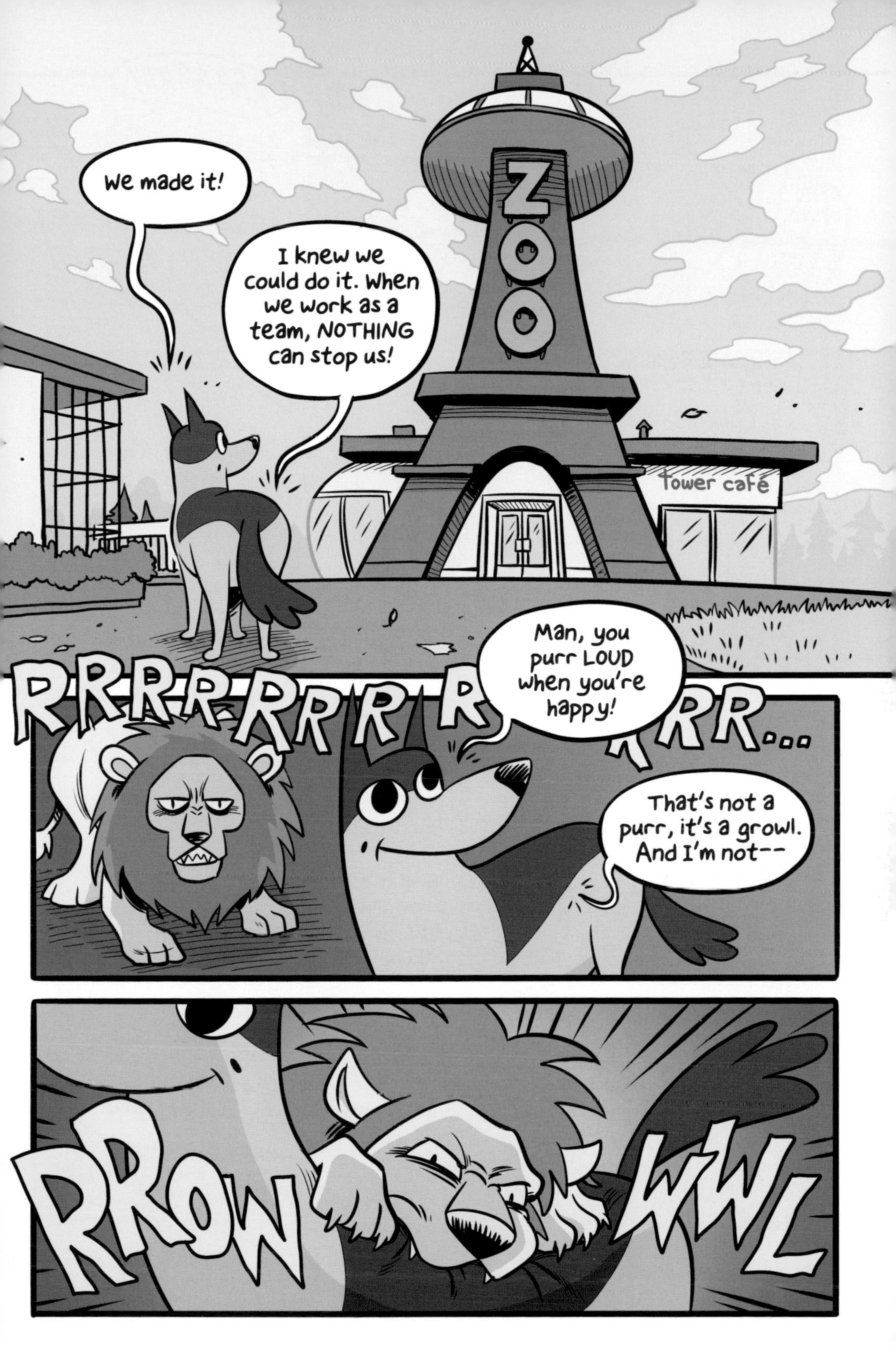

We made it!
I knew we could do it. When we work as a team, NOTHING can stop us!
ZOO
Tower café
RRRRRRRR RRRR...
Man, you purr LOUD when you're happy!
That's not a purr, it's a growl. And I'm not--
RROWWWL

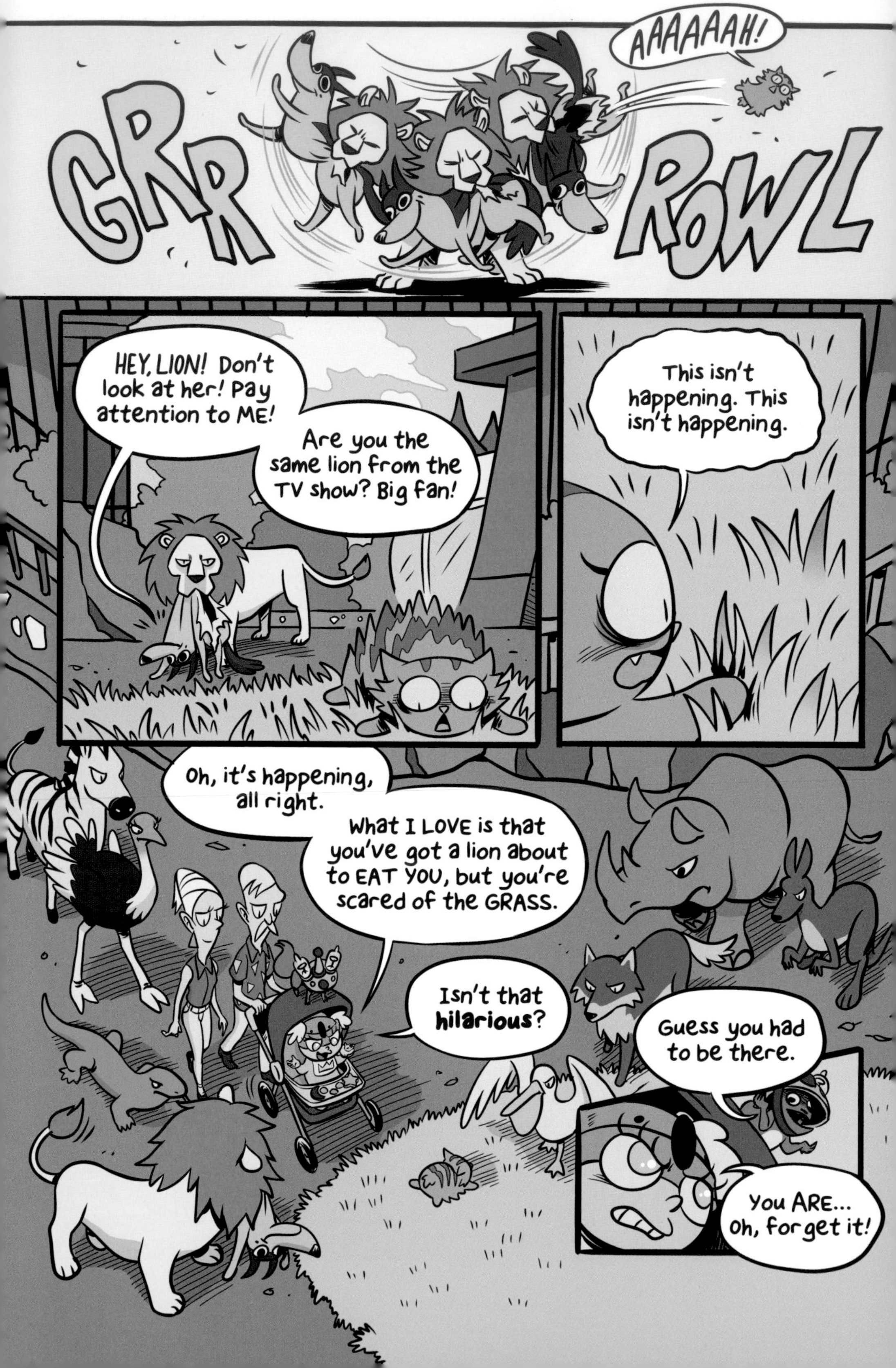
GRR
AAAAAAH!
ROWL
HEY, LION! Don't look at her! Pay attention to ME!
Are you the same lion from the TV show? Big fan!
This isn't happening. This isn't happening.
Oh, it's happening, all right.
What I LOVE is that you've got a lion about to EAT YOU, but you're scared of the GRASS.
Isn't that **hilarious**?
Guess you had to be there.
You ARE... Oh, forget it!

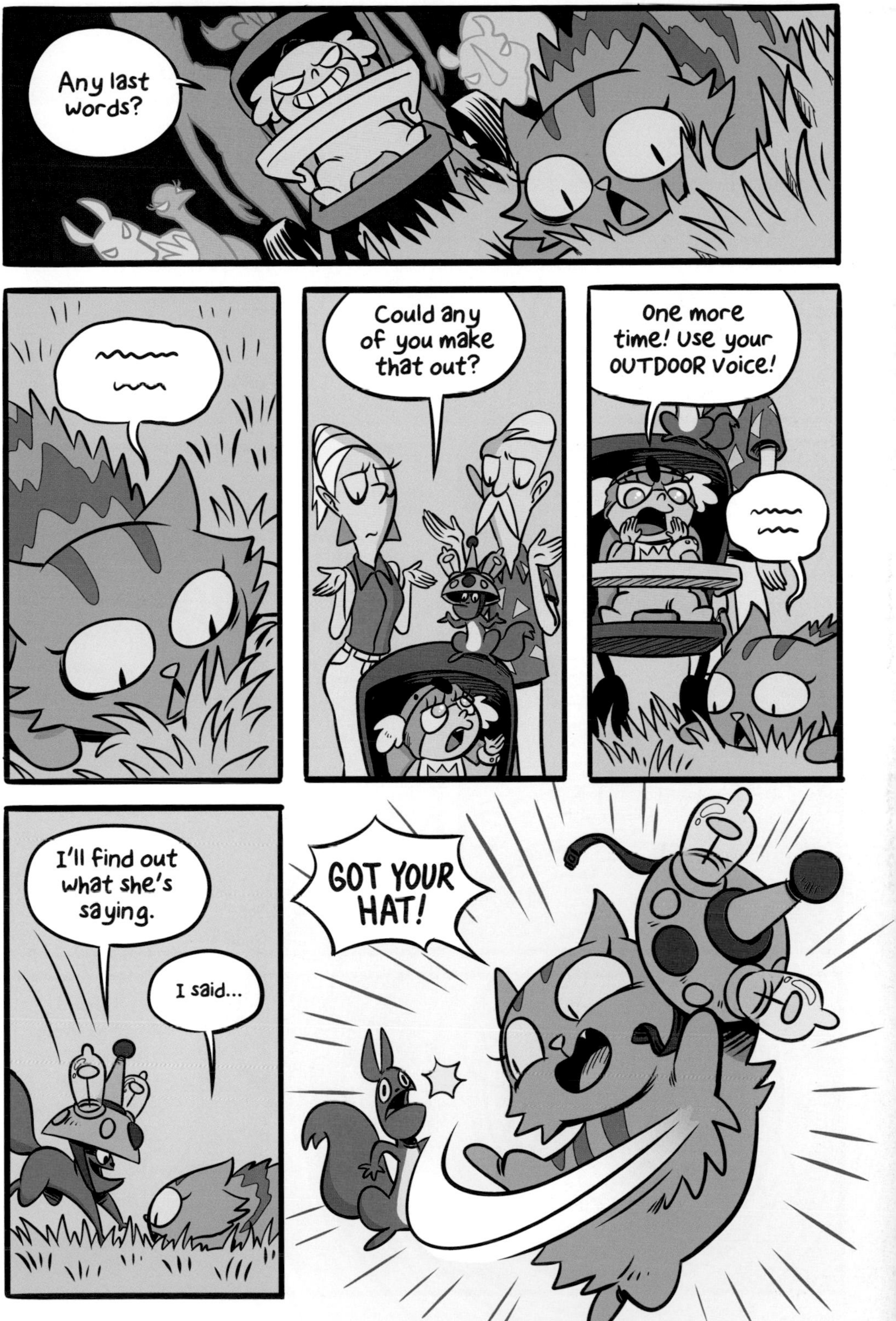
Any last words?
Could any of you make that out?
One more time! Use your OUTDOOR voice!
I'll find out what she's saying.
I said...
GOT YOUR HAT!

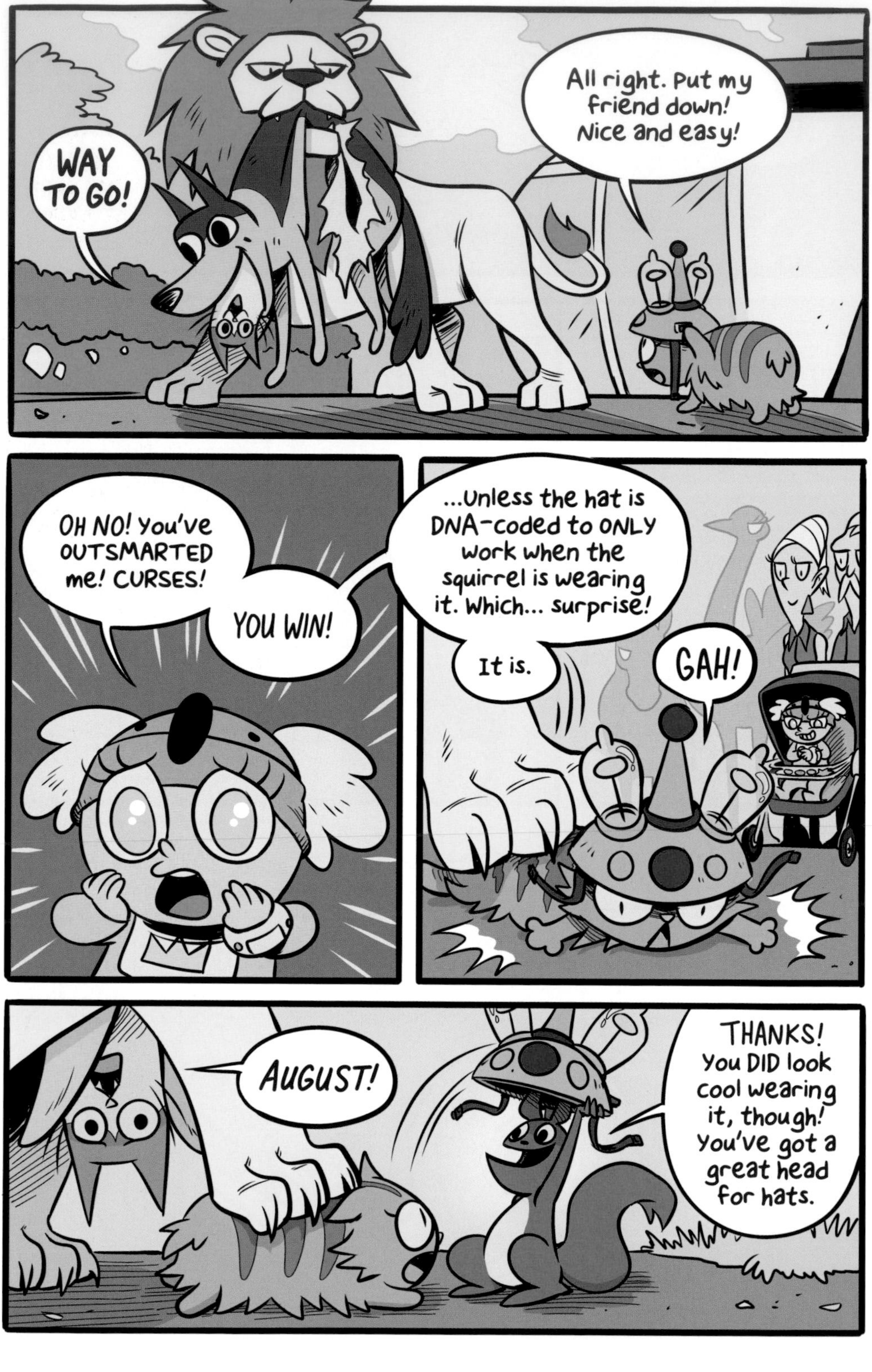
WAY TO GO!
All right. Put my friend down! Nice and easy!
OH NO! You've OUTSMARTED me! CURSES!
YOU WIN!
...Unless the hat is DNA-coded to ONLY work when the squirrel is wearing it. Which... surprise!
It is.
GAH!
AUGUST!
THANKS! You DID look cool wearing it, though! You've got a great head for hats.

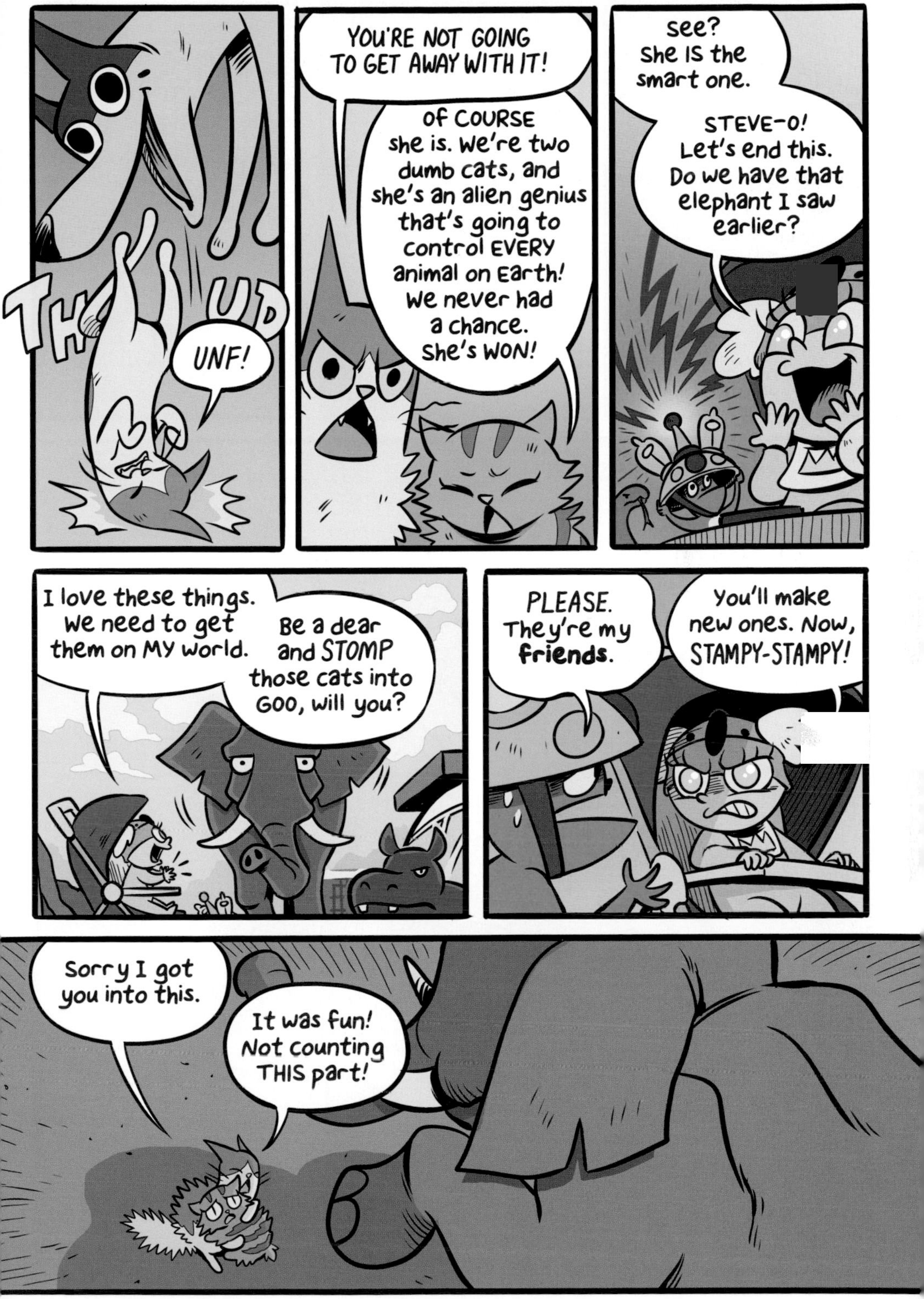
THUD
UNF!
YOU'RE NOT GOING TO GET AWAY WITH IT!
Of COURSE she is. We're two dumb cats, and she's an alien genius that's going to control EVERY animal on Earth! We never had a chance. She's WON!
See? She IS the smart one.
STEVE-O! Let's end this. Do we have that elephant I saw earlier?
I love these things. We need to get them on MY world.
Be a dear and STOMP those cats into GOO, will you?
PLEASE. They're my **friends**.
You'll make new ones. Now, STAMPY-STAMPY!
Sorry I got you into this.
It was fun! Not counting THIS part!

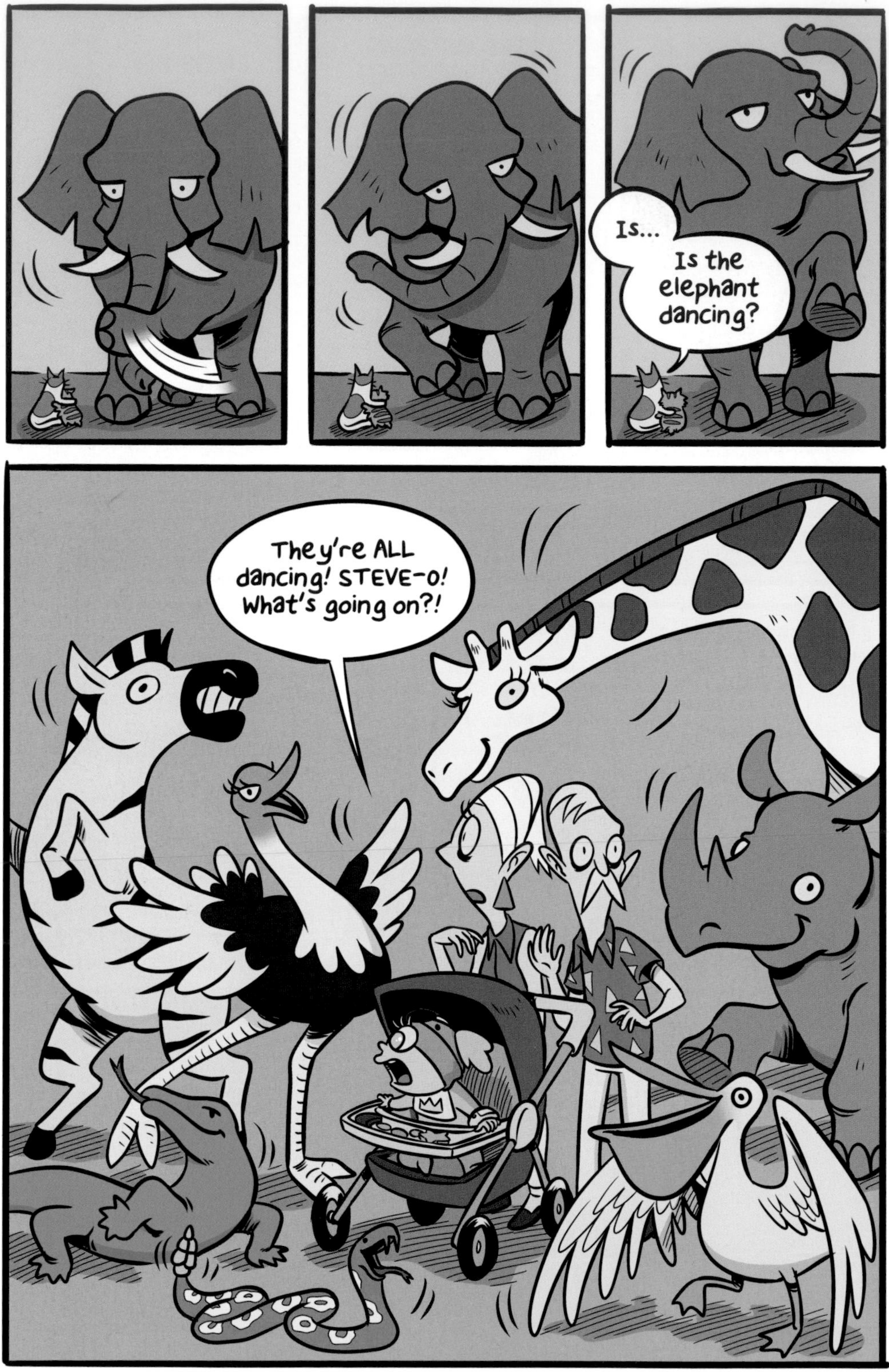
Is...
Is the elephant dancing?
They're ALL dancing! STEVE-O! What's going on?!

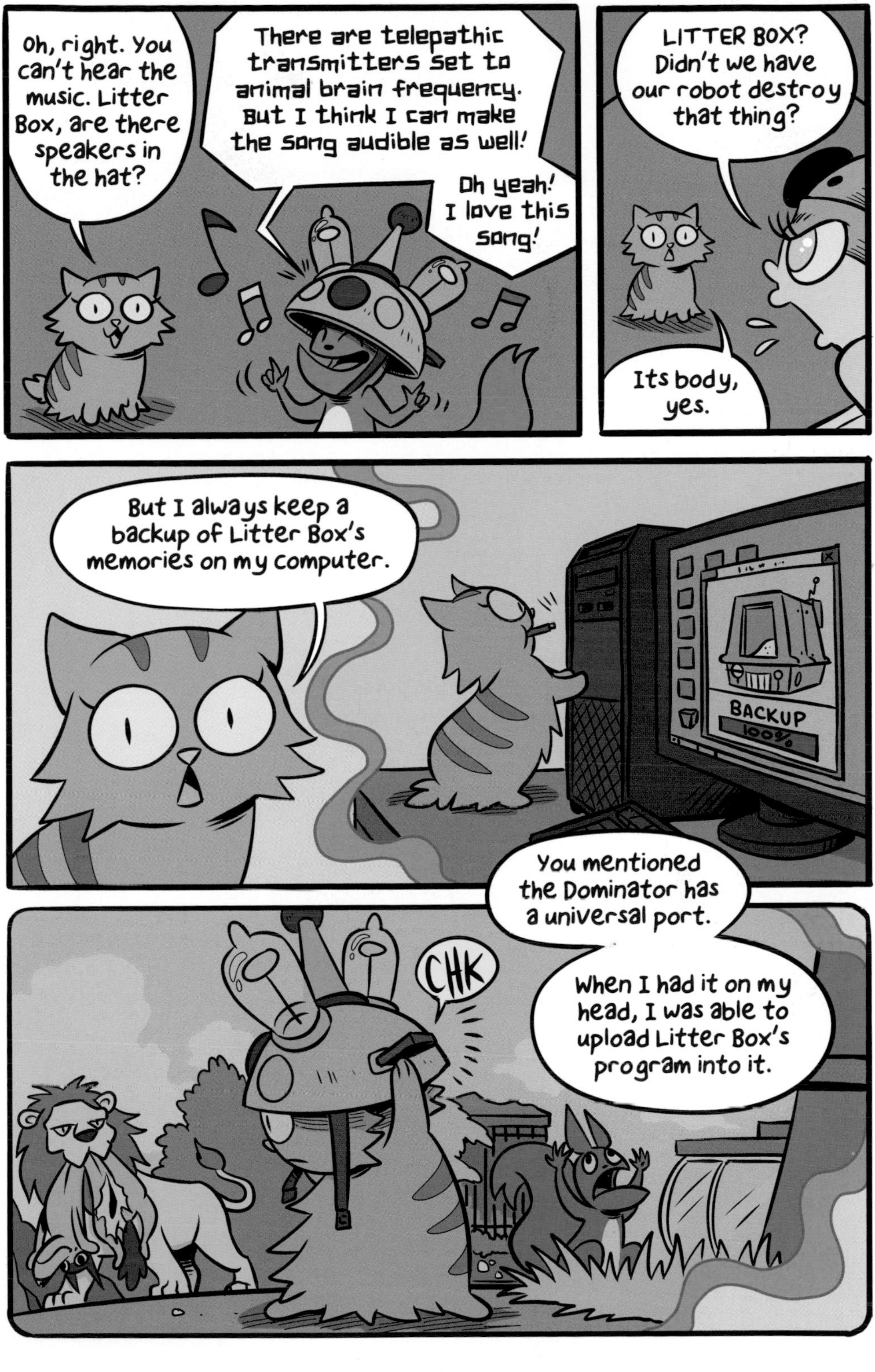

Oh, right. You can't hear the music. Litter Box, are there speakers in the hat?
There are telepathic transmitters set to animal brain frequency. But I think I can make the song audible as well!
Oh yeah! I love this song!
LITTER BOX? Didn't we have our robot destroy that thing?
Its body, yes.
But I always keep a backup of Litter Box's memories on my computer.
BACKUP
100%
You mentioned the Dominator has a universal port.
When I had it on my head, I was able to upload Litter Box's program into it.
CHK

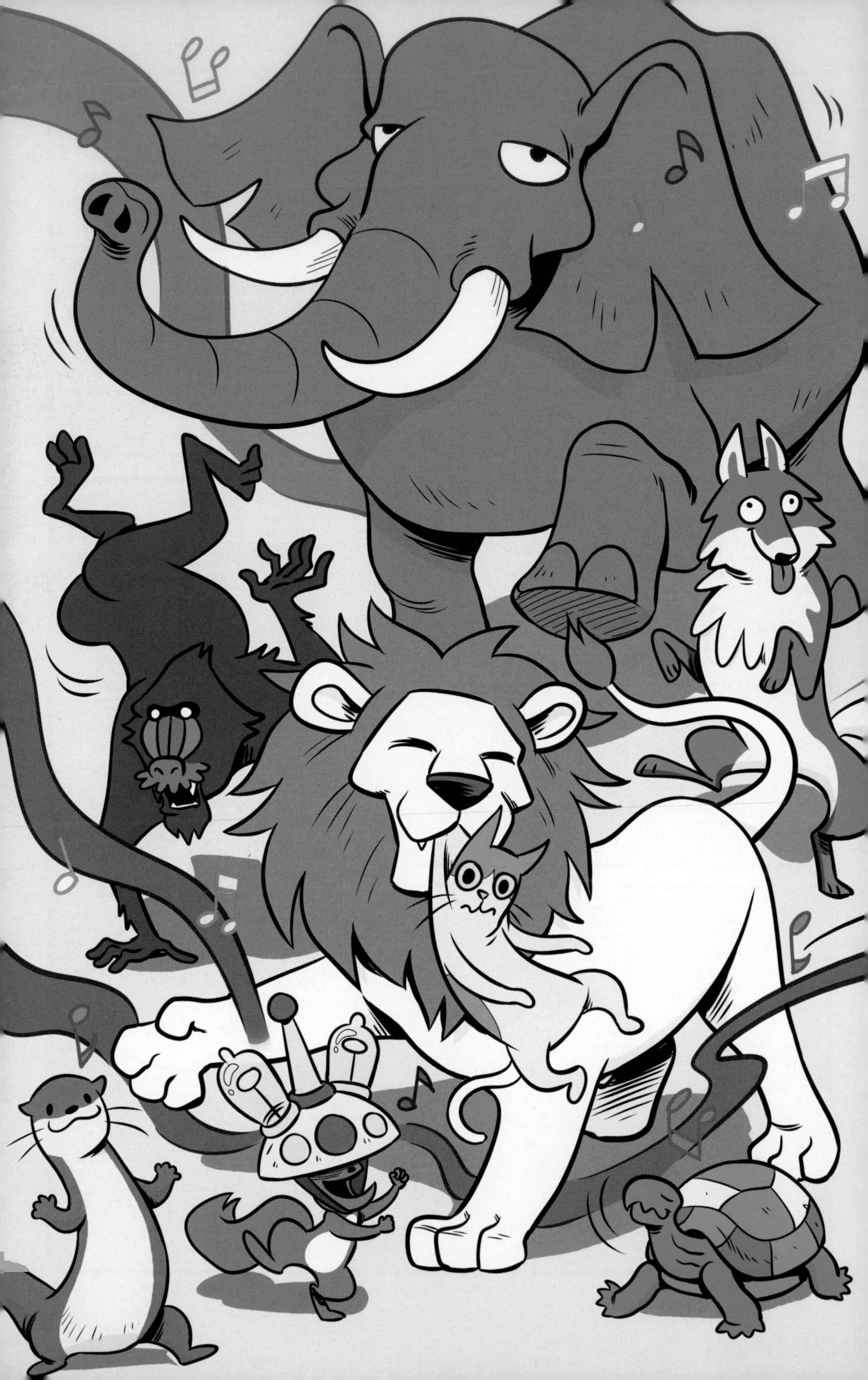

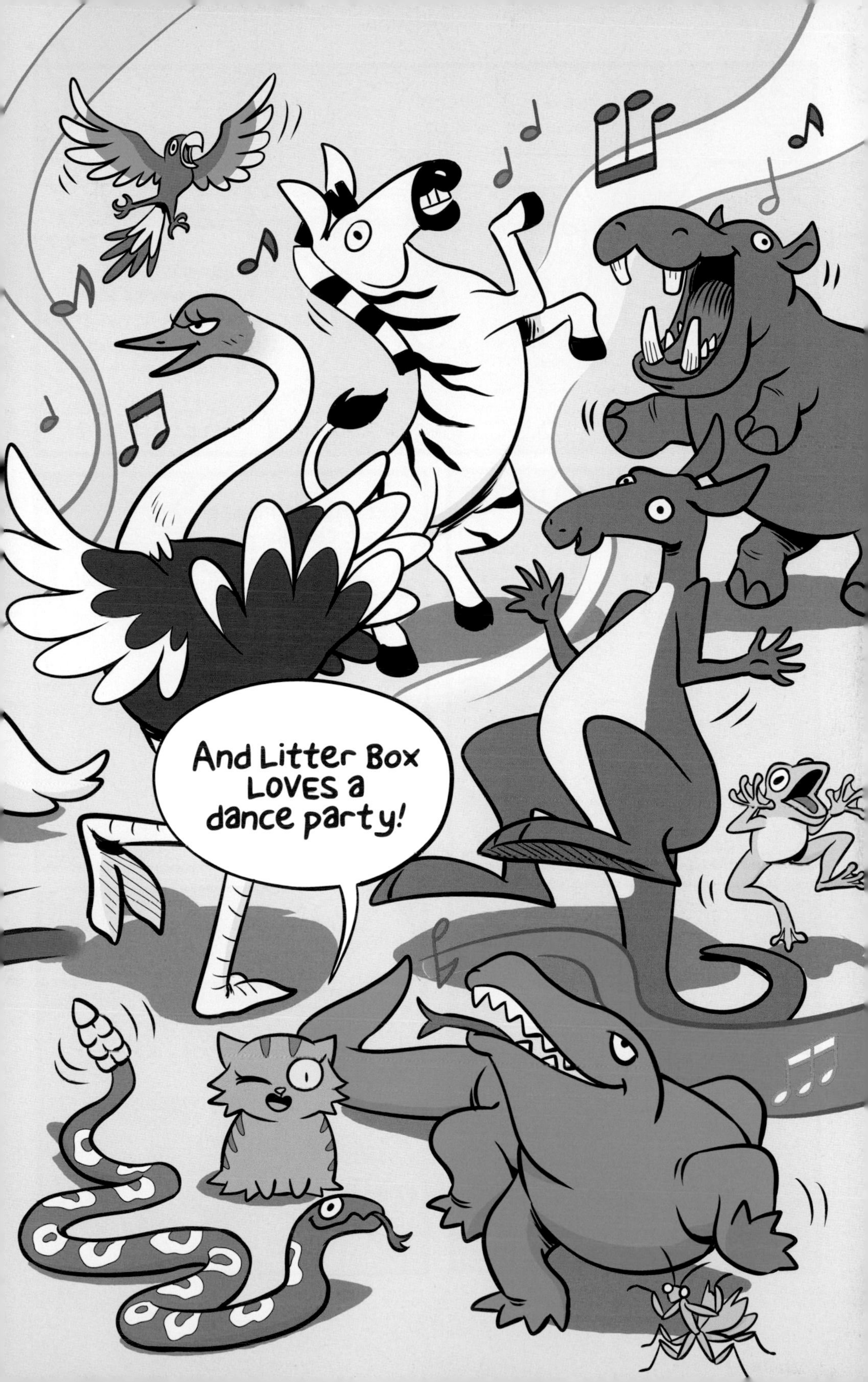
And Litter Box LOVES a dance party!

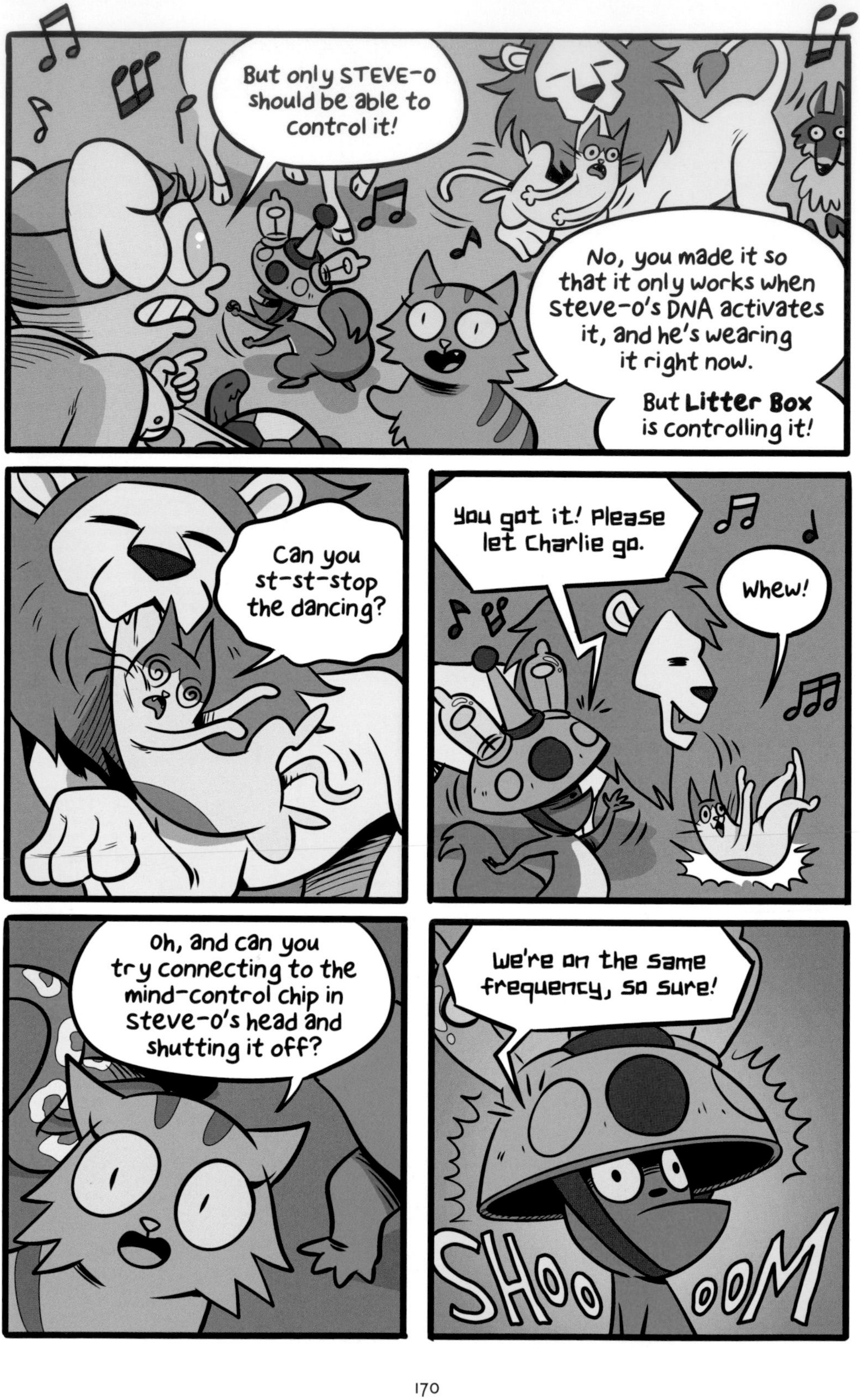
But only STEVE-O should be able to control it!
No, you made it so that it only works when steve-o's DNA activates it, and he's wearing it right now.
But Litter Box is controlling it!
Can you st-st-stop the dancing?
You got it! Please let Charlie go.
Whew!
Oh, and can you try connecting to the mind-control chip in steve-o's head and shutting it off?
We're on the same frequency, so sure!
SHOO OOM

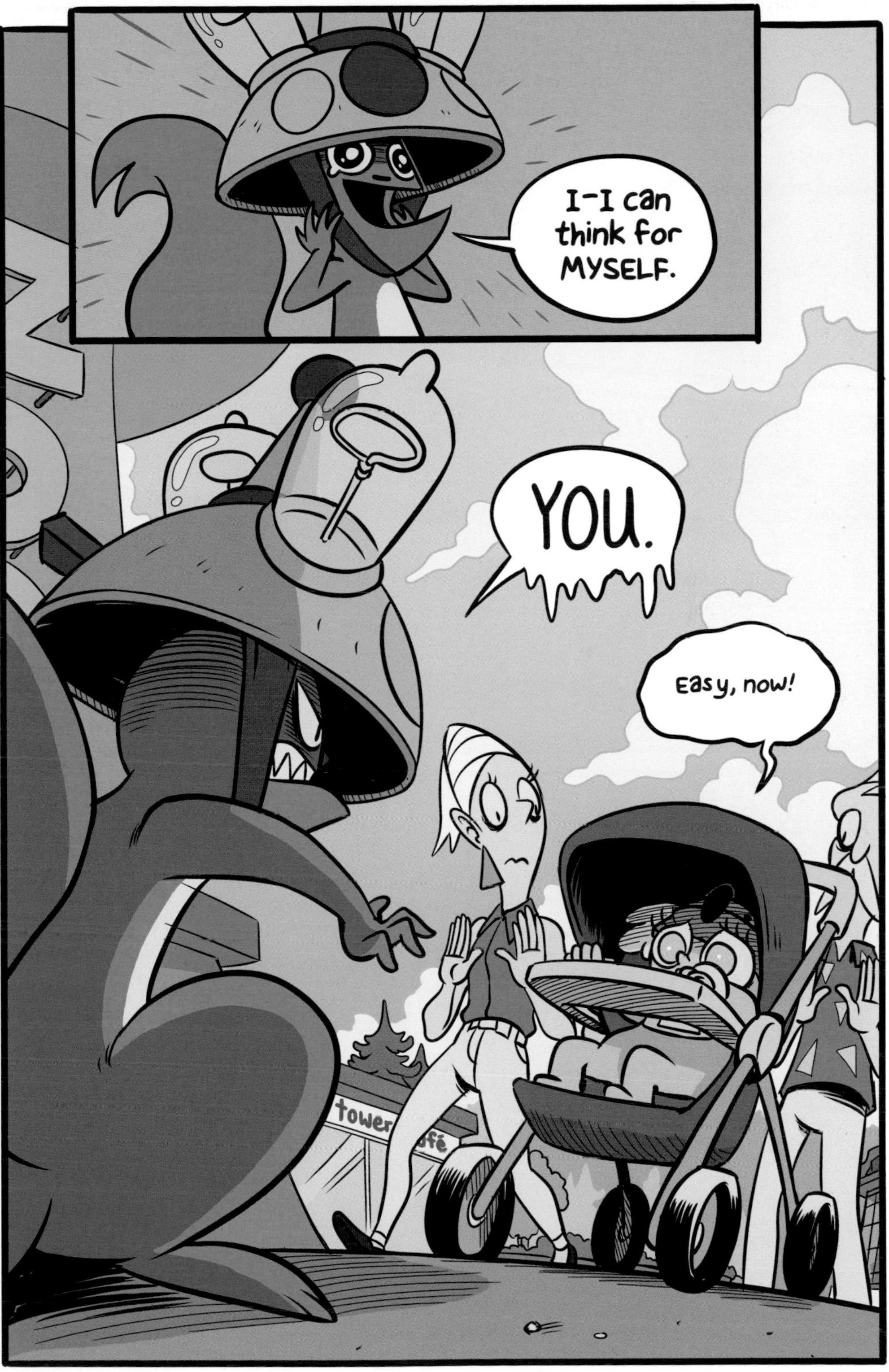
I-I can think for MYSELF.
YOU.
Easy, now!
tower café

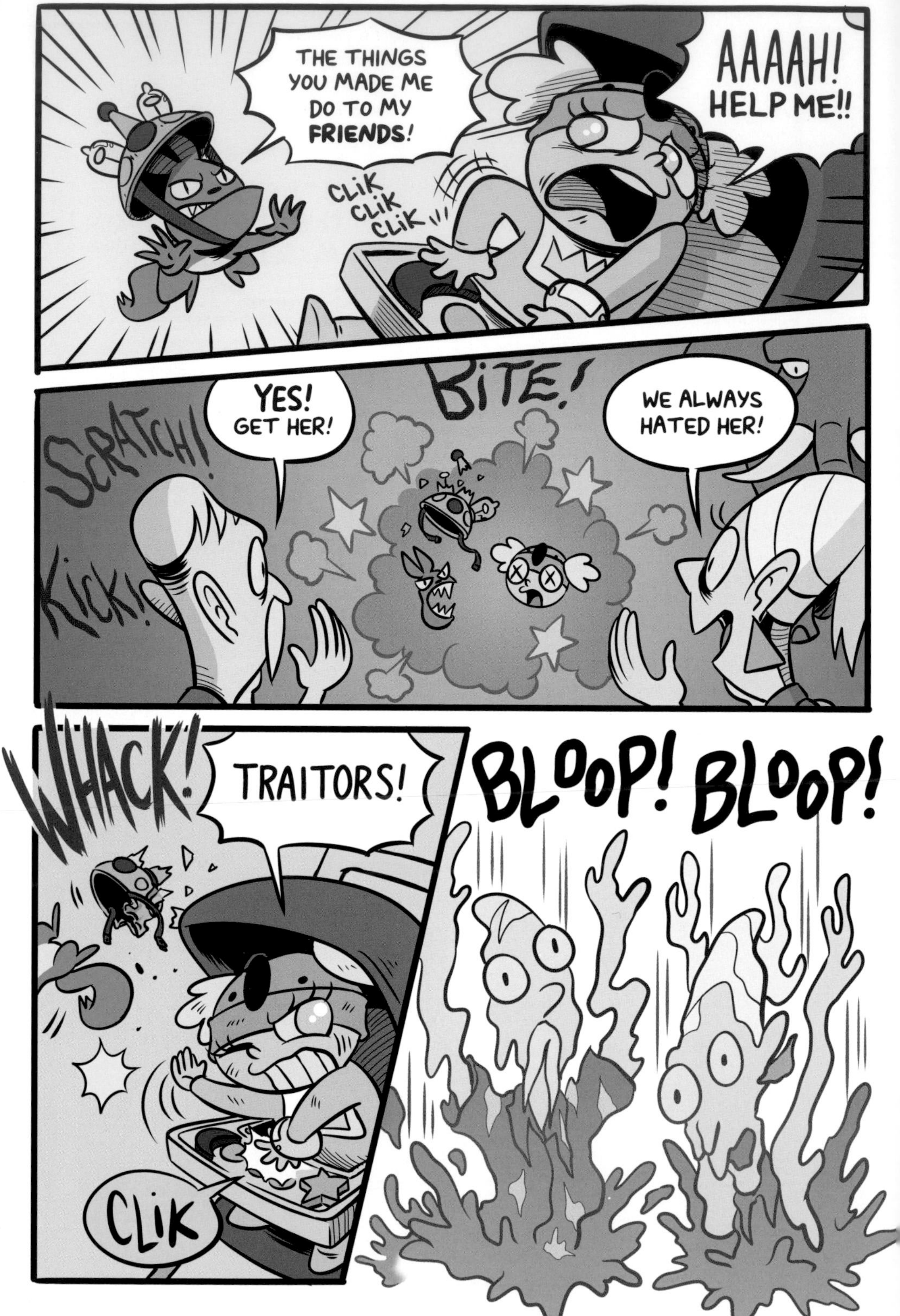
THE THINGS YOU MADE ME DO TO MY FRIENDS!
AAAAH! HELP ME!!
CLIK CLIK CLIK
SCRATCH!
YES! GET HER!
BITE!
WE ALWAYS HATED HER!
KICK!
WHACK!
TRAITORS!
CLIK
BLOOP! BLOOP!

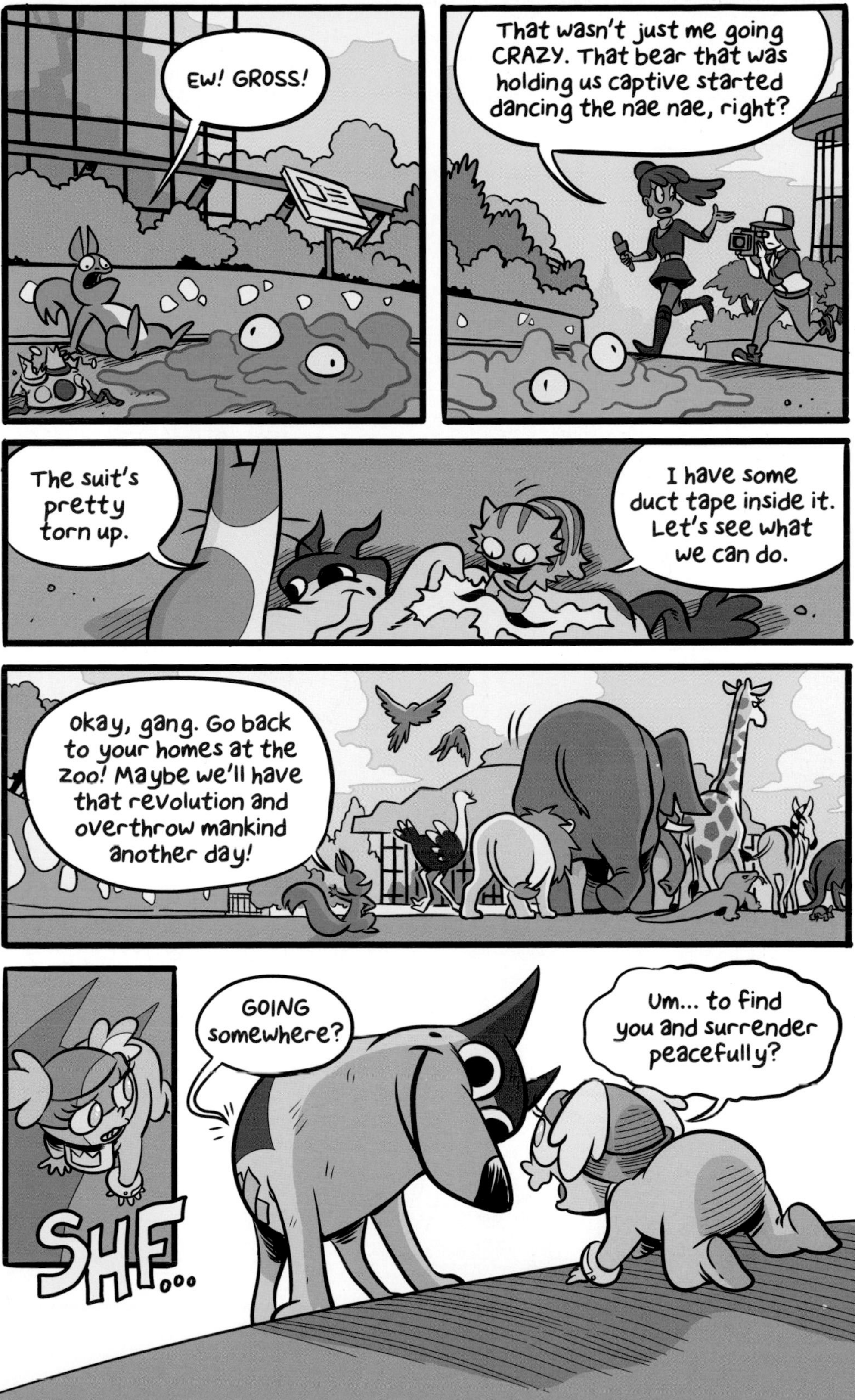
EW! GROSS!
That wasn't just me going CRAZY. That bear that was holding us captive started dancing the nae nae, right?
The suit's pretty torn up.
I have some duct tape inside it. Let's see what we can do.
Okay, gang. Go back to your homes at the zoo! Maybe we'll have that revolution and overthrow mankind another day!
SHF...
GOING somewhere?
Um... to find you and surrender peacefully?

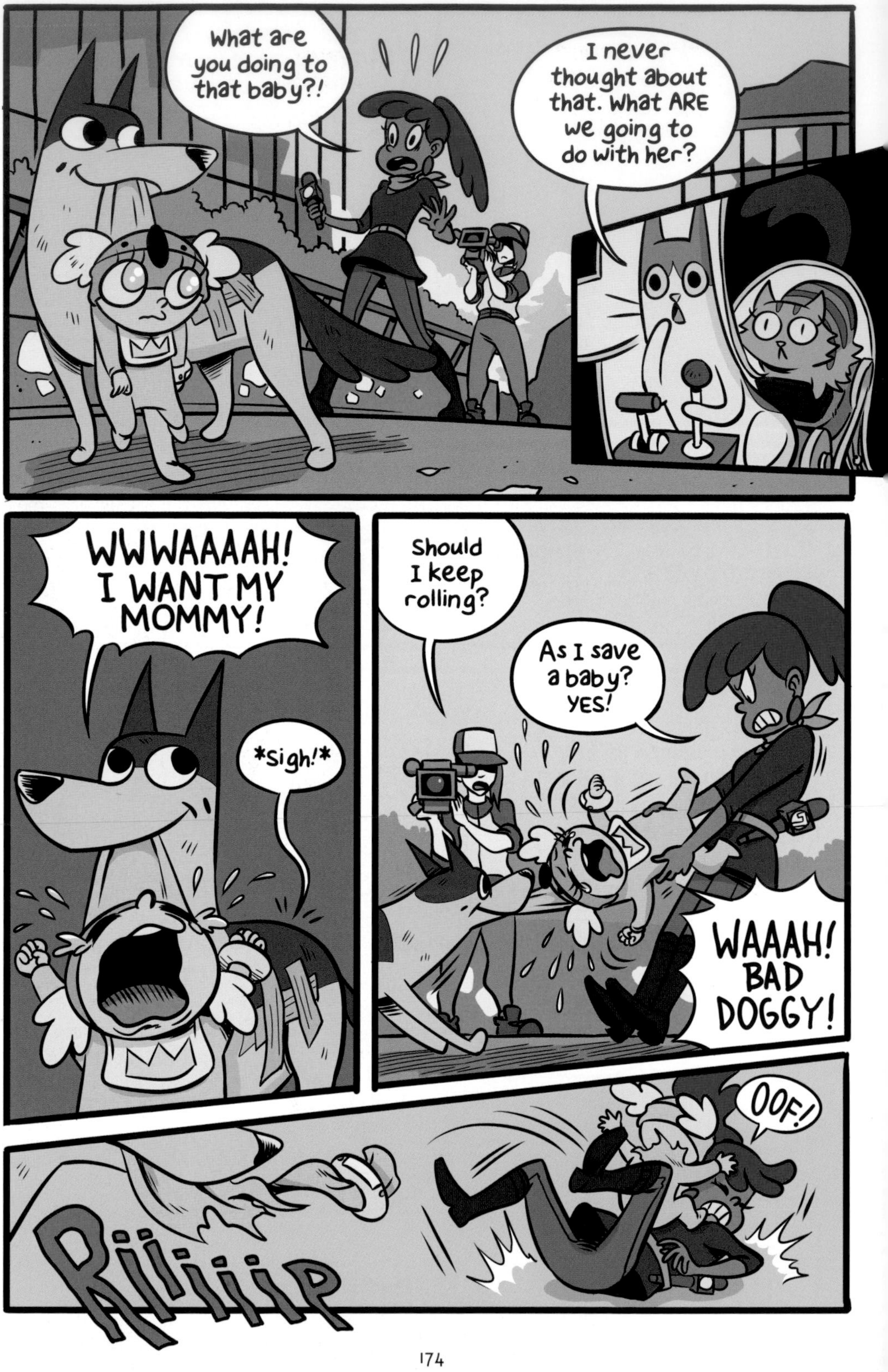
What are you doing to that baby?!
I never thought about that. What ARE we going to do with her?
WWWAAAAAH! I WANT MY MOMMY!
Sigh!
Should I keep rolling?
As I save a baby? YES!
WAAAH! BAD DOGGY!
OOF!
Riiiiip

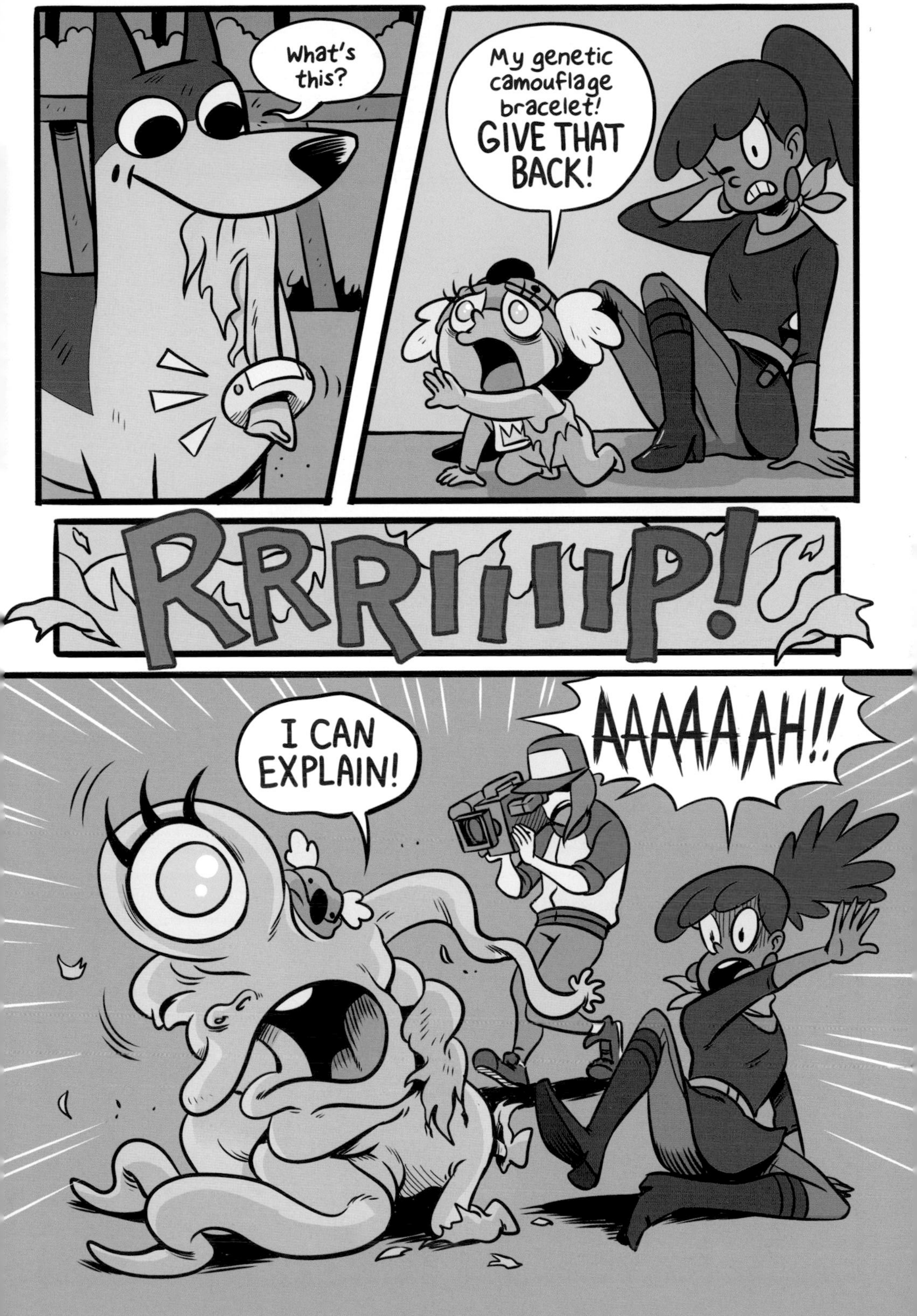
What's this?
My genetic camouflage bracelet! GIVE THAT BACK!
RRRIIIIP!
I CAN EXPLAIN!
AAAAAAH!!

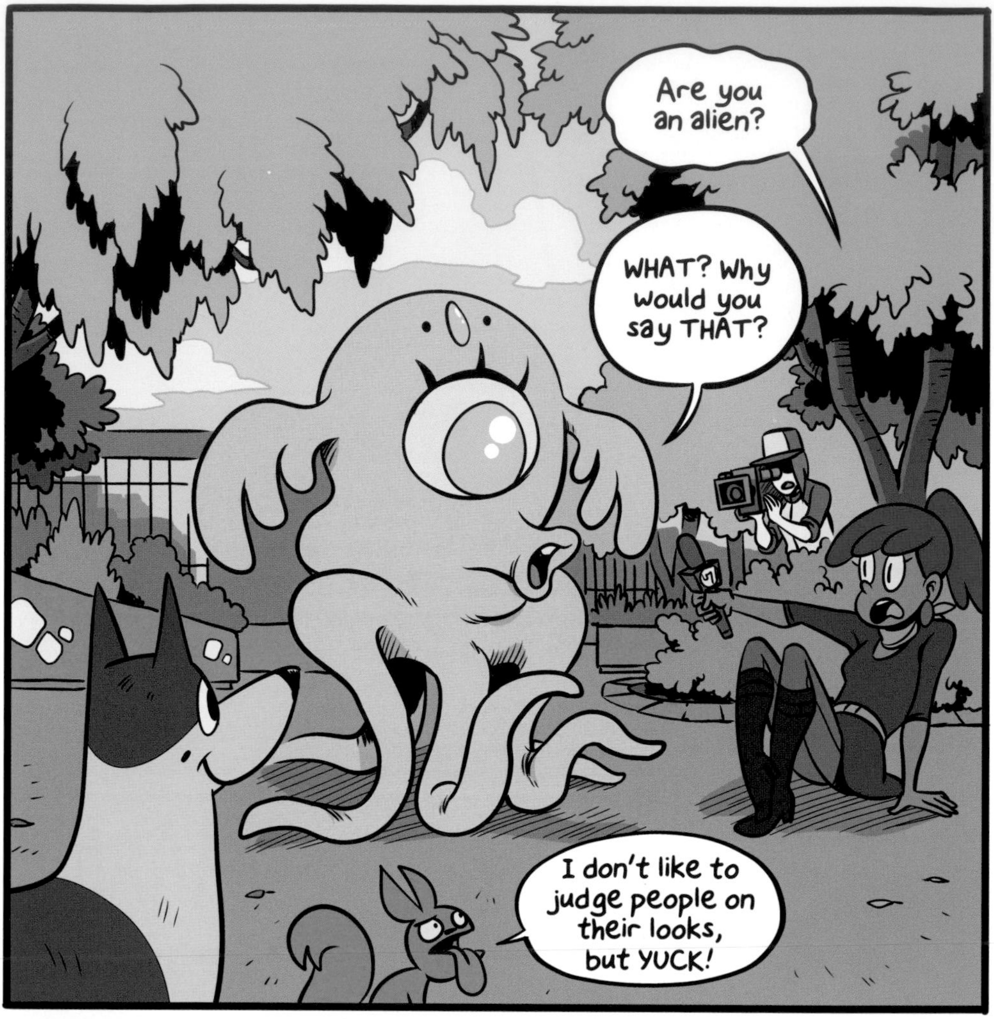
Are you an alien?
WHAT? Why would you say THAT?
I don't like to judge people on their looks, but YUCK!

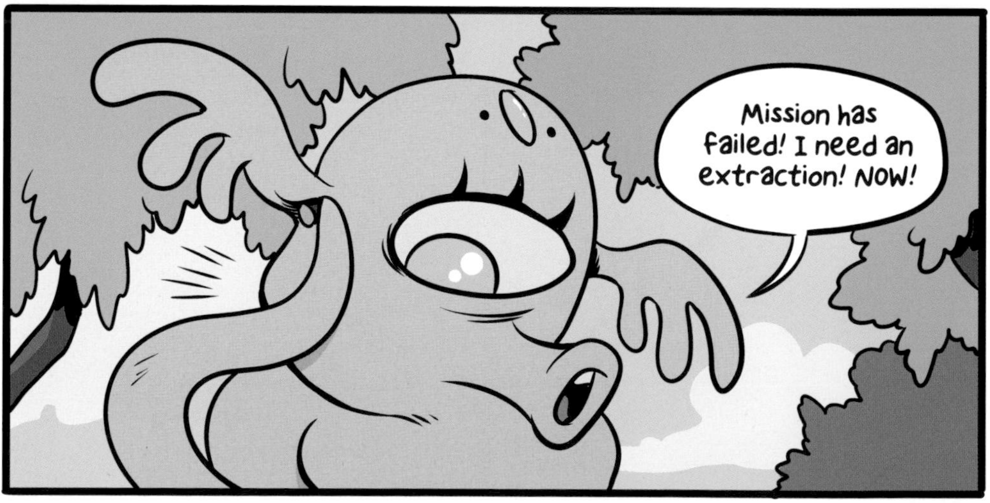
Mission has failed! I need an extraction! NOW!

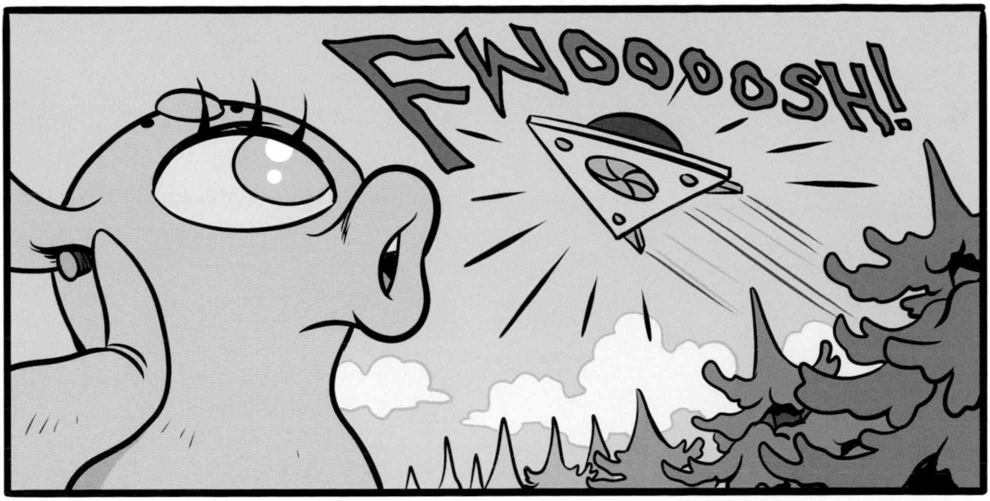
FWOOOOSH!

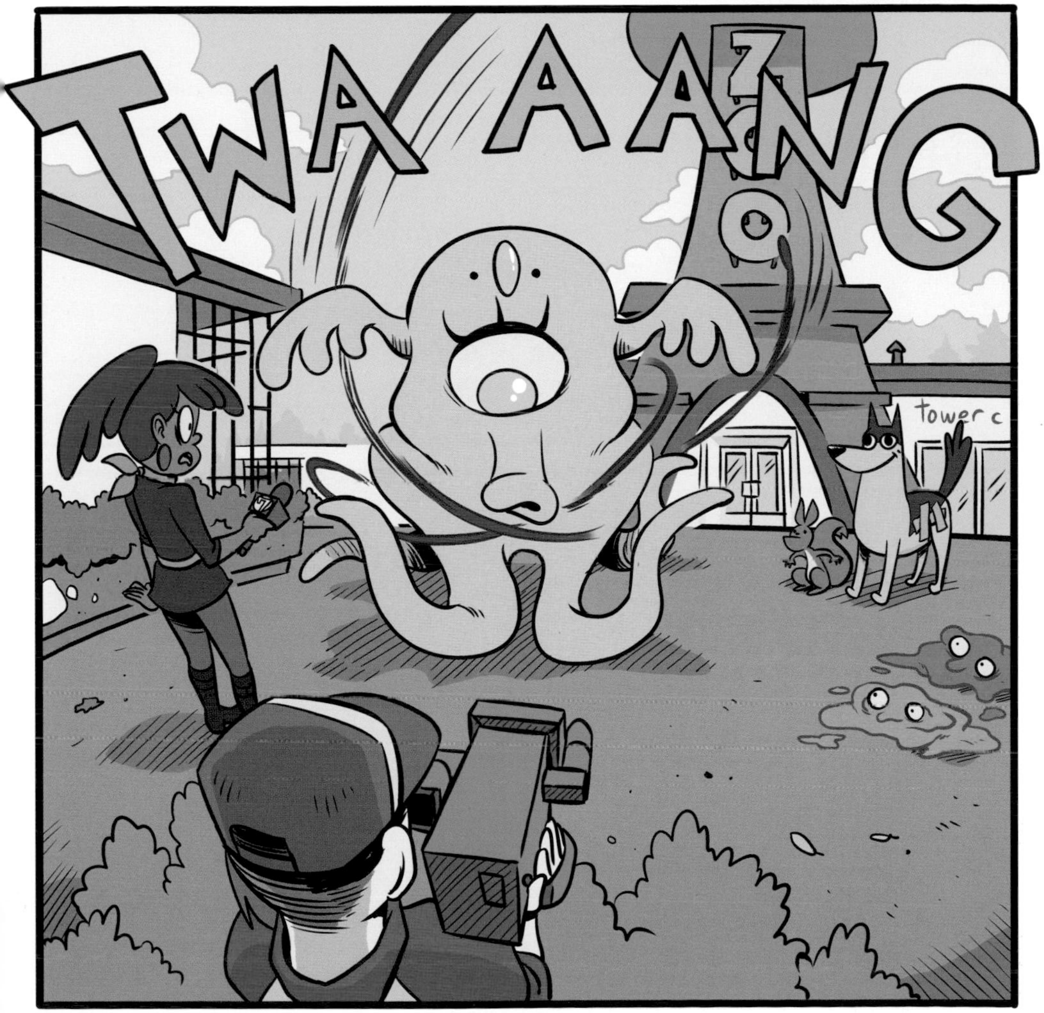
TWAAANG
tower c

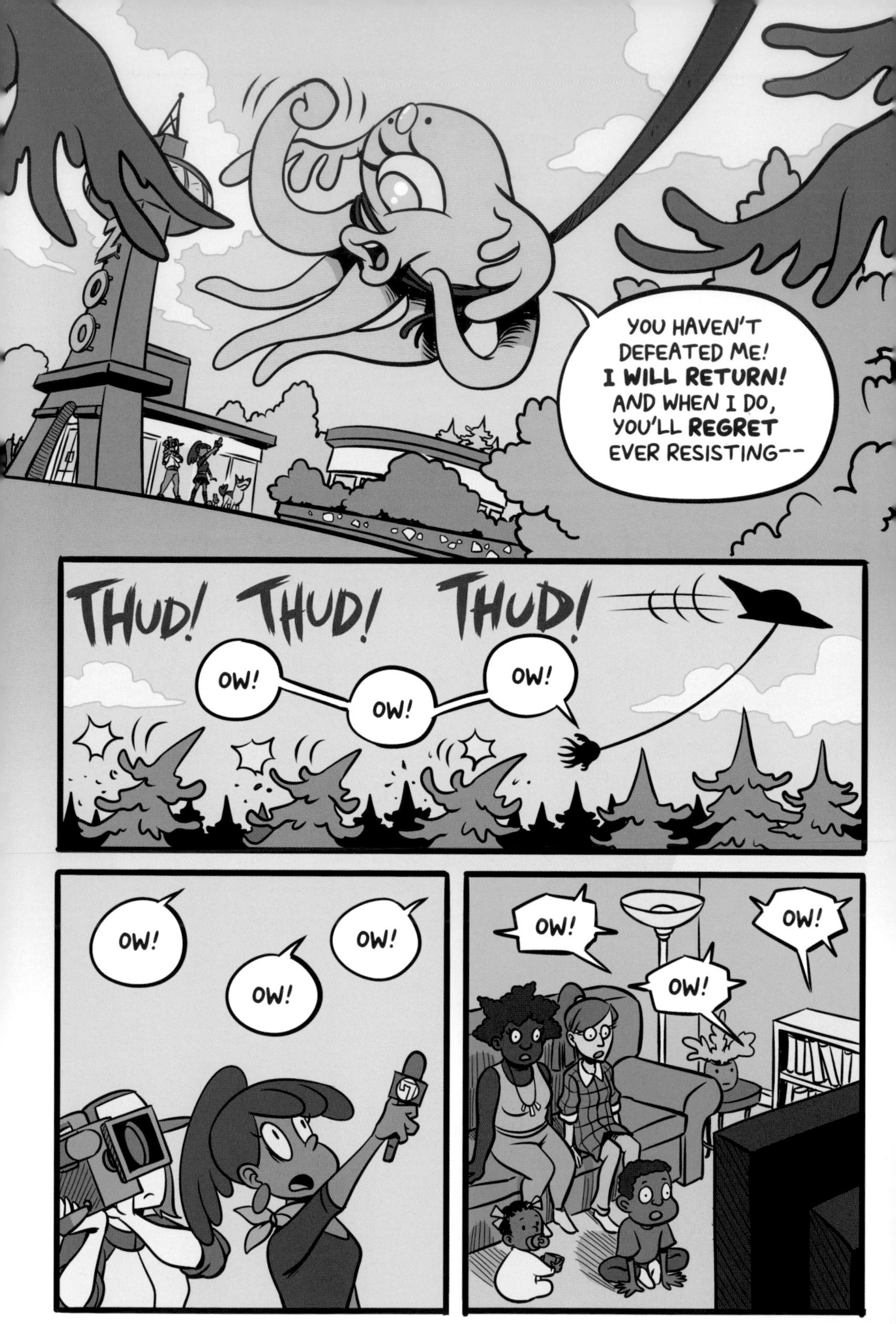
YOU HAVEN'T DEFEATED ME! **I WILL RETURN!** AND WHEN I DO, YOU'LL **REGRET** EVER RESISTING--
THUD! THUD! THUD!
OW!
OW!
OW!
OW!
OW!
OW!
OW!
OW!
OW!

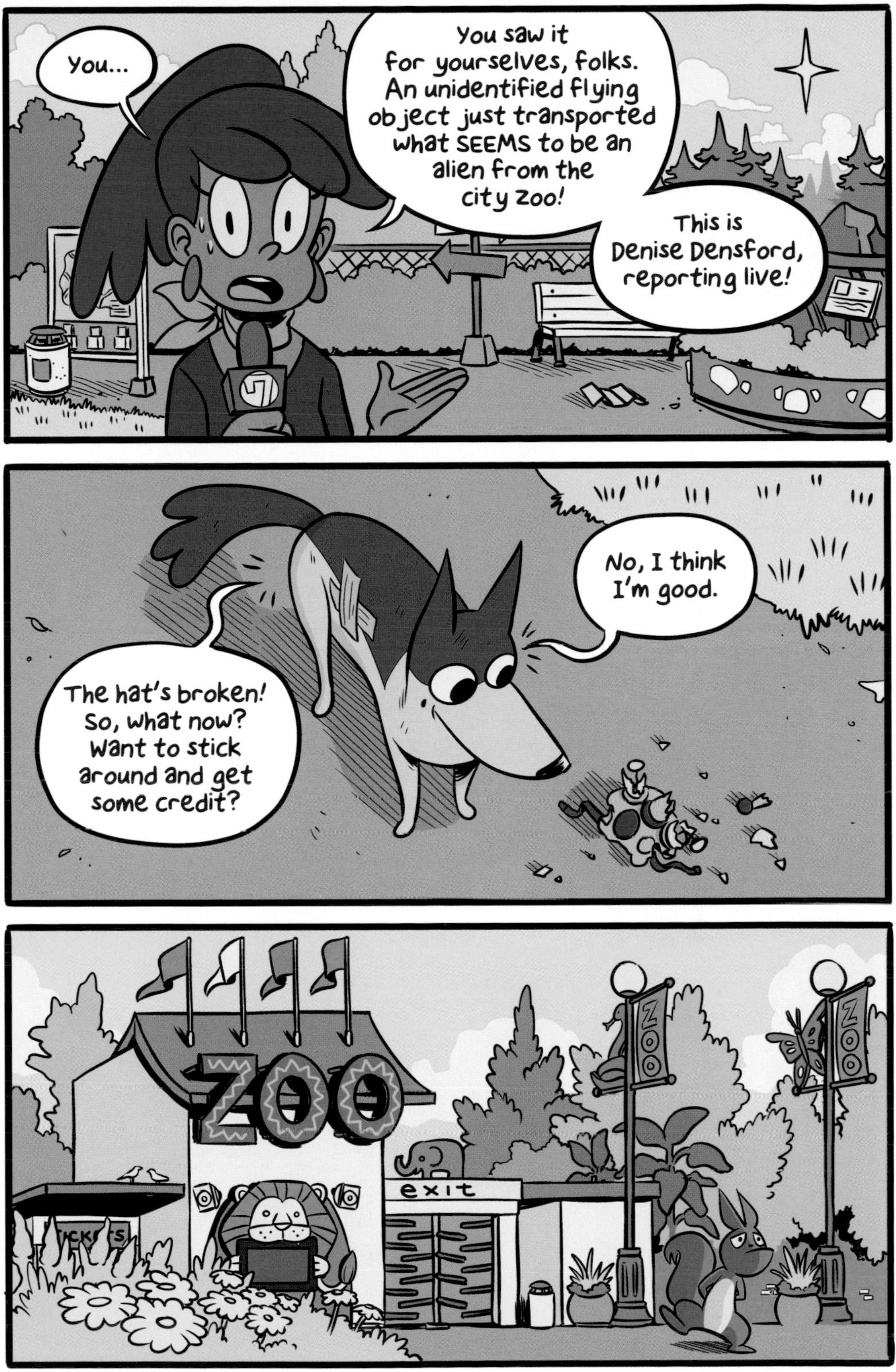
You...
You saw it for yourselves, folks. An unidentified flying object just transported what SEEMS to be an alien from the city zoo!
This is Denise Densford, reporting live!
The hat's broken! So, what now? Want to stick around and get some credit?
No, I think I'm good.
ZOO
exit
ZOO
ZOO

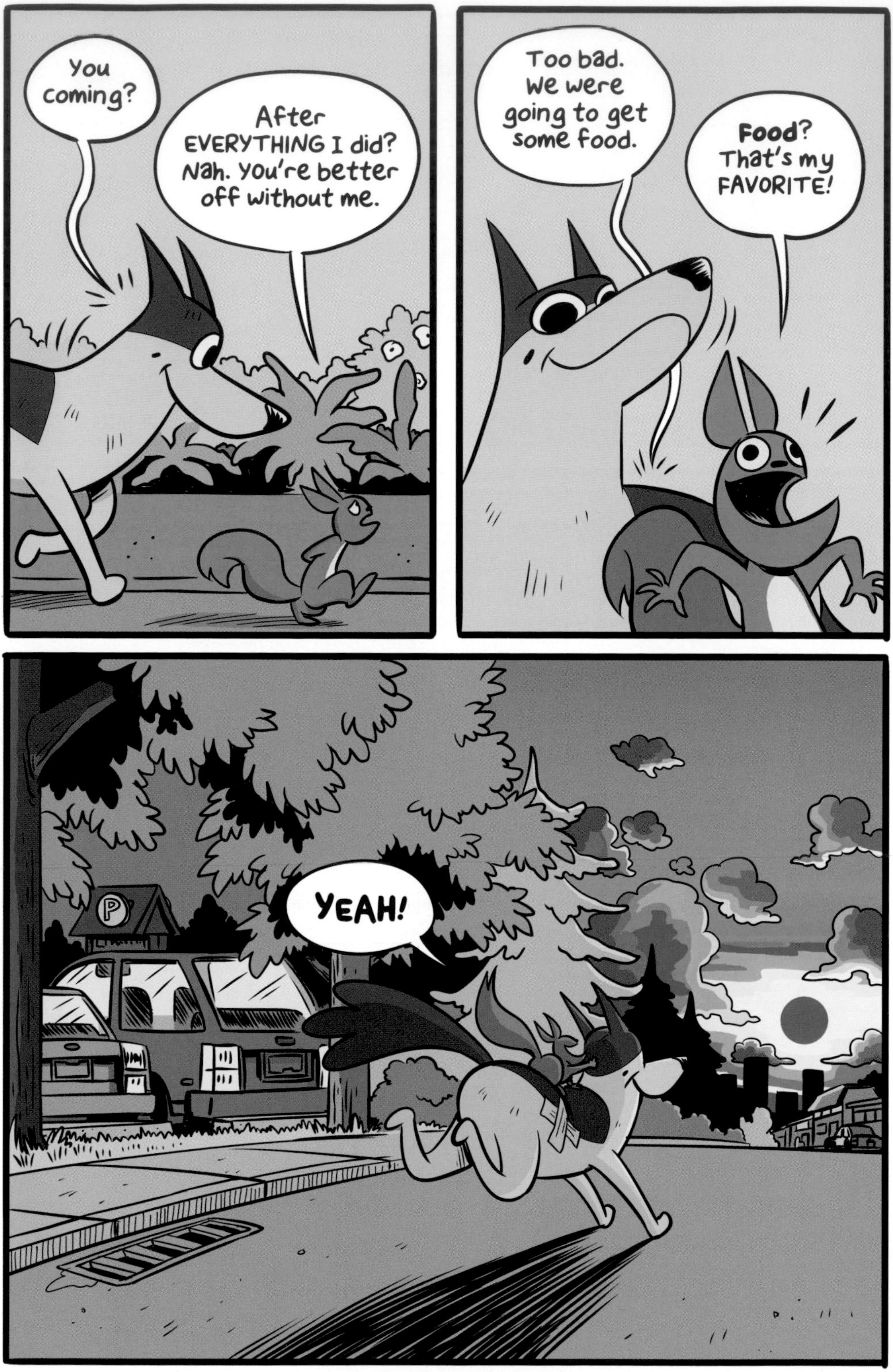
You coming?
After EVERYTHING I did? Nah. You're better off without me.
Too bad. We were going to get some food.
Food? That's my FAVORITE!
YEAH!

CHAPTER ELEVEN

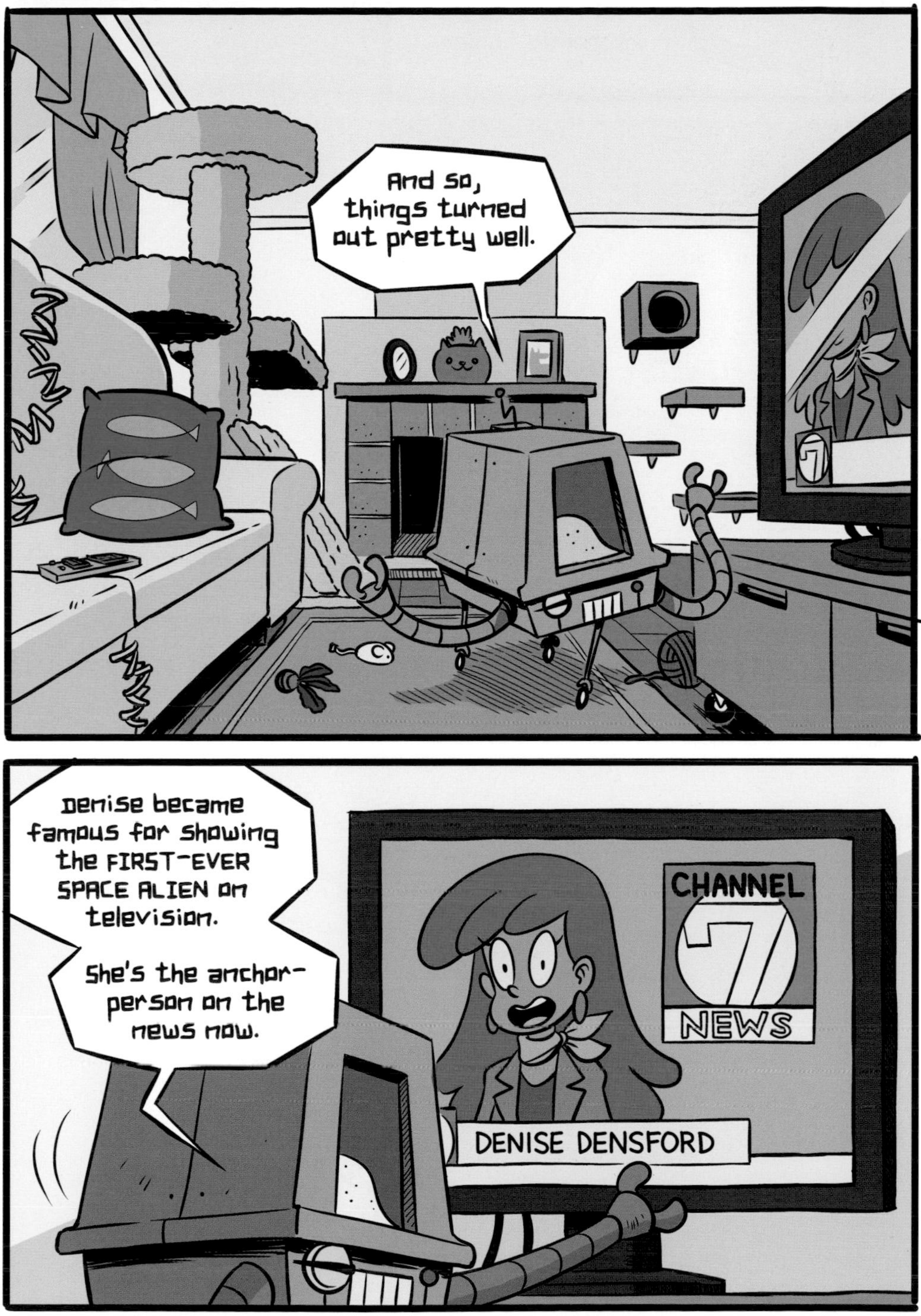
And so, things turned out pretty well.
Denise became famous for showing the FIRST-EVER SPACE ALIEN on television.
She's the anchor-person on the news now.
CHANNEL 7 NEWS
DENISE DENSFORD

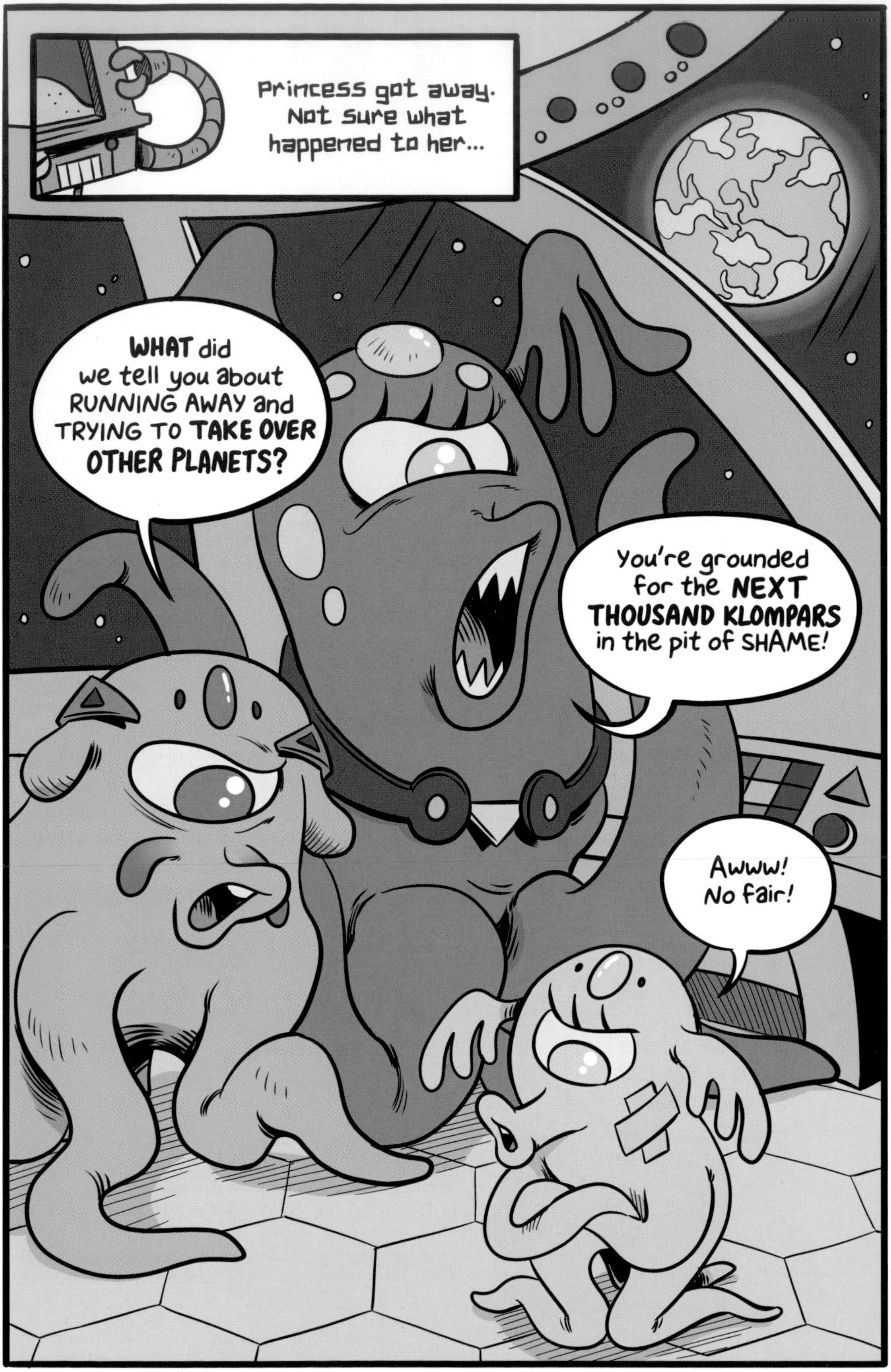
Princess got away. Not sure what happened to her...
WHAT did we tell you about RUNNING AWAY and TRYING TO TAKE OVER OTHER PLANETS?
You're grounded for the NEXT THOUSAND KLOMPARS in the pit of SHAME!
Awww! No fair!

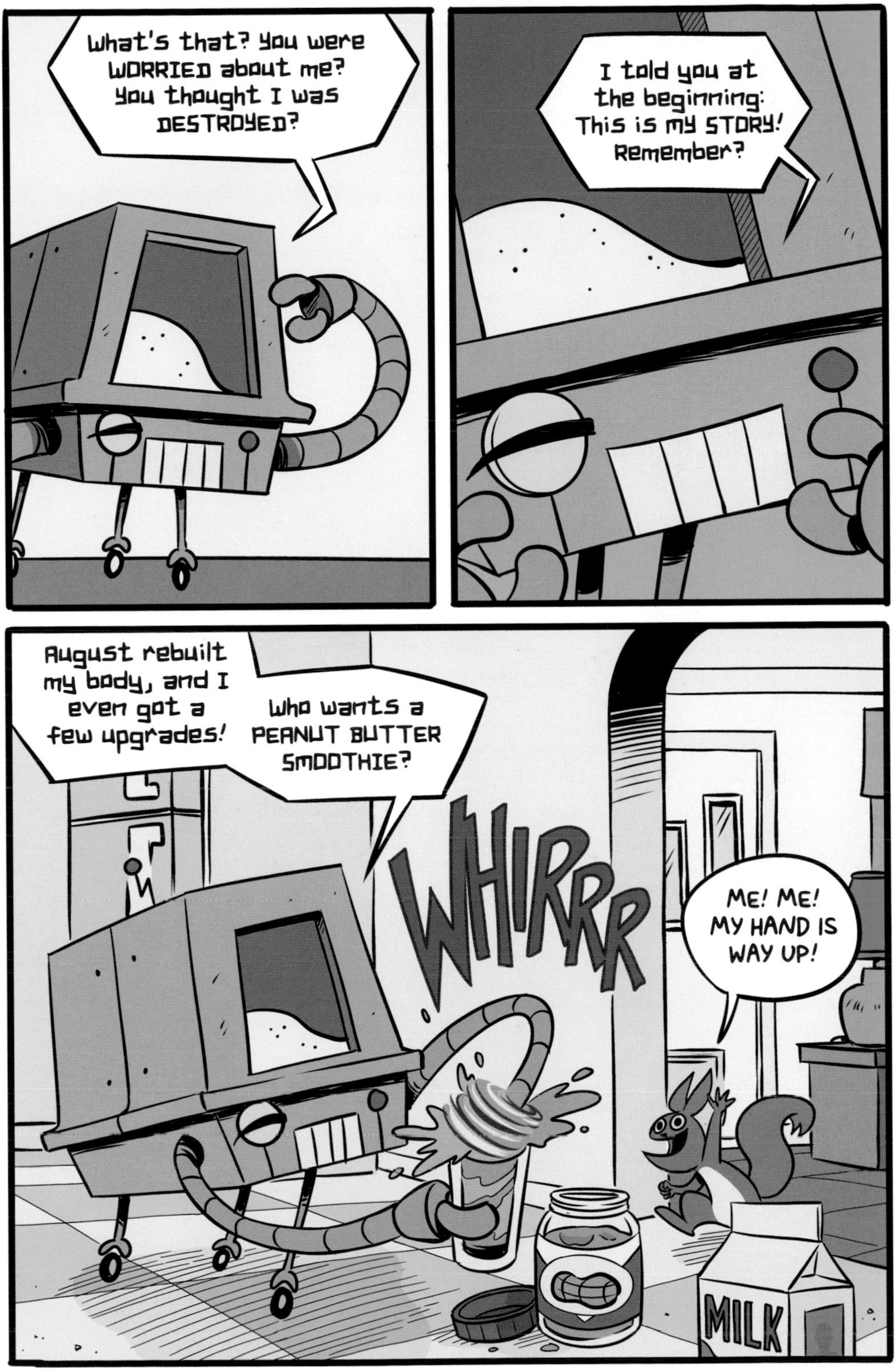
What's that? You were WORRIED about me? You thought I was DESTROYED?
I told you at the beginning: This is my STORY! Remember?
August rebuilt my body, and I even got a few upgrades!
Who wants a PEANUT BUTTER SMOOTHIE?
WHIRRR
ME! ME! MY HAND IS WAY UP!
MILK

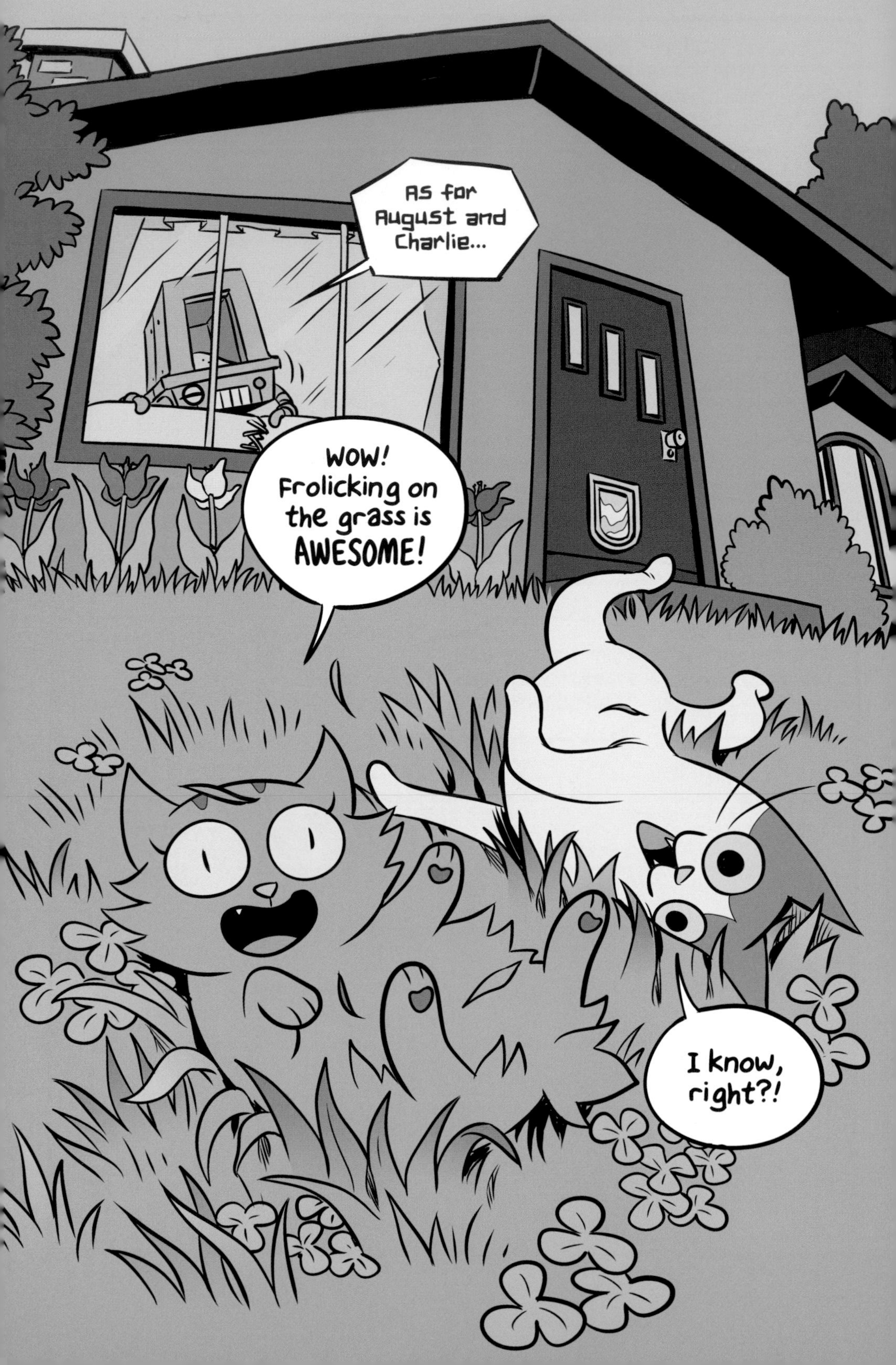
As for August and Charlie...
WOW! Frolicking on the grass is AWESOME!
I know, right?!

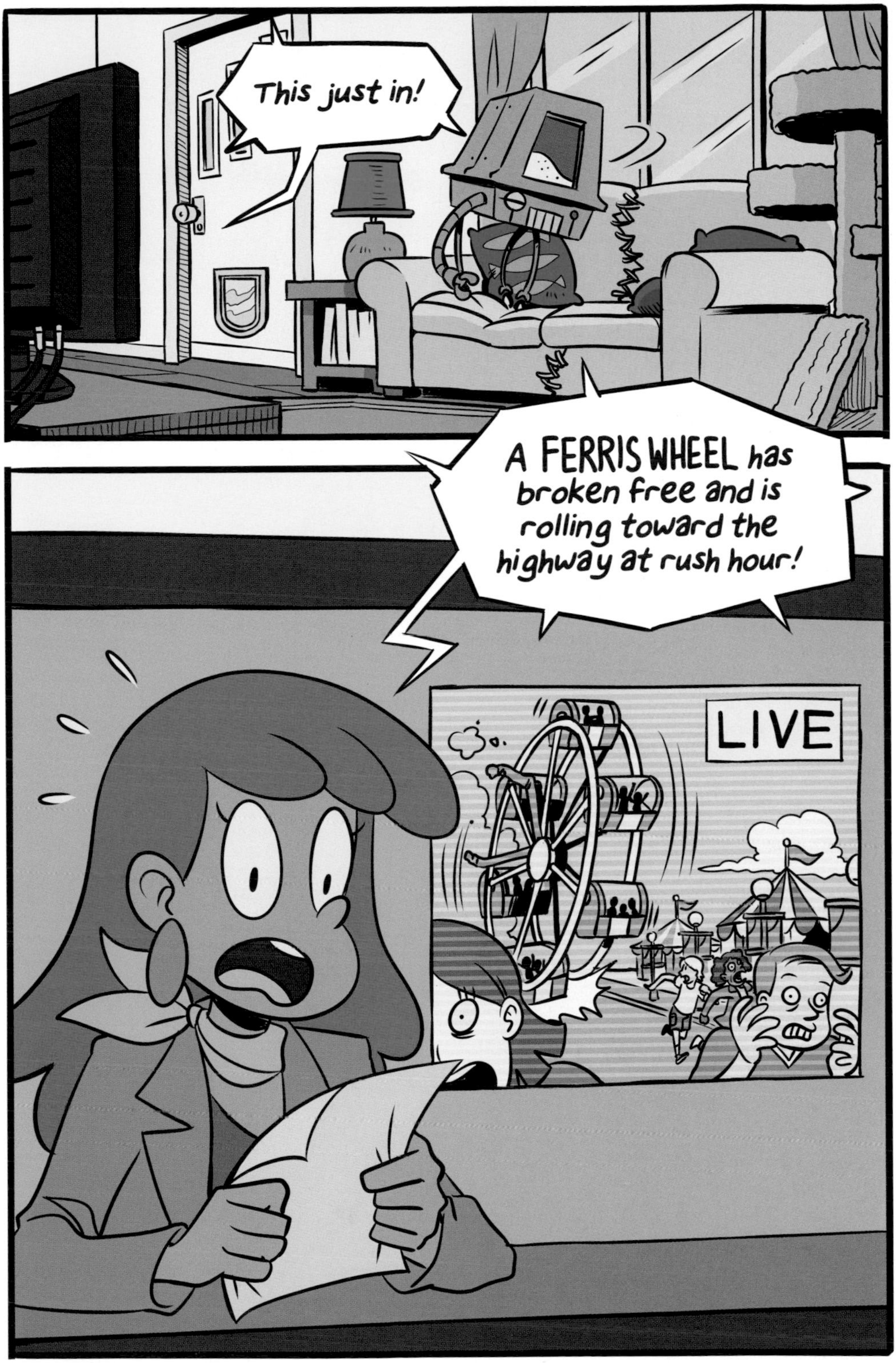
This just in!
A FERRIS WHEEL has broken free and is rolling toward the highway at rush hour!
LIVE

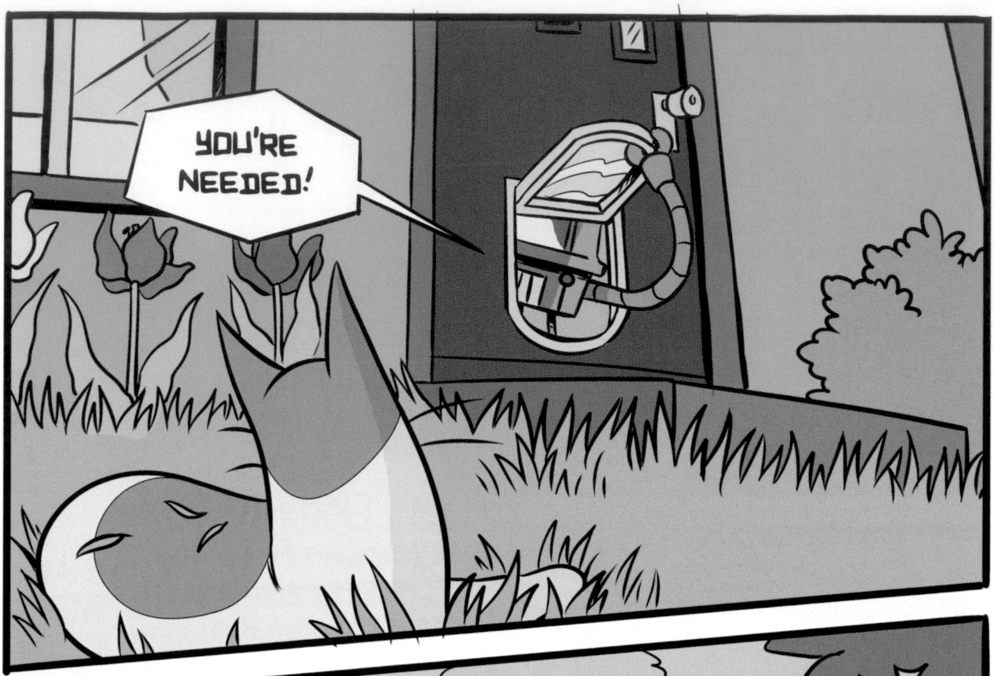
YOU'RE NEEDED!

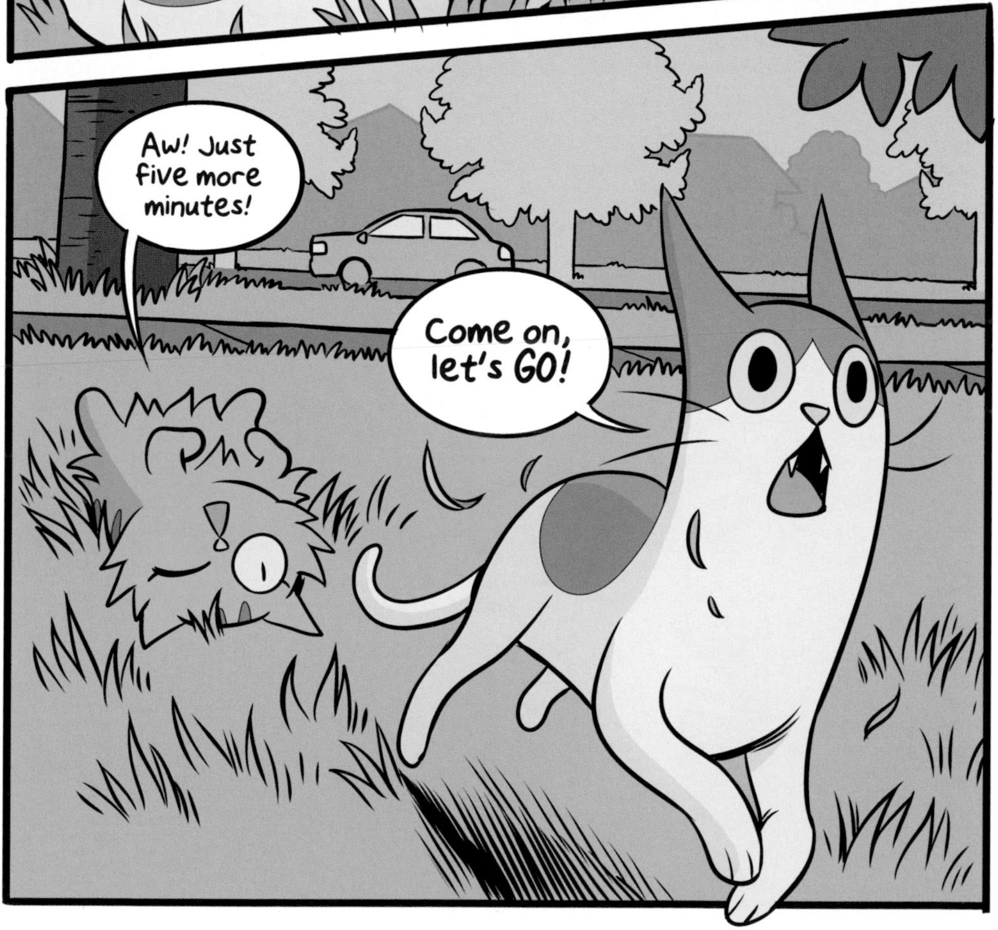
Aw! Just five more minutes!
Come on, let's GO!

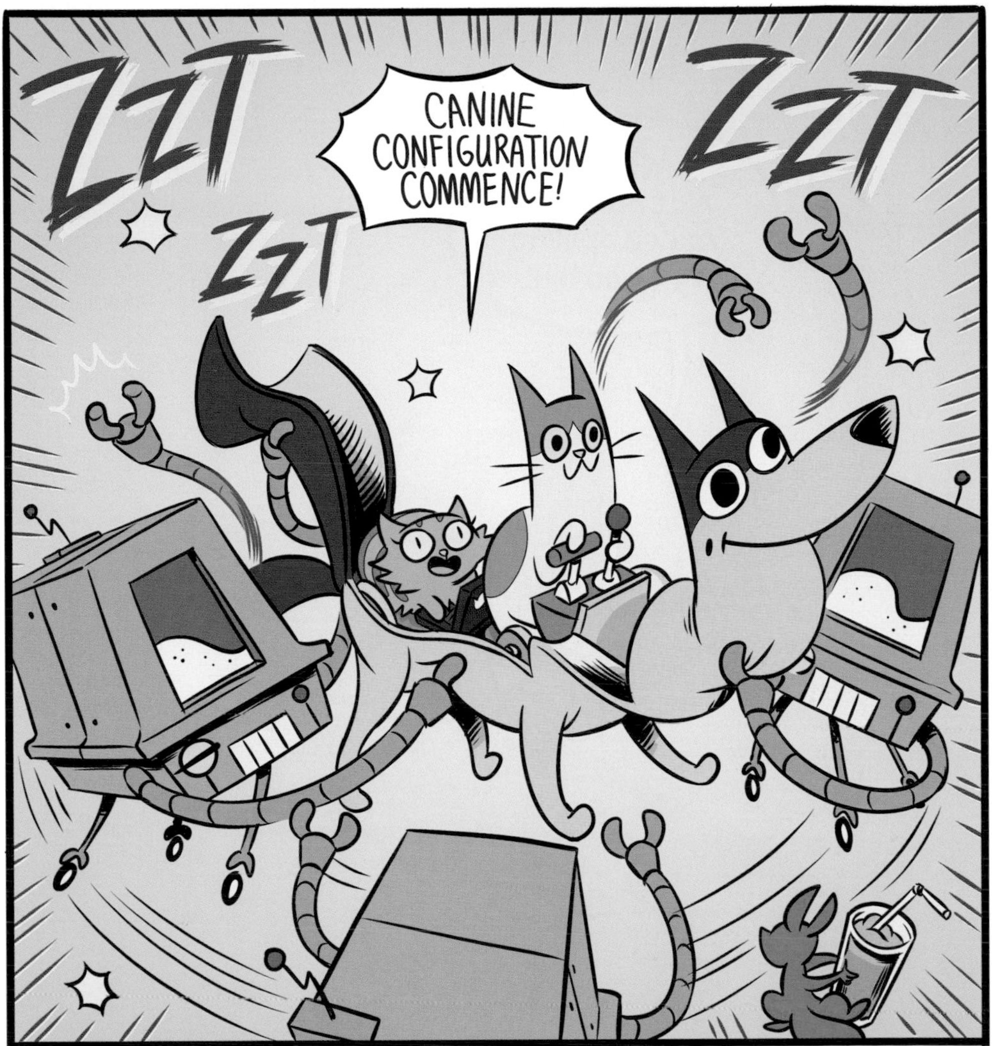
ZZT
ZzT
CANINE CONFIGURATION COMMENCE!
ZZT

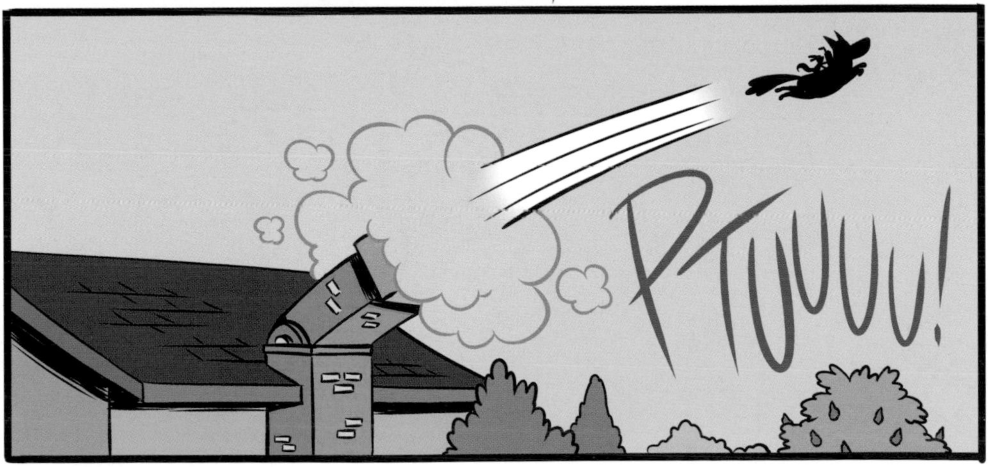
PTUUUU!

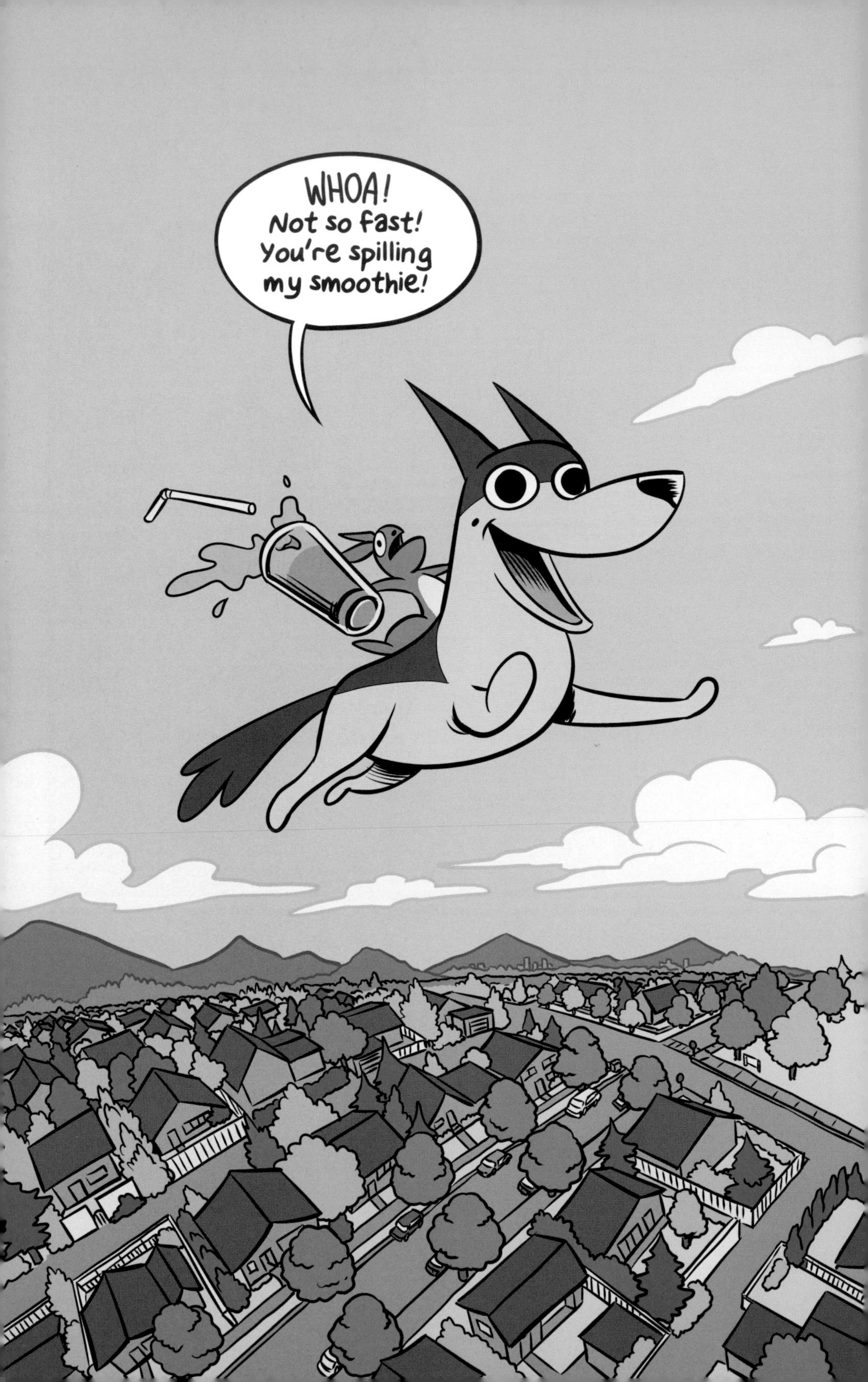
WHOA! Not so fast! You're spilling my smoothie!

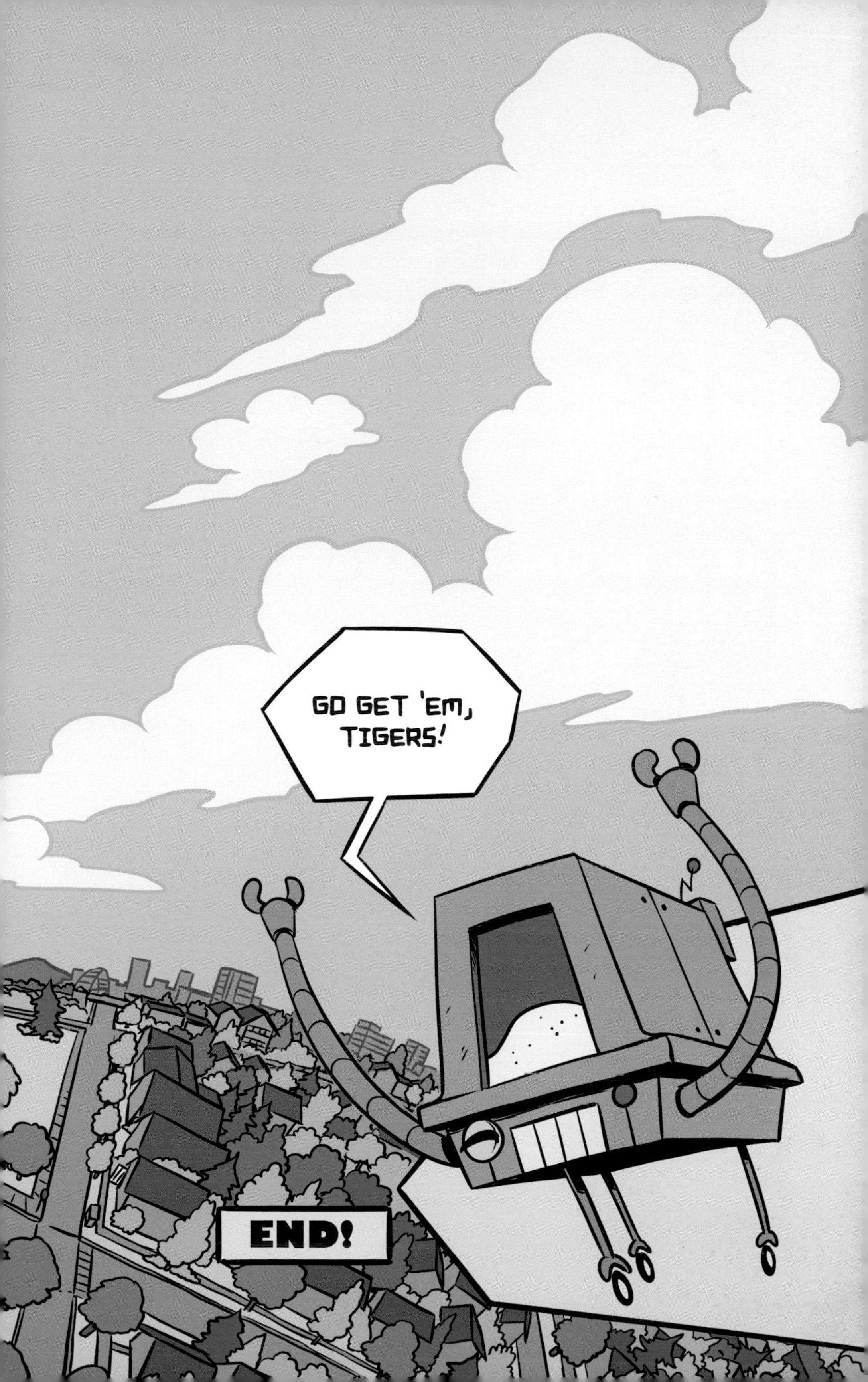
GO GET 'EM, TIGERS!
END!

IAN BOOTHBY has been writing comedy for TV and radio since he was thirteen and making his own comics since he was sixteen. Ian has written comic books for *The Simpsons*, *Futurama*, *Mars Attacks*, *Scooby-Doo*, *The Powerpuff Girls*, and *The Flash*. Ian has also won an Eisner Award for Best Short Story along with Nina Matsumoto, who you might know from being one of the other people with a bio on this page.

NINA MATSUMOTO is a Japanese Canadian who grew up drawing mostly animals, then mostly people, then back to animals again for this book. She pencils for Simpsons Comics and designs video game T-shirts for Fangamer. She created her own English manga series, Yokaiden, and drew *The Last Airbender Prequel: Zuko's Story*. In 2009, she won an Eisner Award with Ian Boothby, and they have been collaborating ever since. She lives with an aloof Shiba Inu that is most likely a cat in a dog suit.

DAVID DEDRICK has been writing and drawing funny pictures his whole life. He lives with his wife, two daughters, two dogs, one cat, and one pony. This is his first time coloring a book. Oh, and the pony doesn't live in the house.